I0636621

The
Chamber
Children

This book is a work of fiction. Names, characters, businesses, organizations, places, events and incidents either are the product of the author's imagination or are used fictitiously. Any resemblance to actual persons, living or dead, events, or locales is entirely coincidental.

Cover: Susan Conditt

Copyright © 2017 by James Riley. All rights reserved.

ISBN 978-0-578-18768-6

The Chamber Children

A Novel

James Tauro Riley

For Miko,
Jade and Grace,
and Ken

PART 1

Chapter 1

To understand the forces that shaped the history of the Chamber family, one would have to go back to the spring of 1853, when Wiltern Baylorson was exploring the southeastern corner of North Carolina. Wiltern was a newly arrived immigrant with ambitious dreams and a vast family inheritance to finance them. He wanted to start a farm, grow a business, build a town, then raise a city ... and that was to be only the start. In the New World, with his new fortune, he felt the possibilities were unlimited. He had found an area that suited him, but was undecided as he huddled under shelter from the occasional nighttime drizzle.

There was a small valley below, with a narrow river at the edge of it, now moving swiftly. Everything about the place looked right to him, felt right to him, but he needed something more. He needed a sign, and he asked for the Lord to guide him.

Only minutes later, he had his sign: a fiery light, streaking afar through the partly clouded sky. Its path was interrupted, and with a soundless burst of light as bright as daylight it collided with something unseen. A fiery plume erupted from the collision, and something of it streaked down from the heavens, slashing across Wiltern's view of the world and exploding into the Earth miles away from him. There was light and fire, and a roar that started after the light and fire, a roar that didn't seem that it would end. The air rumbled, trees collapsed by the thousands along the object's path, and flames sparked to life along that corridor as well.

Wiltern watched for hours as fire raged and then battled the rain, which came down steadily hours after the landfall. The fire lost at last, leaving in the morning a long black scar burned across the lovely valley.

That was Wiltern's sign.

Instead of interpreting the moment as a signal that the spot where he stood, safely removed, was where he wanted to build, Wiltern interpreted the fiery streak and the path it left as if it were a directional arrow. In the next days he ventured to that area, where the ground was deeply furrowed and burned, and the spruce and fir trees were flattened, and followed it along until he found a black crater at the end of it. The trees beyond that blackened spot still stood, a barrier not quite breached, and when Wiltern climbed into the crater, those sentries towered above him. At the bottom of the crater, there was only dust and ash, moistened by the rain into a dirty mush.

And three small, round lumps.

Two of which, when Wiltern picked them up and wiped them off, were perfect spheres, of a black mineral that could have been obsidian except for their light weight. The third was split open, and inside was also ash, although there were notches on the interiors of the pieces where whatever it was that had been contained likely had been seated. The internal structure reminded him of the inside of a plant seed pod. Each of the roughly 3-inch diameter spheres weighed lightly in the hand. He was able to loosely reassemble the broken one, so he did that, wrapped up all three together, and brought them home.

By the time Rose Chamber was born, Wiltern had long since stopped carrying the orbs around. However, when Rose's father Nelson Chamber first came to town seeking a parcel of land years before her birth, Wiltern still had been in the habit of taking out his satchel and showing them to folks, and sharing the story of their discovery as a way of enticing them to consider purchasing land from him. There had even been an article in a local newspaper about his space rocks. It was Nelson who advised Wiltern to be more cautious about flashing his star rocks about, and Wiltern hadn't needed to be told twice to take it to heart. From then on, if he was carrying the stones with him, he no longer mentioned it, and if someone asked him about the stones, he limited the details of both their discovery and their present location.

Instead of purchasing from Wiltern, Nelson had bought land very near to the place where Wiltern witnessed the meteor fall. Although their houses when they built them were miles apart, the Chambers eventually were Wiltern's nearest neighbors.

Rose first heard about the stones from the sky when she was little. When she was twelve, Wiltern had promised that if she stopped by his house to visit someday when she was little older, he would let her have a look at them. Of course, later that afternoon, after Wiltern had left, her father made clear to her that she would never visit Wiltern's house without an armed guard.

Wiltern had spent several years completing his house. Rose's father had long admired the Baylorson homestead—clearly, her father would say, building was where Wiltern's true talents resided. When he finished that structure and a barn, Wiltern set about realizing his vision, establishing his farm, and mapping out in his mind the town that would one day spring up on the land he had purchased, with his home acting as the gateway to that future utopia.

Wiltern's setbacks were numerous, and Nelson had wondered many times over the years at the older man's seemingly endless income in the face of steady losses. The soil was bad, and his plants grew stunted; he convinced himself establishing a quarry might be a possibility, and a source of material for his new town, but digging across the property proved that not to be the case; his one great accomplishment over his first 10 years, carving a grid of roadways where his town would develop, was nearly completely erased by what they called a 20-year-flood, which turned a large section of his property into a near marsh for close to a year.

Too late Wiltern came around to working with animals,

getting the idea from area ranchers and farmers who were doing it successfully. By then those same ranching and farming interests had moved the center of local commerce west of Wiltern's property by several miles. When the first local post office was established far west of the envisioned town of Wiltern, it became clear that his sprawling property would remain a destination with an eventual population of two: Wiltern and his wife.

What Wiltern did have at the far eastern reaches of his holdings was an area perfect for grazing animals, hillsides covered with the green they liked best. After Nelson had moved to the area, and started with the first of his many herds of animals, Wiltern and Nelson had entered into the only agreement that ever existed between those two stubborn and incredibly isolated men. Wiltern wanted Nelson to buy the hillside land, and Nelson did not wish to. Nelson would take his animals there and he thought the land was beautiful, but he had not the desire nor the money to own such a place. They agreed on an annual grazing price that was higher than her father would have liked, and a period of time—50 years!—that it would cover. Wiltern included a clause that would allow Nelson to pay, before a set deadline in the future, a reduced price for the land, so long as the final payment was made in gold.

That Nelson's choices in crops and animals proved to be good ones, and that Nelson made enough money from the animals that over time the rent on the land seemed negligible, those were sore points with Wiltern that her father dealt with firmly and without trying to make it worse.

Growing up, Rose saw Wiltern just about once a year. The forest claimed much of the property between them.

Eventually, Wiltern was the reason her father decided it was time for Rose to start her life away from the farm. The older man, maybe 63 at the time, had come by for his annual collection, and had looked at 16-year-old Rose in a way that set her father's expression into a glower that did not resolve itself until the arrangements for her departure from the area were settled.

Rose's mother died of an influenza when Rose was three years old. Her father had raised her well on his own, but Nelson was aware of the fragile nature of life, and worried what might happen to Rose should Nelson meet his fate before she was old enough to have a voice in her own.

Nelson Chamber considered himself a student of the Enlightenment. He was an engineer and mathematician at heart who had found a deep love of history and literature. He was not, as he would tell anyone who asked, a religionist. He resented the Gregorian calendar and what he saw as its imposition on the world by the Church. To those who inquired, he would say that although he did enjoy a good story as much as anyone, he was not a believer in mythology. He and his wife, Betaan, a tanner's daughter with one quarter Sioux in her blood, had settled in Clay in part because of its closeness to her mother's people. There were great forests surrounding the area, and despite Wiltern's inability to pinpoint it accurately, there was ample farmable land. The two of them, Nelson and Betaan, managed well on their new property.

The Civil War hadn't touched their home county as much as others in North Carolina, although the postal service had been interrupted sometime during the hostilities and local lives were lost in the ranks of both armies. Nelson made smart choices in crops and animals, and enjoyed some contentment in his life. Daily, he recorded the weather, and every night he drew the constellations overhead in a handmade journal. When the mail was restored, he regularly received books and newspapers with the post.

When his daughter Rose was born, she did all these things, too, at his side. She grew up tending to animals and crops, and regularly riding with her father as they herded animals on a circuitous route through the mountains, to the land owned by

Wiltern, and then back.

Nelson schooled Rose on mathematics, science, history, and literature, and she took part in every day's labor, most often working beside him. Rose was not exaggerating, many years later, when she told her son Joshua that he so closely resembled Nelson. Not only was Rose's father a giant of a man at 6'5", strong as could be, with a square jaw line and blue eyes, all of which described Joshua, too; but also, like Nelson, Joshua had a mind where the abstractions of mathematics were decipherable, where the world was a place to be better engineered, and the need to improve on what was now the norm was always present.

The Chamber house of her childhood was a thing of beauty to Rose, the walls built from the giant pines Nelson had cleared from the field, the chimney formed from river rock held together with the same cement formulation he'd used to build what would serve as the kitchen. He told her one day that he'd begun the property by building a storage space into the ground to keep his valuables better protected while they were out in the elements. He built the first room above that, and then the house around it with his exacting attention to detail.

Nelson was always tinkering with things, trying ideas, many of which worked—a weather vane that told them not only the direction the wind was blowing but also about how fast, a hen house design that made it easier to harvest the eggs without disturbing the hens, a varmint trap that impaled its victims with a 3-inch spike. He was a craftsman too, and over time he added his flourishes to everything from the rails in the fence that surrounded their property to the wicker chairs that he built to sit on the porch that looked out over nothing but hills of underbrush and trees.

Rose showed an ability for tending to the animals, and the animals displayed an obvious affinity for her over Nelson. At age nine she assisted with her first calving. At 11, while Nelson watched hopelessly as a pregnant heifer suffered from a complication in the birthing process, Rose stepped forward and reached into the cow and, after a moment, with her arm up to her shoulder inside the animal, did something there that cleared whatever obstacle was preventing the calf from coming out.

For her part, Rose remembered being sure that she could straighten out whatever it was, if she could only tell what was happening. The only way to do that was to reach in, and to find the calf's head, and then feel from there. Doing that, she'd found a hoof, slightly bent but caught on some corner of the heifer's insides. All she had to do was free the hoof, and with a tug the calf turned in the right direction and pushed out halfway without another contraction.

Her confidence in doing what she did was striking, as was the care and competence she exhibited in performing the action, and later, her follow-up with the animals to ensure that both recovered.

One of the brightest memories of her childhood years were the Carolina parakeets, those beautiful, noisy bursts of color that made the area look the way a tropical island might be described in a book. In Rose's childhood, the cocklebur-eating birds had been abundant, although at that time they were already being hunted by farmers who blamed them for destroying their crops and killing their cats—it was thought that the poisons in the cocklebur seeds in their diet made the birds toxic themselves. Rose found it hard to blame the birds on any of those counts. Even she understood that when people cut down the forests the birds lived in, then the birds needed to go someplace else to eat, which brought all sides into conflict.

As the years passed, she saw the parakeets less and less. They fared better in the deep of the forests than in the town or on the outskirts of town. She had watched them in the wild long enough to appreciate aspects of their behavior. They did not abandon their sick and wounded, or their dying and dead.

More than once as a child she came across a wounded parakeet on the ground being tended to by another parakeet, while other members of the flock hovered above the injured, guarding the skies overhead.

Dr. Lloyd was a traveling doctor of animals, and his irregular visits tended to bring him to Clay every nine to twelve months. He traveled with a covered wagon, which he would park in an open space outside of town before beginning visits to local ranchers. He received a government stipend for his efforts, which were seen as an aid to protecting the nation's food supply, and the territory he served included four states. He was well known in the area, and his presence much sought after, both for his fine singing voice, and for his good Christian nature. Although he requested payment in money, he was more than willing to accept barter for his services.

Dr. Lloyd preferred sleeping in a house to sleeping in a wagon, and welcomed near any invitation that included shelter or a home-cooked meal, although neither of those types of invitations were ever considered to be part of any transaction. In fact, if one wanted the good veterinarian to barter for his services, offering him a bed overnight and meal or two was the best way to get him to negotiate a lower price. Once in a social setting, Dr. Lloyd would sing hymns and other religious songs, share his thoughts on smaller, less commented upon stories from the Bible, and generally inspire others around him with his positive faith.

Based on a previous discussion with Nelson, on this visit Dr. Lloyd took Rose with him on his week-long round of appointments. At the end of that week, he agreed with Nelson that Rose could accompany him when he left for the next stop on his route.

This was all negotiated without Rose's knowledge. When told of the agreement, after her initial shock, and some concern at the idea of her father living alone, Rose felt a small thrill that the option even existed as a possibility. Rose had never harbored a great desire to leave her home. There was a completeness to a world with a farm at its center, only diminished by the absence of her mother. Rose was aware of the outside world, and intrigued by it in that it seemed incomprehensibly vast. The possibility that she would be sent out into it had existed up until that moment only as some event years-distant in the future. She did not remember protesting when it was decided, because she trusted her father's judgment that this would be the best for all involved. When she'd left, she was looking forward to seeing what it would bring.

Dr. Lloyd spoke frequently of the Royal College of Veterinary Medicine, but in such a way that decades after Rose had joined him as apprentice and assistant, she did not know in what capacity he had served at the college, although she was sure it was not as a student or teacher. He also spoke frequently of colleagues he regularly conferred with who were engaged in opening a veterinary college in Ohio—from these he received letters and papers that he shared with her as they traveled.

Dr. Lloyd was a Christian man, and was often asked if he was a preacher, because his conversation was filled with prose from the Bible. He regularly could be heard singing hymns quietly to himself. In some areas, his recitations were so well regarded that there would be jostling among locals to be host to his carriage and wagon.

He had a wife who along with four grown children—two boys and two girls—tended to their property in Arkansas during the many months of the year that he was on the road. His territory at different times included Tennessee, Mississippi, Alabama, Georgia, and parts of both Carolinas.

For Rose, the work of caring for others' animals seemed a natural extension of her life growing up. Where she had once walked miles with her animals in a loop, to the pasture and back, now she was working her way through a much greater loop that would circle back to her home once or twice a year. She loved walking alongside the carriage more than she did riding seated. She was awed by the wilderness and then by the country as they journeyed forward. Dr. Lloyd served areas outside the larger communities, sticking to remote, mostly poor areas. The work—caring for animals, identifying their problems—was hard for Rose to think of as work. It became her life.

Mrs. Lloyd was equally taken with worshipping the Holy Trinity, and that spirit seemed to guide her when she welcomed Rose into their household. Having Rose along had allowed Mr. Lloyd to accomplish more from the beginning, and he came home with more money in his pocket and more goods that he'd received in trade than ever before.

When they did return to the Lloyd homestead, Rose noticed that Mrs. Lloyd had the same habit as her husband of singing hymns quietly to herself throughout the day, almost under her breath, but also almost as if it came and went with every breath. When the two of them were in a room together, both focused on entirely different subjects—him in his books and her organizing the shelves, it was an ethereal duet they created as they both sang their own songs of worship.

Growing up, Rose had witnessed interactions between Christian folk, but it was a different view from the inside, as it were. Dr. Lloyd understood that different people seemed to have different understandings of the central text, of their savior, of the role of the church, and he would adjust the language he used when referring to Christian topics to accommodate each one. Their differences, to her, seemed to amount to disagreements about things that weren't necessarily central to the text anyway, or about the exact meaning of concepts that were, as her father had pointed out, imperfectly translated ("Without the nuances of the original text," Nelson would say) to English from Greek, Hebrew, and Aramaic. Rose needed Dr. Lloyd to explain to her the difference between the Virgin Birth and the Immaculate Conception, because that seemed to be a much-discussed topic in some communities. To Rose, it was a great example of what happened when people spent too much time in their imaginations.

One topic she did not have to ask about was the apparent animus they encountered toward the Pope, as her father had many times targeted the existence of such a person masquerading in a role of supposed infallibility, invented by the Church itself, in contradiction of the words of their sacred text. (Nelson would ask rhetorically, "Who died and made the Pope King?")

Rose enjoyed the Lloyd family. She enjoyed having, in the Lloyd children, others of her own generation around, and she appreciated the Lloyds' acting as her guardians. Over the next two years, she returned to her home three times before Dr. Lloyd's territory changed, shifting somewhat south, and eliminating the stops in North and South Carolina. Her father by that time had found companionship, and as easily as the house had once accommodated the family of three, it was too small when it came time to visit with her father and with his new wife, Leanne. Leanne acted like a stray dog who'd found a new home too good to share with anyone.

Rose chose to continue with Dr. Lloyd and her visits with Nelson dwindled to none. Thereafter, they would occasionally exchange letters as their mode of staying in touch.

At Dr. Lloyd's residence, she met Annabelle Findley, daughter of a local rancher and a fixture at the Lloyd household. Annabelle attached herself to Rose shortly after their first meeting, following her into the hen house. In that first meeting, Rose had been on her way for eggs, but to get Annabelle to move on, Rose had dallied, acting as if she were inspecting the chickens.

Annabelle was not put off, and peppered Rose with

questions about her origins as Rose eventually led her back to the house and out to the horse stables. Unused to such attention, Rose started to be unnerved. Annabelle completely misinterpreted the look of discomfort on Rose's face, taking it as some sort of encouragement, and assured Rose that the two of them were going to be friends forever.

"Maybe for the rest of our lives. I knew it when I first looked at you."

Rose remembered standing back and looking the other over. Annabelle appeared to be Rose's age, or even younger, but Rose knew Annabelle was actually several years older. She came from money and seemed like she was bored silly in Little Rock. It also seemed she found Rose to be genuinely interesting.

"I want to learn to do what you do," Annabelle said at the end of that first meeting. Rose hadn't been sure what that meant. "Don't you see? We have so much in common!"

Rose didn't see it.

"We'll be great friends!"

Later in the week, when Rose had been looking after a small herd of pigs where three of the sows were ailing, she saw Annabelle again. The girl shadowed her for the entire afternoon, this time plying her with questions about the things Rose was doing as she spent time with each of the animals. She managed to be more helpful this time, even fetching supplies for Rose when she needed them.

When Rose returned to that farm to help in the birthing of a new sow, Annabelle had been there as well, wide-eyed and clearly not averse to seeing such sights, although she did throw up before the birthing was over. It did make Rose like Annabelle a little more than she did before.

Chapter 2

Rose remained with Dr. Lloyd for almost twenty years. It passed like the wink of an eye. Over that time, it became her territory, too, and the animals under their care became her animals. She enjoyed all of the responsibility, the concern, and the emotion that accompanied such a feeling of ownership.

For the first year or so, she hardly spoke, except when Dr. Lloyd addressed her directly. She stood back and watched as he talked to farmers and ranchers, oftentimes families with only a few animals on a small property. She paid close attention as he worked with the animals, and was always ready to help when he asked. She learned how to inspect an animal's mouth and its feet, which Dr. Lloyd called the gateways for disease, and she learned there were a great many more afflictions that struck at farm animals than she could have imagined. She learned to inspect the animals' environment for possible causes for their distress, which often yielded an answer.

Rose understood after a while that Dr. Lloyd was attempting to educate the people he helped, to get them to understand what was required of them to be successful animal owners. He taught them about proper animal nutrition, about animal exercise, about grooming, and about what signs to watch for if an animal seemed to be behaving in an unusual manner. Everything he told them was so very basic and generic and obvious to someone who had always been around animals like herself, but to his customers it was often a revelation. He gave them recipes they could use to make nutritional improvements in the animals' diets, he gave them tips on handling their animals more effectively, and he advised them on making changes to the animals' living conditions that would lower mortality rates.

Rose was most impressed by Dr. Lloyd's skills as a surgeon. She had cut apart a dead animal before, of course, but she had never seen inside a living animal beyond its uterus. He would go in and set bones or sew internal tears, or clear some foreign object from the stomach or throat. She learned the peculiar geography, the similarities and differences, inside nearly every kind of farm animal. For her part, she was a quick learner and had a gift for assisting him—it wasn't too long before it was easy for her to anticipate what tool or medicine he would be needing next, and what kind of support she could provide to make his efforts easier for him and the animals.

It helped very much that Rose had a good rapport with the animals. She was at ease around them and vice versa. Her presence could instantly diffuse the most temperamental of outbursts from an animal in discomfort. This manner of hers, so calming with the animals, had the same effect on Dr. Lloyd, the result being that he found it easy to begin trusting her with performing certain duties on her own. She became skilled at diagnosing problems, and had what Dr. Lloyd called "a gifted touch," which referred to a habit she had of laying her hands on a sick animal and feeling her way, guided by the body's response, to the area that was causing the trouble.

Rose learned from Dr. Lloyd how to deliver a child—a human baby was how she thought of it after so much time with animals. Whether or not the people they worked with were educated, and they usually weren't, the assumption among them was that she and Dr. Lloyd would have better outcomes than a frightened layperson who hadn't birthed anything, human or otherwise, and so they did make their appeals. Dr. Lloyd rarely would perform any other service than that, in terms of treating people, because he felt that generally people's expectations for their own care far exceeded what they expected for their animals, and that he was not prepared, nor well enough educated, nor trained to meet such expectations. If a birth looked to present unique challenges, Dr. Lloyd would refuse to perform it and urge the expectant parents to seek someone trained in caring exclusively for humankind.

In time, Dr. Lloyd slowed, and Rose took on more of the work.

"Rose," he would say, "To look at you is to think only a year or two has passed since you joined me. But then this great gut of mine, and these aches in my bones, they tell me that it isn't so." He would suggest that the combination of her European and Indian ancestry had worked to conceal the effects of the passage of time where her looks were concerned. Not having access to a mirror, not being a person who invested too much thought in her appearance, she took his words as a kindness and did not dwell on them, although she would admit to being aware of the number of times that people questioned her experience based upon her appearance, or when they were surprised with her physical strength in dealing with the animals, saying things like, "She is so strong for such a young lady." It might have been after hearing comments such as these that she started wearing scarves to make herself look older.

Eventually, Dr. Lloyd's part of the job involved dining, sleeping, and storytelling at each of their stops. He drank perhaps too much, but was never offensive or unkind. Despite these indulgences, despite his widening waistline, his body seemed to shrink slowly, his impish face seemingly growing larger. He retired one season, and left her with the wagon, the carriage, and the horses to carry on the practice, with the homestead in Arkansas continuing to play the part of way station for her.

For the first two trips on her own, she fairly effectively pretended that Dr. Lloyd was in the wagon, at rest, when she made her rounds. Some, the best of his friends along the route, she was more honest with, but other than that she was very quiet about the fact that she was a woman traveling alone.

She was not a fragile woman. She was short, yes, but she was sturdy, almost mannish in the boxy shape of her upper body. She was stronger than a lot of the men she met on her route, and she'd discovered that if she wore a hat when driving the carriage, and slouched forward a little, many assumed her to be a short man, particularly if she put her hair up. Other than that—hiding behind her mannish form—she was an exceptional listener when it came to the world around her, deft at noticing when something was awry, and she had a good instinct for knowing when she should retreat until whoever or whatever it was passed her by. As a general rule, she stayed away from groups of men on the trails, and men in general other than the ones she was working for, and if she was on foot, she didn't mind walking a longer distance if that was what it took to do so.

While it was good for carrying supplies, Rose found the wagon and the horses unwieldy, and less comfortable, on her own than they had been when she was with Dr. Lloyd, even on those last trips when he had been capable of so little and relied on her to take care of everything else. It was not a safety issue, in truth, but more the loss of purpose—not her purpose, but the purpose Dr. Lloyd brought to the endeavor. He believed he was doing that which a higher power and the United States government had wanted him to do. Rose, for whom the animals were her core concern, had operated under the umbrella created by his faith. She did feel her life was less purposeful without his presence.

Annabelle had moved with her family by then to New Orleans, and when Dr. Lloyd died, Mrs. Lloyd chose to follow Annabelle's family. Rose received as an inheritance a small measure of money, and the wagon, carriage, and horses. Annabelle sent her a message, asking Rose to come to Louisiana, too, but Rose chose not to, as she could not envision a life for herself inside a city.

Rose ended the pretense that Dr. Lloyd accompanied her on the road, and continued living this way for five more years.

The sale of the Lloyd property meant that the wagon became her home year-round. The loss of the Lloyds' protective aura extended to some of her dealings with folks who had previously treated her warmly as Dr. Lloyd's assistant. She found that as a woman on her own, they were more wary, more critical, more liable to question her advice—even if it was the same advice Dr. Lloyd would have given them—and they offered less compensation for her services.

She realized, too, that she missed Dr. Lloyd's endless enthusiasm for the wonders of creation, his ability to look at all things in a positive light or else find a passage in his Good Book that lent misfortune the promise that something positive would come of it in the end. The longer she continued without him, the less well she was treated, the less she cared for people, was what happened. The less she cared for people, the more she noticed the way they were spreading uncontrollably, that the wilderness she had wandered for years was being degraded, if not disappearing entirely. Roads, factories, simply the refuse from their daily lives had started to crop up everywhere.

It would have been one thing if the trade-off for the prosperity made from the resources of the land they all shared were used to improve the lives of everyone. But as much as things seemed to change for a certain group of people, the lives of the ones that she spent her time helping—who essentially were farmers, ranchers, and the very, very poor—never seemed to change.

After she finally gave up the carriage, wagon, and horses, she would travel to Tennessee, Georgia, Alabama, and Mississippi by foot over the next years. Daily she would walk miles to the farms where she worked. She was never afraid when she was out in the forests or walking through the countryside; it was the towns and the small cities that scared her: the more people, the less comfortable it was for her. So she tended to avoid such situations.

In those years there were places along her route where the Carolina parakeets could still be found.

In a note from her father's new wife, Leanne, she received the news that her father had passed, without much detail beyond that. Leanne included a letter from her father that he'd been readying to send to her before he died. That letter, typical of messages from her father, was full of information about weather and crops and the book he was currently reading. He'd also written that there were no parakeets left in North Carolina.

Rose grieved for Nelson daily, for many miles. She found great comfort when her path took her through forests in Tennessee still populated by the parakeets and filled with their sounds.

The Carolina parakeets nested on the ground instead of in the trees, and she had seen their creches in her travels, sometimes with as many as 300 birds. She was in the northern part of Louisiana when she came across a nesting area for the birds, with maybe 80 nests tucked into the forest greenery by a river, every one of them hiding silently as she passed.

When she returned by that same trail two days later, the creche had been attacked, decimated. There were bodies everywhere, and she could not determine what they had been slaughtered for—not for food, not by an animal. It might have been 10 men, there were so many dead birds, but then again it might have been only one. He could have attacked one nest and then the next, and the parakeets wouldn't have fled or completely abandoned their mates and cohabitants, and thus the whole creche died right there. Others had likely circled above the destruction, wanting to help the injured as soon as the threat subsided. Instead they were shot with arrows, their bodies left untouched. The barbarity of it overwhelmed her, made her regret for a moment any role she'd played in bringing another human child into the world. What good were any of them going to do, in the end?

When she did see those distinctive green feathers again, they were in the hats of two women on a sidewalk in New Orleans having a conversation that precluded their noticing Rose passing them by.

Seeking some insight on the changes in her heart, Rose had traveled to visit Annabelle. She thought the person who greeted her at Findley Manor's front door must be Annabelle's heretofore unmentioned daughter, or much younger sister, who resembled exactly the Annabelle Findley that Rose had first met a quarter of a century before.

For Annabelle, there was no such hesitation—she wrapped her arms around Rose and hugged her ferociously. Rose, who was not used to hugging anybody, and hadn't in a long time, was touched by the embrace.

"I don't understand," Rose said incredulously, "You look exactly the same."

Annabelle pulled back, but continued holding Rose's shoulders with her hands. She stared at Rose, nodding knowingly. Without a word, she pulled Rose into the house, down the short front hall, to a full-length mirror. She gestured for Rose to look into it.

"Twenty-five years stubborn is how I see it. Are you starting to see the light now? I told you long ago, we have more in common than you think," Annabelle said. "I never thought it would take you so long to see the light."

Rose gasped.

"Unless," Annabelle countered herself, seeing the strength of Rose's reaction, "Unless you're just starting to grasp this . . . ?" Her voice trailed off before her joy at seeing her friend came back into her voice. "We can save that for later."

Rose couldn't remember the last time she saw a mirror, but it wouldn't have mattered. She looked exactly the same as she remembered. She was not the middle-aged woman whose reflection she caught occasionally in a weathered pane of glass or a pool of water. She looked young! She also looked slovenly. Standing next to Annabelle, she was immediately appalled at the way her own clothes looked, as if she had stolen them from an old country German widow.

Seemingly reading her mind, Annabelle said, "You've heard the expression 'Mutton dressed up like a lamb?' Well, you are a lamb dressed up like mutton. If you'll stay for a little while, then we can fix you up a little." A servant appeared at the end of the hallway, and Annabelle told her to prepare tea for them in a commanding yet polite tone that Annabelle had not been capable of before. "It's a much fancier lifestyle we lead here than we had in Arkansas," Annabelle explained.

Over tea, Rose asked if the women she had seen on the street were really wearing parakeet feathers in their hats.

Annabelle's eyes glowered.

"Yes, it's a fashion trend. Not for much longer, though. Even though they only use the adult birds' feathers for their clothes, they end up killing the little ones, too. I've heard the birds are difficult to find already. Next month those hats will go into hat boxes where no one will see them until they're given to charity."

Rose described the scene in the forest at the parakeet creche, and this led to the longer story of the dissatisfaction she'd been feeling these last few years, at the end of which Annabelle closed the study doors and then, when she returned, moved her chair closer to Rose's.

Annabelle explained that her father was in rapidly failing health, and that she had been working feverishly for months to see that her inheritance would be preserved. When her father had first shown signs of serious illness, she had felt set upon by men who wanted to step in "to help her" to manage affairs. The banker, the lawyer, the business manager. And that was not to count suitors who would want to marry into her fortune. She was worried about laws in regards to women's rights to own property, to sign contracts, to even write a will disposing of her inheritance as she saw fit.

"Everyone wants to 'protect' a woman. The federal government, the state, the cities, the random men, armed or not, all of whom 'know' with authority how best for women to conduct themselves for their own benefit. Well, I don't need their protection anymore." Annabelle said she had developed a dream of owning land, and caring for and sheltering that land and all the life that inhabited it.

With her father's blessing and what assistance he could provide as his condition deteriorated, she had worked through a web of intermediaries to purchase an expanse of property. The bulk of the money had already been transferred or spent towards this purpose. The house they were in, upon her father's death, would be transferred to the new owner—she was leasing it back, paying for it out of cash on hand to deter suspicion at the bank.

"When the word is out that he is gone, they will set upon this house," she said, "and if all goes as planned, I won't be here when they arrive." She made it sound settled, but her anxiousness in discussing it suggested otherwise. "Unfortunately, a woman cannot trust what a man may do to prevent her from exercising her own will openly, and the courts here are only too glad to assist. If I were to shout my intentions from the street corner, they would feel obligated to manage things for me 'for my own good.' Although everything is seemingly set, I won't feel it's done until I've started the rest of my life."

Annabelle's forwardness as an adult was the same Rose remembered from when they were teenaged, except that now Annabelle was the one who was brimming with knowledge. She was eager to do so many things, and Rose was still trying to recover some feeling about the world that she seemed to have lost.

Rose stayed for a week that would turn out to be the most luxurious of her life. Daily hot baths prepared by servants, food prepared by a cook, robes warmed before they were handed to her, rides in carriages, and sightseeing.

For all the relief it provided her, she couldn't help noticing the poor and needy outside the manor door, the dirt and filth in the streets, the smoke in the air. She couldn't ignore the brightly plumed hats that the women strutted under as if they were to be admired—she thought it made them look like the ugliest birds she'd seen.

Luxury was not something Rose was accustomed to, and by the end of the week, the life she had long been living gnawed at her, and she made plans to be on her way.

In parting, Annabelle said, "I know you aren't ready yet this time, but also I know your mind is turning. You may not know it yet, but I hear it in every word you say. When you're ready, I'll be expecting you."

She told Rose where Rose would be able to find her, "If all goes as planned."

It was several years later when Rose finally was ready to admit Annabelle had been right. The world was changing rapidly around her as she traipsed across it, and there was no end to the poverty she encountered, no end to the babies she delivered into one dubious existence after another, and no slowing the advancements that were taking over the world—telephones, light bulbs, flying machines—nor the spread of people, metal structures, machines, roads, and factories across the landscape. Nearly seven years after she'd encountered the women with the brightly colored parakeet feathers protruding from their hats, the parakeets were extinct, and the forests less enchanted for their absence. She thought she would make one last trip home, to North Carolina, before she made any great decisions. Her father had been dead a while, and she didn't know what, if anything, had been left behind, or if it held any meaning for her at all. Perhaps her father had left a message for her in the vault? Would he have? Would it have remained undiscovered?

But heading south from Georgia she came across a second scene of wanton slaughter, this time an extended family of panthers, eight of the great cats shot dead outside their lair, three adult females, two adult males and 3 young ones. One of the males had been beheaded. The paws had been cut off of all of the females, even the babies. The ones that still had their heads, their eyes were yellow and open. Although there was blood everywhere, she saw they had soft, white, furry bellies to contrast with the tan coats—which was all she had ever seen of a panther in her lifetime before this sad discovery, a tan form that slid into the woods and disappeared as she had approached. They had black tips on their ears and tails, and were much smaller than she would have guessed—smaller than a large dog, to be sure.

As far as she could understand, for this dead pack, the killers had procured one head and 20 panther paws. For what? For voodoo? For trophies? For good luck?

This was the last that she was willing to bear. She decided that she would not be responsible for helping to bring more people into the world. Instead of continuing north toward home, she turned south and spent each day seeking places where there were no people nearby, where she could camp alone but for the nature that she desired as her only companion. She finally ended her journey in what she thought was Alabama, on the edge of a swamp. The smell of the distant ocean was faint in the air. There were forested hillsides around her, lush fields, rock-covered mounds, and running streams.

This was close to where Annabelle had invited Rose to visit. All Rose had to do was find her. And, it seemed, she had all the time in the world to do it. Little did she suspect this was where she would spend the next 30 years of her life.

Chapter 3

Following Annabelle's directions, Rose found herself moving through a forest. There she came upon the first sight that stopped her in her tracks. Among a stand of birch trees, two tall trunks stood out among the others, being a yellow-orange hue instead of greyish-white. Walking closer, she saw a small house, painted red, twenty-five feet up in the canopy, sitting atop those brightly colored posts.

At the base of the painted trees, the exposed roots of the trees had been painted as well, to look like a hen's webbed feet.

She recognized immediately what it was supposed to be— it was Baba Yaga's house, a folk tale from the Old World. Baba Yaga was a supernatural being with magic powers who sometimes aided and sometimes threatened the heroes of many stories. In the New World, she was identified as a sort of witch, but originally she was something more, something less easily defined, an Earth spirit enforcing a primal moral code. At the end of her stories, she always retired to her home in the forest, a house on giant chicken legs that roamed the wilderness at her will.

Rose found the sight incredibly strange at first, regarding it as if it were a carnival attraction. Why would someone have gone to the effort? Its oddness in those surroundings immediately made it seem less whimsical. She thought, as she walked away from it, that it actually might come to life and start pursuing her. Of course it did not, but it left her with a feeling of disquiet.

From there, she felt herself challenged by the path she was trying to follow. Many clearings she wandered into looked similar to one another. The air was fragrant with floral scents, at times almost dizzyingly so. The canopy grew thick enough that she could not see the horizon ahead of her, and she lost some sense of her direction. She found herself walking toward a stand of trees, among which two were painted yellow. A small red shack sat up on top. Had she gone in a circle? Rose didn't believe so, but she did not know if she should double back the way she came, or if going forward was the path she had already traveled. So before she set off in the direction she thought was forward, she made a small pile of rocks as a marker to recognize should she return to that spot again.

Indeed, after moving forward through similar-looking clearings filled with disorienting scents, again there was Baba Yaga's hut, and she felt not only dispirited, but also slightly panicked. The forest was alive with sound, and she started to feel skittish. Then she saw there were no rocks piled here, and that was even more puzzling, and left her questioning whether she was in another location or if someone was pursuing her for some purpose, and scattering the rocks that she set. She made another small pile of rocks.

She continued forward again, but this time heard a sound she thought she recognized: it was the back-and-forth calling between parakeets, perhaps even Carolina parakeets. The direction the sound came from was clear, so she continued forward.

Their chattering did not end there, and Rose began following their sounds rather than focusing on the trail. When she passed Baba Yaga's hut for a fourth time, and again there were no rocks on the ground, she hardly paid those two details attention as she moved along.

The terrain changed, and the forest gave way to a marshier area where the plants were no lower than her chin. The day was starting to lose its light, but she pushed forward rather than set up a shelter near wet ground for the night.

At some point, she was startled to realize that in her hurry, she hadn't noticed that she wasn't alone out in the dusk of the day. She'd pushed noisily through a patch of reeds and when she came out realized she was standing not ten feet behind a man. He had his back toward her. His hat was that of a confederate soldier, but his coat was not a uniform—it was a dark, heavy jacket. His hand was stretched out to his side, holding a rifle, the tip of which tilted toward the ground.

Her heart nearly stopped. These were not the circumstances in which to encounter an unfamiliar, armed man. She had a knife in her supplies, and quickly and quietly it was in her hand. She thought that if she backed away, then there was a great chance he would fire at the noise. She didn't know why he hadn't turned already at the racket she'd made. Was he a hunter? Was he instead focused on some prey?

She cautiously moved forward, and decided there was something wrong with him, with his stillness, his lack of reaction. When she was close enough, she could see that the hand extending out of the long sleeve, the one holding the rifle, was twigs and leaves—it was actually the end of the branch of a tree. The "gun" was another branch perfectly shaped to suggest a weapon.

She stepped to the front of it. It was a tree. The top of it had been knocked off—it was probably the crumbling wood lying on the ground nearby. The remaining section, maybe six feet tall, was still alive. The confederate cap partially covered the jagged top. Not far below the cap was a blackened knot that resembled a mouth. Maybe a branch had been there once, and fallen off. The bark had swelled around that old wound, and that swelling resembled lips. Above were two knots that would be its eyes. In a way, it looked like art. In another, it was frightening. It looked like either a tree had grown up and into the clothes of a man, or a man had been turned into a tree. It was the pants that confused her more than the rest—the stump appeared to have grown into one of the pant legs. It just wouldn't have been possible to slip the pants over the branches that formed the arms. Someone would have had to have sewn them on that way, which Rose thought could be indicative of a whole world of lunacy.

Perhaps, she thought, it marked a soldier's grave?

Only a bit further, and there it was, a cabin. A large cabin in the middle of a cleared lot, bordered by a simple railed fence. There were several small fields clear-cut for crops. Sounds of the parakeets were emanating from within, through an open window. There was smoke coming out the chimney.

Annabelle stood in the doorway, not wearing the smug look Rose imagined would be part of her greeting. She looked delighted. She clapped her hands together quickly in excitement, and hurried out to greet Rose.

It was almost like coming home.

Annabelle's exit from New Orleans had been more difficult than she had foreseen. In her father's final days, she'd been so put off by most of her father's business associates' advances that the only person to whom she left a bequeathal was the Chief of Police. She forged her father's signature to a note thanking the Chief for his good service in the protection of the city, and for the knowledge in death that the Findley family would continue to be protected by his efforts.

With her father's death, and the appearance of associates to whom the estate owed money, in particular out-of-state banks with whom many of her expenditures had been made, it became apparent that those who had hoped for a portion of the estate were to be duly disappointed. It was likely her gift to Chief Carroll that helped her to escape incarceration. Having failed to disappear into the night, she so feared being followed to her new retreat that she placed all of her possessions remaining in New Orleans into storage, booked herself on a cruise to Greece, and left, vowing never to return.

In Greece, Annabelle had experienced a spiritual reawakening, and as she toured sites far and wide came to believe that she was seeing things with her eyes that some parts of her soul remembered from a past life. On the island of Delos, she wandered among ruins, convinced that in an earlier life she had run among the structures when they were new.

She returned to the United States, and settled into her new property, her purpose fixed in her mind. She was going to create a nature preserve to protect the flora and fauna of the South, separate herself once and for all from the controlling madness of men, and live her life out in peace serving the Mother Planet.

The property she owned was a sprawling spread of land, with forests, fields, marshes, swamps, and a set of three small hills that offered pleasing views all around.

Annabelle was satisfied at hearing Rose's description of the difficulty of the path into her property. She said she'd been working for years to make it as confusing as it was. She was still working on the flowers, chosen for scents that would overwhelm the senses, adding to the disorientation of accidental and unwanted explorers. Once those were planted, she had a collection of less-than-friendly plants—thistles, thorns, cockleburs, and the like—that she would seed throughout, leaving only a narrow and concealed "safe" pathway in and out for herself.

The clearings on the way in looked identical because she'd put effort into making them that way. She'd paid men to paint the Baba Yaga trees, and to build and raise the tiny houses into the canopy. Rose had encountered all of the four of them. Annabelle was also responsible for the tree stump dressed in men's clothing— she'd brought along items of her father's clothing, and had indeed dressed that stump and several others—there was a lumberjack, a hunter in a raccoon-skin cap, a cavalry soldier astride a stump that looked like a wild animal rearing up, and a female, an archer, dressed in Annabelle's proper riding clothes—across the property. It was Annabelle's idea that they served as a way to further discomfort those who might try to visit the property uninvited.

They were not scarecrows. They were scarepeople.

Annabelle had also found and bought what she believed might be the last six breeding pairs of Carolina parakeets in the world. She'd built an aviary of wood and wire for them, so they wouldn't escape. None had yet laid any eggs. Rose knew when she first saw them that they would want a more natural habitat if that were to happen, but held her tongue. There would be time and there would be opportunity.

When in her older years Rose had ever mentioned this time of her life to her children, the picture she would paint for them would have them envisioning their mother as having been a sort of hippie living on a cooperative farm or a commune with her best friend. When they heard of it, they imagined a short-lived adventure. But this was a continuation of the life Rose, and Annabelle to a certain extent, had grown up living. They had more land than they could tame, and the small patch where they lived and farmed required much of their time and energy. They spent most of their time working together, but there were periods when Annabelle would go her own way and be gone for days. Rose didn't mind. She had more than enough to occupy herself.

They kept track of birds they sighted in one journal, where they would attempt to draw accurate pictures of each species they saw. They did the same for wild animals, and there was also a journal for flowers. They grew vegetables and herbs. They raised chickens, goats, lambs, and pigs. They searched out fruit-bearing trees and seed-bearing plants to feed themselves. They tried their best to balance the needs of the animals in the forest around them with their own, and devised ways to protect their domestic animals from being a magnet for four-footed hunters.

Annabelle, who Rose had believed she understood so well, was not at all the person she used to be, no matter her looks. Even those did change some over time, too, although one would probably have to know her as well as Rose did to notice. Annabelle's eyes were a different story. She had a different look in her eyes, one that suggested she was not the open book Rose had once thought.

In her time in New Orleans, Annabelle had been involved in the town's social life. Her father was a sponsor of painters and musicians, and she attended many functions and parties; she also hosted salons attended by writers, artists, and enlightened intellectuals from around the region, as well as those she labeled "theorists and students of the mysteries."

In the shared history theorized by these groups, before life blossomed on the planet Earth it was a home for monstrous beings from the stars, and a gateway to the worlds above, among which heaven could be found, and the worlds below, where each level was darker than the one above. None of these places could be reached after death—"Dead is dead"—but before death they were all accessible if a mind were in the right state when it tried to transition between them. Annabelle believed other beings, too, traveled up and down this existential ladder between the above world and the below world by way of the Earth.

When life was ignited on the planet, the elder gods were driven to the colder places in the universe, or they went into slumber deep in the Earth, or else they transitioned to the lower planes. The way up was not open to them. They left remnants of their stay here to test their successors, and to serve as anchor points should they ever wish to return.

Annabelle believed that a secret guild comprised of a small number of families worldwide had conspired through generations of time to destroy the existence of magic in their world. They could find no security from the intrusions of demons from the lower planes, nor from the giants and spirits that remained here on Earth, and they believed it was magic performed on Earth that drew the inhabitants of the Netherverses here, or else threatened to awaken them.

Magic cannot be destroyed, the guild knew, so their strategy focused instead on killing the practitioners of magic, because they were seen as the bridges by which these other forces accessed our world. In their Crusades, in their witch trials, in their enslavement of the Hebrews, in their burning of gypsies and heretics, their purpose was twofold beyond mere conquest. If there was no one to practice the ancient and hidden arts, there was no one to teach those secrets to others, they reasoned, and the knowledge eventually would be lost forever. Perhaps the bridges to the other worlds, if not severed, would not be so easily opened. The second hoped-for result was that a frightened populace, robbed of their first line of defense against the forces of darkness, would turn for shelter to the only forces left to defend them—the guild members themselves.

"Now," Annabelle said, "with magic cut off from us, our only option is to try to go back to the start of learning it again." She would say she was working at the root of it, where the magic was sleeping, and she intended to rebuild her understanding from there. "That's what I've been doing. Working at the root of it.

"One day, Rose," Annabelle would say, "if women like us keep at it, we can reestablish our connection with the planet. The possibilities will be endless. Mother Earth can save us all."

For all Annabelle's claims that Rose took with a grain of salt, Annabelle was undeniably gifted in the mixing of her powders and salves and potions. She knew plants, herbs, roots, and minerals, and understood their variety of uses. She kept a collection of preserve jars, only a portion of which contained preserves or spices for cooking. The rest were filled with the gatherings from around the property, among them dried leaves, insects, seeds, pieces of bark, parts of reptiles, snail shells, and butterflies. There were different colored rocks, stones, and crystals, and jars of different colored sands. There were more empty jars waiting to be filled in crates in the yard. "The last remnants of Daddy's factory," Annabelle had said of the crates.

Annabelle had also developed an odd habit of talking to herself. Not all the time, and rarely in front of Rose. In fact, Rose thought the only reason she had noticed was that occasionally the conversation was one where something was left unresolved, and Annabelle would continue to make seemingly random comments related to it, as if arguing with herself.

When asked about it, Annabelle had been slightly embarrassed. Then she explained that since she had been in Greece, she'd felt at times as if there was something that was speaking to her.

"You're not telling me you're hearing voices?"

"I'm not mad, Rose. It's not that at all. I've simply opened up enough to be able to notice it's there. And it's not a voice, but it is something that speaks to me. It comes mostly in images. There are times when I see things in my mind. At first they seemed like random objects from my past, but I've realized that each object has specific connections for me. A bowl of sugar relates to food, and has come to mind several times as I've encountered seeds and berries and fruits. A bowl of sugar means it is edible. Other times I don't understand why I'm seeing what I'm seeing, and you might have heard me then, arguing with myself and with the images, trying to figure them out. It doesn't seem to happen unless it is important, and since it has started, it has become clearer and clearer what I'm being told. I'm learning. My senses seem to be expanding."

Indeed, she had developed a close connection with her property. She would know when they would be able to find a herd of deer grazing in the area, whether it was nearby or far away. She had an accurate sense of the severity of each impending storm. She grew more talented with her mixtures and salves and potions. She had a powder that they sprinkled between the rows of vegetables that kept the rabbits and rodents away, and another that kept the ants from the house. She made a liquid, sprayable through an old perfume bottle sprayer, that encouraged plants to increase their size and double the number of their blooms.

Oddly, although Annabelle never advertised her skills, every few years a person would somehow make his or her way to their home. Each one came desperate in need, seeking a remedy— either for their health or for the health of someone who they loved. They never came because they sought treasure, which Rose found interesting. Annabelle, for all her professed dislike of humankind, never turned them away, and in fact never seemed surprised at their appearances. Usually she gave them one herbal concoction or another, either to be taken by the person making the pleading or by the loved one they pleaded for. Once a young couple fleeing their families stumbled into their front yard, where the woman promptly went into labor. But instead of progressing through the stages of delivery, she hovered, with contractions every 6 minutes, for nearly two days. Rose had at first attended her closely, but by the end of the second morning was taking regular breaks to do daily chores like feeding the animals.

Finally, as the sun was setting again, Annabelle said, "That's quite enough, don't you think? Drink this." The young woman, clearly exhausted, took the drink without pause. The father of her child had dozed off nearby despite any noises his beloved had made during the most recent set of contractions.

Fifteen minutes later, she was open and ready to push with what little energy she had left. The baby fairly popped out at the first push. Annabelle allowed them to stay two days before sending them off.

Later, after complimenting the effects of her potion, Rose asked, "Your grand plan, then, is to become a witch? If not for real, then in the eyes of the world?"

"My plan is to accept that I am the sort of person they would call a witch," Annabelle said. "A single woman, gladly eschewing men and Christianity and society, living in the woods, communing with nature, daring to believe I have a right to live my life as I choose? I'll do anything that inspires them to keep their distance. My grand plan is simply to continue investigating the world outside as a way to live my inner truth.

"Rose," Annabelle continued, "I will ask you only one time. I'm already so pleased that you're here. I'm ready to move forward with exploring who and what this," she said, holding out her hands, palms facing toward Rose, "means. I am embracing what I'm capable of being. And I believe you and I are the same. We're both meant to be doing this, learning this together. But I also know you want nothing to do with it, that it goes beyond what you want to believe in, is that right?"

"I'm content living my life as I am," Rose said. "I'm content with you living your life as you wish. I'm content living here. You can go about your witchcraft without involving me too deeply and I won't be hurt. I hope you won't be hurt by that choice."

It was settled. With the qualifier that after many years living together, Rose couldn't help but to have absorbed something of it even without actively seeking to acquire the knowledge from Annabelle. She could prepare many of Annabelle's mixtures if she needed to, the pastes that fed the plants to quicker growth, the potions that she painted on the sides of trees to keep the panthers away, the powder that she could blow into an animal's face to send it off to sleep. She never did prepare any of those actual items, but she knew she could. Perhaps once or twice, while caring for a hurt animal, she might have tried to push the boundaries of what she understood to be possible for a person to do, but both times, despite her success, she immediately felt regret, and the second time she vowed not to do it again.

Rose eventually lost all sense of how much time had passed since she'd arrived. The seasons were clear enough, but the business of living blended them together. Perhaps the strange way that she and Annabelle aged added to that effect. It was a lifetime in paradise by any measure. A respiteful window the world had opened for them.

One day, with the young couple in mind, Rose asked Annabelle whether she'd ever wanted to have children.

"No," Annabelle said without a pause, "I wanted to always be a child. No, no. I'm not built for childbearing. Maybe I can't. Not because I've tried but because I've never tried not to, and it's never happened. And now, I wouldn't do any of that again, even if I did change my mind and suddenly desire a child." She snorted at the thought. "No, I'm done with that. What about you?"

"I've never wanted to be a mother," Rose said. "I've always loved babies, animal and otherwise. Bearing one myself? I never . . . I've never seen that as being a thing that might happen. Never wanted it. Do you think that makes me strange?"

"Not at all," Annabelle smiled wickedly. "I understand perfectly. Witches don't have children. They eat them."

For her part, Rose managed the animals successfully. The fertility of the land extended to all—they raised clutches of baby parakeets, and they expanded the hen house to fit their growing flock of chickens. They had a herd of goats, several cows, two young bulls, and sheep, on top of all the wild animals of Alabama to deal with.

Armadillos were her favorites of the new creatures she encountered. All one had to do was startle an armadillo, and it would leap into the air, sometimes maybe four feet, before running away. It was uncharacteristic for her, but she took great pleasure in the whole process of waiting for them, jumping out at them, and catching them off guard, so much so that Annabelle was sure to warn Rose not to try the same on her.

Rose once found a dead armadillo, killed by a wolf perhaps, and seen in its exposed stomach that it had been pregnant, with four babies. She couldn't understand it exactly as she stared at the four seemingly identical forms. Had they all been attached to each other, she wondered? Did they all come from one egg? It was a new animal for her to study and learn.

Indians had been cleared from Alabama at the turn of the century. With a simple majority vote, the newcomers ejected the region's non-voting original settlers, and relocated them to other states. This had once been tribal land, Rose decided over time. She occasionally came across evidence of their presence, and she left it undisturbed because not doing so would have made her feel complicit in what was clearly a crime.

From their occasional visitors, Rose and Annabelle learned of a town forming 20 miles distant, There were more cars in the world by then, and although roads didn't come near yet, it was assured that eventually they would, and 20 miles would no longer seem so distant. There were also rumors of a factory being built nearby.

They learned that there were people outside of their paradise who believed two witches, immortally young, had long lived somewhere in the forest, offering aid to some travelers while driving the rest away.

What brought about the end of that time in her life? Had the townspeople's crops withered? Had their animals become diseased? Was it a plague of frogs? An overzealous preacher out to rid the world of evil? Would that Rose actually knew the cause, what had pushed the town's population to descend on their property with torches.

Annabelle knew hours before anything happened. She'd stared out the window for half an hour or longer before telling Rose, "I think they are coming tonight to end us. You should gather whatever you have here that you wish to save, whatever you can carry with you." She was assured and calm as she spoke.

The air smelled of chamomile.

"What about you?"

"I'm not leaving, Rose. They'll win, but it will cost them. It will give you time to escape. It's either you, or neither of us."

Rose was torn. There was no apparent threat. Yet, by now, she had learned to have some trust in Annabelle's pronouncements.

She let the animals out to pasture, knowing they would wander some but that she would be able to gather them easily enough if this, whatever this was, blew over. For the hens, she could think of nothing better for them than they already had. When she considered the parakeets, wondering what she could do, whether or not there was truly a threat to them . . . somewhere in her mind, she touched on something, not an image, not a voice, almost not even a feeling, something charged and fleeting, and came to believe there was indeed a physical threat in the air. She didn't try to examine it further. Instead, she decided Annabelle might be right.

Rose had already established several nesting areas for the birds in the wild, and she had continued to supplement their efforts by keeping breeding pairs at the house. She placed the remaining four birds into a reed birdcage so she could move them to one of the other creches on her way out.

What did she wish to save? All of it! Nearly every possession she had was tied to this place, from this place, because of this place. There was no point to most of it without it being here. She settled on a few pieces of clothing, the money she had originally arrived with—the earnings of her previous lifetime—and a few of her favorite stones and crystals. Annabelle gave her what she called her seed wallet, where she had collected a library of seeds. Each different type of seed was pocketed in labeled parchment paper, and the inner lining of the wallet's fabric was padded with cotton to help keep the seeds dry. She also gave Rose a small satchel, filled with jars of various of her potions and powders, which she thought Rose would be able to use. She gave Rose more money, too, and offered her some advice for redeeming that money when she was out in society again. She put a chain necklace around Rose's neck; the pendant on the end was a tiny glass vial with a cork on top. Inside were tiny yellow seeds that resembled sesame seeds, only much smaller.

Annabelle asked, "You know what these are?"

Rose nodded.

Then they embraced. Neither cried, although Rose was on the edge of it.

"We'll meet again," Annabelle said. "Either in this life or on our way to the next."

One of the things Rose remembered most distinctly about that night was the contrast between the inside of the house and the outside. The inside of the house had been so calm, in fact, that Rose would wonder later if the incense Annabelle was burning contained some kind of sedative. Outside the cabin, the air was charged. Night was coming on fast and the smell of smoke was powerful. She heard the echoes of voices shouting in the distance.

Clearly, the townspeople had determined fire was the best antidote to Annabelle's maze. Rose couldn't go back the way she had first arrived. Instead, she'd gone west, in the direction of the hills, keeping to the natural canopy where she could. She heard the sounds of gunfire, and much yelling, but there were also unidentifiable noises—thunderous booms, an unearthly and extended groaning, a tremendous roar repeated again and again, and shrieks that seemed to emanate from the sky.

She was nearly to the hills when she heard, over and over, a loud thumping noise, steady, like a drum. It sounded far off, but it seemed to be coming her way. Thump, thump, thump. It grew louder and louder. She scrambled to hide inside a tangle of bushes underneath a tree, not knowing what path whatever it was might be approaching on.

The sound continued growing louder until she knew it was close to her. It did not pause. It was going to pass right by her. It wasn't chasing her. What she saw moving through the trees nearby appeared to be another tree, or part of a tree. It was wearing the clothes of a lumberjack and holding a great, wooden axe as it headed with stiff, steady steps, in the direction of the house. As it passed by her, each step shook the ground.

She yelled after it, "Protect my baby birds, too!"

In the nook between the first two hills, where three streams joined together to form the river that flowed down to the forest, she delivered the last of the parakeets to a family of their own kind. Trees grew on either side of the river, and she knew she could stay with that tree line until she was off the property and into the wilderness.

She climbed a short way up one of the hills to look back one last time at the place where she'd spent the last decades of her life. The sky was clear. A partial moon was out among the stars. A cloud of black smoke poured up from the forest to the left, billowing into the air beneath the stars. Flames were jumping from treetop to treetop. A fog was rapidly rising around the house. Through the haze of smoke, there appeared to be skirmishes going on all over between fire-wielding townspeople and what Rose believed were Annabelle's tree sculptures. The lumberjack charged into battle with one group of villagers, while in a field close by the confederate soldier collapsed in a burst of flame, surrounded by a large group of pitchfork-wielding men, many of whom appeared to be injured. Across that landscape, there appeared to be many bodies laid out on the ground; however, Rose believed there were too many townspeople left for them all to be stopped.

In one section of the trees where fire raged, a pair of giant yellow legs capped by a red house lumbered wildly through the smoke, randomly crushing and kicking its assailants along the way. Farther back in the blaze, a similar pair of legs toppled, the little red house on top aflame, before being swallowed by smoke.

Rose watched only a moment longer before slipping back under the cover of the trees and heading on her way.

Chapter 4

Wiltern Baylorson's wife, Eva, died at an advanced age with multiple ailments, each of which individually should have been adequate for the task of killing her, but none of which could manage the final blow. Years of submission to her husband's eccentricities, his wanderings, his ego, his lack of consideration, his inability to have any conception of the insufferable person he had become— those had perhaps hardened her beyond the incapacitative power of any single affliction.

The both of them were old; she hardly left the house, and never went beyond the porch, although her husband was still able to work around the property. Neither had been to town, or in public, for many years, and no one had visited at the property in longer than that.

There had been an unsettling of relations between Wiltern and Clay town elders after the City Hall burned down under questionable circumstances around the same time there was a public discussion ongoing about Wiltern's continued meddling in town affairs, the condition of his mind, and the details of his life and his holdings. Among the losses in the fire were one hundred years of the town's birth records. Although no charges were leveled and no evidence found to tie him directly to the crime, the bad will expressed toward him in Clay was enough for him to vow not to return. It was enough, indeed, that the town council voted to disincorporate Wiltern's land holdings, allowing Wiltern to become the independent territory that he had always wished to be.

None of that mattered to Eva. She was miserable and dimly aware that she had lived beyond her time and deserved an end. Finally, when it seemed beyond fate to deliver her, she shot herself through the temple on the porch with her Colt pistol.

Ten years later, feeling only an endless gnawing inside his stomach, which hadn't had a meal in it for months, Wiltern hung himself from the exposed rafters in his living room. He thought when he did it that he was already likely dead, and he placed his star orbs in his pocket so he would not be away from them. He kicked the stool aside, and then he hanged there.

For how long? For several months? For several years? When it gradually became apparent he had not succeeded, he gave it more time. What was time, after all? Then he scratched weakly at the rope with his fingernail, patiently, for whatever amount of time it took, until the rope broke. Wiltern fell to the floor. It would take him a while to stand again. There was no pain for him, and there was no time. He stayed there on the floor. He still held the orbs in his pocket.

He waited.

When Rose left Alabama, she went West. Although there were more modes of travel available to her than before, she traveled by foot. She stayed inland from the coast. She wound up in Texas.

The world she emerged into was a different place, or parts of it were. Bigger, faster, more developed. Parts of it were near the same as she remembered them, depressingly so in comparison to the advances she witnessed elsewhere.

A lone person couldn't expect to pitch a tent just anywhere their trail led them. There were fences everywhere, for one thing. Nearly every piece of land had some sort of boundary around it. Nothing was as open as it used to be.

Following Annabelle's advice, she found a bank that had several branches throughout the area, and deposited a large portion of what she had brought with her from Alabama. She found herself a small apartment at the edge of the suburbs.

She continued to barter for her services in the poorest of areas, where she spent much of her time tending to humans and animals, and gradually moved her way toward a suburban area outside of Dallas. She volunteered at poorly funded nonprofits that serviced the poor and at veterinary offices. She worked as a midwife and, more lucratively for her, as an animal care specialist for two midsized cattle ranches.

The wife of the owner of one of those cattle ranches was a civic-minded woman, and through her Rose became involved with an organization that provided various support services for different groups of the disadvantaged. That was the sort of phrasing that they tossed around, which Rose was never able to adopt as her own. Exactly what the work involved was that Rose brought farm animals to children in hospitals, drove a book-laden truck through poor neighborhoods, delivered fresh produce to soup kitchens for the homeless, and any number of other community services.

She did not do this all alone. There was a core group of eight volunteers, of which she was a member, who performed on most every job. There was a flow of volunteers, always new, always different, who showed up to perform a day or two of work before they were never to be seen again. A woman named Susan had initially interviewed Rose, giving the impression that she owned the charity and was deeply involved in all aspects of its functioning. Susan had told Rose that she had a special spot in her heart for rural folks, because she'd grown up in the country as well. She had even assured Rose that she would be able to help Rose acclimate to the metropolitan lifestyle—she was going to teach Rose everything she knew.

That was the last Rose had heard or seen of Susan.

It was the other seven regulars who really brought her up to speed. Two silver-haired widows, two middle-aged divorcees, and three single women, two in their thirties and one in her forties. Two of the single women would later confide to Rose that they were lesbians, and then, a year or two later, they moved away from Texas so they could be that without being regarded so poorly by their neighbors.

These woman showed her how to use a phone. They taught her how to drive. How to change a light bulb. To turn on a modern stove. They had explained to her what a lesbian was. They helped update her wardrobe and her hairstyle. They helped with her history. One of them figured out the process for getting Rose issued a birth certificate. They believed Rose was in her mid-thirties, and she went along with them, choosing a birth date and year for the first time in her life. She read many of the books on the bookmobile, then tried to learn what more she could from them on any subject she found interesting: Stalin, the two great Wars, the Depression. They helped her find a dentist. They helped her get a license and guided her through buying her first car, a white Nova.

They went to movies together, usually on someone's father's quarters, and she saw her first musical, a movie with Gene Kelly.

The truth was, it was an uglier life than she'd had before with Annabelle, and an uglier world compared with what it was when she abandoned it to live with Annabelle. It mattered little to her how much people marveled at the new, despite her benefiting from the many comforts that weren't available to her at any other time in her life, modernities that made life easier for everyone. She embraced the challenge and the new friends and the unexpected rewards of her work. She thought she would one day be like one of the widows, silver-haired and running tirelessly each day on less than four hours of sleep.

At one of the orphanages where she regularly dropped off baby supplies, she met a child orphaned when his mother shot the child's father and then killed herself. One of the parents had been a Mexican citizen, the other American—Rose did not know which had been which—and the child's mixed heritage had made placement in a home more challenging. The boy was one of 12 babies in the unit at the time, one of 65 children overseen at the orphanage. Because there were new babies coming in all the time, the staff were constantly chasing around leads of openings at other orphanages to shift them around on top of trying to find homes for all of them. Rose would stop by after her afternoons in the bookmobile, where she commonly received multiple donations, to drop off things that people had given her. She was passing by the room where the youngest children slept in rows of pods, when something about that one child caught her eye.

It was a sparkle of light that caught her eye, and when she came closer, she realized it was the baby that was sparkling. Radiating a subtle, golden light from somewhere deep inside of him. She fell in love right there. That was the moment she discovered her purpose, and her true life began.

Instead of dropping off the donations, she brought them back to her car. She didn't think anyone had seen her arrive or leave. She would come back the following day. She would finish her work, and return the following day to visit him again.

That night, she was anxious in a way she had never been before. She had never felt this way before in her life. She nearly cried at the thought that she had left him behind. He was hers, was how she felt, so deeply that it nearly hurt.

The clinic was understaffed, and those on duty were often tasked with any and every job that needed to be done. It wasn't unusual for children to be moved from one place to another by someone on duty, and when Rose returned the next day, she pretended that was just what she was doing, or else she would have pretended that way if she'd run into anyone on the way in. It was as depressingly abandoned as it had been the day before. She wondered, were they off for a cigarette break? Were they rutting away the time someplace? What was it about this state that it cared so little for its most vulnerable?

There were only nine babies when she returned. Her heart lurched when she thought he might be gone, and then was filled with awe and affection when she saw he was indeed there. She picked him up and named him Joshua.

Then she'd walked straight out of the place, baby cradled in her arms, imagining that she looked like she was a mother on the way back to her car from a stroll around the facility.

With the baby lying across the back seat, she'd simply driven off. She would have driven straight out of town from there, but it had occurred to her that if someone noticed the baby was gone, and if someone connected it to Rose's absence, there was one person in the area who probably knew a little bit too much about Rose. A little girl, a neglected and parentified latchkey foster child so in need of adult attention that she would probably reveal everything she knew about Rose if there were someone there to listen. In her time with the girl, what things had Rose shared with her? Rose had mentioned growing up in North Carolina. She had mentioned the clinic and the parent organization, and she had even told the girl where in the area she had been renting a room.

Rose considered taking the girl with her—it would solve the girl's problems, and her own. Rose thought to herself: I might have even told her to be ready to go.

So she'd doubled back to get Lily.

That was the day Rose Chamber started her family.

With Joshua and Lily, she drove to Arizona, where she sought out and found Miriam and Mercy, the two volunteers who had moved to Scottsdale after realizing both their mutual affection and their desire for a place to live where they might be able to be more open about their feelings.

Lily took to Miriam and Mercy, expressive and interesting people and, deprived in their new life of a chance to work with children, they were glad to have little ones around their house. Rose rented a room from them, set about finding work for herself, and Lily started kindergarten. Miriam worked as a receptionist at the office of Pure Heart Confessional Church, and by some method obtained church paperwork that she was then able to use to get birth certificates for both of the children—and eventually, for Carolyn, as well—certificates which would show Rose Chamber as their mother, John Doe as their father, and Scottsdale, Arizona, as their place of birth.

Miriam and Mercy had once questioned Lily about Joshua's father, and her own. They thought it was clear that Lily was not Rose's daughter by birth but rather by adoption. Lily had explained that her mother, as Rose had asked Lily to call her, left her dad because he was too angry. Then she had burst into tears. The two older women both shook their heads seriously, and doubts of Lily's origins were dispensed with, and the subject was not mentioned again, with Lily or with Rose. Lily told everyone that Joshua was her brother, and if someone asked about their father, which people did more than a polite person might expect, she would say, "I don't like to talk about my dad."

Rose started walking again. In Texas, the closeness of her life to all the places she had worked, she believed, had made her lazy. Now, with the children, and it being not too long a time that she'd had them, she'd been afraid someone was going to come after them, track them down, and take them away. Which, she would admit, was giving credit to Texas' childcare system that it didn't deserve. She truly believed they hadn't even noticed Joshua was gone. Lily's foster parents were wild cards, although by what Rose had seen of them, they'd surely noticed she was gone, but not done anything about it. Likely, she thought, they were still collecting whatever payments they were getting for fostering her, too.

But, she thought, suppose word was out about the kidnappings—she didn't like that word, preferring "rescues."

Say someone did stop her because they were suspicious of her connection to those kidnappings? Well, if they arrested Rose, and she was on foot instead of driving her car, they wouldn't so easily find their way to the kids.

But that wasn't going to happen, Rose believed, and she tried to live in a way to ensure it did not. Walking was a part of that. She'd promised Lily they would never have to go back.

Rose spent some hours working at a small, remote clinic near the California border. It wasn't in a building at all, but in one of a set of converted mobile home bungalows. The two units had been divided among four businesses—a dirt bike shop and a sandwich shop were in the first trailer, and the second trailer was occupied by the clinic and an insurance company's office.

There were more patients than one would expect, but that was not to say the clinic was ever busy. Arizona could be so parched and so dry that Rose found the feeling of remoteness was magnified. There might have been a town just a mile away, around that hillside, behind those rocks, but because all she could see was dry prairie, it felt like the trailers were the only structures in the middle of an endless desert.

The remoteness meant there wasn't a doctor within a 30-minute drive and the absence of reliable consistent public transportation meant that a person on the verge of dying might not want to end up there, but Rose was able to perform a lot of services competently, and had not yet found herself in a situation she wasn't prepared to handle.

So the absence of a doctor would not have seemed an issue at the arrival of the pregnant woman at the clinic doors, her water already broken. Rose was, in fact, the most experienced person on the staff in obstetrics, a fancy word for what she could do that she would never use to describe her skills.

The woman seemed unbalanced, but it was hard to tell if

that was an issue that extended beyond the pregnancy—it might be that this was some hormonal surge. She was unable to meet and hold Rose's gaze, and she pulled at individual strands of her hair compulsively. The delivery revealed more of her condition, the thinness of her frame, the bruises around her abdomen, the cuts on her inner thighs.

Rose asked, "You tried to kill it?"

"I'm not supposed to be able to get pregnant! It's going to kill me now! You don't understand. It's a soul-sucking monster. It's a vam," she breathed in slowly, "pire."

"Well, even if you succeeded, you'll still have to push it out of your body. It's the best way to give the body a chance to heal. Otherwise, you're just walking around with a mass of dead tissue attached to your insides."

They didn't have much by way of sedation, and nothing Rose could give to her but a cloth to bite, but once the contractions settled in the woman became fiercely focused on the task.

She showed no signs of relief when Rose held the baby girl in her arms. Rose looked the baby over quickly for damage, but found very little save for a red mark in the middle of the back of her hand, perhaps from her mother's knife or scissors.

The woman asked, "Why is she glowing like that?"

Rose did a double take, and stared at the baby as a whole, instead of inspecting its parts for damage. And it was true. It was just as it had been with Joshua.

It was because of the mark on the hand that Rose resisted a moment passing the baby to her mother, which was normally done as quickly as could be done, to start the bonding, to let the baby know immediately it was out but not alone. Rose stared at that birthmark, which might well have been from a knife or a wire hanger, and she felt a possessiveness that closely matched the emotion she'd felt with Joshua. This woman had already proven herself unworthy, Rose thought.

The woman looked at Rose holding the baby, and Rose looked at the woman, perhaps shifted in a way as to suggest she might pass the baby, and the woman lifted her arms as if she was willing to receive the child. Her eyes were watery, and she moved her lips as if she was saying words, but no noises came out.

Rose hesitated a moment longer. The woman in that same moment grabbed for the baby, arms flailing, with an expression of murderous intent. The pain of moving made her cry out as she lunged. Rose took a step backward, but needn't have moved that far because the woman's legs were still strapped to the table. More than that, in that moment, whatever rage it was that filled her also broke her. She was dead the moment she sat upright, and Rose would guess that her heart had stopped, and when she fell back on the bed again, she was gone.

It was only a few short seconds after the woman died, when Rose was nearly panting as she tried to calm her own heart, that the body made a gurgling noise. Rose looked at it, and would later swear that something from the mother's corpse was released out into the room as her body twitched its last—and in a reaction Rose couldn't understand, the baby grew hot in her arms. Her skin reddened as if to her first exposure to water, and small welts appeared on her chest and hands. When the baby started to cry, Rose walked it out into the night, thinking it was too warm inside, and she blew on the welts and on its reddened face, rocking back and forth, until the color started to lighten, and the welts started to go away. Then the crying stopped.

Rose thought, What just happened?

The rain began not 30 minutes later, dashing any expectation that the doctor might arrive soon to assist. She recorded most everything that happened that evening on a piece of paper, with changes. In her version, the baby was stillborn, having died at the same time the mother was inflicting upon herself the internal injuries that would kill her.

In the rain, Rose dug a small, shallow grave. She put everything that had come out of the woman that wasn't the baby into a cardboard box, along with several rocks, which weighted the box enough to sink into the water that gathered in the grave. Then she had shoveled the soil back into the hole, until it was partially filled. Wouldn't take a critter long to find it, get it out, and make a meal of it, and Rose would be fine with that.

She was able to open the lock to the shop next door, and she cared for the baby there, away from the body. That beautiful, outraged child didn't mind the powdered milk packets for the two days it took the doctor to arrive in his converted army Jeep.

Rose told him the story as she had written it, while he took notes and examined the body, which by then smelled. She had considered wrapping it, but knew the doctor would want to see the corpse.

The baby slept next door, and Rose was prepared to lie about it and its identity to the end should there be a need to do so. In her mind, it was already her baby, little Carolyn.

With a body to be disposed of, paperwork to be filed, a death to be recorded, and not another potential health need in sight because no one was out there in the rain, the doctor opted to load the body, with Rose's help, into the bed of his pickup. And then he was off.

Although Rose knew the clinic management did not like for the office to be closed, she was also aware that they knew it happened from time to time, because out in the middle of nowhere it was not always possible to have a full-time staff on hand. She knew someone on the next shift would be along soon, but the more time passed, the less appealing the prospect of keeping the baby out of their sight seemed to be.

She left a note on the door reading, "Back in Five Minutes," although she had no intention of ever returning. She wrapped up the baby and started the long walk home.

There were stunned looks all around when she returned with a newborn. Miriam and Mercy could only gesture with their arms to ask questions. It was not long before Lily embraced the whole concept and tried to hug her sister.

"Where did she come from? Is she ours?"

"Yes," Rose said, "She's ours. I guess yours and Joshua's father left me a little parting present I didn't know about. I just thought I'd gained a little weight. I didn't realize she was there until the contractions started."

Strangely, Rose found that explanation was enough. She herself, if presented with such a story, would have questions. Perhaps, she thought with some guilt, it spoke to how much they trusted her. After all, why would Rose lie?

Chapter 5

The Chamber family stayed in Arizona another year, and then moved north, to get away from the heat. They lived in Washington, and then in Oregon, where they found a rustic, off-the-grid town not far from the coast.

Rose plied all of her skills there, working for a pig farmer one week, and as a midwife the next two, then at a health clinic the next. With a small, two-room house as her base, and relying on local girls for childcare, she found work that was at some distance from her home, and she would take extra precautions, such as parking her car miles from a job, and then crossing the last distance by foot, to keep anyone from following her home. Her car, she'd realized, decades old, made her easier for anyone and everyone to find, so she traded it for a nondescript brown sedan that seemed to match what everyone else was driving.

At one of her jobs, she covered evening shifts at a family planning clinic in Eugene. One thing she had missed was the camaraderie of her group of women in Texas. Those sorts of connections had made her life easier, but everyone she encountered in Oregon seemed so young. Even the middle-aged seemed like children to her, with their own age-appropriate issues.

It was in Eugene where she met a man seeking someone to serve as a midwife. She'd known he was an odd one from the beginning, and she refused his offer of a ride to his ranch, instead collecting the address and promising to visit the next day. She drove a good portion of the distance the following afternoon, then parked her car beside the road and walked the remaining distance. About a mile-and-a-half in, she was startled to find the man seated in his truck, parked beside the road, waiting for her.

He asked her, "Where'd you walk from?"

This was when Rose realized she was in a worse situation than she'd anticipated. At that point, she felt there would be no backing out of it for her. Something had started.

"Oh, I like to go everywhere on foot," she said. "Just let the husband know which route I'll be taking and where I'm headed—that way he can check on me if there's any trouble." It was the first time in her life she had invoked a husband as a ward.

Until Lily was engaged, it wouldn't occur to Rose that a wedding ring would have made that lie more convincing.

"Ride you up to the house," he said.

"Made it this far," she demurred. "A little more will be over in no time. I'm still working out something in my head. I'll see you at your house. Thank you for the offer."

She soon arrived at a spare ranch-style house on a large piece of land in an area where the neighboring properties seemed distant. Inside were two girls, in their early teens at best. In conversation, it would emerge that they had been told not to tell Rose their names. This restriction, which they obeyed, had the effect of making the girls more comfortable sharing information that didn't include their names. One girl, Rose would discover during the third visit, was the stepdaughter of the man who'd hired Rose, and the other was the stepdaughter of his friend and business partner, with whom he shared the ranch. Over the next months, she would learn that the two men had taken each other's stepdaughters as brides in some ceremony sanctioned by traditions and beliefs invented by the men themselves. Their mothers had run off before that, according to what the stepfathers had told the girls, leaving them behind. Rose thought immediately the mothers must be dead, but then told herself not to jump to conclusions.

There was no stopping the visits. She could have notified the police, but she didn't. She suspected this was something he had understood about her before he first approached her, that a person like her wouldn't want to get involved with the police. Regardless, Rose couldn't abandon children in such great need.

When Rose thought the girls were nearly ready to give birth, she was prepared. She brought a small jar from the collection Annabelle had given her in the satchel. This was the herb that would hasten their progress from labor through delivery. Rose was very much concerned that when the children were born, the men not only would no longer have a use for Rose, but also they might be highly motivated to keep her from leaving and possibly sharing what she might have seen or learned about their homestead.

On her way to their ranch, she stopped at spot where a creek ran beside a hillside covered in yellowed grass and tumbleweeds. She had cloth pouch filled with balls of lint held together with pine resin, each with a match tip at its center. This she hung by a string from the branch of a tree. She had also made a wick, and coated it in wax, of a length that she believed would burn for an hour or more, and that she attached to the cloth patch before lighting the end of the wick on fire.

She did all this several miles west of the ranch. She then drove to an area east of the ranch, and parked there before walking in.

There was no smoke visible as she entered the house. She did not know if it had caught. She did not know if this would work. She gave both girls a mixture of water and the birthing powder half an hour apart, to stagger their deliveries. The men were not about, apparently working at different ends of the ranch.

For the older girl, it was less of a problem than Rose had ever known it to be; the baby was out in 20 minutes. The mother was well enough to lend a hand with her friend and fellow prisoner, whose extreme anxiety seemed to be countering the effects of the herbs.

Suddenly and at last, while the younger girl labored, Rose

heard the sound of sirens. The sound of a car driving down the main road, calling for hands to help battle a nearby fire. The sounds of the two men returning to the property, shouting at each other as they gathered tools in the yard, and finally, the sounds of them setting off together.

The air soon smelled of smoke.

With the older girl's coaching, and the example she'd set, things eventually moved along. The younger one was a smaller girl, and her baby was larger, and both of their cries would surely have been heard were it not for the klaxons sounding fire alarms across the area, and the trucks thundering by.

For the rest of her life, Rose would puzzle over her nearly irresistible attraction to a handful of children out of the hundreds she had brought into the world. It hadn't been about any baby's particular circumstance—after all, the first time she saw Joshua, there were eleven others beside him and none of them had appealed to her so irresistibly as he had. It wasn't a matter of sympathy for the mother or the mother's circumstances— she'd worked with the poorest of the poor, people who were in difficult circumstances, and she'd never even once considered offering to take one of their children from them. It might have been something about the mothers of these specific children, although she did not know them well enough to know what those women might have had in common. Or was it simply the children themselves, each special in his or her own way, each something more than they appeared to be?

The head emerged without her having to cut the mother, for which Rose was thankful. Then a baby boy was there next to the girl, both of them glowing faintly in her minds' eye.

She faced the hardest part of her plan, which would be to sedate the girls and be on her way—but she found she had some doubts inside her about leaving the two teens with these men if that was not where they wished to be.

The answer presented itself in the form of the 14-year-old, fully dressed, a backpack in her hand, confronting Rose.

"We're leaving."

"You're leaving the babies?"

"No. You're taking the babies. Wherever you need to take them to give them a better life than this. Drop them off at a fire station."

Rose turned to see the younger one rising from the bed. She thought, Where do children get the energy?

"Do you know where you're going?"

"You think we haven't had enough time to map it out? Yeah, we know where we're going." The girls wouldn't offer any more than that, and Rose wasn't sure she wanted to know. In five minutes time, her estimation of them had changed radically.

Finally, the 14-year-old said, "They'll catch us if we're all together. If we separate, we make it harder for them."

There was no debate. Rose used a sheet to fashion a bundle for the babies to held them fast against her chest. They all left the house out a window facing the direction opposite of the fire, and went straight into the fields. The plants were just starting to grow, so they offered minimal cover. Better was a neighboring plot filled with rows of small Christmas trees, which concealed them without requiring them to crouch or crawl. They passed an intersection, and then another intersection, and were not far from her car when the girls told Rose they were going their own way.

"My car's not far from here."

"No offense, but we're not getting into anybody's car again for a while."

And that was that.

Could it have been that simple? When she had nearly reached her car, she heard the sound of a familiar engine approaching. Her first fear as she listened to it was that it would turn down the road in the direction the girls had headed; her second fear came true when it didn't turn, and continued in her direction, not driving at full speed but rather at the speed of someone who was checking the sides of the road as he drove. She didn't think he saw where she had parked her car, but she did get the feeling that somehow he'd known she was nearby, and she was sure at some point he would be doubling back.

This was the start of a daylong chase.

Rose went farther from the road, which slowed her down, making a wider circle through near-wilderness to get around to her car from the other direction. She fed the babies powdered milk while sitting on a log near a bank of wild blueberry bushes. She decided their names would be Ben and Zoe. Then, feeling that she was still being pursued, she began the drive back to her home.

She avoided Eugene entirely. Still, he seemed to have a better idea of her route than she suspected. She saw him by chance pulling out of a gas station on the road about six miles from her home when it was dark. She pulled into the same gas station, filled up her tank, and placed a quick call to the sitter at the house.

"Jill, I'm up at the Rayso gas station. I'll be home in about 10 minutes. I think it'll be okay for you to head home. I'll toot my horn when I pass your house, so you'll know it's me. If Lily is up, tell her she's in charge."

"Okay. She'll be delighted. Thanks, Mrs. Chamber."

Rose knew he was ahead on the road, but she didn't believe he knew the area well enough yet that he had taken the unmarked turn-off that led more directly to her home. He would start at one of the two marked exits further down the road, and work his way back. By the end of tonight, maybe by tomorrow morning, he would know the area street by street, and he would find them. Her only choice would be to stop to pick up the kids and anything that might tell anyone looking who they were and where they had been, and then be on their way. But their way to where? Back to

Arizona? Rose would decide that later.

Finally, after a panicked frenzy of packing, the kids were in the car. Lily and poor little Josh were wide awake in the back seat in a shocked and frightened state. Rose was afraid neither of them would ever sleep restfully again.

It wasn't long before she knew where she was headed. North Carolina. Home. The only safe place she had left.

Chapter 6

At the moment Rose saw the walls of that grey rectangular structure at the end of the winding driveway, she felt both relief and awe. Empty and abandoned in the middle of a stand of 80-year old trees, there was no glass in the window, no doors in the doorways, and inches of dirt and leaves covering the floor. That it stood made it seem indestructible and enchanted.

It was home. This was where she came from. It was still here. This was where she and her new family belonged.

There had been no paved roads when she had last been here, and she'd found that the most confusing new element when trying to locate the family plot. The spot was more remote from the town center than she'd remembered, although much of the land between those two points had been sectioned off with chain-link and barbed wire fences, and looked to be undeveloped property owned by someone. The farther from town, the fewer the number of properties that appeared to have houses on them.

When she'd stopped at a gas station to ask for directions to the Chamber property, the cashier had no idea. When he asked for a street name, she realized the street she lived on hadn't had a name, or at least one that she remembered anyone ever using. It had been a dirt road.

"I don't know," she said.

When Rose drove away from the station, she was sure he wouldn't wait long to repeat the question to someone else, starting a conversation that would crawl across the town.

She found the right area finally, north and west of the flood plain, with a mountaintop visible to the north, and the river they'd just driven past to the west. Nature had been left more to its own course the farther they went from town.

Then they were at the property. She turned onto what looked like a maintenance road—all dirt and not maintained at all—and when they drove around a small knoll, and she started to think that the trees were too close together for this to be it, then they were suddenly there. In the time since she'd seen it, much of it had been reclaimed by the forest.

The children were bewildered as they walked around among the trees. Rose went to what was left of the chimney, looked inside the mouth of it, and then up. There was a small metal ring there, clipped to the wall inside, above and behind an inner edge. She pulled the ring free, and later put it into the glove box compartment of the car. Then she set about creating a shelter from their belongings.

Rose had money left, although she would have to go to a bank in town to start the process of transferring it. It was enough to get them by for a while, figuring for the added expenses that would come with rebuilding a home here. What she had with her, the portion she'd always kept on hand for emergencies, that was all they had for now, thinned, of course, by thousands of miles' worth of gasoline and food.

It wasn't long until some curious passerby came around the hill that shielded the property from the view of the street, and saw the straits they were in—a single mom with five kids, two of them babies, camped out in a weathered car. This first passerby apparently shared what she had seen, and a local couple soon stopped by to take stock of the situation.

When they discovered she was a daughter of Clay returned home, and saw the challenges she faced, they left for a short while, and then they returned, followed by other people from the community. The first day, people brought them food, blankets, and a couple tents. The next day, they came with supplies. After that, more came to work on building them a better shelter.

In those first few days, Rose updated her history yet again, adding details here and there until at some point she realized she was creating the history that she would have to live by, and that she had better keep it simple. Also, she had better pay close attention to what she was saying.

She became Rose Chamber, granddaughter of Nelson and Betaan, daughter of Roslyn, the mythical mother to whom Rose bore a striking resemblance. Rose decided she was in her early forties—once again, she thought. She told them she worked as a midwife and farm animal care specialist. She told them the stories of the fathers, which of course had to be shared if she were to earn anyone's trust or sympathy. In those stories, Lily's father died in a car crash—which could have been true, for all Rose knew. In Rose's grieving, she'd fallen in with a man that she realized, too late, had a violent temper, and had been forced to flee him with Lily and two new children, Joshua and Carolyn, after annulling the marriage. And finally, in Salt Lake City, where she met the twins' father, and discovered he was a polygamist. He'd started a family with Rose before telling her another family already existed. She had packed up her brood, Rose told whoever asked, and, with nowhere else to go, brought them home to North Carolina.

Her story then, was not one of a young woman who'd gone out into the world with hardly a look back, who managed to live a good life on her own. Instead, she became a figure deserving of sympathy for the bad choices that brought her home.

She stuck to that narrative for 28 years, and it was a background story that most had heard. Rose was aware that people from town had gossiped extensively about her difficult "situation" in the early years, and she took some comfort in witnessing the effort they put into making it seem like they hadn't.

In a few short days, her new life took on a hopeful shape. There stood a small structure, essentially one general living room and two bedrooms, attached to the ruins of the old house on one end and the refurbished chimney on the other. Many trees had been cleared, and the wood was stacked in the area that would someday be the vegetable garden.

They had also received some donated and needed household items—a stove, a sink, a table and chairs, mattresses, cribs, and diapers. More importantly, after many conversations with many different folks, there were leads for work for Rose.

Less than a week after their arrival, Lily was enrolled in third grade at the local school, riding the school bus and seated next to one of the children of one of the men who'd worked on the house. Joshua and Carolyn were at a pre-school program at one of the local churches, and Rose had a morning at home with Ben and Zoe.

While the twins slept, she went to the oldest part of the house. She brought a chair with her and a length of rope. She set the chair in the middle of the room, stood on it, and carefully removed the rusted metal fixture from the ceiling, exposing a thick, circular, metal hook. After setting down the fixture, she pushed one end of the rope through the hoop.

Then the floor. She pushed aside the rug in the middle of the room, revealing the stone slab underneath. There was a hole in the center, as if for a post or a flag. Around that hole was a ring cut into the hard, concrete-like material. She took out the ring she'd found in the chimney. There was a collapsing arm on the back of the ring, and she stood it up and pushed that into the hole. As the arm slid into the hole, the ring fit perfectly into the indentation around the hole. When it was pressed flat, there was a click, and the entire cylinder pushed up about half an inch. She held onto the top of it and turned it to unscrew it the rest of the way, at which point she pulled and the cylinder came out.

She looked down into the hole in the floor. There was a hook at the bottom, through which she looped the other end of the rope, which she tied into a knot

Grasping the end of the rope, she pulled, and the section of the floor gave way with surprising ease, although the effort to set the piece down in a place other than back on top of the opening proved challenging because her arms were not long.

It wasn't a treasure trove, but that wouldn't have been obvious if a person were judging by the look on Rose's face. Her father's journals were there, and a couple of the books which he had used for her schooling. There were a few pieces of jewelry, which might have been her mother's. There were folded pieces of paper tucked into various journals—the old fashioned variety of a handmade envelope, each of which contained something—a stamp, a rock, a coin—which carried significance for her father.

She went back and forth through the cache, trying to decide what she might take out that would be useful, before she came across her father's birth certificate and a copy of the land covenant—each filed in the chronologically appropriate journal, with her birth document in the front of his first journal. She took those three documents, and then sealed up the rest, promising herself to return to her father's papers when she had a chance.

Afterward, she felt strangely satisfied. She felt as if, for a moment, she had visited with Nelson, and he was just as she remembered. She also knew that she herself was in there, hidden away in one or more of those books, the real her, the original Rose, in some form or another. That was another reason to keep it a secret, at least until she could see what his journals might reveal about her.

Later that evening, when the kids were home and asleep, Rose sat feeding Zoe on the porch. She was gobbling down the milk—this one would be a healthy eater—and her eyes were closed. Rose started to doze off, but a touch of something warm startled her awake.

Zoe was still drinking, but her skin had started to redden.

Small hives formed on her face, on her nearly bald head, and then down her whole body. Rose gasped, but Zoe kept drinking, her eyes closed. The baby's skin heated up, and turned an even deeper shade of red. Rose reached her fingers into her glass of ice water, then touched her damp fingers to the baby's forehead, so drops of water fell on her skin. Zoe reacted to that by twisting her head a little, without releasing the bottle. Rose blew lightly on the baby for several minutes until the heat started to release, and Zoe's skin started to return to normal. The hives faded as quickly as they had formed.

When she was done eating, and had her burp, Rose held her close until the baby was asleep. If Rose understood what had just happened, Zoe's birth mother was dead. Rose tried to picture what fate that young girl might have met, but there were too many to choose from for her to manage it. She hoped it wasn't at the hands of her "husband."

Rose knew what it felt like to lose a mom.

"I'll be your mother, little one," she said quietly to Zoe. "We'll do fine."

It was several years before she thought of the journals again. Her new life, her new family, it swallowed her for a while, and she embraced it. Life was full and happy and secure, and she was no longer contemplating where the next step in her journey would bring her. She had visited her father's grave, which had a marker that only bore his name and the year of his death, which Rose was certain was a date at least ten years later than Leanne had told her he had died. Rose wondered: Had the woman lied to Rose to discourage her from coming home again?

Rose also wondered why her father's grave was in the town graveyard instead of the cemetery closer to their family property. But she hadn't thought too much about any of those details until she had a long conversation at the market with a man who had served with local police more than 40 years before.

Then she learned the circumstances of her father's death. Nelson's was one of three unsolved murders in the history of Clay. Every generation or so, a change of administrators or the appearance of an eager recruit would lead to the case being reexamined, yet nothing new had come of it.

The first version of the story she heard was that her father had a meeting with Wiltern Baylorson, and on his way to this meeting he had stayed overnight at a small cabin owned by a local farmer, whose name was Havers. In that remote cabin, he was shot, killed, and robbed.

The next version, which she read in an archived copy of a local paper at City Hall, had more detail. Her father was thought to have been interested in purchasing land from Mr. Baylorson, and so was traveling with an unusually large amount of gold. He stayed in Havers' cabin. In the morning, Jericho Pinter, a local man who was harvesting lumber in the area, said he heard a gunshot, ran to investigate, and found Nelson had shot himself, but was still alive. Pinter ran for a doctor, and when Dr. Malls, who Rose remembered from her youth, made it to the cabin a short time later, her father was dead. The doctor found none of her father's possessions—as described by his wife, Leanne—in evidence, and because of the blood and the damage to his face from the gunshot wound, might not have been able to identify the victim had he not known Nelson personally and recognized his regular clothes.

In trial, wherein Jericho Pinter, who first reported hearing the gunshot that killed her father, was charged with second degree murder, Mr. Havers cried at the loss of her father. Pinter proved to be of such limited intelligence that he would repeat anything that was said to him and would say "Yes" to any question asked with an animated expression.

Dr. Malls testified that he had inspected the cabin after finding the victim dead, and found no weapon that might have been used in the murder. Trails of blood on the floor, lack of blood on the bed itself, and a lack of blood spatter evidence inside the cabin indicated the body had been dragged into the room and placed on the bed postmortem, rather than having died in the room. Dr. Malls believed the murder had taken place elsewhere and then the body was moved to Havers' cabin. He noted an absence of blood evidence on Mr. Pinter when speaking to him, although clearly the man had not washed himself nor cleaned his clothes for an extended period.

When the doctor returned to the scene of the crime the following day with the head constable, there were two bullet casings on the floor next to the spot where the body had been placed, where the day before, clearly, there were no casings—as the Doctor had written in his notes after a careful examination of the cabin's interior. After hearing the doctor's testimony, the jury did not convict Pinter.

Attention fell on Havers, and then on Mr. Baylorson, but the lack of evidence kept any from being charged.

It angered Rose to hear of the way her father died. She thought surely he'd been on his way to buy the grazing property from Mr. Baylorson before the end of the 50-year lease. She didn't recognize the other names involved. The vagueness of the description of the crime and the time that had passed added to her feeling of helplessness, and to the sadness she felt for her father.

Over the next months and years, Rose would work her way through her father's journals. She would talk to different people throughout the area, all of them older, most of them elderly and in homes, about their different recollections. There were more folks who were around at the time than she had initially believed would be so, gentlemen and ladies of the old South, in their seventies, eighties, and nineties. They were in their teens and preteens at the time of the murder, but with spectacle trials that dragged out several years, and the crime's notoriety as the region's (at the time) one unsolved murder, the story had left impressions on many.

The journals, in the end, revealed very little, other than the methodical nature of her father. Up until his last entries, he'd been keeping his almanac, recording weather conditions, sunrise and sunset times, and constellations in the night sky. There were sketches of everything he built—the additions to the house, furniture, feed bins for the animals, new tools he would like to have or make. Each sketch was covered with equations and measurements and descriptions of materials.

There were notes about her in some of the journals. He always referred to her as R: R born today. Took R on the trail for the first time. R rode horse today. Letter from R. The references were quick, elliptic, and never elaborated on, but it was satisfying for her to know that she was present in his mind.

There was a tally kept on the back page of each journal, the last number of which was transferred to the following journal. Since his receivables and payables for the ranch appeared on other pages, she decided this was where he'd kept track of the money he was saving to buy the land from Baylorson.

Rose wondered about Leanne. She remembered receiving the last letter from Leanne, the letter telling her that Nelson had died. It had only been a short time later that Rose had gone to live with Annabelle.

She found a few notations referring to Leanne, such as "Engaged to L" but gathered more from the accounting—which included added expenses for decorative fabrics, a new stove, a subscription for beauty supplies, among other things she couldn't imagine her father having ever wanted—that L enjoyed a greater measure of comfort in her daily life than had long been the custom in Nelson Chamber's house.

She wondered idly if Leanne had anything to do with her father's death. Throughout the newspaper articles and the trial, she was referred to as his grieving wife, nothing more. Perhaps she'd wanted more than a life in North Carolina. Perhaps she was well aware of the small treasure he had saved to purchase the land.

However, those mentions of Leanne were all that Rose could find out about her on the public record. Although she had found a notation indicating an engagement, she could find no reference to a service or a document recording their marriage. There was no certificate in the county records. The City Hall fire had obliterated it if it existed. The ninety years in between his death and the modern day was a veil she could not penetrate.

Rose worked in a clinic in Tennessee for a while. She didn't know why it was so, but this particular clinic at this particular time served more poor, young girls than she could believe lived in the entire state. People liked to put it all on them that they were in the situations they were in, but they didn't get that way on their own. Rose had started to think that young men should be required to have some kind of condom surgically attached to them until they were married.

One day she met a college-aged woman very different from her regular clientele. Kendra was fit, fashionable, middle class, and not long from delivery. She was in the last year of her Masters degree program, but was off classes for a semester because of the baby. She'd met the baby's father at another University. He was from a country in Asia; his family was living in the United States, in New York, while he was attending college. They were in love, and she had no doubt about that. What she hadn't understood was the control his family had over him. Two years into their relationship, when he revealed the relationship to his parents, and they disapproved, all his talk of love and independence and making his own decisions had turned out to be theoretical; in practice, his obligation to family was absolute, and the relationship ended.

Except that she was pregnant.

She didn't tell him. She put in the paperwork for time off

just as she was beginning to show. She hadn't known what to do, whether or not to keep it, whether or not to tell him, whether or not she wanted to be a single mother. At some point, she decided she would have the baby, and that when she did, she would let him know. Perhaps that was the sort of familial obligation he also could not ignore.

Kendra otherwise had considered having an abortion, but Rose told her it was too far along for it.

A month later, Rose delivered that baby. The moment she held him, Rose knew he was meant for her. She was so confident of this that she placed the baby into the mother's arms, and could fairly well feel the mix of emotions that raced over the woman's expression. Rose gave Kendra the paperwork she would need to file with the city, filling in all the information except the names of the father and mother.

Two months later, she contacted Rose at the clinic, and asked to meet Rose at a restaurant near the clinic for lunch. She brought the baby to the lunch, and explained that the father, upon hearing the news, hung up on her. Within a week, his entire family was on a plane headed back to their ancestral land.

She was despondent to the point of suicide, a state she had remained in for the duration. She had received $25,000 in cash from his parents one week after the phone call. Kendra explained to Rose that she had been considering walking into a lake with weights in her pockets and the baby in her arms. Rose would have felt sympathy for the younger woman but for the fury in the woman's eyes. Kendra did not want pity.

This was what the mothers of Rose's found children had in common, or the one obvious thing that they shared. They were all angry. Wronged and angry. Kendra's fury, masked by layers of depression, reminded Rose of Carolyn's mother—and it was once again anger directed at the only innocent in the room.

Kendra left the baby with Rose. She gave Rose the envelope

with the money, and she handed Rose the birth papers, where the names of the child's parents were still not filled in. She stared Rose in the eyes and said, "Never give up this child." When she left, Rose, in turn, telephoned Lily to let her know she would be away for a few days.

"Really?" Lily paused a moment. "Okay. Really. Um . . . "

"What is it?"

Lily said, "Is there something you want to tell me?"

"What do you mean?"

"Ummmm . . . hello? The last time you said those words to me we moved across the world! Are you pregnant again? Are you coming home with another baby? We don't have room for another baby!" Rose smiled. Lily was mature in word and so very young in what she knew of the world.

"We'll make room," Rose said.

One last time, she would try to get away with this. She chuckled to herself, thumbing through the money inside the envelope. These were the children she was supposed to watch over. There was a reason for them to be with her. Would Annabelle have been pleased or horrified?

Rose continued to visit her father's grave on occasion, often leaving flowers. One day after a visit, she got it into her mind that she wanted to visit the Baylorson property. She drove home, parked the car, then set out in the direction of the flood plain. They'd been here six years, and she'd never turned her attention in his direction. The land had been swallowed by forest, much as the Chamber property had been, but an effect spread upon a far greater acreage of land.

There were very few she spoke with who remembered the Wiltern name, or knew who he was, or were aware that there was once a large ranch and farming operation on the flood plain. Those who did remember the name just shrugged, not knowing what had happened to that fellow Wiltern. Some recalled him being suspected of having something to do with the City Hall fire. Others said he and his family had returned to Europe.

Parts of the trail to Wiltern's property overlapped with the path she and her father had taken with the herds. All one did at some point was veer left and cross the cracked plain. She thought the plants and trees on the other side of the plain seemed not well, but wasn't sure if that impression wasn't a symptom of her bad feelings toward Mr. Baylorson.

By the time she'd stepped in sight of the house, after a long section walking through the quietest, most still stand of forest she'd ever crossed through, Rose knew it wasn't her mood—it was the environment. The center of it was the homestead itself. It was warding life away, she thought.

There were no animals, no birds, no insects, nothing around except an old Fordson tractor in front of the house.

The trees were old, and alive. But one look at an infected tree next to an uninfected tree was all it took to see which ones were sick—the bent ones, greyish in hue, with the crumpled, wrinkled leaves. Her determination to go forward faltered. This was not what she had expected here. Still, she had come this far. She continued up toward the house, but the closer she got, the greater the desire to turn around and flee.

What was behind that desire, she wondered as it intensified. In Alabama, Annabelle's plants along the route of her maze increased the confusion of the person lost along the route. This was not a magic of that illusionary sort. This was not a natural magic. The feeling struck her at an instinctive level. Her body wanted to leave this place.

She went up to the house, believing it abandoned. She wondered what had been left behind. She pushed open the door and her eyes wandered around the room. It looked so intact. Her eyes were wandering over the books on a shelf when she froze, and realized the house was not empty.

In the corner. Standing there with a noose around his neck, the frayed end of the rope hanging over his shirt, was Mr. Baylorson. There was a chair on its side in the middle of the room. His skin hung loose from his chin. He was staring at her, but she couldn't tell if he was seeing her or if he was actually dead and this was just the expression on his face. He did not react to her, but he was staring at her, this nearly two-hundred-year-old man.

Rose turned and fled the Baylorson property.

Later that evening, under the new moon, she opened the vial she'd long worn as a pendant on the necklace Annabelle had given her, and began the process of planting the tiny seeds inside. She needed two pairs of tweezers to separate one seed from the other, and although there appeared to be thousands in the vial, she did not believe there were enough to seed the perimeter of the entire property.

She briefly considered sending the police to the Baylorson property. She did not know then that the town charter had specifically been amended to place all things Wiltern out of the town's jurisdiction. Regardless, she decided not to stir it up. She did not want to be responsible for anyone going into that place.

She divided her property into two sections: residence and fields, with the residential section including the house and the small vegetable garden and the fields section including the farmed lands and Joshua's slowly expanding back house. She would make a wall around the residence area. As she sewed the seeds, she imagined a wall that would deter threats against her family's well-being, a defense against that which would harm them. She would leave openings only for two doorways. The work occupied her evenings for weeks.

It was the only thing she could think of that might truly give her a feeling of security in her own home from Mr. Baylorson, or whatever was left of him.

A few years after bringing Cole home, Rose returned from a day of work to find a small package had been left on her newly built porch doorstep, addressed to her. By that time, the seeds for the perimeter wall had taken hold, and a square of greenery several inches tall marked half the property. She brought the package inside and opened it on the kitchen table. First, there was a note:

"Dear Ms. Chamber. There is no preamble adequate for this message. Very simply, the deathbed confession of an estranged family member has led to the revelation of the role another long-deceased family member played in your grandfather's death. Enclosed you will find what we believe are the last remaining personal items that were stolen from him. Please know your grandfather Nelson did not commit suicide, as was conjectured in court at the time, and that, thankfully, the innocents originally charged with this crime were released. Our family, already buffeted by the revealed deficiencies of our deceased relatives, is devastated at this further news. We cannot make adequate reparations in any form beyond what accompanies with this letter. Please forgive us for retaining our anonymity. The truth once revealed would only allow terrible persons opportunity to reach from the grave to bring further shame and harm upon their innocent descendants. God Bless you and your family."

Rose considered the note carefully. It didn't give her anything more than she had already, she told herself as she examined it.

There she was quickly proved wrong. She reached into the box to see what else was there. It was a small canvas bag, which held eight gold coins.

Chapter 7

The summer before Lily started at the police academy, Rose took the whole family on the route she had once traveled with her father to graze their animals. She told them that she had remembered her mother describing the journey, and that she had read notes from her grandfather about the trip as well, and that she thought she could find her way from the information they had provided.

She borrowed horses for the week, and the children and she took turns riding them and walking. As they traveled along, she shared her memories with them, telling them stories as if she had memorized all the stories her mother had passed on to her. When they came to the path that diverted to Baylorson's she didn't mention it at all. Three of the kids being boys, a stern warning to avoid that area surely would have brought them there shortly after they returned home. Zoe would probably want to be in on it, too— she wouldn't be left behind if adventure awaited. Instead, she led them across the river, heading up the first of many mountains.

In her mind, she kept returning to her father making this journey the last time. She wanted to retrace his steps. If Annabelle were here, Rose would have asked her for a magic that would help her replay the past, so she could know what happened. Even then, what would she know? She would not know if the person who killed Nelson Chamber was employed by someone else. She would not know if there were other ways a person might have benefited from his death.

They reached the area that used to be the site of Havers' cabin. Instead of the cabin, there was a lodge with newly built cabins spread across the forest. They chose to set up camp a short distance beyond the lodge, and by the campfire she told them an abbreviated version of the story of her time with Annabelle, which they all listened to eagerly.

After they went to sleep, she stayed by the campfire, thinking of her old friend. Of all the people she'd met and spent time with, Annabelle was the one she would most like to have the chance to see again. She missed Annabelle. Simply to see her face would be so satisfying.

In the whole of her life, Annabelle was the only one who made Rose feel like she wasn't alone in the world. She wished she could speak to her friend again. Over the years, Annabelle had lived on in her mind. At different times, Rose would recall her opinions on different subjects, phrases she had thrown out regularly in conversation, ways she would approach different challenges, lessons she had taught Rose about the way people behaved in society.

Staring at the dying embers, Rose said quietly, "Where are you, Annabelle? If only I could see you, hear your voice, it would be a relief."

After a moment of silence, in her head, she heard Annabelle's voice say clearly, *Rose, I've been waiting to hear from you.* It was such a reassuring sound.

It wasn't easy finding my way without you, Rose thought. I wasn't prepared for any of this.

I told you I would always be here for you. You never believed it, no matter how many times I proved it to you. I told you that I knew it the first time we met.

I often wish, Rose thought, that you'd left Alabama with me. Or that I had stayed, and we had figured a way out together.

I looked for you, but you were gone. I was mortally wounded in their attack.

The thought surprised Rose. Why would her mind wander there? There was nothing good to come from that kind of morbidity. She looked at the children. The three older ones had picked their own spots to sleep under the stars, a bit farther from the campfire than Cole, Zoe, and Ben, who were sleeping in a cluster closer to the light.

I have a family now, Rose thought.

There was another moment of quiet. The fire, nearly out moments before, flared back to life.

Rose!

Annabelle's tone was quite displeased. For the first time, Rose thought it was not her imagination she was having this conversation with. *What have you done?*

What do you mean?

They're cursed children!

That's daft, Rose thought. Children are not born cursed, despite their mothers.

What are they then, if not that?

I don't know. They're something special, Rose thought.

Nothing good can come of this, Rose. It's not too late.

Rose tried to imagine where such a sentiment could come from. Because she had children and Annabelle never did?

You should kill them and be done with it. Kill them all. I told you once, that witches don't raise children, Rose. We eat them.

Rose waited until they were at Baylorson's grazing hills, the halfway mark for their trek, to tell the children the story of her father—she referred to him as her grandfather, the man they knew as their great grandfather—and his murder. They were seated on the land he had intended to purchase once and for all. She did not go into details of the trial eighty some years ago, but she did mention her suspicions about Leanne.

When she was done with the story, she gave them each a gold coin, calling it a gift from their great grandfather to each of them. She didn't tell them about the package the coins came in, or the note that came with them—although a few years later, when

Lily decided to conduct her own independent investigation, Rose did share that information with her. Instead, she let them all enjoy the moment as the past reached out to give them a last embrace.

When they returned from that trip to their regular family life, it was a while before she had another conversation with Annabelle. Never again did they discuss the children. Most often when they spoke, it would be when Rose was in the garden or in the fields. Rose knew that she was showing more of her age now, and that the children would be on the lookout for behavior, such as talking to someone who wasn't there anymore, that would mark her decline. She was always sure to take it outdoors.

She wasn't crazy. Not yet.

She told Annabelle about her visit to Baylorson's property.

He reminded me of one of your tree soldiers, Rose thought. Waiting to be called to action.

Did you plant the seeds I gave you?

I did, she thought.

Later, when Rose was inside making the paste that Annabelle had used to encourage plants to grow faster, she felt as if Annabelle were instructing her each step along the way, to make sure she remembered it correctly.

It needs to set for 20 minutes before the next step.

It needs to sit in the dark for a week

Make sure it coats the stem down to the soil.

One night Rose awoke from a troubled sleep because she heard Annabelle calling to her, urging her awake. Once Rose opened her eyes, and stared through the darkness of her room, she immediately felt there was something amiss.

Rose whispered to the darkness, "Why did you wake me?"

Can't you feel it, Rose? Something is happening.

Rose wasn't sure what she felt. Something would seem to be happening, if she were blind and deaf and just feeling the air. She looked in on Lily, and found her asleep, breathing deeply. Joshua, however, was sitting up in his bed, his head turned her way, and seemed to be awake, so Rose whispered to him as she approached his bedside, "Everything all right?"

He didn't respond. She drew a sharp breath. His eyes were wide open. She didn't try to wake him, but instead backed out of the room. Strange, she thought. Even stranger when she looked in on the other four, and found Carolyn, Zoe, Ben, and Cole in exactly the same posture as Joshua, seated up in bed, eyes wide open, minds deep asleep.

Rose wondered, What is happening? Something beyond what she was seeing here was happening.

Wherever they are, they're together, Annabelle said.

Rose asked, You think they're communicating with each other?

Perhaps plotting your overthrow.

They stayed that way for an hour, maybe a little longer. Ben was the most restive of them, pushing at the sheets covering his legs. Rose didn't know how long it had gone on before she'd awakened to notice, whether it had been minutes or hours. She resisted trying to wake them up, instead making a routine of sitting at the kitchen table for five minutes, and then looking into each bedroom to see if anything had changed.

She heard it when it ended, because all of the five of them must have put their heads back on their pillows simultaneously, judging solely by the resulting sound of their bed frames and mattress springs creaking in concert.

In the morning, none seemed aware that anything had been amiss the night before. Only Carolyn mentioned anything out of the ordinary. She reported in the morning over cereal that she had experienced an unusually vibrant dream the night before, wherein she had at first been with a group of people, but then gotten bored of it and started walking along the train tracks. On a bridge over a valley, she came to a train car that appeared to have been abandoned on the tracks. She couldn't walk around the car, so she climbed in through a vent that was very dark inside and filled with unexpected corners and edges, receiving numerous cuts and bruises, and even a black eye that looked curiously like a handprint, before she emerged into the interior of the car. Inside was treasure piled to the ceiling—gold, silver, all kinds of antique objects and fancy, expensive clothes. She said she'd played in there for hours, and that was what she'd still been doing when she woke up.

In the next days, Rose heard gossip about a small California coastal town where all the population disappeared overnight. The talk of terrorism and increasing security in Clay was wagging the lips of the locals. The mass disappearance had happened on the same night the children had gone into their united trance. What connection could there be, with so many miles distance between here and there? Likely none she would be willing to believe, because in life things that seemed connected often didn't turn out to be.

But she couldn't forget Annabelle's words that night, either: *Something has started.*

When it was only a few months away, Lily's wedding to Richard had the effect of putting Rose in a reflective mood, which was unusual. She didn't believe in dwelling on what was done. After all her years on Earth, after the many phases of her life, she was coming to the realization that this was the beginning of the winding down of her time.

Her life with her children, with her family, was the most exhausting, thrilling, unexpected time of her life. It had taken her by surprise when she'd suddenly found herself in the middle of it, and now, with Lily finally completing her move out of the house, she could see the end of it. Joshua would marry or move off on his own, Carolyn would be marrying herself off as soon as she had a good prospect, Zoe and Ben would probably go off to a state college together, and then Cole would go off to the university, and it would be over. Oh, there would be grandchildren, and maybe one or two of the Chamber kids would want to move home for a time, but by then, the center of the family would have shifted, expanded beyond her. Beyond their home.

She really wasn't ready for it to end.

Other parents told her that it never ends, that just when you think it's over, one of them returns, needing you more than before. But Rose thought maybe not only was this the end of this phase of her life, but also perhaps the end of her time. She couldn't walk as far, she couldn't walk as long, she couldn't move as fast. If she couldn't reach the people she wanted to help, what would she do? She could probably find someone to drive her, and stretch that arrangement for a while, until even the driveway would be too long to negotiate even with a walker.

This was the first wedding Rose had been a part of in her entire life. In her younger days, weddings had been simple affairs—a scheduled ceremony at a church followed by a lunch with sandwiches and coffee at the new couple's home. Nowadays it was a big, seemingly never-ending procession of events—the engagement party, three bridal showers, a brunch for the two families, a cocktail party for the bride and groom, a rehearsal dinner, and then the ceremony itself.

She was only midway through the week, and was so tired of all the questions—about her history, about her family's history, about the children's fathers—all of those subjects which she had long tamped down by being resolutely circumspect and vague. Yet suddenly, with a new crop of strangers eager to befriend the Chamber family, strangers they were going to be joining with through marriage, the questions had all returned. By then, of course, she'd realized that some of the questions would never stop being asked, the very same ones she would never answer.

When Zoe and Ben ran away, the perimeter wall was a foot tall. Everyone in the family tripped over some portion of it at one time or another. Stalks of green would shoot from the top three times a year. When they grew long enough, about five inches, the shoots would droop and from there tangle with other shoots from the same plant and from neighboring plants, and then grow into each other, thickening and knotting, for months, until they lost their green color and turned a color that was greyish and beige while new shoots started at the top. Once knotted as tight as possible, the tangled shoots would harden.

Those two children leaving unnerved Rose more than anything else. She could understand only a little of it—that Ben, not an athlete, not a stellar student, not a lot of prospects that might help lift him out of here—might see it as a window of potential escape to a better life. For Zoe to go made no sense at all. She tried a little harder than Ben did, and she was going to find things she wanted and then find a way to get them. There was no need for her to leave off for anywhere and make the challenge that much harder.

Who was out there who could potentially wreck this life of theirs? Lily's foster parents? Rose didn't see them as being up to it. No skin in the game for them. Perhaps Cole's mother and father. Ben's mother would have to have had a dramatic change of heart which Rose did not foresee happening either. So it was Ben and Zoe's fathers left—they were the ones she worried about most.

Ben, she thought, had a bit of his father's temper, and when he lost it she could see that he didn't understand where it came from, or why his reactions to things were much more extreme than his siblings.

Rose wasn't one to blame a child for their parents' sins. What she had seen in her lifetime, though, was that the parents' strengths and faults were often to blame for their children's failings. The single teenage girl giving birth is the daughter of a woman who gave birth in her teens. The pregnant single woman, who, abandoned by her boyfriend, is the daughter of a single mother abandoned by her spouse, a situation she vowed never to repeat with her own children. The father who abandoned her, in turn grew up in a home where his father abandoned his mother and him, and always swore he would do better by his kids.

What was that, if not that acorn falling next to the oak?

Lily's worldview, for example, would seem to have been defined by her foster parents, in that she wanted to be the opposite of everything they were. A good person, a good parent, a good daughter, a good sister. But there was no way of knowing whether or not Lily, the Lily she knew, resembled her biological parents in any way, either in physical appearance or in behavior. She could very well be exactly like them in her emotional makeup.

Carolyn, well, it was too early to tell. It was hard to connect Carolyn's socializing, her vanity, her concern about appearances to anything that Rose had observed in Carolyn's mother that night. Zoe not only looked like her mother, but also had the same quiet and observant demeanor. For Joshua and Cole, it was harder to tell—although, was it coincidence that the only one whose parents attended a university was the only Chamber who looked like he had a chance of attending, too?

Of course Ben's anger might have nothing to do with the genetic material contributed by his father. That might just be the way Ben was, fifth child and middle boy, running off for another venue so as not to get lost in the crowd.

Rose wondered sometimes if despite most of them being with her from birth or shortly after, if there were someplace in their consciousness where they were aware of all that had transpired, down to the last detail. She wondered if underneath it all, their souls recognized the contradictory messages they'd received about who they were and who they seemed to be. Did Carolyn know somewhere in her heart that her birth mother would have killed her, and find that irreconcilable with the good intentions of the mother who raised her? Did the twins know one of their mothers wasn't dead, that their fathers were likely still out there? She thought and hoped both were in jail by now. More likely they'd tried to repeat their scheme with some other unsuspecting women.

Was it possible Ben, struggling with the contradiction, had set out to explore something that in his heart he knew was not true? All of the children were like that about nearly everything else in the world—they had a way of seeing through things. Rose thought it was part of what made them special. They saw through everything but their mother, she would have said to Annabelle, and everything but the stories she'd told them about their lives.

In every story where she imagined Ben and Zoe establishing contact with either of their parents, Rose could only see sadness and regret and a wish to never have succeeded in finding them. She would actually pray, to no entity in general but for the world to hear, that such a thing would never happen.

What gnawed at Rose was that answers might still be there for anyone who had an inkling of the right questions to ask. In her mind, with a clue or two, maybe a word she'd let slip—a town Rose had called by its real name instead of a name she'd made up, the name of a school one of them attended—with those clues, if they remembered them and held them closely, maybe they might find a trail they could follow. In the case of Zoe and Ben, well, finding their ways home would be very bad for everyone involved.

Rose slowed down her work schedule when Carolyn started preparing for her nuptials, while Cole was getting ready to go off to California, a place which she was nervous about any of her children visiting. She enjoyed spending more time at home, in her gardens, which were much admired by visitors for the variety of unusual flowers.

Her eyes did start to bother her more. She had a visit from a woman, now in her early thirties, who Rose had helped with the delivery of her first child, when she was 15. The woman was working to get her PhD in biology. When Rose mentioned during tea that her eyes had been bothering her, the girl gave her several hand-rolled marijuana cigarettes, which she explained would help with the pressure in Rose's eyes.

Rose found they had the desired effect, and continued to smoke three times a day for the rest of her time living in her own house. She smoked what she was told was a very mild blend. When she found some seeds, she started to grow it herself in a corner of the garden.

In this last phase of her life, Rose hardly left her home. She had a steady stream of visitors, many of them people in the area whom she had cared for or whose animals she had cared for, and other folks whom she had met through the years. She'd spent so little time at home for most of her life, but she developed a routine for entertaining, down to the nap she said she had to take—but never did—if they overstayed their welcome.

On what would turn out to be one of her last weeks of roaming the region independently, Rose was on a walk through town when she passed by a teenage girl sitting on a city bench. Hours later, returning from the market on another section of the same road, she saw the same girl, this time standing on the sidewalk of the overpass above the road, leaning against the chain-link fence, looking down at her.

Rose returned home, and set about her evening routine, but after it was dark, unsettled by concerns for the girl's safety, she set out for the overpass. She didn't go to the top where she had seen the girl—instead she went into the short tunnel, and found the girl curled up under a large, tattered coat there.

She sat up as Rose approached.

"Come with me, honey," Rose said. "This is no place for you to be."

The girl stood slowly, with some confusion, some concern on her face.

Rose said, "Let's go," and started walking away.

The girl followed at a distance. Rose only looked back once or twice to be sure she wasn't walking too fast for her.

"What's your name?" Rose didn't think she would answer.

"Emily."

"Oh, good. Emily. Nice to meet you." Rose looked over her shoulder at Emily's face. "My name is Rose. I don't see as well at night as I used to, so we're going to hurry to my home." Emily stopped walking. Rose did not. She said loudly, "If you don't want to come in the house, you can sleep in the yard, and you'll be better off than out there. Come on, girl."

Once they were home, Rose made up a meal for the girl, who was not very responsive to questions about where her parents were and where her home was. Rose believed the girl was being evasive, but also thought it was likely she was covering up for her mother, her father, or both, regardless of their neglect. She said only that they'd left her in the parking lot at the convenience store, her mother and maybe her mother's boyfriend. They'd never come back. She was from out of town, maybe out of state, and seemed, at least to Rose, to be a little slow in the head.

In the morning, Rose told herself, she was going to bring Emily to the local church, to see if they could help to figure out what Emily's story was. She told Emily this was her plan.

Emily looked down at her feet, disappointed, when Rose

said she would have Emily back with her parents in no time.

While looking down, Emily said, "Can I ask you a question, Rose?"

"Yes, honey, Please, do."

"Who is the golden lady who follows you around?"

Rose's eyes widened in surprise. She studied Emily more closely. When she lifted her eyes from the ground to look at Rose, Rose realized Emily was being serious, and she was being sincere.

"Is she here now?"

"No."

"When did you see her?"

"I've seen you before. Before today. Sometimes she's with you."

"How long have you been on your own, Emily?"

"For a while now. I don't know."

Rose continued staring at Emily, so much so that Emily looked back down at her feet, until Rose made up her mind.

Rose lost control of her life around this point. Her children met in front of her and decided that she could no longer be in charge of all her decisions. She needed to be accompanied when she went out on a walk. She needed to be driven when she wanted to shop in town. She needed someone to live with her, or maybe she needed to go live with other people. She needed a caretaker. She got Carolyn. They took Emily away.

Rose felt betrayed.

I told you, that voice said in her head.

She lived with Carolyn for 20 months. Heaven and hell that was. At her best, Carolyn was amazing. She and Rose cooked dinners together and gardened together, which Rose enjoyed so much more than doing those things alone. Carolyn kept the house and worked in the fields, and there wasn't any chore that Rose asked her to take on that she didn't manage. She gave Rose more freedom than maybe Lily had envisioned, letting her go for walks on her own, within some limits. Carolyn loved to listen to show tunes, something Rose enjoyed as well.

At her worst, Carolyn was a drunk. A loud, unpleasant, braying drunk. Every once in a while she would tie one on, and those nights, with the way Carolyn would bellow out songs into the late hours, Rose would end up wishing she'd never owned a record player at all. She got in the habit of hiding the records out in Joshua's back house when Carolyn pulled out the wine bottles. It was the one place on the property where Carolyn was hesitant to go without his approval.

Rose lived with Lily, Richard, and her two grandkids at the end. She had trouble remembering things in the right order, but had great fun just being around the little ones, more amazed than ever by the potential held by every child. Who knew what they would grow into? Who knew what lives they would lead? There was simply no being sure about anything.

Rose Chamber died shortly before Lily came in with her afternoon tea. Alone in the room, feeling herself slipping away, she said quietly, "Annabelle?"

I'm here Rose. I told you I would never leave you.

PART 2

Chapter 8

Cole Chamber tried to get comfortable on the eastbound bus, his thoughts turning to home in a way they rarely had during five years of California living. It had only been nostalgia then, or something to keep him moving forward if he needed inspiration. Now it was going to be real again. North Carolina. Home-cooked meals and open space and a chance to be someplace where there weren't so many people to watch out for.

When the first text message came through, his phone chirped, then buzzed, then let out a chortling laugh. A text from Trina: Just talked to Tony. Are you FUCKING around with my BEST FRIEND and her boyfriend? You SUCK.

Cole quickly texted Zane: Heads up she knows.

Zane texted right back: Shit!

That was that. Cole's Amazing Life in L.A. was over.

Cole could guess exactly how this train had derailed. Worlds had collided. Three roommates—Tony among them—his best college buddies, had been fronting his part of the rent and utilities and looking the other way for six months while Cole hunted with increasing desperation for his first post-college job. For nearly all of the last two months it had been ugly and tense, and he'd hardly been back to the apartment they shared. Most anything that was important to him he carried around in his backpack, while the rest of what little he had acquired over years on an extended poverty budget was held as collateral. Amid ultimatums and threats, they'd insisted he not remove anything, fearing he was thinking of pulling the roommate version of a dine-and-dash.

There'd never been three happier faces when Cole finally landed the job at Aardner & Associates, but his personal property restrictions had not been lifted. The roommates had all extended themselves as far as they were willing to go. They knew he'd be getting his first paycheck this last Friday—he had to remind himself that was yesterday, because it already felt like it happened a week ago—and Tony, his former best friend, expected to hear from him before the weekend was over. Tony had in fact threatened to make a scene in the front lobby of Aardner & Associates on Monday morning at 9 a.m. if Cole didn't check in with him over the weekend.

Tony would have had Trina's number at the ready for such an occasion, too. Tony prided himself on his vindictiveness. If he knew he was in the right, and he had been wronged, nothing was out of bounds. Cole, in this case, was clearly in the wrong.

Tony could be a good guy, with some qualifications, and he had been a reliable friend, but since Cole had started seeing Trina eleven months before, and spending so much time with Trina and her friends—thus spending less and less time with Tony and the roommates—Tony had grown increasingly impatient with Cole's shortcomings. Tony didn't like being ditched for a girl. Tony didn't like vouching for someone who didn't show up at the bar like he said he would. At this point, only ten percent of it was about the money—like Tony, the other guys were all earning good money now and weren't hurting for his cash. The other ninety percent was the hurt magnified by hours and hours mulling over Cole's transgressions. Or, as Tony would refer to it, emotional principal.

Cole's first paycheck had come in, and instead of being $3,000 minus taxes, it was $1500 minus taxes, because apparently the payroll system required holding back two week's pay from an employee's first check. Minus taxes, it was $1,200 and change. Cole had spent the afternoon Friday doing the math to calculate how long it was going to take to pay everyone off, and to determine if he could make everyone happy by giving them each a smaller portion until the next check. It didn't take long to figure out he would likely be out on the street because waiting another month would mean everyone putting more money into Cole than he was paying back just to keep him around. Then he did the math and figured out exactly how long it was going to take him to pay everyone off, even with a full paycheck.

After that, he went online and put a hold on a bus ticket home, leaving early Saturday morning.

He felt surprisingly content with the decision, and that feeling had stayed with him into the next day and onto the bus, where he sat alone a couple seats back from the front. When he'd seated himself on the bus, the only other passengers had been two Goth girls with black and purple hair seated near the back of the bus and an older woman seated in the middle. He'd pretty much avoided looking directly at any of them, perhaps a reflection of the feeling that he was fleeing, and a failure or worse.

As his situation in L.A. had grown increasingly tense, he'd spent so much time worrying about how he was going to keep his life going. His options narrowed, and there were times he'd felt not only broke, but also hopeless. It simply had never occurred to him, the idea of going home. Not until the moment he decided to do it. When the idea struck, it felt not only like a great solution, but also like the only thing to do. It was what his mother would say: *There is always home.* It was exactly what he should be doing—getting back to his real life, to the real person he was, instead of compromising everything in the scramble for a foothold 2,500 miles away. He didn't recognize this person he had become—this wasn't the way he'd ever lived his life before or that he'd ever thought he'd live his life. This wasn't who he was. He was better than this. Or, he thought with some disappointment, maybe he wasn't.

He owed Zane and Alexa nearly a thousand dollars, so he had put that in an envelope that he set on their mantel before he left. That was the only relationship he hadn't trashed or neglected. They were the ones who had really kept him going the last few months.

The phone laughed. Ha-Haa! A message from Trina: You shit. CALL ME.

Cole assumed that Tony had pulled the trigger early, not waiting until Monday, instead starting early this morning with a phone call to Trina to voice his suspicions about the nature of Cole's relationship with Zane and Alexa.

How did his next conversation with Trina go? Cole already had some idea of his side of it. He had been ready for it since the morning after the first time he and Alexa and Zane got together. At the time he'd been feeling so wounded by Trina's abandonment that he'd wanted the story to hurt her. From his point of view, she'd all but dumped him without letting him know.

He would say: Remember when we went to Big Bear with Zane and Alexa? When we stayed at the hotel with theme rooms, rented ourselves the Cave Room, a suite with two bedrooms where the walls were covered with dark faux lava rock? We dropped mushrooms, and you and Zane and Alexa wanted us all to sleep in sleeping bags on the floor in the shared area, in front of the faux fireplace, and you all thought it would be fun to do it next to each other—no cross-touching between the couples involved— to see what that would be like. I was against it, because I was threatened and insecure, and I hardly knew them, and it just wasn't anything that I was into doing.

Also, there's no denying, Cole thought, that Zane and Alexa are much better looking than average. The idea of being naked in front of their perfectness still made him cringe a little.

He would say: But I went ahead with it, and I focused on you and did my best to hide our parts from their view, just let them see my butt, and I also tried to mentally block them out, and somehow I managed it, although clearly you did not, even though you kind of half-pretended you had. And when we were done I looked over at them and they had stopped completely whatever they had been doing, and they were lying there, Alexa on top of Zane, their beautiful naked model bodies right there, their blond hair and blue and green eyes staring at us, their faces side by side. I couldn't even hold their stare, and it made me even more aware that I was the only one in the room that had actually done what we said we were going to do. It was like my bare, sweaty ass was the floorshow. You didn't seem particularly into it either, during or after, despite the buildup, but I guess at least Zane and Alexa enjoyed it.

So flash-forward to the middle of summer when, I believe, you more or less decided you were done with me, although you weren't quite ready to cut me free. Clearly you were unimpressed with my level of ambition. You bailed on me and your best friends repeatedly while you were "establishing helpful college slash career connections" with your incoming law school classmates. Then you just disappeared. At some point, I guess because you were tired of all my calls, you encouraged Alexa and Zane to "play with me" until you got the school thing more under control. Well, what ended up happening when we got over the fact that you really weren't ever going to be joining us was that we ended up having a fun, fun summer after college.

Who wouldn't have fun playing with Zane and Alexa? They're plugged in everywhere in the city. They get into trendy clubs, sold-out concerts, parties in the mansions on the cliffs at the end of Sunset Boulevard, dinners in private rooms with television and movie stars, all the things that a Southern boy like me would be dazzled by.

He would say: When things went really bad with the roommates, I ended up crashing on Zane and Alexa's couch for a few days. I finally got this job, and to celebrate, they made me dinner at a house they were looking after for some industry friend. We drank a lot, we jacuzzied, we sat next to the jacuzzi and stared at the stars and talked about our childhoods. I was so not prepared for it to be anything other than that I was wearing the oldest underwear I had, underwear I'd owned since I was twelve, my Aquaman Underoos. And when they stripped down to soak, I kept on the Underoos when I jumped in because I was feeling shy. Zane's not the kind of person you want to be naked next to in public, unless you have a lot more self-confidence about your body than I do. So we're sitting there, talking, laughing about something, and the next thing I know one of them is kissing me on the lips and the other is pulling down my Underoos. Everything progressed from there.

And then, despite the reprieve presented by the new job, there was another epic fight with the roommates. I ended up on Zane and Alexa's couch again, this time at their invitation, for about three weeks. The thing between us all only happened twice more, and totally at their discretion. When they were in the mood, one of them would just come out of the bedroom at night and ask if I wanted to join them.

What did we do? You name it, we did it twice, everything you can think of, and everything we could think of, first time just to see, second time to work out any kinks. I know you will want to focus on the fact that it was Zane and I, to make it into an XY thing, but it was XYZ the whole time. It was never about Zane and me alone, and wouldn't have happened without Alexa's approval or presence. Just so we're clear, every time you go with the XY when we're discussing this in the future, what I'm remembering in my mind is all XYZ.

I think what you will be searching for will be times that we lied to you, or deceived you, to keep this going, and there weren't any, because we've hardly heard from you the last six weeks. Except for the conversation we had about the three-pack of designer boxer briefs that I charged to your Macy's account. I know you took it as a sign of me growing up, and maybe it could be looked at that way, but really it was because the jacuzzi night was the last sighting of that pair of Underoos and I could only go commando for so long.

I know there's no way around this (and me) being an irritant for you but I hope that by removing myself from the equation, you can figure things out with Y and Z, and that this can be the cautionary tale that brings your relationship with them back from the brink. Right now, they both still like you far more than I do, and I honestly think you need them in your life if you want to stay connected to the best parts of yourself. If you can look at it this way, they've done us a favor and forced us to move on.

Of course, Cole told himself, it would never go like that. Trina would be a nightmare times ten and wouldn't leave him time for soliloquies. He would actually be okay with it if he never had to talk to Trina again.

Beside that, if he told Trina that story he would feel like he'd hung Alexa and Zane out to dry. When at this point they were the only ones he still cared about.

Instead, Cole would disappear, and not say another word to Trina. This would allow Alexa and Zane to blame him for everything, and Trina could hate him, and maybe the three of them would salvage the relationship they'd had long before Cole came along. Maybe Trina would get over the fact that Cole and her best friends had gotten so close—and maybe even be glad that it happened that way. Although he doubted that—Cole would bet that part of Trina's anger was because she was jealous that they'd done this with him and not with her.

Ha-Haa! Zane: Just got home. You out?

Cole texted: Yes. Thank you to you and Alexa for everything.

Zane: Stay golden, Pony boy.

Ha-Haa! Cole's heart jumped a little. This must be Trina

again, he thought. Instead, it was a message from his sister, Lily.

Lily: Mom died. Come home when you can.

He gasped, maybe said something out loud, but only was aware of it because when he looked around both of the Goth girls were watching him with curiosity. He looked to see if he'd disturbed the older woman, too, but . . . she wasn't there. It was just him, the two girls, and the driver on the bus. One of the girls in back was crouching on her seat, making her look taller. She was wearing a black t-shirt, sleeves cut off, with a large, thin, white circle on the front, like a hoop.

In the middle, in white letters, was the word Syzygy.

He stared at the phone for five minutes in silence, stunned, before he returned Lily's message. The message was similar to the one that he'd been hesitant to send to his mother for the previous 12 hours, knowing that if he told her out of the blue that he was coming home it would cause her concern and raise questions he wouldn't want to answer honestly. In his mind, he saw his brother and sisters, looking the way he remembered them from the last time he was home. Joshua, Lily, and Carolyn. He had a harder time summoning memories of Zoe's and Ben's faces.

To Lily, Cole texted: I'm on my way. Don't know how long it will take. Don't wait for me to do what you have to do. Sorry, Lils. My love to everyone there.

The phone sounded off again. The events of the morning prior to Lily's message were not present in his mind. When he saw the incoming call was from Trina, he found that she mattered even less than before.

Trina: Call me or I'm going to come find you.

In the right hand corner of his phone screen, he saw the tracking app being launched remotely.

Trina continued: You suck. I'm going to find you. You faggot.

Cole sighed. Not just XY. Without the Z, X and Y would

have been playing video games, fully clothed. XYZ, he thought. XYZ. And Y and Z are both really, really good-looking. That mattered in this kind of math equation, right?

He turned the phone over. He couldn't get into the battery pack without a miniature five-point screwdriver. The phone was off-market, to be kind. He looked at the screen with some consternation, wondering what sound effect she had attached to the tracker. Would it be Godzilla? Would it be an electric chair? A voice screaming murder? A police radio? The *Jaws* theme?

If he threw it out the window, she'd know he was on the road to Vegas. She might guess he was going home, not that she had more than a faint idea of where that might be, because he'd always been vague about it. Cole had been the same with everybody, Zane and Alexa included. Simply saying "North Carolina" was usually enough, because it was enough to send the typical Californian inquiree off on a tangent about where in the United States North Carolina is actually located. In Cole's case, because of his quote unquote drawl, and his being half Asian, his place of origin came up regularly in conversation when he met new people.

Cole turned off his phone. He set a napkin on the floor mat in front of the seat beside his, and then set his soft drink cup next to the napkin. He took the top off his soft drink, and then dropped the phone into the cup.

That was a shame, he thought.

He fished it out immediately, set it on the napkin, and dried it off. To make sure it wasn't transmitting anything, Cole turned the phone on. It started to power up. The screen image wiggled a little, signaling the short, and then the phone clicked off and would not start again. He pulled another napkin out of his backpack, wrapped the phone in it, and slid it into the side pocket of the backpack.

It was going to be a long ride home.

Joshua Chamber stood out in the small orchard on his four-acre property, tree trimmer in hand, sawing steadily at a branch that had been hit by lightning but which had not broken free. It was late afternoon. Birds were settling in trees all over and their chatter was all he heard in the pauses between sawing.

He felt something he would describe as a fluttering of wings at the back of his head, a sensation that had him feeling something was about to happen or was already happening somewhere around him. He lowered the tree saw slowly and looked around the spot where he was standing, toward the back of the plot of trees . . . and didn't see a thing out of place. He listened, and the afternoon sounded no different than usual.

Joshua wrapped his hand around the pole, looked up at the tree branches above him, and gasped. His mother was there, at the fork where the great tree trunk split into two arms. Her hands were joined in front of her. She was dressed in a simple black dress, and her steely eyes were locked on his.

Unsteadily, he said. "Momma."

Wordlessly, she nodded slightly at him. Joshua couldn't read her expression. Was it satisfaction? Was it amusement?

He could have said that when he blinked, she was gone. But he didn't blink, and still she was gone.

Joshua turned and started walking to the house. He understood what this meant he had to do. He had already long since broken it down into steps. He would have to assemble the pieces of the coffin. His mother had said she did not want a coffin, that she wanted to decompose in the Earth and for her body to go back into the soil and feed the Earth. Joshua had convinced her that her children and grandchildren would have nightmares for the rest of their lives about it if they tossed her body into a deep hole and then shoveled dirt down on top of her while she stared back up at them.

They'd compromised, and he'd found biodegradable

materials to use to build her coffin. His blueprint called for lining the bottom of the box with a bed of moss and grass, with pansies from her garden planted as pillows for her head, shoulders, hips, and heels to rest on. The coffin sides would be aerated, so that insects would be able to get in and out. Joshua even had, stored away in his freezer, an array of bugs—ladybugs, caterpillar pupae, worms, pill bugs among them—that he would seed in the soil beneath the grass and in divots in the sides of the coffin. They would be there with her when they put her in the ground.

He would reinforce the corners and the middle with strips of local pine so the coffin wouldn't collapse immediately after 6 feet of dirt was dropped on top of it. He didn't know how long it would hold, but Joshua hoped it would be long enough for the caterpillars to turn into butterflies. Eventually her flesh would be gone, and her clothes would break down, and the box would decompose, and her bones would be resting the way she wished for the rest of time.

Joshua was still debating the crickets. Those were easiest of all to acquire, as he owned a small-scale operation that raised them for tackle stores and protein bar makers. But it was the noise he was worried about. On the one hand, it would lend to the natural effect he was trying to create; on the other, they were likely going to eat at least a few of the other bugs, and they were going to make noise until they died. Which posed a question: Once a person was dead, didn't she deserve a little peace and quiet? Or would relentless chirping be preferred to the sound of a body breaking down and being consumed by the organisms around it? Joshua would have to think about it a bit longer. There was time.

He heard the phone ringing in the house. That would be Lily calling with the news. Joshua hurried to answer the call.

For Carolyn Chamber, the decision to return to the family home was fraught with considerations. On the road there after she'd heard the voicemail from Lily, she'd only just started out when she actually did a U-turn and turned back and decided not to go. She did that not once, but three times, before turning her car right around again and continuing on her way. But she wasn't headed for her childhood home after the third time—instead, she drove to the restaurant she personally owned.

A half-hour later, she pulled into the Southern Baked parking lot. It was only five minutes later that she was making herself the first of what would be three hours of drinks. It was dead quiet inside, and after an hour Carolyn told Maddy—the only one left up front serving—that she could leave for the night. Of course, five minutes after Maddy left, the first customer of the night showed up. Turned out, he was one of the nicest men Carolyn had talked to in years, and he listened as much as he talked, a rare balancing act.

As Carolyn would likely explain to anyone who asked—and she did to this gentleman even without the inquiry—she had a history replete with the wrong kind of men. She didn't know why they turned out bad, she just knew they didn't seem to be that way at the start. She didn't believe she was looking for anything different than any other woman—here, for example, was a fellow in her restaurant, a man she found attractive, and he was a man who asked the sorts of questions a person might ask only if he were really paying attention to what she was saying. Why wouldn't she or any other woman like that?

Unlike any other person in the world lately, this man seemed to be in agreement with the positions Carolyn had taken in some family disagreements, and he was very sympathetic about the passing of her mother. He told her it was important to take care of herself first, because she wasn't going to be any help to anyone else in her family if she didn't have her own head together.

"Riddle me this," he'd said, this mister strangely perfect, when she approached his table to take his order. "The beginning of eternity, the end of time and space, the beginning of every end, and the end of every place. What am I?"

Carolyn couldn't think of anything but Death.

She hadn't planned on listening to him more than she needed to pass the time. He wasn't drinking, just eating appetizers, which just meant he was lingering. Probably killing time before a big date. She thought it was strange for people who weren't from around the area to linger. First off, people didn't come to the restaurant unless they lived here or knew someone who did, or else they had a reason they weren't being truthful about. Generally, this wasn't one of those places a person just came across.

Whatever he'd said, it went over her head. She hadn't known how to respond other than to stare at him vacantly, holding her drink, thinking about Death.

He'd smiled. That charming smile.

"The letter E."

Hadn't he shown interest too? Holding in his smile a glimmer of something more?

Then how come, after two hours, he just up and vanished? Said he was going to the bathroom, walked toward the bathroom, then never came back? She had even asked Rodrigo—he wanted her to call him Roger now, but that proved a challenge—to check the bathroom, to make sure he was okay, and Rodrigo had returned to tell her the bathrooms were empty.

Carolyn had never learned the trick that her mother managed with people in general—not just with men, but with women, too, which was not letting them in. One smile was apparently all it took nowadays to crack Carolyn's lock, which only showed the toll had been further reduced in the favor of newcomers. She went from resisting them as a kid to being desperate to see a smile like that. It was funny, having believed for so long that her mother sacrificed so much to raise six kids, and then suddenly Carolyn was old enough to understand that having children, for her mother, meant not really needing anything else in the world, particularly a man. So she never had to face her fear of them, or the truth that she deserved more in terms of adult companionship than she dealt herself. Her mother had deserved a life mate, a lover.

It wasn't good for us kids, Carolyn thought, no it wasn't, the attitude in our house about men. Lily used to joke around so much, calling us after the states we were born in and whatnot. Was she supposed to be modeling what it was like to be okay with not having a dad? Who knew what effect that had? Not having fathers left us all wanting a father in our lives in one way or another, no matter what the cost, no matter how much any and all of us deny it. All of us but Lily, it seemed like. She was fine not knowing her dad. That was the only explanation for why she would make jokes. It never bothered her. But for the rest of us, Carolyn told herself, it meant having it constantly being pointed out that was what we were lacking.

Caught up in her frustration, Carolyn told herself that maybe it was the sort of teasing that Lily did that drove Ben and Zoe, the two "missing" Chamber children, away.

But she knew that wasn't true.

No, that wasn't why they left, she knew. Better than anyone else, because she'd been the only one who saw them kissing each other. Carolyn shivered at the thought of it. That was why Carolyn didn't fuss when they left—it wasn't because she understood or was sympathetic. What was anyone here going to do with that kind of thing? What was everyone going to think? Because of what she'd seen—not much at all, truly just a kiss, but enough—it was already too late to do anything but bring shame and condemnation from the outside world, and a stain on their whole family. No, no, Ben and Zoe did the only right thing taking their business out of the house and away from Clay.

What if they sauntered in here some day, the two of them,

married and with children? What would the family do then? Even when everybody was most despondent about them being gone, Carolyn never hinted at what she'd seen. It wouldn't do anyone any good to know, as she saw it. She could keep a secret, if she wanted to.

Carolyn finally stumbled out of the diner after the rest of the staff had clocked out. She opened the car door, climbed inside, decided she was fine to drive, and put on the seat belt. Before she could put the keys in the ignition, however, there was a moment that made her flinch, a flash of a moment, where she felt like she was already driving the car, where she felt like there was some sort of impact, as if someone had slammed into the left side of the car. Was her car spinning out of control?

But she wasn't driving yet.

What was that?

Carolyn shook her head a little. She did not put the keys in the ignition.

Not after that. Not going to risk that was about me, she thought.

She set the keys in her lap. Then she reclined her seat.

Getting home tomorrow wouldn't be much different than getting home today. It wasn't as if she had been away from the family home for long. Just three weeks this last time. Just long enough to convince herself that her new boyfriend Harris wasn't going to end up being worth the time—if he wasn't already stepping out on her.

The timing of everything had really not worked in favor of Carolyn and Harris. She'd been living back with her mother for 15 months already when she bumped into him at the market. They'd rekindled their high school romance on the sly during Carolyn's last three months caretaking for her mother. About two months into their relationship, Harris lost his job. That was around the time that Carolyn and Lily had started talking about bringing in hospice, or possibly moving their mother to Lily's for her last days. So Carolyn had known her time living in her old home, nursing her mother, was nearly over, and that she would be moving back to the house she'd lived in with her husband Don, which had sat empty since Don died nearly a year before.

Carolyn had moved Harris into her house for the short term, thinking she would likely soon be returning from living with her mother. She'd thought they could try living together. Carolyn wanted that—she wanted to come home to someone, not to an empty house.

Then it happened—the dominoes started to fall. Mother moved to Lily's, and hospice started their visits. Carolyn moved home with Harris, which was not what she had expected it would be. How could she return home to live with him, and the last thing he wanted was sex? Even if he wasn't seeing anyone else, she could tell that he'd decided in her absence that maybe life was easier without her. Which she was sure it was easy for him to think, as while she had been living with her mother, she was fronting the rest for him, so to speak. He would say it was her drinking, too, but she was sure it was some other slut he was chasing. It wasn't the drinking, she thought as she closed her eyes and the world spun.

Then Carolyn was asleep.

Lily Chamber also sat in her car at the side of the road, although she was only a couple miles from her family home. Coming down the last stretch of highway, she'd been tailgated by a blue Toyota pickup truck. Despite wanting to take the guy to task, she was also worn, worn, worn by the day's events. Her mother had died hours earlier. The doctor had come to confirm it—the first time a doctor other than a dentist had attended to Rose Chamber in all of Lily's life. Her body was still in Lily's house up north, on the guest bed. Lily had left it there to figure out what one did next in that situation—in terms of what to do with a dead body. She'd taken care of notifying the others, checked in with her own family, and now was in a hurry to pick up some "dead" clothes for her mother and get back to her body. Strangely, she felt guilty leaving her mother alone when she was dead.

The Toyota pickup had come up too close behind her, honked his horn, flashed his lights, given her the whole business. Wanting no kind of confrontation, Lily had signaled to switch to the right lane to clear his path. Well, the car that was traveling a car length or two ahead of her on the right decided to move left without signaling as Lily was moving. The Toyota, seeing her move, surged into the open space, only to find the car ahead of Lily cutting into his intended path. The Toyota swerved to cut into the space the car ahead of Lily had just abandoned, the back of his truck crunching into the driver's side door of Lily's car, sending her spinning across the lanes while both of the other cars raced away.

She ended up off the paved highway, on the opposite side of the road, facing toward the coming traffic.

Dammit, Dammit, Dammit, she thought.

She picked up her phone as she stepped out of the car. The station was still on her speed dial.

"Police."

"Hi, Claire. It's Lily."

"How you doin', Hon? Sorry to hear about your mom. She was one of our hidden treasures."

Lily paused. She had to swallow the lump of feeling that rose up in her. She wasn't ready to receive sympathies yet, apparently.

"Thanks, Claire. Listen, I just got clipped by a blue Toyota, maybe 1993, on the Interstate about a mile before the turn-off."

"Oh, well, you almost made it."

"Yeah, really. He's heading north at a tear, with a banged

up right bumper. State plates, but didn't get the number."

"You gonna wait there? Elias is on patrol tonight."

Lily was sure Elias would find a way to get someone else to check it out. Even if he was two blocks over, she understood that he wouldn't come himself. Still, she thought it would be nice to see his face. It was too bad he had to be stubborn.

"Car still runs. Think I'll head to my mom's place."

"Okay, Hon."

In the middle of the driver's door was a wrinkled divot, and there was a four-foot-long, 3-inch wide scrape on the side of the car emanating from the divot and ending at the front wheel well. She didn't care that much about her car, because it was an old piece of crap, but she did care about the driver of the blue Toyota getting away with that behavior.

She got back in the car.

She'd gotten a text from Cole and spoken to Joshua. She hadn't heard from Carolyn, and wondered if she would. Carolyn would know that Lily was going to get done what needed to be done whether Carolyn wanted to help out or not. Carolyn would also have her input on the service and the wake, and she would know that if she spoke up in a timely manner, then Lily would listen to her. What Lily wasn't going to do was change everything when Carolyn did finally show up—probably the day before the service—and started complaining about the arrangements.

Lily wished she could send a note to Zoe and Ben, too, to let them know—it made her feel bad to think of them out there in the world not knowing their mother was gone. Whatever it was that made them decide to leave, Lily was sure that they'd loved their mother and she imagined that they'd always planned on one day seeing her again.

Oh, Mom, Lily thought, How much am I going to miss you? I can already feel it, that part of me that will always be adrift without the shelter of your love.

Imprinted in Lily's memory was that hot Texas day, more than thirty years before, when she finally started the life she was supposed to live. Most everyone was inside because of the heat. Lily was inside, in that foster home, safe for the moment because foster dad Steve was at work and foster mom Winnie was at the store. They left her alone there every day.

Lily had been so sad that day, just sitting and staring out the window thinking that she would never again see the sweet lady with the short wavy dark hair whose name was the same as a flower. Rose. The day before, speaking in a whisper while she took Lily's temperature and iced a bruise on her arm, Rose had explained how she was taking her new baby and running away from the baby's father and from Texas, to go where no one would hurt them again.

The next day, that hot day, Lily was sure that Rose was gone. She truly believed that it was over. That her friendship with Rose had been just a moment with a friend—and then it was done. Lily's life with Winnie and Steve would continue as it was. No one would make it better.

In the next breath after accepting her fate, she watched as the front of Rose Chamber's white Nova swung around the street corner several houses up. It couldn't have been all but a few seconds later that Lily was letting herself out the front door of the house, carrying Winnie's amazing little lipstick-pink suitcase, just as the car slid up to the curb.

The passenger door opened. Lily climbed in. Off they went.

Rose promised to take care of Lily always. To protect her. To raise her as her child as much as she was going to be raising little Joshua, who was asleep in the back seat.

The trick was not to worry too much where you came from, her mother would later tell her, but to have a good idea that where you were headed was going to be a better place.

Chapter 9

Struggling during the 20-mile walk from the bus stop to his old home, long since overwhelmed by the feeling that instead of moving forward with his life he was really just undoing his glorious escape five years before to California, Cole considered just giving up, at least for a while, and sitting down until someone came along and offered him a ride.

It was seven weeks since he'd set out from Los Angeles. That he was this close made the last leg intolerably long. He'd been on this road a hundred times in his life, and yet it seemed to have stretched, grown new curves and higher slopes.

The most comforting thing about it was that he couldn't go on a long walk without thinking of his mother. On this particular road, the feeling of being closer to her was stronger. She walked everywhere, and it never seemed like it made her tired. She was like a machine when she got going, locked into that perfect pace, arms swinging, cylinders firing, the brim of her sun hat shading her view of the road ahead.

Cole could have followed the train tracks home, and shaved off at least a mile of his trek, but a ways in, he saw the reason he'd chosen this route: The long driveway leading to his friend Sean's home came into view, and when he walked past the first turn in the driveway, there was the hammock, between two longleaf pines that were five years taller than he remembered. There was a kid's play table next to one of the pines. Most of the paint had peeled off its red and blue wooden legs, and the circular piece of wood that formed the top was slightly warped.

Without another thought, Cole climbed into the hammock. He was asleep before the swinging stopped.

Waking up there the next day, the sun on him, roosters crowing, birds in the sky, not even a breeze—that was the right way to be coming home. Even the fresh smell of it! He hadn't smelled a place like home since he'd left it. It was cleansing to have it all fill his senses in a way that didn't leave room for the memories of wherever it was he'd been coming home from.

Cole wished that were so. Although it was still nice, he thought, to experience some of the better things about home.

As if to affirm that idea, when he rolled out of the hammock he saw there was a glass of iced lemonade on the play table, sweat near the rim of the glass. A handwritten note next to the glass read Welcome Home, Cole.

The note couldn't have been from Sean—Sean would have just turned him over in the hammock, spilled him onto the ground and then pointed at him and laughed. Maybe Sean's mom? But she was a character too, Cole remembered. She probably would have done the same as Sean, and laughed twice as long.

Cole would come back another time to find out. He was going to have all the time in the world. He savored the drink as he walked back down the driveway. He felt much better after sleeping. Replacing his exhaustion was a growing anticipation of seeing his home again.

An hour later, Cole sat on the front porch of his home, staring vacantly around the yard, memories of his mother swimming in his mind. The yard needed work, but the fruits and vegetables were still doing better than the weeds. "None of them are weeds," his mother would say, "they're all volunteers. Almost all of them can be useful in one way or another."

After only a few steps inside, he'd had to step back outside. Not only because he hadn't been prepared for the strength of the emotion he felt at being inside, wanting beyond everything to see her again, but also because the place was a terrible mess, and he couldn't imagine why it should look that way, and he didn't know whether or not he should go about doing something about it. He thought it looked like they'd been robbed.

His last text from Lily had been two months ago. No doubt they'd had a service—wouldn't they have had some kind of wake at the house? Why did it look like the place had been abandoned for longer than that?

When he'd come up the driveway far enough to see the house, he'd expected it to look smaller. But it was the same. The absence of everything he'd become used to—cars and shops and people everywhere—made it all look bigger than he remembered. There were no street signs and no parking lots, just some old fences between properties that looked like they could be pushed over with a little effort. It was so big it filled him with a calm he hadn't felt in longer than he could remember.

On the way along the driveway, he passed by a tree that he very specifically remembered standing in front of, but which he'd otherwise forgotten even existed. It was at least seventy feet tall, and at the base of the trunk it was a good six feet around. About thirty feet up from the ground there was a lump in the trunk, like a giant ball, and there were at least ten branches of various thicknesses that stuck out of it. As a kid, Cole had always thought that lump looked like a giant spider's body, and that one day it would do something that would show it was really alive and not petrified wood. He'd never liked walking past that tree in the dark.

When he was closer to the house, he noted the hedge that marked the perimeter of the house and the spice garden. His mother had planted the slow-growing seeds for the hedge at least ten years before, maybe more. It had grown in, but still looked to be only about three feet tall.

And the house! It was a patchwork of additions made over the years from whatever materials had been available at the time to his builder brother. The house and the property seemed bigger than they'd been in his memory, but the structure itself was just the way he remembered it, just as he had described it to his friends, one of the very few things he'd been comfortable sharing about his home life. That caution had proved useful—he truly felt he wasn't going to be an easy find for anyone—but at the time there had also been a basic reticence about sharing his less-than-sophisticated origins. One of his concerns in arriving in California had been his being characterized as the Asian Appalachian.

He stared at the house. All it was missing, he thought, was his mom. Its heart.

When he'd decided to go to California, his mother at first held back her opinion, but after he'd put in the papers she'd gone to worrying out loud. She didn't know much about California that she hadn't heard from other people, but she did know that ten years before, a whole town full of people had disappeared in some unexplained way, and so she was convinced the same thing potentially might happen to Cole. Cole had visited the town, in fact, which had been designated a ghost town, and the park surrounding it, which was now a state park, but had planned not to tell his mom about it. That was a moot point now.

Thinking it was inevitable that he would have to go inside and decide how to proceed, Cole stood and considered walking around the property a little to see what had changed and what had stayed the same. He had seen some flashes of color in the gardens—flags or banners or maybe some leftover decoration from the funeral service—and told himself that maybe they were worth an investigation.

The sound of a car coming up the road interrupted the thought. He paused, listening as he remembered he used to, to hear if the car was going to come up the driveway or move on down the road, generally the more usual outcome.

But no, it was coming up the driveway. After rounding the

last turn, it pulled up to and parked outside the hedge wall.

The car door opened, and out stepped Carolyn. Cole rose from where he was sitting, but waited for her to close the car door, to start up the path from the driveway . . .

. . . when a rock slid under her foot, and her foot slid back and away from her, and boom, she was lying there face down on the ground.

Cole sprinted across the yard as Carolyn fairly quickly pushed herself up to a sitting position. When she looked around, seemingly worried that someone else had seen, he almost felt bad about having been present to witness it.

She looked at Cole in confusion as he approached. There might even have been a hint of fear as he got closer to her.

"Carolyn! Hi! It's Cole! It's me!"

It took a moment to sink in before a broad smile lit up Carolyn's face.

For many of her early years, Carolyn seemed to be the shyest of the Chamber children, maybe even a little slower socially. She was always very awkward at the beginning of any kind of event that involved people other than immediate family. She never seemed at first to recognize anyone beyond immediate family, could never remember who her teachers were, and she frequently made mistakes when it came to identifying her friends at school or telling one adult from another.

If the family ran into someone on the street who recognized her, like the school librarian or the mailman, Caroline wouldn't have the slightest idea who the person was when they greeted her. They once ran into her fourth grade teacher, who had also been her second and third grade teacher, at the post office, and that had set off the teacher's search for a diagnosis.

When Carolyn did seem to be able to identify someone, it was only because of some obvious physical feature—large ears, a big nose, a sharp, pointed chin, a square head with no neck. She would watch animated movies at school, and clearly follow who was who, because the characters tended to wear the same clothes throughout. Not so the live features, where actors and actresses quickly became confused with one another, and unless their dialogue called for them to repeatedly state each others' names in conversation, she would always spend time playing catch-up to figure out who was who.

That schoolteacher (who Rose Chamber thought must have been some sort of genius for figuring this out) realized Carolyn was face blind. Prosopagnosia. She really couldn't tell one person from another, and until the condition was noticed, never knew that other people, her siblings included, could tell people apart solely by their facial features. She'd spent years mystified at their ability to know who everyone was. She'd assumed that they, like herself, relied on other clues—clothing, hairstyle, accessories, voice, posture, and just about anything else that might fill in an identity.

Once the diagnosis was made, Carolyn bloomed. They couldn't correct the condition, because it wasn't treatable, but they could help her develop strategies for dealing with it, most of which began with Carolyn speaking up and interacting.

Cole held out his hand to her to help his sister up. Instead of taking it, she pushed herself up to her knees and rubbed her hands together, sending bits of gravel back to the ground. She looked at her hands and laughed—she was laughing at herself, he thought—and then she looked at his face, and there were tears welling in her eyes.

"Baby brother, is that really you?"

"Hi, Carolyn."

She stood, a bit unsteady at first, as she stared at him. Her hands went to her cheeks. She looked older, much older than he had expected. The skin on her cheeks looked weathered, her waistline had doubled, and her hair, which she had once prided herself on, was darker than he remembered, and stringy and unevenly cut.

"All the time you've been gone, when I think of you, you're still the age you were when I babysat you."

"I was nineteen when I left, Carolyn."

"And look at you," she said, ignoring his words, her voice mock sexy, "Now you're a man. You're a handsome man! You know what the secret is to our good looks, don't you? Symmetry. Our features are balanced—Mother's gift to us. You know it was her and not the fathers because we all have the same thing going on. Except for Lily—she's a little crooked."

Carolyn shrugged, moved in closer and wrapped her arms around Cole to give him a great, long hug, patting his back gently the whole while. She smelled faintly of alcohol.

"Welcome home. I wish Mother were here to say that to you."

She let out a great, dramatic sigh.

"I'm waiting for it to really feel like home," Cole said. "I think Mom has to be here for that to happen."

She sighed again, and stepped back from him. He wanted to ask questions, and wondered if now was the right time.

"About six months ago," Carolyn said, staring past him, toward the garden, "she wanted me to dress up some of the trees out in the garden."

Cole thought he had misheard her. "What?"

Her eyes focused on him, and she smiled and stopped herself. Took a breath.

"Come, look," she said, and she started off toward the garden. "We had four newer trees, all variegated apples, that didn't make it through the winter frost. They were just dead there, and I came over with some bolts of fancy fabric I found in Don's trailer, because, you know, I thought it would be fun to make her a pretty dress. I didn't tell her that if it turned out good and she really did like it that we might dress her in it after she died. But she saw those bolts of fabric and right away she had me out in the garden wrapping it around those dead trees."

Cole caught sight of one of the trees she was talking about. An apple tree, maybe fifteen feet tall, its trunk maybe six inches in diameter. The trunk split into a Y, with long branches extending to each side. A third branch at the split had been cut to a short nub.

Raspberry-colored, sparkly fabric had been wrapped around the trunk to resemble a dress. The dead branches of the Y looked like long, jagged arms coming out of the sleeves of a fancy outfit, raised in celebration. A dark red belt was wrapped where the waist would be. The stump of the third branch made it look as if whoever it was in the dress with her arms raised up had lost her head.

Cole chuckled. So did Carolyn.

"Can't help laughing," she said, "even if it's spooky. Mother loved it."

"I bet she did," Cole said. "Just needs some of those masquerade masks."

"I said that, too! Especially since the whole reason I thought she liked it was because it reminded her of New Orleans . . . " Some stray thought in her head made her pause, but more important was not losing the thought she was in the midst of. " . . . but Mother thought the masks ruined it. Too much like a masquerade, when she just wanted a ball."

A few steps further, and two others, in shimmery green and glittering blue, came into view. Not funny or spooky, really, Cole thought, more like scary. He laughed some more. The other two were similarly designed, with variations in the way the fabric was wrapped giving the appearance of other dress styles—the green one had a collar around the head stump, and long, fake (he assumed) white pearls draped down the front. He saw there was a fourth tree off a bit in a long dramatic yellow dress with long flaring sleeves and rhinestones in the shape of a flower on the front. The positions of the largest branches gave the forms different poses—the way the branches resembled arms raised up to the sky at various angles and bent in different angles, the dressed trees seemed frozen mid-celebration. Altogether, the four looked like a quartet of Erté models had wandered into the garden and been magically transformed into trees.

Cole came upon a cherry tomato plant covered in fruit, and his hand shot out, plucking a handful. When he popped the first one into his mouth and bit into it, he smiled, closing his eyes.

"That's the way they're supposed to taste," he said.

Carolyn watched him as his eyes scanned the garden, looking for other edibles, and they were literally everywhere. He'd forgotten that about Carolyn. The way she observed the details. Even, apparently, when she was drunk.

"Don't have to run a restaurant to see that you're hungry," she said. "When was the last time you ate?

"This is the first and last thing I've eaten . . . for a while." He didn't want to say it was the first thing since the Snickers bar this afternoon. "Had some water. Lots of water. Lemonade. Fruit I picked alongside the road."

"Well, that's why you look like skin on bones. More like someone coming back from the peace corps than college. Let's go inside and I'll make you something, start fattening you up."

When Lily had called Carolyn a year-and-a-half before, asking her to come back home to look after their mother, it had come as a godsend to Carolyn. At its most basic, it was something that Don would likely allow, a way to spirit her out of the house with his approval and right under his watching eyes and to get away to a place where he wouldn't dare come to find her. That was how far out of control things had gotten in Don and Carolyn's marriage. So even though Carolyn was purportedly going to stay with her mother because her mother couldn't take care of herself, Carolyn was also going because her mother was the only one who would be able to protect her from Don. Her mother had put some fear into Don along the way that made him keep his distance from her. Don wouldn't mess with Rose Chamber.

When Lily had called Carolyn about looking after Momma, Lily hadn't gone long on explaining, just said that Momma shouldn't be living alone anymore. She was checking with Carolyn and then with Joshua to see what they could do, and if they didn't have anything to offer, she was either going to move Momma into her house, or else look for another living situation for her.

As Caroline and Cole walked away from the garden to return to the house, Cole said something about not feeling right about going into the house when he hadn't been there for five years. Carolyn waved it off as silliness, then found herself reliving the moment twenty months before when she had crossed the threshold to find Lily, Josh, Mother, and that girl she had never seen before, and hadn't seen since, waiting for her.

Carolyn was coming from a place where she had been scared for her life just driving away from Don and their home. Scared he was going to chase her down the street with a rifle—and she'd been overwhelmed with shame at them, her family, standing together and seeing her the day after a fight with Don. None of them had tried to understand what she'd been going through.

So she came into the house not caring to hear whatever story Lily had that day for why Josh couldn't take care of it himself or who the hell the unknown girl was. Nor had Carolyn bothered to explain her own appearance, specifically the slightly swollen and reddish area on her cheek just below her eye, which would bruise up more over the course of the day but hadn't yet had time to fully bloom.

Clearly, whatever it was with the girl was one of their secrets that they weren't going to share all of, or Lily already would have on the phone when she asked for Carolyn's help. Josh and Lily were always so busy taking care of things themselves, and Carolyn had come in that day feeling she really had no more time at all for it. The secrets of her own marriage were out in front of them at that point, for all of them to ignore. Caroline remembered thinking: Let Lily and Josh go and do whatever they had to as long as they went away. She had come home to stay.

Walking over the threshold with Cole, Carolyn surveyed the disarray inside, and felt that familiar anger—frustration at her older siblings for being so selfish, for not following through—rising up inside her. It always fell to her to clean up after them, she thought to herself, clenching her left fist.

"You know," Carolyn said, "I kept this house clean when I was here. Drinking or not, sick or not, busy or not, this place was clean. And when I left it this last time, I cleaned up everything. Because Momma went to Lily's for the last few weeks and we didn't want the vacant house to be filled with quote unquote valuables, we went through and packed up everything that was most important to her and sent it off to Lily's to store. Then I went through the house and straightened and put back in place everything that was left. When I left it was spic and span."

As she walked through the rooms, starting with the kitchen, she found she could pretty easily put together a picture of what had happened. "Lily and Joshua held a service, or maybe just a visitation, at the house. Probably went and buried her in the yard instead of doing something more decent because it was easier than listening to what I thought would be more dignified. Lily cleaned up most everything, except for what the lingerers and Joshua and his friends were still working at. Lily had to leave because her kids and Richard finally had enough, and Josh promised to clean up the rest of it—then he and his crew messed it up more, and this here is the best shape he was able to put into it before he left promising himself he'd be back to finish it 'the right way.' Darn him.

"With him knowing," she said, "or hoping, of course, that at some point I'm going to come home and finish up for him.

"And see the book case here?" She pointed at the bookcase, part of which had been pulled away from the wall. "About a year ago, we started getting these little clusters of quakes. People say it's fracking. Mother would just say, 'Earth's up to something these days.' But some of this mess here looks like it came from that."

She continued, "It does look like someone's gone through some things in the bedrooms, but that could be anything— someone who was here looking for something Lily asked them to find, that sort of thing. Maybe it's so noticeable because there just isn't a lot left here. I know that anyone who might have come in here to rob the place was sorely disappointed."

Carolyn returned to the kitchen to look through the cabinets. They were the least disturbed part of the house, and she was pleased to see that so many of the jars remained sealed. There was more than enough here to cook something up. She started up the fire on the stove.

While Cole ate, Carolyn fidgeted. She put all of the dirty dishes in the sink, filled it with water, but didn't start washing. She was eyeing the alcohol at the back of the cabinet. Before she started anything in earnest, she wanted another drink or three. Then she could get lost in the cleaning. But she had been doing wine earlier, and the cabinet was full of the hard stuff. Following up with hard stuff was likely to make her sick, she knew from experience—not that she wouldn't chance it if there wasn't another option. She still had a couple of bottles of wine in the car, but there was a whole awkwardness associated with drinking in front of Cole. If she stuck to the hard stuff, she could sneak shots and Cole wouldn't know, she told herself. Otherwise, she was going to have to make an announcement and just put it out there, then head out to the car.

She blamed her discomfort on Lily and Josh. They had both made it clear they didn't care for her drinking, making her feel that she had to be secretive about it around her family.

Cole pushed the empty plate away from him, stood from the table. He brought the plate to the sink, washed it off, and slid it into the dish rack beside the sink to dry.

He turned to her.

"Should we get cleaning?"

"Guess we should," she said.

"Do you have any more of whatever it is you're drinking?" He had an awkward look on his face.

"You bet," she said, eyes sweeping the room for her car keys. "If you can find my keys. You'll find bottles of wine in the trunk. I'll chill a couple glasses."

Cleaning had always fallen to them, Carolyn and Cole, especially after the twins, Zoe and Ben, went wherever it was they went. Before they ran off, the workload was this: their mother worked; Lily was either working or in school or at the police academy earning for the family also, and later, married and taking care of her own house; Joshua took care of the property outside the house; and the other four—Carolyn, Zoe, Ben, and Cole—shared the housecleaning chores and the animal care, jobs they divided different ways each month.

In those days, the only music they had was played on a record player. The only records to choose from were their mother's, and there were two genres available—New Orleans jazz and Broadway shows. Mother had an old 78 player in her room, and kept her New Orleans records in a crate nearby. The player for 33s was in the living room, and that one belonged to the kids, and so the music he was most familiar with growing up were the musicals of the 50s, 60s, 70s, and 80s.

Carolyn started with *Phantom of the Opera*, singing along as Cole made his way to the back of the house. He went to his mom's room. What greeted him inside was cold, stale air, and dust. The daylight, filtered through browned and thinning paper shades, cast the interior in a yellowed hue, making the walls look like aged parchment.

Maybe it really was this small, he thought.

He went to the dresser, pulled open the drawers quickly to see if there was anything left behind that a thief might have gone through. But the drawers were empty, except for a black box in the bottom drawer that smelled like an ashtray.

It's hard to believe she isn't here, Cole thought later. Lurking somewhere, ready to jump out from around a corner and holler and make me piss my pants. It was hard to believe she wasn't just going to come walking up the road, back from a day of working wherever they needed her.

The feeling was like a breath caught in his heart. He'd thought something here would feel the same.

Maybe it was him that wasn't the same. Or maybe it was just time away that made it seem like someplace other than the one he remembered. Or maybe that had been his own pretense— believing that living like he was someone other than a poor boy from the country meant he didn't have to be that any longer.

Up at the front of the house, he found a glass of red wine waiting for him—he took that with him as he stepped back out onto the front porch.

The distance from the house to both the main road and town had appealed immensely to his mother. In a region once populated with swine farms, she'd justified the remoteness of the property by saying it was the only patch isolated enough that it wasn't downwind from a pile of pig waste. The driveway had been his mother's warm-up for a day of walking that might have taken her 10 to 15 miles round trip. It was another measure of how far she would go to keep them safe from the world and hidden from any of the fathers who might have been out there looking for them. And who still might be, he thought.

Six years of schooling aren't going to have any relevance in these hills, he thought. My impression of who it is I have become isn't going to matter much in a place where everyone is going to treat me like the person they remember I used to be, as if those are two different people in anyone's mind but my own.

He drank down the wine in three gulps, and then returned to the back of the house, setting the wine glass back on the table where he'd found it.

Many of Cole's last memories of home and everyone there had been of Carolyn's wedding, which took place three weeks before he left for California. Just about everyone he'd ever known in his life up to that point was at that wedding, most of them looking the best they'd ever looked. Don's father, who always acted like he had money to burn, invited just about everybody in town.

The moment Carolyn had reached the front of the church escorted by their mother and stood beside Don, tears started to run down Cole's face. This had surprised him, because even though Don wasn't necessarily his type of person, Cole had been happy that Carolyn had found someone she could love and who seemed to love her back. He wasn't sad at all, in fact—but nonetheless, he was wiping tears from his eyes and cheeks for the entire hour the ceremony lasted. His nose didn't stuff up, he didn't sob, emotion wasn't welling up inside him, but he could not stop crying. Afterward, Don's father told Cole how touched he'd been to see Cole's reaction during the service. He'd had a strange look in his eye when he said it, and Cole hadn't been sure what had been behind it—he assumed the old man was thinking Cole very well might be the biggest wuss he'd ever seen in person.

The modern-day Carolyn was a world of different from the one he'd last seen five years before, in her wedding best form. At that time, she'd dieted down to the size of her high school cheerleading uniform, wore long, curly princess tresses, and any signs of aging had only required a light application of makeup to smooth.

Now he had to remind himself of the number of years between them—five—and then recalculate her age to realize that she was still not yet 30. She looked at least ten years older than that. Her hair wasn't terrible, but it looked like she might have cut it herself—shoulder-length, very plain. She looked 30 to 40 pounds heavier. Her skin looked sunburnt and leathery. The winning bit was the smile, which she'd flashed only once outside—it washed away many years when it appeared, and lit her face. Otherwise she looked stern.

The front of the house smelled much better than the part he'd come from, and he wondered if Carolyn would have more for him to do in back to rectify that. The glass he'd emptied before had been refilled, and as he drank it down Carolyn crossed into the room and dropped a bag of trash by the door. He was relieved to see that she looked more like the Carolyn of old to him. She had put her hair up into a scarf, clearing it away from her full cheekbones. She wore a cleaning outfit that looked like a modern-day version of what she used to wear—an apron and a long sleeve plaid shirt, with long plastic gloves on her hands.

When she saw him drinking, she said, "Oh, hold on a minute," and hurried to the kitchen and back with her glass and an open wine bottle. She didn't seem too drunk—no worse than he'd seen her this afternoon. She refilled his glass, touched her glass to his and then downed hers before refilling.

"You've got your Asian blush on," she said, nodding knowingly at him. Alcohol made his cheeks red.

"I can feel it already," he said.

Cole set the small black box he'd found on the table between them. Then he unsnapped the button latch, and lifted off the top to reveal a box filled almost to the rim with the ends of hand-rolled cigarettes.

"These are smoked joints," he said. "They were in Mom's bottom drawer."

Carolyn chuckled knowingly.

"Mother started smoking those for her glaucoma. She was something of a pot smoker for a while. One of her patients, or maybe someone's kid she helped deliver, talked her into trying it."

"I can't imagine Mom smoking." He laughed, maybe from the wine.

"She liked it, too," Carolyn giggled also. "She did it every day, at set times, and said it was about her eyes, but I know her eyes weren't bothering her as much as she did it. She even got kind of paranoid about her 'stash,' you know, moved it around all the time so people wouldn't steal it."

"No way."

"For about a year-and-a-half, there wasn't anyone but me around most of the time, and I know that she knew I didn't even really like to do that stuff, but when she was high on it I could tell that she would get a little suspicious that I was getting into it. She would take one of her hairs off of a hairbrush and tie it around that little box, or this other little silver box she kept her new cuttings in, and then leave it out on the counter, thinking that a broken or missing hair would be evidence that she was being robbed."

"Was she being robbed?"

"No, she was just too old to be smoking so much of that stuff. We finally did have to take it away from her, when she moved to Lily's, because Richard wasn't having any of that in his house. I think they finally agreed to let her have some pills with ingredients that had a similar effect."

Carolyn shook her head, "Oh, she was so mad about that, when we told her she would have to stop smoking that stuff."

"It's like you're talking about someone other than Mom," Cole said.

"When she was pushed too far, she could be wicked."

"Mom?" He found it hard to believe.

"She'd say things with that blank face, like she wasn't saying anything out of the ordinary. I'm telling you Cole, it was like living with someone other than our mother those last few months." Carolyn laughed, almost a cackle. "She could be a mean old mule. You know what she said to me when she finally realized she wasn't going to get to smoke any more? She said to me, 'You know, you were adopted. Your mother was a whore and she didn't want you. And now I don't either.'"

"Oh my gosh!"

"Boy, she was mad. Lily and Joshua laughed about that for a week. She'd said mean stuff to both of them, too. Called Joshua a tit suck for hanging around the house as much as he did. Called Lily a know-it-all slut tease. We were all laughing by then, Mother, too, even though she really was angry."

"Geez." He thought about it. "Did Don live here too?"

She looked at him incredulously, then looked away. Again, he couldn't tell if he was witnessing sincere emotion, or if these were drunken dramatics.

"Don's gone, Cole. He died. Drowned."

"What?"

Carolyn nodded, held her right hand against her heart.

"For real?"

"Oh, yeah, we had some bad storms last year. You know we have a house up in Elmer, where we moved so Don could open the store in West Bank. Not too far from here. He had a thing about wanting to walk to work, and the road he took crossed the river there. They think he got swept off the bridge."

"Fuck, I'm so sorry," Cole said, and he regretted the way he slurred each s, because he was sorry, even though he'd never cared for Don or thought he was a good match for her or their family. Carolyn had loved him enough to marry him, so Cole had always kept those feelings to himself.

All the time Carolyn had spent in her own head, entertaining ways to teach Don a lesson or two, none of them had been as good as the way it had worked out, because every other scenario she'd envisioned eventually ended with her arrest.

"Don and I didn't have a good marriage. He did not treat me well, is just about all I want to say about it. When Mother needed help, it gave me a way out of there—and by the time I was out of there, I pretty much didn't care what happened to him, long as he stayed away from me. So this was for the best. Because I didn't believe he really was going to stay away from me."

There had been only one evening session with the investigators from West Bank. That was all. A short session at that; she had an alibi for the evening, witnesses galore, and no reason to help them with anything other than directions back to town. This too she thought of as an act of the angels, as little as she cared about religion. In the time she'd been married, she'd never gone to the emergency room for care, so there was no record that might have been used against her, innocent or not. She'd been back at her mother's long enough that her complexion had cleared up, so there was no reason to think there'd ever been anything wrong with the relationship, except for the quiet Praise the Universe that escaped Carolyn's lips when she first heard the news.

Her time with her mother she took as a respite, and as her penance. For not being wiser.

Caroline had never known her mother to have any close friends. Didn't foresee having the time for them, she would say. She had her patients, and there were neighbors she got along well with. The people they would see regularly in their daily lives were the only other people in her mother's life who the children had ever met. Socially, she had been an island. Her mother's parents were gone and there were no uncles or aunts as far as anyone knew. She'd never mentioned there being anyone else other than a friend from when she was younger, Annabelle. But it was only in returning home that Carolyn realized how alone her mother was in her life. Almost as alone as Carolyn was herself.

Eventually, too quickly, her mother became more confused. Carolyn would catch her using important papers—her driver's license, pages from her journals, old address books—as kindling for a fire on a perfectly warm evening. She would mix up their fathers' occupations in her stories, or the name of a city or a state they lived in, and when Carolyn would innocently correct her, her mother would become very frustrated, and there was no telling what she might say when that happened.

None of the rest of the kids could have done it, Carolyn believed. Lily had her kids, Cole was in school, and Joshua was off somewhere, fighting forest fires in the northwest, or at boot camp, depending on Lily's story of the day.

There were a lot of things Carolyn had never told anyone else about mother. But then there were a lot of things she would never say out loud to anyone.

Her mother had been dead for two months. It was a slow recovery from that sad event, and it was still ongoing. This upcoming reunion felt to Carolyn like picking at the scab. There were so many things gone unsaid in their family. What if this was the time they finally all come out? She wasn't ready to face all of that right yet. Why would she want to? Before it came to that, Carolyn was going to insist on the silver set in its entirety. Mother promised it to her. It was what she deserved.

They could have all the rest of it, for all she cared.

"It worked out for the best. Don always was a Daddy's boy, and when Don Sr. died, part of him was lost without his Daddy. Don inherited both the stores, so I got them when he died, and I sold one and bought into the restaurant, because I always said I was going to own that place and then die there."

"So you're rich now?"

"I'm comfortable for a while, if things stay alright. Far cry from rich—still have to work all the time. Best thing was that Don Sr. had a trailer on his property, and it seems like what he did was take the very best of the things that came through the thrift shop and stored it all away in the trailer. Damn thing is packed, and it's all valuable stuff. I never understood why he shot the wheels on the trailer—until I understood that he was afraid someone might steal the whole thing."

"Well, I'm going to have to borrow some money, Sis— because I got nothing right now. It took the last of what I had to get home."

"Don't worry about that. Not having money was never an issue in this family, right? Now we've got more than we ever had. We'll manage. Is that why you're so serious now? So grown up that you're worrying about everything?

"No, I just . . . it's weird to be home. And I think I left everything so bad in California that I can't imagine going back there again." He told her about the money issues he'd left behind, glossed over the breakup with his girlfriend, and sort of hinted about the less than desirable person he thought he'd became.

"You know, Cole, you left here with one goal: to graduate college. And you did it. And you started out with just about nothing. However it was you managed that, don't let it get ahead of the fact that maybe all of it was just the cost of reaching that goal. I tell myself that nearly every day. That's maybe even a better life lesson than anything you learned in school. Sometimes you've got to do what you got to do to get where you want to be.

"Now you're home and it's over," she said. "And you can start fresh, taking in everything you've learned and applying it to doing better in future. You know what needs to be done, and you do whatever it takes to get it done. It isn't always a pretty business, being a Chamber. That's how we do it."

When they were both in the back house, just getting started cleaning, Carolyn ranted a little to herself as she washed down the walls, and it wound into a slurred soliloquy.

"No surprise there, what with our lack in positive male role models. None at all. Best she could give us was that Josh's and my dad was a do-nothing, Lily's father left her," she was counting off one, two, three on her fingers, "Ben and Zoe's dad was so abusive that we ran across the country to get away from him. Your dad was probably the nicest one, but he was in the wind just the same. How are any of us supposed to make a decision about picking the right person when those are the best examples we've been given?" She went into the next room, still talking.

Cole set about opening the windows throughout the place. He thought that what really frightened his mother after Zoe and Ben left was the idea of all of them not being a family anymore, that they could all just leave, after she'd worked so hard to keep them together. As if family were anything but forever. Moving away didn't make that any less so.

When Carolyn returned, she had apparently forgotten that she'd already blamed Mom for the types of men that she, Carolyn, was attracted to. The reprise rendition was less linear than the first, and Cole thought he heard a hint of something in the way she delivered the narrative that suggested she had long since embraced the idea that the end of her marriage had nothing to do with anything she had done—it was the result of forces beyond her control.

That was how drunks worked, Cole knew, never taking the blame for anything. It also occurred to him that the spiel about their mother was something she repeated frequently.

"How was I supposed to know anything? Gosh, I was so ignorant," she laughed harshly as she walked out of the room again.

Wherever Ben and Zoe are, Cole thought, I hope they are at least still taking care of each other.

Chapter 10

"That'll be it then, Josh?"

"Yes, Sir, Mr. Hazeltine."

"Cheryl saw your brother Cole crossing through early afternoon."

"That right? About time he made it home," Joshua said. "How'd he look?"

Mr. Hazeltine looked at him blankly, licked his lips, then said slowly, "Well, I'm guessing he looked like your brother Cole." Joshua waited for a something more, but that was it.

As he stepped outside, Joshua lit a cigarette while gripping the paper bags in the crook of one arm. He was late getting back from a long round-trip drive, and he had to tend to the critters at the farm, so he decided to put off heading to the family home until the next day. Wasn't as if Cole had called him yet. Maybe he was still getting settled, Joshua thought. There was a lot to get settled with.

Joshua couldn't deny being excited to see his brother.

Earlier in the evening, Joshua had driven over to the University for what in the flyers had been called a seminar but which had actually turned out to be a movie followed by a question-and-answer session. Now the story from the movie was swimming around in his head—what it was about, what it was trying to say, why it was made.

That Joshua had gone there at all he took as a major slip in his mental state. When he first met Christy, she had been handing out pamphlets from the same organization, The Framework Foundation, that was sponsoring the lecture. He'd thought there was a chance she might be at this one, too.

What was that group about? Was Christy one of them?

The tag line on the flyer said, "Developing a framework for understanding the universe." Did they want people to join? Did they want people to believe? With that movie, were they just trying to take a poke at religion? A little bit of all three? Was it a religion? A cult? A nonprofit, as it said on the flyer? A moneymaking venture with a product to push?

Joshua was relying on dumb luck to bring him into Christy's orbit again. He was not only steadily on the lookout for her, but also apparently now chasing around to places near and far, however dubious, where he thought she might make an appearance. Without knowing whether she lived in the area, or much of anything else about her other than her first name, he didn't see that he had any other choice.

He thought she just might be the One.

Of course, she hadn't been there at the University movie night. Of course, afterward he'd picked up a flyer listing upcoming Framework events in the region. Because now that he'd chased after her this once, likely he was going to continue to be desperate enough to do it again in the future. None of that was rational.

Nor, he thought, was the movie.

The story was about a spaceship of scientists who traveled through space to explore a planet. They were in pursuit of an even more advanced race that they believed had left its fingerprints all over different corners of the universe. In the exposition early on, it was explained that although sites occupied by the elder aliens had been discovered in different parts of the universe, none of the younger races of aliens searching for them had encountered them yet. The elder aliens were believed to be still in existence, but hidden someplace the younger aliens hadn't yet discovered.

Part of the scientists' efforts to understand the elder beings involved studying the works they had accomplished, which included the elders having seeded life on various planets across the known universe. The younger beings had taken to exploring these seeded planets to better understand what their predecessors had done, how they had done it, and most importantly, why.

It was suggested many times that the older race had responded negatively to the presence on other planets of scientists from the younger races, and that their responses to such meddling had been nothing less than cataclysmic, and so the characters were often saying things like, "Who knows who is watching us?" or "I hope this doesn't piss someone off," and looking up at the stars in concern.

The spaceship that they traveled in broke apart into separate modules, each holding a separate team of scientists, and they spread across the planet. The film generally followed one team, male and female, who became a couple as they collected samples of every kind of organic matter they came across. They came to enjoy their lives on this planet, particularly when they discovered a region so rich with organic diversity that they made it their home. The male, in particular, developed a taste for fermented fruit and the effects it produced.

Occasionally their paths crossed with other teams who were each conducting different types of experiments. Some teams were dissecting flora and fauna, other teams were cloning them, and still others were mixing and combining DNA elements from existing organisms to create new, different organisms. Samples from every one of the experiments happening worldwide were transmitted to the male and female protagonists, who stored them in a black rectangular box.

One team combined DNA from things that resembled lizards, rats, insects, birds, squids, and monkeys, and they created an upright-walking creature that seemed like it could be a distant ancestor of the scientists themselves. These creatures became the laborers that many of the scientists tasked with their more challenging physical endeavors, although the protagonist male and female eschewed their use.

Shortly after the upright creatures' creation, the original planet seeders—who were never shown—reacted to the scientists' efforts by throwing a meteor at the planet, splitting land masses apart, stranding all of the scientists in distant places across the planet, and causing the continent on which the hero and his family lived to sink below sea level, resulting in the beginning of a flood that would engulf the paradise in which they lived.

Someone said pointedly, "Is the whole world flooding?"

"It must seem like it to the primitives," the heroine said, in what Joshua interpreted as a jab at Bible believers, "But that's really not possible. It's only happening around the impact zone."

The debris kicked into the atmosphere by the impact warped weather patterns, resulting in months of grey skies and rain. Their craft was too damaged to fly again, but sturdy enough for the hero and his family to seal themselves inside as the floodwaters rose. They had food and supplies, they had each other, and most important, as salt water rushed around their vessel, washing away everything in this paradise, they had the storage box filled with genetic samples from every living thing their scientific mission had managed to catalog.

Their craft reached land outside the flood zone, the rains ended, the skies cleared, and they set about preparing for the rest of their lives on the planet. With a home established, the lab in their vessel restored, and a refreshed fear of the elder race, they used the genetic samples in the box to begin recreating the life forms that had been destroyed. Beginning, of course, with the much-beloved alcoholic-fruit producing tree.

The hero and the heroine, and then their children, for the rest of their lives continued creating animals, birds, insects, plants two by two, male and female. The couple lived to be hundreds of years old, as did, somehow, descendants of the first-version cavemen-looking creatures, which had managed not only to survive, but also to thrive. These creations spread and evolved, and eventually started to worship the scientists. When the creatures began to hunt and kill the scientists' other creations and offer their remains to the scientists for tribute, the hero and his mate moved away from them, into a hospitable valley located in the midst of an inhospitable mountain range. They lived out the rest of their lives surrounded by, protecting, and protected by some of their creations. The box carrying the genetic material ended up damaged, and instead of being carried by its handles, they slid poles under the left and right sides of it, which required two people to carry it—one holding the sticks while walking in front, and one holding the back ends of the sticks while walking behind it, with the box held aloft between them. The movie ended on an image of the box being carried up a hill.

There was enthusiastic applause from the audience. Joshua thought maybe a few of the actors were in the crowd having their backs patted. The lights came up, and the writer/director stepped up to the podium to take questions, and Joshua scanned the room for that one face, which he hadn't seen during the intermission or when he scanned the crowd during the film, and which he did not find when the room was lit again.

As the film's director took the stage for a question-and-answer session, he opened by saying, "Thank you for joining us— I'm so pleased to see so many unfamiliar faces here! Is everyone planning on gathering someplace for the Sizzy-jizzy?" Joshua looked around curiously at the sound of the last words, to see if it made anyone else want to snicker. All he heard were cheers and applause, and all he saw were nodding heads all around.

These were believers, Joshua thought.

"Before I say another word, I do want to offer my thanks to the Framework Foundation for the financing that made this film possible." Scattered applause. "I know this organization is the subject of a lot of controversy these days, and I can't speak for anyone's experience but my own, but from what I've seen, the Framework Foundation is dedicated to answering the questions 'What is out there and how is it connected to us?' and 'What is our role in the Universe and how can we achieve it?' They were not interested in influencing my story; they were interested in contributing to the overall discussion. That said, no, it was not solely my intention to make a sci-fi retelling of the story of Noah . . . " the director was saying as Joshua made for the exit. He noticed as he walked toward the lobby that more than a few people were wearing black t-shirts with a single word on them, set inside a black circle surrounded by a band of white flames, which must have been what the speaker was referring to: Syzygy.

Lily received the text from Josh just after she'd finished washing the dishes.

Joshua: Think Cole's home. I'll go by the house in the morning to see. Any word from Carolyn?

Lily: No, but that's just because I haven't tried lately. I think she'll come if I ask her to. Let me know tomorrow.

She filled a cup with hot water, dropped in a tea bag, then walked to the front door, out to the porch, where she sat.

She was having mixed feelings about going home again.

Two weeks before, she'd gotten a call from Al, the owner of the body shop where she'd had the work done on the damage to her car. Al had always taken care of their family's car needs in exchange for her mother's veterinary services for the animals on his property. It was a long and inconvenient extra distance for a working wife and mother to drive, but Lily trusted Al and he always undercharged. The car, which she and Richard had decided to keep when they got the new one, had always been great for running small errands that didn't require an SUV. Really, it didn't matter to her for anything other than sentimental reasons—it was the first car she'd ever bought and paid for by herself. It wasn't a problem to leave it with Al, knowing there was no way of guessing when he'd get around to finishing it.

Al reminded her when she got on the phone that he'd kept some of the paint flecks that had been left on the side of her car—light blue paint. He said that he thought he'd found the match—that the owner had the pickup towed in. Did Lily want to come have a look?

She did, of course. She wanted a name, but she wanted to see the truck first to be sure. So two days later, after hugs and more sympathies for the loss of her mother, Al led her around the work bays to a fenced-in area behind the building, where ten cars were parked in a dirt lot. To the right of the car were three bays, and in one of them, a blue Toyota.

It didn't just have headlight and front bumper issues. It looked as if it had been on the losing side in a demolition derby. Someone had gone to town on it—the windows were broken, the side view mirrors smashed and dangling, the tires slashed, the doors gouged, and the hood was covered with deep dents and jagged holes.

"Goodness," Lily said.

"When he hit you, did he flip and then roll across a field of boulders before righting himself and driving off?" Al was looking at her, watching her expression. "Or did someone go and teach him a lesson?"

"I don't know anything, Al. Did he say anything?"

"Too scared. Had his brother bring it in. Brother said he woke up one morning and saw someone had gone to town on it. But it's clear to me, that sort of thing," Al gestured toward the truck, "isn't the kind of thing anyone sleeps through. Not when the car's parked five feet outside a person's bedroom window."

Oh, please, Lily thought, connecting the dots that Al was drawing for her. It can't be that.

"You know . . . I haven't . . . I didn't spend more than 20

minutes thinking about it after it happened," she managed to say, "and then another ten minutes two weeks later when you called. This is the first I've heard of any of this."

"Well, someone found their man," Al said. "Maybe you weren't the only one he was messing with that night." The way he said it, Lily knew Al was thinking of the same person she was, although he would never say it.

When Lily started at the police academy, she'd quickly gravitated to the small group of classmates who were neither good old boys with connections to the department nor their friends or sons. One member of the group she was part of was Elias Morales, and the two of them had an instant rapport. She would later attribute that to the similarities in their backgrounds—raised by a single mother, oldest of several children, in the program itself half because they liked the idea of being cops, the other half because they wanted to be breadwinners for their families.

She'd early on vowed not to be one of those women who lived up to the worst stereotypes of women in the program: That they became involved with their male counterparts whether they were married or not, disrupting life in the ranks, and that they were looking for husbands more than badges. In the case of Elias or anyone else, the point was moot: Lily had been seeing Richard for a year before the academy, and the strength of that relationship, still in its early phases and going well, made it easy not to attempt to be too personally involved with anybody at school.

Over the course of time, as their study group bonded, she and Elias had become friends—the fact that they both had significant others and family responsibilities seemed to put them into a subgroup of the study group, the subgroup that didn't have the time or spare change for nights of bar hopping and eating out. The others in the group started to refer to them as Mom and Dad, or the Parents.

Early on, she'd thought that if not for Richard, if not for Elias' girlfriend, Chloe, maybe something would have happened between them, despite her pledge. However, because they were in the friend category and part of a group where he felt open to talking about himself, he shared details of his life that she thought would be issues in a relationship. Elias was very flirtatious. Not with the best-looking girls, not girls he would ever date, but with girls who took him too seriously and spent time trying to spend time with him while he spent time trying to evade them. Every single one of them believed the only reason he was talking to them at all was because things maybe weren't as solid with his girlfriend as he acted. But he was never going to leave Chloe for any of them; it was simply that she was at school in Ohio and he needed a way to pass the time while they were apart. He liked their attention, them wanting him. He would go to a family barbecue with a secretary from the office, and then joke with the group afterward about the way she'd kept his drink full and how she had reminded him five times that she had a spare bedroom if he wanted to crash there for the night. All that really mattered to him was that he'd found an enjoyable way to pass another night. He'd had fun hanging out at the barbecue with her friends—but that was about it. It didn't matter to him that the secretary thereafter would occasionally practice writing her first name with his last name in cursive on the Post-It pad at her desk.

After some time knowing Elias, Lily thought she was grateful that nothing had happened between them. As for his feelings toward her, other than the way he called her "old pal" and "buddy," she had no idea what he truly felt about her, though there would be glimpses that his feelings ran deeper. She was glad when he was assigned to the same department that she was, glad to have someone in her life who could understand what she was experiencing—who valued that first paycheck as much as she did, who was trying to learn to look at the world the same way she was trying to learn to look at it. The group would joke that he was her work husband. She was happy to have him as a friend.

When Chloe came to town to visit, Lily and Richard often went to dinner with them. Richard and Elias got along well—any discomfort between them had more to do with the differences in their backgrounds than anything else. Richard didn't know people like Elias, and vice versa. It was Lily who felt at least a little uncomfortable on these double dates, because she could tell there were many aspects of Elias' life with Chloe that he really hadn't shared with her or the group. He was, for example, quite an obedient puppy when he was in Chloe's presence. It made Lily wonder who he was being truthful with. His excuse for not following through on any of his flirtations with other women was his deep commitment to Chloe. But for all the attentiveness he showed toward Chloe he also seemed to be simultaneously holding her at arms' length, too, with the excuse that he was deeply committed to his career objectives and the life he needed to be living to reach those objectives.

When Chloe broke up with Elias, and it turned him into a most pathetic man, Richard would go out to drinks and happy hour snacks with him and let Elias just ramble on about his inability to understand the end of his relationship. He couldn't fathom what went wrong, when clearly the problem was that Chloe wanted a deeper commitment than Elias was willing or able to make. He wasn't single for long, but his relationship with the new woman— who had a young son—seemed to hold the center of his attention for an even shorter period of time.

There were odd moments in their friendship that stood out to Lily. Like when Elias had commandeered a delivery cart at an agricultural processing facility they'd had to check out after some graffiti artists decorated a couple of exterior walls. He'd taken Lily on a joyride around the facility, speeding between the sheds and buildings in the cool of the morning, and it had made her feel young and silly. Several times during the ride, as he went to shift gears, his hand grabbed at her knee or her thigh instead of the gear shift, and each time, with an "Oops," he pulled it back instantly and awkwardly and then grabbed the gear stick. By the look on his face, she couldn't tell if it was a sincere accident or just a high school level pass at her. He giggled almost guiltily the third time it happened, and then smiled broadly while avoiding her eyes. It just felt like something was going on that day.

Richard had gone abroad for a semester at some point. Lily had been displeased about being left behind, about his failure to consult with her before committing to his plan, and his unwillingness to propose or make promises before he left. Instead he acted as if, with the prospect of their impending engagement seeming inevitable, he needed this one last experience before he would be able to commit. She felt it was his belief that she should be waiting expectantly for his return.

Maybe he didn't say that exactly, but that was how Lily interpreted it. In the days immediately after he left, she decided to view it as a window of opportunity to do as she wished. She thought then, because she really was hurt by Richard's abandonment—however temporary—that what she wished to do was to try to see how things would go with Elias. It didn't have to be anything serious, she'd told herself. Just a fling. But even after she decided to try, she felt strangely unable to do much of anything without more of a sign from him.

From then on, their timing didn't work at all—she would be awkward one day and then he would be off the next. He would talk about girls he thought were hot and their pathetic efforts to pursue him, and she would just clam up. She would catch herself wondering what it would be like to kiss him, what he would look like undressed, what his penis might look like, and then she would catch him staring at her from behind, or sneaking a glance at her chest, at her lips. It was the most baffling relationship she'd ever been a part of—she was quite certain he was as attracted to her as she was to him, but expressing those sentiments presented a barrier neither seemed to be capable of crossing first.

Her resolve sort of fizzled from there. They couldn't break out of the holding pattern. Her anger at Richard lessened—she started to miss him, to crave honest and open affection, to look forward to his letters, to hope for his early return.

One night Elias had asked her to meet him at the river, where he had invited her to sit in his car with him and listen to some "verse" he had written that he wanted to share. (She had known he wrote "verse" and thought that although it sounded poetic, it was also some kind of rap thing that she wouldn't be into.) It turned out it was indeed poetry. And he wanted to share it with her. Even though they'd sat side by side on many occasions, in classes, at work, on patrol, at that moment, it felt different. She believed she was sending him a strong signal that night in her willingness to drive to meet him, to be sitting in the dark in a car by the river with him, someone who was not her nearly-to-be fiancé, and who was reading her poetry.

The poem was about a man who wanted to be adored and desired, but when he had those things, his heart dreamed only of finding his true love. The universe granted his wish, and his true love came knocking on the door, but afraid of answering, he hid inside. While he was inside, he pretended to be everything but who he actually was—he barked like a dog, he squawked like a parrot, he brayed like a donkey, he pretended he was the phone ringing and the answering machine picking up and a caller leaving a message, and he yelled out finally that he was sick with a fever and couldn't come to the door. Love kept knocking patiently the whole time, and waited even longer after it stopped knocking before moving on. In the end, the man blamed his heart for making wishes he was afraid might come true.

When he'd reached the part of true love knocking on the

door, Lily started to wonder who this was about. Was it about Chloe? It couldn't have been about the one after Chloe. Was it about Lily? Was he telling her he thought she was in love with him, but that he was afraid to make the first move? Was that what this was about? Were the song's lyrics a message to her not to bother? Or was it supposed to be romantic? Was he finally taking a shot at her, knowing the window of opportunity would soon be permanently sealed with a ring? Or was this really supposed to be about his latest artistic achievement?

She'd looked around, a little panicked, thinking of opening her car door. Behind the car and to the right, the giant, fading Dutch windmill that marked hole 10 in the weathered Whizland Golf Course rose into the night, blades turning slowly.

By the serious look on his face as he stared at her after he finished speaking, she did not know quite what level of enthusiasm she should show that wouldn't disappoint him.

So she'd asked him to read it again.

When he finished a second time, Lily thought it was a sad story he was telling, and she still returned to her questions. Why this? Why now? She thought for a moment about asking him those questions, or asking him about his feelings for her, and immediately in her head she recalled just a few of the many times he'd told her that a pathetic woman had posed him that question, and stopped herself.

Lily wasn't available, not for this, her ire rising. She wasn't one of his easy catches. She wasn't going to be the one who kissed him tonight and then waited in vain for his call in the morning. He had a new girlfriend and, Lily told herself, she was soon to be engaged to Richard. She was sure of it. Did Elias really expect he could get her to alter the course of her life—because that was what would happen if anything happened between them—without even having to tell Lily that she was what he wanted? Without having to admit he was in love with her? They knew each other well enough that giving in even a little to those feelings wouldn't be dipping a foot in the pool. It wouldn't just be a blowjob in a parked car with a scenic view, much as he might prefer that simplicity. It wasn't something that was going to happen lightly. Not without something more concrete.

That night, she told him the poem was funny but sad.

As she said it, she realized that unless he actually had the nerve to express his feelings toward her, to say whatever it was he was feeling clearly, to open it up and let her at least know it was there, then she was going to let it lie there and move away from it before it could do any damage to her life.

Was he disappointed at her reaction? She thought so, but again, she had lost some confidence in Elias' ever being up front and honest about his feelings. Lily had long since come to think of that night as the beginning of the end of their time as close friends. She remembered coming home that night and thinking, "Well, that window is closed."

It wasn't until much later that she realized that what she should have asked, probably what he'd wanted her to ask, was who the poem was about, who it was that had made him feel so desired and then left him destroyed. Then he would have said, "You," or "Us," and that might have at least given them a place to start from. Or maybe not. Who knew? In the end, she was as guilty of not speaking up as he was.

It wasn't long after that Lily was engaged, and even less time after that when she accepted a dispatch job with the department that served the town where she and Richard bought their first house. She and Elias didn't stop being friends. They didn't stop talking to each other, but it was more at a safe distance. Making jokes, laughing, helping with work, all of that still happened. But whatever it was that had happened or didn't happen that night, whatever was said or left unsaid, it was still there, and they both continued to pretend it wasn't until she transferred.

Elias' mom took ill before the wedding, so Elias didn't attend, and she died while Lily was still on her honeymoon. She sent a sympathy card from Italy asking Elias to call when he was ready to talk, but stayed away when he never responded. At work, Lily would send him a message once in a while related to the job, and he would always respond with a message within a day or two, but never strayed far from business and always kept it short.

It wasn't that she spent days wondering what her life would have been like with Elias instead of Richard. It was her impression he would have wrecked her and then not understood why or how he'd managed to do that when all he was doing was just living his life the way he always had. The difference between Lily and every other girl who threw herself at him was that she'd understood that basic fact—he was not ready to change.

She did spend time every once in a while missing having him to talk to. She missed hearing his take on the current goings-on. She missed having him as a friend. More than once, she'd wondered if she had just romanticized those aspects of their relationship to an extravagant degree. But she always returned to wondering: If everything was as he indicated, and their relationship was only platonic from his point of view, and there was no undercurrent of unspoken feeling on his part—then why wouldn't he talk to her anymore? Why did he put so much effort into staying away from her? She thought he knew that at this point they wouldn't be able to reestablish direct contact without having an honest conversation first. And he still wasn't ready for that, evidently. Maybe he never would be. And maybe, she thought with some reservation, she shouldn't be so quick to hope for it. *Don't let your heart make wishes you're afraid might come true.*

She'd long since decided to honor the space Elias seemed to want between them. He had his life, she had hers, and, seemingly, up until now, he preferred if never the two did cross. Perhaps that was why the bashed-up truck filled her with concern.

Chapter 11

The gist of what Joshua had been hearing lately was that someone had been asking around about the Chamber children. The fact Joshua knew this was a good measure of the family's status in town. The Chambers were no different than the rest. Every living soul in the hills here had something in their family past they didn't want held against them. The Chamber family had been here long enough, and they'd fit in well enough, that people would let Joshua know someone had been asking about his family. Not long enough or well enough that they were going to check with Joshua before they started answering the questions they thought they knew the answers to, but still, that was a hard-earned ounce of protection.

Joshua once believed that no one in town cared a bit about the Chamber family, beyond the fact that his mother provided good care for people and their animals, practically for free. Otherwise they might have to go someplace else and pay for it. Now he understood that his neighbors' distant and formal public manner masked the depth of their involvement with all that transpired within and along the borders of their small town. Although there existed a heartfelt desire to make any newcomers feel welcome, most of the hard-working people in the area tended to keep to themselves. It wasn't that they didn't care; they really only got involved if it was something they judged bigger than one person or one family should rightfully be able to handle on their own.

It was a message he'd first witnessed in practice when they'd first come to town. His mother had brought them to the neglected lot that she said had been her family's property—nothing but a stone room and a chimney left on it—and they'd pitched a tent made of old bed sheets while they figured out a plan. It wasn't long before random folks were dropping by with food for them. At that point, anyone looking at their family could see the need was great. So they all just up and stepped in to help.

Josh parked his truck next to Carolyn's car.

If a person came down here from a nicer area, he thought, they would look at this place and see it as slightly nicer than a hovel. But if a person knew what the property looked like when the Chambers first got here, and knew how little they'd had to work with, a person couldn't not be impressed. Joshua was going to keep fixing it up—couldn't help himself, always looking around the place and thinking about what he would like to do next. He used to pretend it was for his mother that he kept working away at it, but now that excuse was gone. The truth was, he felt the property had developed a life and personality of its own, and after all the hard work he had already put into it, he wanted to make sure it became the homestead he'd always wanted it to be.

Inside, Cole was asleep in his room and Carolyn was slumped over at the kitchen table, a cell phone in her hand. The house was as clean as Joshua had ever seen it, except for the wine bottles here and about—it seemed that there were empty bottles in nearly every room.

He knocked on Cole's bedroom door and then opened it a crack to see his brother still asleep, although the knock had him stirring. Joshua was surprised at how happy he felt to see Cole. He had to stop himself from picking his brother up out of the bed.

Cole opened one eye.

"Josh."

"Yippy-yi-yay. You made it back, brother."

Cole was groggy. Clearly his head hurt. Joshua thought he might have some hangover powder in his truck.

"What happened to me?"

"You let a drunk get you drunk, is what I'm guessing. Drunk leading the misled."

"I think she was singing 'Totally Fucked!' from *Spring Awakening* on the roof of the back house at three in the morning."

"Good thing you didn't look. She was probably topless when she was doing it."

"So she's an alcoholic."

"And unrepentant. She thinks it's everybody else who needs to get off her ass and drink more."

"Who slept in my room?" Cole lifted himself up, but must have moved his head too fast, because he winced. "I can almost feel that somebody else was living in here. Ouch."

"The only one I can think of is Emily. But I don't know that she slept in here."

Cole asked, "Where did I hear that name?"

"I have some BC Powder in the car. I'll go get it for you, then we can tell stories, okay?"

Cole looked at his brother with a puzzled look.

Cole said, "Okay?" Like he didn't understand what was happening.

"I'm glad you're home," Joshua said.

"You are?"

"I missed you."

"You did?"

"Of course, I did. I . . . " He looked up, saw Cole was messing with him.

"I missed you, too, Bro," Cole said.

"It started with the stories I was hearing," Joshua said, "stories I never gave any weight to; wasn't ready at all for the idea that Momma might be slowing down, that she might need some looking over. People said she was getting behind in her appointments, forgetting things here and there. Never missed a birth but came close a couple of times, according to them. I thought it had more to do with the fact she couldn't say no to people, no to their kids, and especially not to an expectant mother, and that she kept taking on more than she could handle.

"But then, not long after that, the stories had mom running her appointments with a girl in tow. A girl out of nowhere. Although at the time she was living in the next county over, people were telling Lily the same stories, and asking me if I had a cousin or a niece they hadn't heard about and otherwise, you know, where might this girl be from?

"I finally just had to go over to have a look."

Joshua remembered, but didn't describe to Cole, the way his mother had tried to flex her mom muscles, and how, for once, it hadn't worked, although he'd been as polite about it as possible.

"What do you mean, who is she?" Then she said, "Don't raise your voice with me."

"Sorry, ma'am." He hadn't raised his voice at all.

"That's better. Now don't you recognize your own sister?

"My sister?"

"Emily. This is Emily. Emily, this is your biggest brother, Joshua."

"Mom said to me, 'Don't you remember Emily?' and she nodded at me, and by her expression she was encouraging me to agree that I did remember her. I was thinking it was hard to believe mother could ever start to show her age. I guess at some point, you have to choose between the truth as you hold it in your heart and what your eyes are seeing in front of you. She looked old to me that day, Cole, and not all together in her head.

"I was thinking, 'Did Emily look like us?' and, you know, there not being a generic family look, it's hard to say. Had she adopted a child without telling us? Had one followed her home from her daily rounds and she'd just decided to keep her?"

"Emily," Joshua said slowly at the time, "It's nice to meet you." *Emily was shy, no voice.*

"You haven't been around much lately," Mom said. "She's

gotten big already."

Joshua didn't mention that Emily was a teenage girl.

"Who is she, Momma? Where did she come from?"

"She is your sister. We'll leave it at that. Do you want to argue with me about it?"

"So I drove into town, called Lily. Lily called Carolyn, who I guess had been too busy getting drunk and then getting beaten up by Don to check in on her own mother.

"That was the last time the three of us were in a room together. Carolyn having just come in through the front door looking like Don's punching bag, Lily and Momma there beside me. The three of us and Mom. And that Emily. I couldn't look my one sister in the eyes without seeing the handprint her husband had left there beside them, or the other sister and the girl without facing the fact that I was ready to run away and hide, leaving all of it in Lily's lap for her to solve. It was just too hard for me to see Momma like that.

"When I walked out the door that day, Momma was saying, 'For me, Lily.' She was holding the girl's hand, and begging. 'For me. It's not too late for me. An Emily for Rose.'"

"I still don't know where that little girl came from, or where she went. Lily took care of it all."

When Rose Chamber died, a good part of the area's population came to the funeral, out of respect for a woman who had served her hometown and asked very little in return. She was a stoic and beloved figure known for resolutely traipsing the countryside day after day, caring for animals and people. It seemed like it had been the same wherever she'd lived before this place. She would move them under dire circumstances into the poorest and most remote of places, and then set out on foot the next day to take care of anyone who needed her help.

Joshua had idolized his mother.

He tried hard to live by her words, and by the example she set. She wasn't going to let the world stop her from being who she was.

When they were younger, the family took a trip to town for an afternoon at the dentist's office. Joshua brought along his homemade bow and arrow, to show his little brothers he was going to protect them from the Hamilton boys, two boys with an older bother who together had been making Cole's days at school that much harder. The Hamiltons had promised to hassle with Cole if he ever stepped inside the city limits. Joshua knew his brother had put up with more than his share of razzing as a kid, on account of Cole's father being an Asian. It made him an easier target.

That day, their mother had dropped them off for their appointments while she did the shopping. Sure enough, that day, the timing was that Joshua was in the chair when the Hamiltons arrived on the scene, and he had to sit listening to endless rounds of taunting going on in the waiting room while his teeth were being scraped at and shined. When Joshua came out, and Ben went in for his turn in the chair, Joshua and Cole and the other three boys were out the door and down the stairs to the parking lot in a flash and without a word spoken between them.

In no time, Hugh and Jimmy Hamilton had Cole pinned to the ground while Joshua and Tommy Hamilton were still pushing each other around. Little Hugh was soon taunting Cole to get him to cry.

But Joshua was bigger, and better with his fists than Tommy. As soon as Tommy went down, Joshua pulled out his bow and arrow and aimed the sharpened metal tip at Jimmy Hamilton, who was across the parking lot on top of Cole. He would surely have shot Jimmy in the eye right then and there, if not for the arrival of Mr. Hamilton, who appeared from nowhere, suddenly grabbing a fistful of Joshua's shirt and then lifting him up off the ground. Joshua struggled and twisted around as he went, and was nearly horizontal when he let the arrow go, just as Mr. Hamilton slammed him against the building.

The arrow stuck in Jimmy's hand for a moment, and then fell out when he saw it and started to shriek.

Mr. Hamilton ranted at Joshua as he held him there against the wall of the convenience store. He threatened to beat Joshua senseless, and as he settled into a litany of curses, Joshua felt the color run out of his face. Joshua saw the frightened, helpless look on his little brother's face, and every other kid's face there, and then Mr. Hamilton shook him again, telling Joshua to look at him when he was talking to him. Joshua looked back at that old, angry, distorted face just in time to see a fist smash into the side of Mr. Hamilton's head, catching the man completely by surprise, hitting him hard enough that it knocked him off his feet. He dropped Joshua as he went down.

It was his mother coming to his rescue. And she was angry.

Joshua jumped on Mr. Hamilton, swinging his arms, repeating many of the curses Mr. Hamilton had just directed at him. His mother joined in, circling Joshua and Mr. Hamilton, kicking at Mr. Hamilton's legs and sides, and stepping on his hands, as he tried to fight off Joshua.

His mother recomposed herself and reined her son in before real harm was done. Gathered the children up, picked up her bags of groceries, and walked off down the road with her family without looking back at the Hamiltons crowded around Mr. Hamilton in the dirt. None of the Chambers said a thing about it, although Joshua and Cole wanted to crow the whole way home.

Zoe ran ahead to be the first one to tell Lily, which was exactly what she did, finishing just as the others came in through the front door, and finally their mother behind them.

Cole burst into the kitchen shouting, "Mom kicked Mr. Hamilton's ass!"

Lily asked her, when their mother set the bags she was carrying down on the counter, "Is that true?"

Momma, unapologetic as she unbuttoned her coat, said, "He was a grown man hurting the boy. I took care of the situation." She might even have cracked a little bit of a smile, although if she did, she turned away from them so they would not see it.

When Cole was upright again, and he'd pulled on his clothes, he took a moment to be amazed at Joshua's size.

"Dude, I gained 10 pounds at school, and I still feel like I'm standing in front of a giant."

"Yeah, I know. I'm not lifting any weights, but I think day-to-day I'm working my body harder than I ever did in a gym, and I don't have to watch my diet the same way. So I've grown."

When Joshua graduated from high school, and decided not to go to college, one of the things he threw himself into was competitive bodybuilding. He went on a diet that had him eating a plain piece of chicken and a cup of rice eight times a day. Joshua was already a big guy, but from there he grew like crazy, and would get thick veins on his neck and arms after working out.

Cole remembered the family attending two amateur events, one where Joshua finished runner-up, and another that he won, which qualified him to move a step up from regional contests to national competition. Cole had never seen anything like it, hundreds of muscled men in bikinis performing posing routines to music ranging from classical to country to pop, like talent auditions for the local gym. Carolyn went crazy at those shows, screaming wolf calls at the athletes until her voice was horse, constantly fanning herself with her hand while she talked about their muscled thighs.

But Joshua had cut it off there, dropped out of the whole thing because he said going further was going to require him to put in a lot of money, a lot of time, and maybe call for him to use some kind of "supplements," which he didn't want to do.

Ten years off and he was still huge.

"Any time you want to hit the weights, little Bro, just let me know."

"Right," Cole said, looking down at his comparatively small chest.

After a minute, Joshua asked him, "What are you doing?"

"Flexing my pecs. You couldn't see it because of my shirt, but I was."

Joshua smiled at him.

"Puny arms rule," Cole said, flexing a bicep, then frowning at its lack of size.

Joshua set a bag of groceries on the kitchen counter and started unloading it. He pulled out a BC Powder pack, filled a glass with water, poured the pack in, and passed it to Cole, who drank it down.

Carolyn finally started moving around. Without lifting her head, she opened her eyes and stared at Joshua without a word. She was still drunk, morning-after drunk, and whatever mad-on she had against him was still there. When she stood up, he noticed that the cell phone she'd been holding was nowhere to be seen.

She turned toward them, then just stood there watching them through the strands of hair hanging over her face.

Joshua said, "I heard you were here, Cole, and figured that meant we'd be having a family meal soon. I miss me a family meal more than you can know. So I stopped and picked up some food items that might be used for that purpose. Figured sister here would be so busy making sure we had a good wine list that she wouldn't think of the food."

Carolyn said, "Who did you picture would be making this meal, Mr. Helpful?"

Joshua shrugged. "Well, you or Lily. My plan was that I would start cooking, and whichever one stepped in to stop me would be the anointed one."

She walked away.

"Lily can't cook for shit," she yelled from the next room. "The only thing she knows to do are four dishes, and it's only because she memorized the way Mom did them that they taste any good at all. She could burn a pot of water."

"I figured maybe Cole didn't have a phone," Joshua said, "and couldn't call here because the house line is disconnected. But I do know that Carolyn has a phone, and thought she would have called to let me know Cole was home . . ." Cole could tell by Joshua's face that he was poking at Carolyn, trying to get a reaction.

It worked. "I was just waiting until I could get your last mess cleaned up before I called you over to make another," she hollered.

Cole added in, "We figured the local gossip network was still faster at delivering relevant information than the Internet. And we thought you'd be here first."

Joshua continued, ignoring them both, " . . . I figured, if the rumor was true, I could bring you out to my farm."

"You have a farm? What do you farm?"

"Bugs," Carolyn yelled from the other room. "Nothing but bugs."

Joshua was amused by her caustic tone. "She's right. It's crickets, and mealworms, and night crawlers. I have a few accounts I sell them to—bait-and-tackle stores, pet stores, like that."

"That's awesome. But . . . "

"Yeah," Joshua said, "I think you'd just throw up a lot if we did that on a hangover."

It was just the insects Joshua was raising now, but he planned to be farming pigs soon enough. He wasn't going to tell Carolyn that, though. She'd just remind them that their mother always complained about "the smell of swine-a in North Carolina."

Joshua was glad his brother was home. Now there is another diploma in the family, he thought with great satisfaction. Right there was a reason to celebrate—to know that if he ever had a smart kid, that she might be able to do the same. Even if that meant Joshua ended up being the dumb one in his own family.

"Seeing as how you're not in the right shape to visit my place—and I don't mind at all," Joshua said, "but if we're going to stay here, then I'm going to do a little work in the back while you sober up."

Chapter 12

"Do you remember that girl, Christy, the one that Joshua had such a great crush on way back when?" Carolyn's voice was conspiratorial. She'd come back into the kitchen soon after Joshua stepped outside.

This was her dishing voice, which Cole hadn't heard for so long that he'd just about forgotten it. She lowered her voice, drew you in, then let it all fly. Cole couldn't help smiling as Carolyn spoke.

He'd forgotten the wicked that ran through the women in the family.

"Not really," he said. "I only remember Roxanna."

"Well, before Roxanna, there was this supposedly amazing little blonde that he met at a book store, who he spent an afternoon talking to, who he felt he had a connection with, and who seemed to feel the same way about him, but because she had a boyfriend she wouldn't consider it."

"That sounds kind of familiar," Cole said slowly. "I have a hard time remembering any of the girls before Roxanna."

"Bless her heart—I'm not even going to get started on Roxanna." Carolyn really drew out every word in "bless her heart," so Cole knew there was a lot about Roxanna that could be said. "Well, about three years back, which would be three years after Joshua first met her, he ran into this same girl at the motor vehicle office. All that time had gone by, and because he didn't know anything personal about her—like where she was from, what her last name was—he didn't even know where to start looking for her.

"So this time, they talked while they were waiting in line, and they hit it off again. She was newly single, and he was nearly engaged to Roxanna, and he was honest about it, but while that didn't stop him from trying to find out more about her, it did stop her from telling him too much about herself. What she did tell him was that she was going to be at some 'Mysteries of the Unknown' seminar in Haverford the next week, and that she loved pecan pie from a restaurant other than the one I now own.

"So it turns out the seminar was the same night Joshua had dinner plans with Roxanna. He was supposed to be home at 5:30. The seminar started at 5, or so he thought, but when he got there he realized it didn't start until 6—the doors didn't even open until 5:30. Of course, he didn't realize that until he'd bought a piece of that pecan pie, had it wrapped in a box with a ribbon, and brought it over to the community center where the seminar was happening. So he set the pie on the front passenger seat of his car. And since he was in town at 4:45, he parked his car and went into a bar for Happy Hour.

"When he comes out of the bar half an hour later, no one else but Lizzie Hamilton herself has his car hooked to the bar of her tow truck because he's parked in a red zone."

"Oh, no," Cole said. "Is she still huge?"

"Big enough now to have eaten the Lizzie you remember. Can't say she's the 'little' sister without laughing. She's enormous. Anyway, they go back and forth about the towing, but she's already got him on the lift. Then all he wants is to get into the car, but he doesn't want to tell her why, until she goes over and sees the box with the pie in it. And however much of the story behind the pie she had no way of knowing, there was one part of the story she seemed to instantly understand, and she was very satisfied when she came back from looking to see what was there, according to Joshua."

"Probably wanted to eat it."

"No doubt. Instead she towed the car to the impound yard and locked it up. And because he'd left his wallet in the car when he went into the bar—just brought his cash with him—she wouldn't let him sign for the car. She made him call Roxanna.

"And when Roxanna came to pick him up, her heart was full of anger at Lizzie, thinking Lizzie's pettiness had ruined the long-anticipated date night. Lizzie, of course, took the time to point out how badly Joshua wanted to get to that ribbon-wrapped pie in the back seat."

"Why didn't he just say it was for her?"

"Roxanna is allergic to pecans, and she knew that Joshua knew it.

"Ouch."

"Yes, that was near the end of our time with Roxanna. It took about two weeks for the whole episode to settle in with Roxanna, and then she said she was done with him. I think she expected he would go after her when she broke things off, but he didn't. He was relieved." Carolyn snickered. "She was just a ball of anger for a while, but Joshua always knew she'd be hell on wheels if he dumped her. He got off easier because she was the one who ended it."

"Did Josh find the girl?"

"Not yet. Mom told him he wouldn't find her until the universe allowed it to happen, and that he should focus on other things while he was waiting for that to come to pass. I think he still goes out looking for her places where he thinks she might be . . ."

"Oh, that's sad. Drive-bys when you don't even know where they live."

"Right." Carolyn shook her head. "And according to him, I'm the one with problems."

Although she couldn't share as many details of her mother's life at her service as she might have wanted to, Lily did feel that she had a firm grip on the highlights of her mother's existence from the time Rose Chamber started raising her children. However, putting together the facts—like, for instance, the year her mother was born—had proved harder than she expected. Her mother's life before they met in Texas was an empty file. She couldn't try to contact old friends Rose had mentioned at one time or another, because she only knew vague details—a first name, for example, or the city an unnamed hospital was located in. Nothing complete enough to follow. As for social contacts outside of town, Lily could only remember the first names of the lesbians in Arizona. Miriam and Mercy. That just wasn't enough information to follow any lead very far. (Lily recognized it was wrong to be referring to them by their sexual preferences, and as a general rule she did not refer to other people this way. However, Miriam and Mercy, long a part of family lore, had always been "the lesbians" and Lily had never shaken the habit.)

There were many reasons for this disconnect with her past, but Lily was sure her mother was so secretive mainly because of the fathers. Any friends she might have made while with Joshua and Carolyn's dad, or with Zoe and Ben's dad, might go and tell someone that they'd heard something about the wife that ran away all those years ago. The risk was the same with any of the fathers. Her mother wasn't ever going to do anything to risk that the fathers they'd left behind might find them.

Lily had always been mildly aware of the possibility of Steve and Winnie seeking her out, although by her recollection of them they had likely missed the state support payments more than they missed Lily. Searching her out would have required more money and effort than they would have been willing to expend. She guessed that after she'd left, they had pretended to be raising her for as long as they could, probably until kindergarten age, then they cleared out of Texas the night before the government scheduled its first appointment to talk to the foster family together.

Lily hoped to never see them again. Which is why she had

so loved growing up where they did, far from everything.

She parked her car next to Joshua's, turned off the engine.

When they'd left Texas, it had been Joshua and Carolyn's dad her mother was leaving behind. Rose never said much beyond the fact that he was quick-tempered and didn't treat her right for too long of a time. She'd also said that once she'd found out she was pregnant with Carolyn, she'd realized she needed a change to make a better life for her family than she'd had with her husband.

Lily was so young that at the time they left Texas, she didn't know about the baby Rose was carrying. Rose was short, and a bit stocky, and on her feet 18 hours a day when she was working, and her pregnancies didn't show so obviously.

All Lily knew at the time was that Rose was taking her away from the rotten life she'd endured.

They'd driven all the way to Arizona, where they rented a room in a house owned by Miriam and Mercy. Just about all Lily could remember about that time was that partway through it her mother disappeared for about a week without a word to her. Lily didn't know it then, but that was her way, like a cat going to litter someplace where it wouldn't be interrupted. Lily thought she remembered there being a storm at the time, too, adding to their anxiety at Rose's long absence. But the lesbians looked after them, cooking breakfast for every meal because that was all they liked to cook, and they kept telling Lily and baby Joshua not to worry.

Rose finally called from somewhere along the road to say she was all right. It was the rain that had kept her away, she said. What she did not say on the phone, what Lily and Miriam and Mercy were all surprised to discover, was that she was not coming home alone. Any hurt feelings over the worry caused by Rose's absence went out the window the instant Lily met Carolyn.

Family was all that Lily wanted, and it was what Rose gave her.

Joshua, Cole, and Carolyn stood facing the grey concrete gravestone that marked their mother's grave, in the far corner of the property. They were quiet.

"All the time I was in California," Cole said, "coming home was an emergency option only, way in the back of my mind. To me, that felt like it would be failing. Even though things got pretty bad, leaving was never really on the table because I told myself it wasn't that bad. I kept thinking I would get through it, but then it kept going on and on. It made me feel like a failure. Now I'm here and it seems like none of that mattered. I don't know why I was fighting the current so hard. It was such a relief to just get on the bus and give up. I should have just let go when I got my diploma. It never occurred to me that it was even possible that Mom wouldn't be here when I got back. She was always supposed to be here. I should have been more worried about getting back here as soon as possible. Now she's not here and you all have your own lives here . . . and I've just got nothing. Nothing, nothing."

"You've got a bed, you've got a roof over your head," Joshua said. "You've got family. You've got a history here. You've got a diploma, Cole. People have started out with less."

Carolyn said, "You've got your coin still, don't you?"

"I do. If it's still there. When I left here, I had two items of value to my name: this belt buckle, and the coin. One I brought with me. I was waiting for the right time to look for the other."

"You hid it before you left?" Josh whistled, teasing. "Pretty risky."

"I used mine for the wedding," Carolyn said.

"I remember," Cole said. "How much would it be worth now?"

"Probably about $7,000. I got a little more than half of that 5 years ago. Gold's gone up and up. I know a dealer who will buy it."

"Did you spend yours?" Cole looked at Joshua.

"I did," Joshua said. "Helped me with setting up my property."

Carolyn snorted.

"And if you're feeling lonely," Carolyn said, "you should visit at the Whelan house. Young lady there is a nice-looking girl now. And she has pretty friends."

"Erin Whelan? Sean's sister?"

"Yes," Carolyn nodded, "Didn't you date when you were younger?"

"Everybody around here dated everybody when we were younger. We were kids. Small-town social scene. Do you know if Sean is around?"

"Don't know. You'll have to go ask yourself."

Finally, Cole said, "Why are you so mad at Josh all the time?"

Quiet for a moment.

"For one thing," Carolyn said, "look right in front of you. Our mother is buried in our back yard, like the family pet. She deserved better, something more proper. We could have buried her near her grandfather. They're always deciding things between themselves, him and Lily, always deciding they're the ones who know best. Our family's deciding committee of two."

"Carolyn," Joshua said, "they put him in a grave at that cemetery because that was the nearest place to bring his body, and there wasn't anybody who asked for anything different. He's not there for any other reason, certainly not because it was proper. Momma said she thought he would have preferred to be buried on this property. She also said she wanted to be here. Besides, I wasn't going to drag her across the county and be a spectacle to be witnessed and reflected upon by the fifteen or so folks we would pass along the way. To the so-called family plot. This wasn't about them. This was about Momma."

"She should be with her mother and father."

"We don't know where they're buried. We only know where our great-grandfather is buried."

"Shouldn't she be with what family she has?"

"That is where she is when she is here," he said.

Silence.

"You weren't here anyway," Joshua said with finality. "You forfeited the right to vote."

Carolyn, "Well, how was it?"

"I think the service was okay. When they asked people to speak, lots of folks had kind thoughts to express. It was as good as it could be without the rest of you here."

Silence. Joshua wasn't accusing them of anything, just stating the facts.

"We did the best we could," Joshua said. "I think she would have been fine with it."

While Cole and Carolyn went to work in the vegetable garden, Joshua focused on the grave area. He moved a bench, and dug up a couple of plants so he could replant them in a row so as to form a border for the area. When they all grew in, the hedge would make it more private, with the corner of the wall on two sides, the bench on the third, and the boxwood hedge on the fourth. There was a peach tree in the corner, arms extending over the wall, and clover ground cover around the stone marker plate.

In the middle of the hedge was a green PVC tube. Anyone else looking at it would only see the plant, but when Joshua looked at it, all his eyes did was seek out the pipe. When he'd dug the grave, he'd added a length of piping that aligned with one of the vents he'd cut into the top and bottom of the coffin. The pipe ran five feet up from the bottom of the grave, and then 6 feet over, where it vented out the green tube.

As he watched the tube, the head of an insect came out the top, followed by wings that it unfolded to reveal a violet, white, and yellow design.

At the last minute, Joshua had decided to seed the coffin with an extra group of butterfly cocoons.

What he'd most worried about was that some odor from the body would make its way out and stink up the garden. But that hadn't happened yet. Or maybe it had happened while no one was here, and two months was enough time for the odor to clear up. Or, he thought, maybe all the additions he had made to the interior had acted to reduce or even eliminate the odor.

Later, with Cole standing next to him by the grave, Joshua yelled out to Carolyn, "Can't we take down the damn dresses?"

"Leave 'em be."

"Whenever I ask what she wants," Joshua told Cole, "It's never what I want. Is anyone really surprised that I stopped asking?"

Joshua had never thought much of Carolyn's husband Don as a person, and he'd liked him less as family, but that was what he'd become, and Joshua had tried his best to figure out a way to connect with him. Tried fishing with him, tried watching football, things they both liked to do, but it never took.

Twice a week Joshua would make the drive into town for various supplies, and if the timing was right, on the road home there was a good chance he would come across Don, who had a thing for walking home at the end of the day.

Joshua's theory had been that the walk gave Don a time zone after the store closed and before he got home where he could do whatever he wanted—Joshua had imagined drinking, carousing, that sort of thing—but indeed Donald did always seem to be actually walking home. Maybe Don had noticed the days Joshua was more likely to pass him by, and those days he made sure to be doing exactly what he said he was doing. Joshua didn't buy into anything Don said too deep, and toward him felt only a significant expectation that his true nature would one day become apparent.

When Joshua did pass Don, if there weren't any cars behind him—and there rarely were other cars on the road— Joshua would slow, roll down his window, and ask Donald if he wanted a ride. It had happened maybe 30 times in a couple years, and Don had never accepted the offer, and the awkwardness for Don in declining each time was obvious. Joshua would nod at him, roll up the window, and then drive off. At some point he'd accepted that Don wouldn't take that ride, and although he was strangely and continuously irked each time by the refusal, Joshua so enjoyed the discomfort it inspired in the other man that he always took advantage to make the offer.

Several months after Carolyn had moved in with their mother, on a rainy afternoon, Joshua had been on his way home, the back of his truck covered with a tarp, when up ahead, about to cross the bridge over the Cairn River, he spotted Donald, headed onto the bridge, rain coming down steadily.

Today he's going take that ride, Joshua thought as he slowed, rolling down his window, nodding his head at Don. This one time, because the rain's not getting any easier, Don would say yes.

Don got that look on his face, the one that said he couldn't quite ignore or wave off the offer much as he might want to— because, of course, it was family making it. Don stepped close to the car window, without even waiting for the invitation.

Joshua had realized, by the sameness of the posture, that Don was going to turn him down again.

Joshua had lifted the door handle and pushed open the door as hard and fast as he could. He hit Don square across the middle of this chest, with the top of the door catching his forehead. The strength of the hit threw Don backward, and then over the edge of the bridge, and, as would later be confirmed by news reports, against the rocks, before the swollen river swept him away.

That was for the handprint on his sister's face, Joshua thought, and all the bruises she'd had to hide from us.

He'd wanted to settle it up for a while. His mother had let him know a while back she expected him to take action against something that was so wrong. So now it was done.

He'd closed the door, rolled up the window, and continued back to his farm.

Chapter 13

Cole was the first one Lily saw when she walked into the yard, following the sounds of voices.

"About time we saw your face again around here, Cole Chamber."

She gave him an extra long hug, what her own son would have called a super. She almost felt like Cole was her son, too, all grown up.

"Look at you. Look at you! Not taller, and not wider, that's for sure, but your face! You're a man now."

"Geez, Lily," Cole protested.

"I am sorry, Cole, but I'm a full-on mom now, twenty-four seven. Hard to turn it off." She hugged him again. "Took your time getting here, didn't you?"

"Best I could, Lily. No money—had to stop and work a bit just to make enough to get the whole way home . . . "

Josh and Carolyn emerged from different sides of the yard.

" . . . and then my phone died. I've just been carrying around the husk."

Carolyn said, "I think you should check it again. I thought I heard something making a racket last night. Hi, Lily."

Joshua, who was staring at his foot as he kicked some dirt off the path, looked sideways at Carolyn for a moment.

"My goodness," Lily said, sounding just like their mother. "We're finally all here. Should we make a dinner? Just the four of us? Richard won't mind looking after the kids."

Joshua and Cole both smiled. Cole said, "Did you really need to ask?"

Before leaving her house today, Lily had decided to finish

the special gravy base for a reunion dinner. She hoped Josh had been of a like mind, and that he stopped by the store on his way over. Cole might appreciate a traditional family meal, she thought. Everybody here would. Maybe everyone needed one.

For a few hours, it was like the old days—but because they were older and the best parts of it harkened back to fond memories, parts of it were better. They spent an hour-and-a-half in the kitchen making a meal that should have taken them half an hour. They had a lot of questions for Cole, and Cole was glad that there was someone who cared to ask.

"Money, money, money," Cole said, "Everything in California was money. Five hundred a month for a small room in a 4-bedroom apartment." Joshua whistled. "Four bucks a gallon for gas. Ten dollars to walk on a beach. Fifteen to walk on the shore of a lake, and you weren't allowed to go in the water. One-eighty for one textbook. Even trying everything to cut corners, even with the scholarship money, that was the hardest part. I still owe a few people some money there. I wish I'd come home right when school ended, but I sort of had this idea I was going to be able to make it there. There are jobs that pay a lot just starting out. I thought I could really make some money."

"People treat you all right?"

"Turns out that a Southern-speaking half-Asian is just another thing in Southern California. In terms of that, I think at first I did end up hanging out at school with a lot of Asians. Mostly good people. Not Southern people, really not like any people I'd seen before, but they were all as out of place as I was."

Cole watched Carolyn take a swig from the sherry, and the look of irritation Lily shot in Carolyn's direction. Carolyn stared back at Cole, ignoring Lily.

"In the dorms, there were a lot of people like me, who didn't know anybody, and that made making friends easier. But outside of school, I don't know how to describe it exactly. People out there were really nice on top of it all, but not always so much deep down. Not really open to letting people in too close. California Cordial is a good way to describe it."

Later they talked about their mother.

Cole, Joshua, and Carolyn were all sitting in the spots they used to occupy at the dinner table, with their mother's seat empty and the chairs for Zoe and Ben on either side of the window, where they'd been moved on the one-year anniversary of their leaving. Three chairs occupied, four chairs empty.

Lily came in through the doorway and Cole nearly jumped.

"Sorry," he said, "Had a little flashback. It was like we were back then and, not saying you look old or anything, but I thought you were mom bringing in another serving." Cole could feel something different between the others and himself—they had all processed it more than he had.

Everyone was quiet for a moment.

"Do you remember," Lily said, "she used to do that thing, and say something like, 'I remember when they made the first airplane.'"

"I remember when they made the first movie," Cole said.

"I remember when they made that Titanic," Joshua said.

"I remember when women got the vote," Carolyn said.

"Exactly!" Lily laughed. "She did that all the time when she was living with us. My kids think she was some kind of time traveler. Richard and I would just stare at each other and let her go on as long as she wasn't lying. And there was stuff we had to look up ourselves to see if she was really lying or not. 'I remember when they invented the light bulb. I remember when they forced all of the Indians out of Alabama. I remember the first time I heard of a clothes washer. I remember when all we had was a telegraph,' and I would be like, how the hell does she know that? I mean, do you guys remember her studying, or reading, or watching the news? Ever? Everything she knew came from talking to other people, it seemed like to me. I tried to convince myself that she was secretly reading from our encyclopedia set, but really, she was nearly blind by then."

"All I remember her reading was her Faulkner. She had that giant book of his collected works that one of her clients gave her. She used to read me those stories all the time," Joshua said.

"How old do you think she was?" Cole asked.

"I really don't know. Those last few months, she just seemed so, so old. I started to think that maybe she really was old enough to remember all those things happening."

Joshua was tempted, as he had been over many years, to share with his siblings a story he had never told anyone, about a time he went with his mother on her "visits," one of which was for the birthing of a pony. He'd been goofing off in the Thorpe's stable while she was taking care of business. Then his mom brought the horse in there, too, and instead of making his presence known he'd waited silently up in the loft and watched.

He'd seen her do animal births, and this went very much the same as they had gone before. When the foal emerged, it wasn't long before it stood and started looking for milk. Joshua's mother had cocked her head to listen to something that he hadn't noticed, and then she picked the animal up and laid it on its side. There was a whistling noise coming from it, Joshua had realized. Its breath almost squealed, and it sounded so sad that the mare turned to watch in concern.

His mother ran her hand over the foal's chest and stomach as it breathed and whistled, and then her hand stopped over the chest. She felt around the area, to double-check herself, and came back to that same spot on the chest.

She arched her hand in a way that left her fingertips on

that one spot, in a way that looked to Joshua as if she were just going to reach her hand into its body.

Then she did just that, pushing her fingertips slowly into the animal's chest. When her hand was all the way in, she did something with it, and moments later the whistling noise ceased. Joshua looked away from her for a moment, toward the animal's face. It was lying there, eyes open, breathing, absolutely still, as if it were hypnotized. When he looked back from the animal's face, it was already over. Her hand was no longer in the animal, and she was wiping blood off of her fingers with a rag. He expected there would be a cut that she would need to close, or an incision, or some kind of opening left in the animal's chest, but could see nothing but some small spatters of blood on its light-colored fur.

The foal then got up again, and went to its mother to nurse. Joshua's mother stood, and walked to the stable door. Right before she opened it, she paused, and without looking at him, said, "This will be our secret, Joshua." Then she stepped outside.

Something about her voice just about made him piss his pants.

"I think some people around here thought she was a witch after we first got here," Joshua said instead of mentioning any of that.

"More like a witch doctor," Carolyn said. "They weren't afraid to come and ask for her help. Not like she wouldn't try to help anybody that asked."

"Any way you look at it, she was magic," Lily said.

"Hey, Carolyn," Cole spoke up, "Speaking of magic. Can you still do the card-guessing thing?" As Cole remembered it, someone could stand across the room with a deck of cards, and Carolyn could stand with her back to that person, and she could name each card from the top down as the person holding the cards flipped through the deck.

Carolyn chuckled, "It's been a long time since I tried it,

but I assume so."

"It wasn't a trick you were doing that I just hadn't figured out? I told all my school friends about it and none of them believed me." He looked around the table at their faces, nodding, looking as if he was expecting them to confirm there was more to it. "Told me you must have been fooling me."

"No trick. Not that I know of," Carolyn raised an eyebrow mischievously.

"Did you ever think about going to Las Vegas or Atlantic City to see what you could do with that?"

"Don would have tried to make me do that. I didn't ever do that trick for him, because I thought he'd get carried away with it. It was a can of worms I didn't want to open. I'm keeping Vegas as a back-up plan."

Everyone was quiet.

"Those dresses in the trees, Carolyn," Lily said.

"She *was* like a witch, in a way," Carolyn said. "Like Baba Yaga, without the chicken leg house." She giggled a little, and the others laughed, too, because Carolyn's giggles sounded the same as they had when they were younger. "Maybe she just managed to pass on little parts of it to us. Magic is supposed to pass through mothers, isn't it? What did you get, Cole? I already know Lily's power is knowing everything and keeping secrets . . . "

"I'm not going to start with you when you're drinking, Carolyn," Lily said, rolling her eyes. "Be civil. Be cordial. Tonight let's be family. Tomorrow we can fight."

As Lily pulled away from the house in her car, there were many thoughts running around in her head—snippets of conversation that were significant, that needed to be followed up on, questions that needed to be addressed that they hadn't even touched upon, like what to do with the house and the reading of the will. Or the finding of the will. None of that had happened.

She thought it was better that Cole hadn't seen their mother's decline. She envied the way he was able to remember her—strong, active, supportive, and tough. For a while, she thought, Momma wasn't a part of the same world as the rest of us, even though she was walking around and talking to herself among us.

That was the way Lily Chamber had explained it to poor little Emily Cantrell a while back, as they made the long drive to a small community church in West Virginia, where they were going to take Emily in until they figured out where she came from. Lily didn't find out Emily's real family name until months had passed.

Thinking about Emily reminded her that Ben and Zoe had been gone for more than nine years, run away and never been heard from again. Momma had never able to completely relax after that, not the way she had before.

If you went back in the story further, Lily had to consider the way her mother said she went out on her own, leaving her Daddy behind, at about the same age as the twins. Rose hardly saw her father again after that, and that was never a point of sadness with her. Maybe it was just the cycle of life repeating itself, once a person stepped away far enough to look at it and not be hurt by it.

Still, no note, no phone call, nothing. There was no idea who they were with, or what had happened to them, or why they left. Did they run away? Had someone lured them away? Were they alive?

With them gone, and Rose Chamber's other four grown children living away from her, Lily thought her mother had wanted to have someone in her life who really needed her, too.

Thus, Emily.

Not knowing the fate of her missing children was a burden Rose Chamber carried to her grave. Why would Zoe and

Ben do that to their own mother? To all of them? There had to be a reason—neither of them were idiots.

As if there were a better sort of freedom than their mother gave each and every one of them.

Lily Chamber tried to live a quiet life. Her phone number was unlisted. She paid for everything in cash. No credit cards. She used the name she always had since her "adoption," although she'd been married for many years now, and she'd given their kids his last name. She didn't belong to any organizations, or clubs, only the parent group at the kids' school. For many years after leaving the force, she had done temporary and part-time administrative support work at different law enforcement branch offices across the state. Her employment history otherwise included part-time and temporary childcare.

Lily liked to check in on her children and husband regularly. Currently the cell phone was in her jacket pocket, on the back seat, next to the bag with the Tupperware, and she wasn't going to stop the car to get the phone because she was already running an hour behind schedule. She smoked a cigarette instead.

As I have done since I was a child, she thought to herself, I tell myself all my loved ones in the world at this moment are fine and safe, and I trust in it. The kids are fine with Richard.

It was good for all of them to learn to manage together and without her, regardless.

Richard had thought it was just raccoons going through the trash a couple weeks back. But Marnie up the street said she'd seen a man park his car in front of her house and then walk toward that side of our house while Richard and I were working and the kids were at school. Marnie also said that Karen, out for her morning walk, had scared the man off. But who was to say he wouldn't come back another day?

Who was checking up on the Chamber family? Who was it bending Carolyn's ear at the diner, getting the family gossip in exchange? Going through things at the house?

Her mind wandered to Elias. It couldn't be him, could it? Acting out maybe a little louder, loud enough for her to notice?

She dismissed the thought, focusing instead on the feeling someone else was watching them. It reminded her of the way it was growing up: When a new baby arrived, they hit the road for a bigger place, and they usually did it with a nervous eye on the rear view mirror.

The ruin of Lily's mother was her taste in men. One of the best things Lily could say about those men was that her mother kept that part of her life separate from her kids. She didn't carry on her affairs in front of them. They never even saw her with a man she was involved with romantically, for that matter. Her children were her escape from their fathers—their safety seemed to be the only thing that made her reconsider the quality of the men who fathered them. Joshua's father had been verbally abusive and very controlling, and she'd had no question that it wouldn't do to raise Joshua in a house like that, and then Carolyn came nine months later like an exclamation point to their escape.

Even though her mother never brought a man around with her, sometimes Lily would just know something was coming, something was going to happen. Her mother would become evasive, even dismissive. Arizona wasn't the only time she just up and left them for a short block of time.

In Oregon it was three times she disappeared, and it was nearly a week she was gone each time, returning at last in a crazed panic with Ben and Zoe in their swaddling clothes. Oregon was a terrible night. You would have thought soldiers were coming to murder us, Lily thought. That was how she returned.

Rose woke them barking out orders as she swept through the house picking and choosing the essentials and throwing them into the cardboard box they used as Carolyn's playpen. Her dress was ripped and soiled, her shoes soaking wet, her face and arms cut and scratched. There was blood on her from the scratches all over. She looked like she'd walked through a tornado. She told them all to pack as much as they could manage and in no time at all they were all running together with the box out to the old sedan, and then running back to grab more to throw in, and then speeding off into the night. Josh was huddled in the passenger seat wearing just about every piece of clothing he owned—his method of packing his clothes—Lily was in the back seat with the littlest ones, and mother drove. They drove all the way to South Dakota before they stopped. Josh watched the road behind in the side view mirror for hours as they went and Lily watched it with him, her neck sore from swiveling around in the seat, sure every set of approaching headlights was their unknown pursuers about to catch them.

Mother always told her she'd never found a man good enough to raise her kids, but they had all somehow managed to pass the test for fathering them. Lily was glad not to have met any of them. She'd had nightmares about Steve for years after they left Texas. Her mother was right to protect her kids that way, even if she couldn't always do as a good a job of protecting herself. She knew none of her kids needed more bogeyman to haunt their nightmares.

Lily was sure she had been looking forward to this family reunion more than the rest of them.

Lily once believed her mother would never slow down. But then, there was never a way of knowing how old Rose Chamber really was. Lily thought she was sixty-five when she retired, and seventy-one when she passed, which is how she had them record it on the death certificate. But with all the exercise she had over the years, good eating, flossing all the time, it could have been ten to twenty years more than that. There were no records on her mother's mother, Roslyn Chamber, that might tell them something, because of the fire that destroyed the city hall many decades before.

Here Lily was for a month spending her evenings at the department trying to track down some hint as to who exactly this Emily was because she knew her biological mother was not Rose Chamber, who at the time of birth, by Lily's estimation, would have been roughly 65 years old, and well over a decade past menopause. If a junkie hadn't eventually found God and sobered up in West Virginia and remembered that somewhere along the line she'd abandoned Emily in exchange for drugs, Lily might be raising three kids today instead of two.

To this day there was no doubt in Lily's mind her mother saved poor little Emily's life by keeping her that little while.

Lily turned, driving onto the main road, and then stopped her car just before the asphalt ended. The house was not visible from this vantage point on the road, only the trees in between.

She wondered, should she try to see Elias? Not let him get away with hiding away behind his phone and his e-mail screen and that battered old pickup—just have a face-to-face conversation, to clear up any issues that needed to be cleared up. She couldn't imagine how that would go. Would it be cordial? Would it be comfortable, like they had once been? Old friends happy to catch up on the details? Could they just be friends? Would they hug? Yes, she would want a hug from him, however awkward it might be for him. Would they kiss? She didn't think so. Did she still wonder about kissing him? Maybe on occasion. Would she want to kiss him? Would Elias want to kiss her? How far would it go if they were both of a like mind? A make out session, a hand-job? Would they lock themselves somewhere and screw all night? And then what? Be serious, Lily told herself.

What if there was something left over between them—was she ready to face it? To ignore it?

Thoughts of Richard filled her head. Her husband, her kids,

her house, her pets, her whole life. She never wanted to hurt them or lose them. Not ever. Lily realized she was holding her breath, and let it out slowly. They were real in her life. Elias was not—he was a phantom. This was why, she thought, despite the fact that she resented Elias' keeping her at a distance, despite the fact that she told herself she would be content for some time to catch up on life with him, she knew his tactics were the best to adhere to. There simply wasn't a lot of good for anyone else in their lives that would come out of she and Elias spending time alone together. She felt a small twinge of appreciation—not for the first time—for the respect Elias had shown for her relationship with Richard. Still, she did wonder briefly, as she often had, what it would be like to love Elias without reservation. To be loved by him.

' A moment later, as she had many times before, she dismissed those thoughts from her mind. It wouldn't lead anywhere useful, she thought. Elias wasn't the one who was spying on the Chambers.

Lily knew her mother had worried at least once every day of her life in this house that one of the fathers might track them down. It wasn't ever Joshua's and Carolyn's dad or Lily's foster parents she worried about most; despite Lily's anxiety about that happening, her mother insisted that being born poor and unwanted in Texas was tantamount to not existing at all as far as public records and government oversight went. No one from there would come looking, her mother would say. But Ben and Zoe's dad, the idea of him finding them was her mother's greatest fear. Lily had never forgotten the look on her mother's face that night when she introduced them to their new brother and sister in one breath and then told them to get packing in the next.

Lily's greatest fear was that her brothers and sisters might somehow discover the truth, that she wasn't their sister by blood, and that the invisible bond that in their eyes joined her to the family, their family, would be irreparably broken.

Momma was always true to her word, Lily thought. She raised me as if I was her own. There was never a gesture from her, never a word to suggest she considered me any more or less her child than any of the rest.

Before Lily had her daughter Annie, her mother told her that having a child required putting your universe in order. The lies, the contradictions, everything that might have gone on before, all of that vanished, and the slate was wiped clean the first time you looked in their eyes. It was a feeling you could get addicted to, she said wisely.

Eventually, Lily's car rolled forward. She would be seeing her siblings again soon. They had agreed to drive to Richard's family's cabin the following weekend. There was going to be a big lunar eclipse going on, something like that, and the kids wanted to see it. It would be a good time for family

Past the trees and through the tall grass she caught a glimpse of light from the house before she drove off. Like her mother, she would be keeping their secrets.

"You decide who you're going to be, and from that point on," her mother had said, "nobody can tell you otherwise. The rest of what is left behind is history, and it will fade. There's no need to talk about it anymore, is there?"

PART 3

Chapter 14

Of the parts of the country Ben Chamber had lived in since he left home, none of them practiced the art of sitting out front— of a home, or a business, or a local diner—like they did in the South. Sitting was about staying, not just resting or falling asleep, and it generally involved two things. The first was watching and commenting on the world going by like it was a television program on in the living room, and the second was telling all kinds of stories. If a person were lucky, the stories were entertaining, or else the view offered some kind of show worth watching. Sometimes it was a bonanza, and there was a lot of both—things going on that had people's interest, and stories that a person couldn't stop listening to.

For the first two days of Ben's stay at the Galaxy Park LandMar Hotel, there was no bonanza, but there was a lot of entertainment in listening to folks. With the weekend started, and thus his appointment later today with the private investigator whose services he had engaged, he hoped his time away from Zoe was just about done.

Ben thought he'd been ready to head back home as soon as he'd finished checking into the hotel on Thursday morning. There was no reason for him to be there nearly two days before the meeting other than him being dramatic in the middle of another argument that he had instigated about this very trip. "If you're going to be doing the silent treatment till this is over," he'd said to Zoe, "I might as well get started now."

When this was all final, when he finally had some answers, he told himself he would never waste a minute thinking about it again. Maybe he had thought about it too much, continued to care about it too long. He had literally already started a new life so he wouldn't have to be part of it anymore and yet, here he was.

Uppermost in his mind, Ben was worried about the state of his relationship with Zoe. He wasn't being dramatic when he worried that he didn't know for sure if she even wanted him to come back home to her when this was done. They'd hardly spoken on Tuesday, and she'd slept in the spare bedroom Wednesday night so she wouldn't have to be near him.

Her last words to him? "Make sure none of it follows you back here."

What could he do? He would go home tomorrow and crossed fingers were about all he had to ward off the fear that she would be gone. His obsession with their family DNA had absorbed so much of their time and energy already. Dwelling on the state of their relationship while he was away and unable to do anything to make up for it was a pointless exercise in self-doubt and self-abuse, he knew. Deep down, he believed that Zoe knew that his being here was the best for both of them, because even though she was done with it already, he needed to be done with it, too, before they could move on together.

Being at Galaxy Park and in the doghouse with Zoe, he couldn't help remembering similar emotions during their trip to Dollywood a couple years before. It had been a fine day, a fun day, until they'd gone to watch a band perform, and this loud, sort of obnoxious guy standing behind them started dancing around to the music and bumping into Zoe. She said it was fine, but at some point Ben had enough and told the guy to back off, and then shoved him hard, which caused the guy's drink to spill on Zoe, and which set the guy's 6-year-old daughter to crying. Ben hadn't even known the girl belonged to the guy or that the guy had been dancing like that to entertain her. The park security came and walked Ben to the gate, and Zoe had been forced to follow them, walking 10 feet behind, her back wet with soda. He didn't know why he had lost control, and then he didn't know why it was wrong that he'd put the guy in his place, except for the drink spilling. Even now, Ben thought the guy was out of order.

Like any couple, the two of them had shared high points and low points in their relationship, and that typified a low point, with her not talking and him with nothing to do about it other than apologize for something he didn't feel all that sorry about.

If Ben had left on this trip when they were at a high point, he was sure he'd be feeling better about everything. The fact that it had been tense when he'd left, that she had been distant, that made being away from her that much more challenging.

In the early sixties, a businessman developer purchased property west of the Appalachian mountains, not too long a distance from the Chamber property, if there were a road that went straight from one place to the other—which there wasn't. The parcel of land the developer bought was large enough to hold his futuristic and space-themed amusement park, as well as a housing development for park employees who wished to live nearby, and the business district he envisioned being developed around the park, driven by the amusement park's projected steady growth. The brochures he distributed emphasized Galaxy Park's proximity to the borders of five states, and convincingly argued the region could support a venture similar to the amusement parks opening on the American West Coast. He postulated an industrial zone dedicated to future technologies, large enough to include portions of those five states. Located inside that industrial zone, Galaxy Park would be serving the parkgoers of the future. He emphasized the area's historical links to the nation's space program—through the not-too-distant U.S. Space and Rocket Center in Huntsville, Alabama—and suggested a surge of space and technology business in the area was underway. In his brochures, he cited Galaxy Park as the prime example of evidence of the postulated growth surge.

He then proceeded to spend a million dollars leveling the land, building roads that far exceeded the quality of the roads in the rest of the county at the time, and installing some parts of his vision, including nine miniature planets, each one suspended on a set of metal rods thin enough that at a distance, the brass-plated orbs appeared to be hovering in the air. The driveway to the park entrance started at Pluto and went down the line to Mercury. From Mercury, if a person were on foot, they could continue in a straight line to the admissions area (where the booth was never built, but where a grid of pipes that were supposed to frame the booth was still evident). By car, drivers turned left into a large parking lot, under an arch that read Tomorrow Beckons.

From the parking lot, visitors could choose a short walk to the area intended for admissions or they could take another path, also a short walk, which would bring them to the Galaxy Park business district, a small, one-block paved street. No motor vehicles were allowed on the actual business district street— everyone in Galaxy Park used the parking lot.

Ben had explored the whole area in the last two days. He'd spent some time imagining what it might have looked like had it been completed. Outside the intended admissions booth building was a park legend, a faded but legible map hand-painted on a board that had been mounted in a case on top of a small post. If there had been glass over the top of the case, evidence of it was long gone.

The legend showed that beyond the admissions booth, inside the park, visitors would walk along an area labeled Training Camp, filled with traditional carnival games which had been renamed to match the space theme—Planetary Ring Toss, Shoot the Star, Rocket Dart Throw. At the end of the arcade was another gate, this one labeled Mission Control, where attendees would climb a ladder and then select one of several slides to ride into different zones in the park: the Lunar Village, the Adventure Planets, The Lost Dimension, The Space Mines, and, oddly, Stonehenge and, even more odd, The Old South. From the illustration in the legend, The Old South was where space adventurers would find a food service and crafts zone.

Ben surmised that the age of space exploration hadn't really kicked into gear when Galaxy Park was in its planning stages, and thus many of the "futuristic" terrains pictured on the legend seemed very much like exotic earthly locales—the Space Mines were clearly modeled on the subterranean caverns in Kentucky, while the terrain of the Lava Planet roller coaster ride looked like it took place on a beach covered with volcanoes, and in the Lost Dimension zone the denizens were pictured dressed in early American Colonial Garb.

There were elements that had been built or installed before the businessman vanished without explanation. For many years, those totems were the only features to be seen on that plain other than the perfectly paved street on the western end of the lot.

Nearest to the park entrance were metal girders and pieces of rebar shaped into the form of the back end of a crashed rocket-shaped space ship. Once it was probably covered with paint and/or papier-maché, but only the dark metal underneath remained. According to the park legend, this was for the Stranded in Space ride. Although it appeared to be right next to the admissions booth, there would have been a tall wall between the two sections, and to get to Stranded in Space one would have had to go through Mission Control first.

Colored lines for multiple guide paths were painted on the concrete. They started at the end of the arcade, and led in the different directions that the slides would have taken customers. The yellow paint was cracked and fading where it hadn't disappeared entirely. There was one blue line he'd seen in multiple places in the park; from the legend, the blue path seemed to touch every zone in the park before it returned to the admissions booth.

Not far from the crashed rocket ship was an elaborate square arch, made of metal, but then overlaid with a gold, metallic-colored paint. There were hieroglyphic-like images carved into sections of the arch—eyes, strangely shaped letters, ankhs, crosses, and people with heads of animals. In the intervening years, many an individual apparently had become convinced that the arch was made of gold, and had scratched at the paint until they'd reached the metal underneath and realized their mistake. Only the very top of the arch, the sculpture's high point, was still gold. The rest had for the most part been scraped clean.

Further back on the lot was the astronaut, probably the best-preserved artifact in the area, and this was likely because the statue was made of solid steel. Clearly it was a statue of a man in an old fashioned diving suit where the diving suit had been painted white.

One of the waitresses said it wasn't unusual to arrive for work and discover the astronaut had been repainted overnight. Whoever did it always chose different colors, and sometimes used a design—for instance, college kids regularly painted it a checkerboard pattern using their school colors—and every once in a while someone came along who just painted him white again.

In the middle of that great empty park space was the Stonehenge section, which seemed to have been planned to be some sort of concert area. There was a large ring of concrete blocks, each one 4 feet by 4 feet by 4 feet, each block spaced about 6 feet from the next. Outside this low ring of blocks there were several more blocks, these seemingly more randomly placed. These were twice as tall as the blocks that formed the inner ring, and they didn't form a complete outer circle. Ben guessed they'd planned to make it some sort of amphitheater. It looked like a sculpture in progress. There were more concrete blocks of similar dimensions scattered at the eastern side of Galaxy Park, like a bunch of giant, granite dice spilled across a barren prairie.

In the decades since the businessman developer disappeared, a company had finally purchased a section of Galaxy Park, the business district, and had recently built the modern-looking three-story professional services office building. Across the street and half a block up, the LandMar, part of a national hotel chain, had sprung up. The hotel had a restaurant on its bottom floor, and an attached patio area with tables that looked out into the street. Basically, it offered a view of the never-completed amusement park. The hotel property had been lushly landscaped with trees and plants, a meandering walkway, a gazebo, and blooming flowers at every turn. It was lovely, but incongruous with the lifeless plains of concrete and dirt that surrounded this pocket of green on all sides. There was also a gas station at the far end of the block, which cars could only access from the parking lot, and the gas station held a small convenience food mart. This was the whole of the Galaxy Park business district.

As Ben stared across the empty amusement park property, he could almost imagine that one day the whole place would all be filled in with tract homes and fast food places. And Starbucks. He'd seen it over and over in South Dakota since he'd landed there. This place, where everything had already been plowed and reinforced and paved, even had the benefit of being ready to go.

For now, it wasn't much to look at, but it at least seemed as if it was getting started on its way to being someplace new.

Galaxy Park was apparently the place to be for the coming night's total lunar eclipse. Ben had heard talk on the patio the day before that some kind of event was happening on Saturday, driven by a flyer someone had found with the word "Syzygy" on it. But no one present on the patio had any information about what it was all about.

It seemed like just about everybody from the day before was back at the patio tables the next morning, hoping to catch a glimpse of what it might be, and maybe find out how much time they had before it got started.

They didn't have to wait long. Over early-morning coffee, before the city newspapers were dropped off, what looked like a rental car pulled into the lot down the street. A man and a woman stepped out, both brightly dressed. The woman was older, a bit heavyset, and the man was tall and skinny and wearing glittering leg warmers. They walked out to the street, and from there gestured toward the empty amusement park property while they both spoke on their own phones. The guy couldn't stop fussing with his hair.

When they got off their phones, they pulled several folding chairs from the trunk of the Camry and then started carrying them from the parking lot to the street. Of course, had Galaxy Park been built as planned, there would have been no direct access to the amusement park from the business district—people staying there would have had to walk toward the parking lot to catch the path that led to the admissions booth. For these two, though, all they had to do when they reached the street was cut west across the dirt lot, and they were within the park boundaries. This was where they would eventually set up a row of seven chairs.

"A good size trunk on that model," said one old guy, Ed, who was seated to Ben's right with another old guy, Martin. They were on a fishing trip, down from Asheville. Martin agreed with Ed via a grunt.

Ben assumed they were talking about the woman's butt, not the Camry. That was how they were.

Shortly after they were set up, a white transport van pulled into the lot, and after it parked a group of college-age guys emerged. At the woman's direction, half of them seated themselves in the chairs, and then she started working on their makeup while the man who was with her started working on their hair.

Another van rolled in. The side door of the second van

opened, and once each guy was done getting his hair and makeup taken care of, he went to the parking lot, into the second van, where he would apparently change into the clothes he was supposed to be wearing. When the process was finished, they were a group of very handsome guys wearing t-shirts, some of which featured the faces of different North American serial killers. One black shirt appeared to read GBH in white letters on the front and another white t-shirt had the letters BGH on the front. They were all wearing black shorts of varying lengths, from mid-calf to mid-thigh, some with black vests over their black t-shirts, a couple of them in jackets. They looked like some kind of boy band or dance troop when they were assembled together.

The makeup artists then swung into action again, covering tattoos, making little adjustments to their faces while the hair stylist spent more time on their hair. The both of them would be busy doing this most of the morning, whenever the models were at rest.

Meanwhile, the two men who'd been driving the second van had gotten out and walked around to the back and started unloading photography equipment and then a whole bunch of toys—scooters, pogo sticks, skateboards, dirt bikes. They hauled the whole collection over to the amusement park property.

The patio tables provided great viewing for the members of the group that had stuck together on and off for the last two days. Ben, Ed, Martin, Dot, and Walt were all there.

Essentially, for the next few hours, the people on the patio watched while the models frolicked and played and posed for the cameras across Galaxy Park. They hung from the planets on the front drive, pretended to ride on them, pretended to be holding them aloft or carrying them on their backs. They played Frisbee and tossed footballs, and chased each other around on scooters and bikes around the rocket ship. They played hide-and-seek among the 4 x 4 cubes at the back of the park. The models were followed everywhere by a group of four photographers who never seemed to stop shooting photos, a coterie of photography assistants, and the hair and makeup pair. Whenever they went too far away from the patio to be viewed clearly, Dot and a new woman (who'd come in after them and sat at a table away from their group) both broke out binoculars and continued to watch and report.

A steady stream of new t-shirts with new slogans (Union Carbide, RU-486, WD-40) were given to the models, each one intended to offend at least someone. Ben realized that in addition to the group on the patio, all of this was being observed from afar with great interest, literally by everyone in town who was awake, which was just about everyone in town. The groundskeepers were watching from the hotel's garden, and the front desk receptionist was standing in the hotel's front doorway with a waitress, and Ben could hear the women on staff tittering at the sight whenever the models changed their clothes out in the open.

When the photo shoot reached the astronaut, the photographer became inspired and photographed a narrative string of photos. First the models "discovered" the astronaut as they approached it on their scooters. Then they raced around the statue. Shirts were changed, and then the models danced in a circle around the statue. Some of them stepped out of their shorts and continued roughhousing in front of the statue in their various styles of underwear. A group of them lounged around the astronaut for a while, seated at his feet. A series of photographs taken at the end of that session featured the whole group of them lined up in three staggered rows facing the statue. A t-shirt with the word GOD on it had been pulled over the astronaut. The whole group of guys dropped their pants simultaneously and then continued standing and staring at the astronaut while the photographer shot pictures of the tableau from behind the models.

Ben heard a few shrieks emanating from elsewhere in the hotel. The make-up lady walked in between the models—

examining all their behinds, applying makeup to . . . what? Ass pimples, Ben hoped. Then they just stood that way, staring at the astronaut, making adjustments according to the photographer's orders, for at least 15 minutes.

It was sort of hypnotic to watch. Ed summed it up for all of them.

"Never seen so many men's asses together in one place. I just don't know what to do with that. I want to stop watching, but I can't."

Around 9 a.m., two pickup trucks with eight college kids and two loads of lumber pulled into the parking lot. The college kids soon began unloading large pieces of wood, which they carried in and dropped off at a spot in the large open lot between the hotel and the gas station. Another truck showed up with chairs and tables, and while part of their group began unloading them, the rest of them began work on assembling a platform with hammers and nails, stopping every once in a while when the photo shoot came distractingly close to their location.

Because it was hard not to watch good-looking people having staged fun, Ben thought.

An hour after the college kids arrived, a van with the letters K-NOX pulled into the parking lot. A man wearing a baseball cap stepped out of the van, followed by an Asian-looking woman and a stocky, crew-cut man, who was carrying a camera. The three of them spoke briefly and then split up, whereupon the guy in the cap, who looked like he might be a reporter, walked up the street toward the college kids and the camera guy started looking for spots to film from.

Ben found all three of these people fascinating, but couldn't explain why. The guy in the cap looked a little older than Ben, and the other two a little bit younger. There was something about them that really made them stand out—he wasn't sure if it was their clothes, their posture, or their mannerisms, but of all the people he'd seen in town on this trip, they were the most clearly not in any way connected to this area, this region, this state, or the South at all.

Ben watched them closely as they checked out the area. The younger two walked to the far end of the block and started working their way back, each on a different side of the street. In several places they stopped to take something off of a piece of paper each was holding and stick it to something next to them. The girl stuck one on a signpost, the guy put one on the exterior of the office building, and then another on a dumpster at the very end of the street.

Ben saw Dot on the sidewalk outside the hotel, a cigarette in her hand.

As the K-NOX girl approached, Dot waved her over. The two had a short conversation, and then Dot waved goodbye, saying, "Go on back to your work. Sorry to bother you."

When she returned to the porch, Dot told them that the girl said they were putting out some cameras so they could capture the event tonight from a lot of different angles.

"You should see them! The cameras look like those googly eyes that kids use in their crafts. She said not to worry about eavesdropping, because they only record images, not sound, and that all of the cameras were aimed at public areas." She asked her husband, "Does that make you feel any better?"

Walt shrugged. "Sure, if that's what it really is."

"I'd feel better if this place weren't such a sausage fest," Ed said. Martin chuckled.

Ben considered how many people were in the Galaxy Park business district at the moment. With the employees, the hotel guests, the photo shoot participants, the college kids, he guessed it was about 80 people. Maybe a third of them were women. More than two men for each woman. But then, if you thinned out the herd—took out the ones with obvious boyfriends, the ones who were married, the available woman pool went down to about seven. Eliminating those whose first language was not English, nor did they understand English—surely a requirement for Ed—then there were four. None of them were near Ed's age group, dropping his odds considerably. His best bet, Ben thought, was with the middle-aged makeup artist—but he didn't say that aloud.

The most attractive of the women was a blonde with the college contingent. She had seemed at first to be a college student, and she seemed to have some authority, as people continued calling for her attention. Once she had her clipboard in hand, the picture was complete. She was the event manager, and they were her crew.

She was small, but she had big, blonde hair. Looked good in her jeans and her tank top, although she covered up her arms after not too long with an open, long-sleeved plaid shirt. She looked like a cheerleader, but that she wasn't one was quickly apparent. She was the one driving the giant four-wheeling truck carrying the sound equipment. She got in there with the hammer and nails while setting up the platform. She talked loud and cursed and yelled at people on her cell phone, but she did so while continuing to work, pounding metal posts into the ground so she could hang lanterns from them. When a truck didn't start, the driver popped open the hood and she was the one to lean in and fiddle with something for a few minutes before giving the driver a thumb's up. Voila, the truck started. When a man in an old brown Toyota Celica parked in the lot, and began unloading what looked like food supplies, she was there with him in no time at all, and helped him by carrying whatever he couldn't.

So the way Ben saw it, the blonde, if she were interested, likely could have her pick of the sixty-two men up and down the street who had checked her out. Maybe a bunch of them were actually thinking they had a chance, until the photo shoot ended and suddenly there were 12 models standing outside their van not far from the platform changing back into their own clothes out in the open and tossing their t-shirts and black shorts back into the van. All the women within view up and down the block paid attention to this when it was happening, blonde event manager included, many of them nudging each other and whispering. The models, by that point, didn't really seem to care who was watching them, making no effort to cover up.

To Ben, who really wasn't that interested in any of the girls because he considered himself off the market, it seemed that the odds were in the models' favor. He was, in fact, glad that Zoe wasn't there with him. Not because he thought she would run off with one of them if she had a chance—although he wondered, if things were as bad as he'd started thinking things were, would she?—but because she would spend the next week telling everybody about how gorgeous this guy was and how gorgeous that guy was and his chiseled abs this and his cleft chin that and ohmygod I saw all of their butts! Ben wouldn't be able to stand it.

Ben left his seat on the patio to go to the front desk to see if he'd received any messages, and when there were none, he went to his room to see if by chance a note might have been left there. Nothing.

He wanted to call Zoe, even though she'd said not to while he was here. He wanted to tell her that it was almost over, but he knew she would tell him not to make promises he couldn't keep.

The day Zoe left their family home with him, she'd meant to be done with it all. The way she looked at it, they couldn't come back from what they were doing, and there wasn't a point in putting themselves through it if they were going to come back. That life was closed off to her with a finality that he did not feel. His periodic relapses into obsessing over the Chamber family history were the opposite of the way she wanted to proceed.

What was she doing while he was gone? What if she was done with him? What if his leaving was the opportunity she'd been waiting for to leave? What if he came home to find that she was gone? What if she decided the only way to really be done with it all was to be done with the last remaining part of the life she wanted to forget? The last remaining part which kept her from forgetting it all. Ben was guilty as charged on both counts.

He could pack up his stuff and be on his way home in no time, he knew. He could leave whatever answers were awaiting him, and go back to his life with Zoe, and forget about all the familial lies and deceptions.

It didn't need to rule his life the way it did.

He put away his phone. He knew he wouldn't be going, at least not for another day. Tomorrow, when the hotel transport picked up out front, he would head off and then take the train home. He knew that Zoe knew that was the choice he would finally make. What did it say that he did not know what choice Zoe would make in the end?

He looked at himself in the room's bathroom mirror. He looked good. Well . . . he looked okay? He lifted up his shirt, stared at his belly. Damn! Last night, getting out of the shower, he'd checked his reflection as well, and his stomach, he thought then, looked pretty good. Now, after seeing those guys, it looked soft. Doughy. No lines or cuts to mark off anything. No pot belly yet, thank goodness. But just all soft and doughy and no definition. Even the models' belly buttons looked better than his. How does someone go about making their belly button look better?

Usually he looked in the mirror and he could understand, at least a little, why Zoe might have thought he was handsome. He was okay looking. Really. Sadly, Ben thought, I'm only able to compete with guys like that if my clothes are on.

He knew he was kidding himself about that, too.

But really, clothes helped, he thought.

Damn. He shook his head a little to clear the self-pity.

Zoe, he thought to himself, Please don't give up on me.

Chapter 15

When he returned to the restaurant, the place was packed. Lunch at the hotel restaurant was definitely its busiest hour, but in general, on a normal day, that seemed to mean roughly a quarter of the place was filled. There just wasn't anywhere else to go other than the vending machines in the lobby of the professional services building or the food mart at the gas station.

The whole photo shoot crew was there, models, photographers, the photographers' helpers, the make-up lady, and the hair guy. The two college girls had a table from which they were ogling the models, and some of the other guys from their college crew were there, too, but Ben noticed, not either of the girls' boyfriends, who had likely decided to continue working rather than watch their girls ogling.

Ben wasn't sure about this tactic: Shouldn't the boyfriends at least make it clear that they were with the girls by making an appearance? Or were they showcasing their security by letting the girls enjoy the eye candy without them? It was a fine play, unless one of the models started hitting on one of the girls. Maybe that wasn't so bad either, because people liked to flirt, but what if it was a potential start of something? Wasn't it best not to take chances?

The hotel staff was backing up the wait staff, because the three girls on shift were overwhelmed by the sudden influx of customers. One of the front desk clerks was at the host stand, and the man who delivered room service was behind the bar, mixing drinks alongside the bartender.

Ben's table and his great viewing spot were lost when more tables were brought out onto the patio from inside the restaurant, and everything got rearranged.

He grabbed an open two-seater at the back of the room, looked at his watch, saw it was after 12 now—12:02—so it was okay by his own rules to have a beer. He surveyed the room as he looked for a waitress.

It was going to be a while.

A table had been pulled up behind Ed and Martin, and one of the end results was that people moving through had to squeeze between Ed's chair and the chair behind him. At the table next to Ed's table sat three models, who seemed to be acting up, maybe being a little out-and-out flamboyant, talking in exaggerated voices, tittering noisily at whispered jokes. The dynamic Ben could see going on was that having Ed and Martin faced in their direction, with looks of such obvious distaste, had introduced a little nervous tension into the model threesome. They, in turn, started to act up. When they started doing that, Ed and Martin got even sterner looking. On top of that, every once in a while, someone needed to pass behind Ed's chair, and sometimes it was one of the models, and sometimes when they were sliding by they turned sideways and their backsides brushed against the back of his chair as they went. Ben knew Ed just couldn't not think about the fact that if he turned he was going to be face-to-face with someone's butt. His distaste for the situation was apparent.

Dot and Walt, on the other hand, were mixing it up, talking to a couple of the guys who must have grown up somewhere Dot was familiar with, because they were having a good time talking about the town and the people in it.

One of the models, blond and unfairly handsome, was seated near Ben, talking to one of the photographer's assistants. The model was clearly aware of Ben's position in the room—that is, he knew that Ben was close enough to hear them and was possibly listening in.

The assistant, who Ben thought sounded like he might be gay, said, "Are you going to the sizzy jazzy with everyone tonight?" Ben couldn't understand the word the assistant said—it sounded like sizzy jazzy.

"I don't know," the blond said. "I guess it depends who stays. If the van goes back, I'm going back with it. I want to get a rental car later. I have a couple days before my flight back to Cali. There's a friend out here I want to look up, and that might be a little bit of driving."

Ben waited for an explanation of what a sizzy jazzy was, figuring it was some kind of code word for a sex/drugs/model party. Were they both gay? He didn't know about the model, but the photographer's assistant seemed more than likely to be. Ben didn't know a lot of gay people, at least as far as he was aware. He didn't know why it would make him more comfortable to know that the model was gay, too. Was that just the most comforting way for an average-looking guy to respond to the potential threat of a better-looking male in his vicinity? To reflexively assume they're not really competing for the same audience?

"I don't know," the model said, "I guess I don't have to see my friend on this trip. I kind of took the job in the first place because I knew it would put me within driving distance of him."

The assistant said, "This friend. Is it a . . . special friend?"

"Yeah? No, not like that. It's just . . . it's just that I did something that I feel sort of helped mess up his life. His life was a little messed up by that point, anyway, but I think I made it worse. Well, better and worse. I want to apologize. I want to make sure he's okay."

"There are cheaper ways."

"He's not calling me back. And really, this way proves to be pretty inexpensive. They paid for my flight, my room, three meals . . . "

"Maybe he's mad at you. Maybe he doesn't want to see you again."

"And I thought of that, but I feel kind of like I need to see he's okay, and find out if he's done with being friends because of what happened. I need for him to say that to me. Otherwise, I just have this unresolved guilty feeling . . . "

"He's supposed to make you feel better about how things turned out? How's that work? And you're sure you don't have something going for this guy?"

"No. And no."

"No, you're not sure? Or no, you're not gay?"

"I'm starting to think I don't understand what that means. I've got a girlfriend, and I love her. I've always liked girls. I like all the parts, and that was what I thought about growing up and that was what gave me boners. I love pussy! I miss pussy. Just sitting here with you makes me want pussy that much more."

Ben looked away to smile.

"That's not what it's like for gay guys, right? I mean, you know what you've always wanted or preferred and that has always been guys and guy parts, right?" The blond continued, "I'm just starting to think that maybe it's not sensible for people to define themselves by where they place their penis for what percentage of the time or who they're rubbing against their vaginas for a happy ending," he said.

"Maybe some people know what they want," the assistant said. He smiled wickedly, raising his eyebrow suggestively, and the blond laughed.

"Right. But if I blindfolded you right now."

"Ooh." The assistant closed his eyes.

"And one of these guys kissed you, . . . "

"Ooh."

"And then one of these girls kissed you . . . "

"Eyuh."

"You wouldn't know which was which."

"Whiskers."

"Shaved."

"Cologne."

"They both just got out of the shower, then came down to breakfast. Used all the same product. Can't use your hands to check things out."

"I would know," the assistant said confidently.

"You would try to guess. But you'd still get turned on, maybe?"

"Maybe." Lifted the eyebrow.

"And if one of them gave you a blowjob, you still wouldn't know which one it was. Do think you'd be able to tell?"

No answer.

"You wouldn't. Believe me."

"Eyuh."

"Doesn't that mean that maybe gender orientation is partly a mental construct? I mean, you can function in a lot of situations."

"If I knew when I put on the blindfold it was room full of girls, nothing would happen."

"But if they blindfolded you and then lied to you and said they'd snuck a handsome guy into the room and he was the one diddling you, then maybe something would?"

"I don't understand your point. I would still feel molested. Don't invite me to your parties, okay?"

"I'm not talking about you. About being gay. If we flipped everything and it was a straight guy blindfolded and balls deep inside someone, he wouldn't know if it was a guy or a girl either, and probably wouldn't care."

"There's a psychological component."

"Something so deep that it can be fooled by a blindfold? I think it's more likely the result of an intent to categorize behavior, capture it at as a point on a line instead of recognizing it might occur over a spectrum. A person might be at one point at one point in his life today, at another point two weeks later, and another point 10 months after that. How do you categorize that behavior? And the sociological part of it is, even if you enjoy it, even if blindfolded you come in that girl's mouth, or I shoot up that guy's ass, that no matter how much we enjoyed the physical part of it, as soon as the blindfolds came off we're . . . what?"

"Eyuh."

"A little bit, yeah. Right. I mean, at least at first. Why is that? Is it trained into us or is it instinctive?"

"Maybe you're bisexual." The assistant was teasing a little. "But maybe instead of like 50/50, you're like 70/30 or 82/18 or something."

"You know, it only happened a couple times, and it was all because of my own insecurity. But once I committed mentally it wasn't a problem, even though I'm pretty sure I'm not oriented that way. There isn't anyone else I'd even consider that with. It was situational. I stepped up and it wasn't bad. What kind of label do you use for that?"

"Why don't you just go with versatile," the assistant said, "and stop worrying about labels. You're a versatile man. It's an adjective, not a noun. Relax."

"Yeah, right. I thought I was versatile, but maybe I'm not so much. It probably describes my friend more—he just went with the flow, let it happen, and then moved on."

"Hah. You think you bagged him—maybe he bagged you and your pretty girlfriend!"

The model caught Ben's eye again, and this time addressed Ben directly.

"Hey," he said, "Do you know which road will get me to Mason County in North Carolina?"

Ben, of course, did, but because the sudden nature of question startled him, he said, "No, sorry, I'm just visiting in the area." He thought about it, and then, contradicting himself, added, "Although I think if you take the 40 you'll be okay." For some reason, as he spoke, Ben wished he could hide his drawl. The blond looked at him curiously.

A beer at midday would, of course, lead to a cigarette break. On the sidewalk outside, Ben encountered the three people from the radio station. As he stood in front of the hotel, looking for a place to have a smoke that wasn't in the middle of people who might complain about it, the three were caught up in a quiet conversation when a woman in a beige, floral-printed outfit approached the man who looked to be the oldest of the group, and tapped him on his arm. She pushed her wide-rimmed hat back so he could see her face.

Seeing him up close, Ben figured the guy was maybe 10 years older than him, with facial stubble that had grown long enough to qualify as a beard in progress. He was skinny, and slightly pale, blue eyes, short brown hair and thick-rimmed glasses. He had the look of a person who spent his life in front of a book or a computer screen, away from the light of day.

"I know who you are, a lot of people here do," the woman said to him. Not in a loud voice, but in a firm voice. "I know about that book. You should be ashamed of yourself! They should lock you up."

In a flat, dismissive voice, he said, "I'm working on a diet book for dogs next."

The woman scowled and walked away from him as soon as he started speaking.

The guy saw Ben watching, and immediately stepped forward, hand extended.

"Hello, good sir." he said. "My name is Art Sinclair. These are my co-workers. We're here for National College Radio, doing a human interest piece on tonight's so-called Syzygy."

Ben's immediate reaction was that parts of Art's story were true and parts of it were not. He wasn't sure which. He made a mental note to look up the name Art Sinclair on the hotel Internet when he got back to his hotel room later.

Art said, "You live around here, or are you here for the event?"

"To start with, I don't know what the event is."

"The full lunar eclipse," Art answered.

"And the so-called Syzygy is . . . "

"This type of eclipse is a type of celestial alignment referred to as a Syzygy. That describes when three planetary bodies are in a line. There are celebrations going on all across the country tonight. We got sent here to cover this one."

Something about it made Ben feel suspicious.

"What that lady said before—are you a writer?"

"No. Once I helped a writer get his book published. It feels like a lifetime ago. I don't want to talk about that right now. She's just a worker ant, anyway—mad because someone told her it's her job to be mad. Otherwise, she would have taken some sort of swing at me. Happens all the time. My own mother wants to murder me for it. Literally."

There was nothing to say to that. "Sorry, that sucks."

"Do you live in the area, or are you a college student out for experiences?"

"I grew up nearby. Now I'm just here on business."

"Well, maybe we can interview you later."

"Yeah, maybe not," Ben said. "But good luck tonight. I'm sure I'll see you around."

They shook hands, and Ben continued walking away from the restaurant, toward the stage set-up. When he was a good distance away from anybody who might care about smoke, he lit up a cigarette.

Then he saw that flyer again, with that word on it, Syzygy. Sizzy jazzy. Sizzy jizzy. The eclipse. Now he got it.

There wasn't much going on yet. A few more cars were

parked in the lot, a few more people sort of loitering around up and down the block. When he was close enough to the blonde event planner's truck, he saw there was a decal on the door that said MadCap Productions, and underneath Special Events Management. He wondered if it was her company, or if she worked for someone else. As he was standing there, she walked around from the other side of the car, cell phone to her ear.

She said, "Well, I planned on you being here. If you're not, you're not, and I'm still going to get this all done.

"Yes, I know there are other things. I know those other things are important to you. But no one made you offer to help.

"Listen, it's one thing for you to flake on me, but it's another thing to just keep dragging this out until you get me to make you feel better about your having flaked on me. It's not okay. It's just the same thing over and over.

"Yeah, you say so, but I don't see that anything is different. And listen, the longer this conversation goes on, the less I'm appreciating you. Do you really want to keep going?

"Right. Well, I don't.

"Bye."

When she hung up, she stared at Ben's cigarette, and inhaled deeply.

She said, "Did you ever wonder how it is that you ended up with someone who is so not right for you?"

He held out the pack.

She ignored his gesture. "Once, I met the perfect guy, and I had a boyfriend at the time, and I didn't switch horses like I should have."

"Grab that brass ring," he offered.

"Right? But I didn't. Boyfriend didn't last."

"Sort of guessed that."

"Then I met him again! This time he had a girlfriend and I wasn't dating anyone."

"So he had a shot at the brass ring, too," Ben said. "Maybe it wasn't meant to be. Maybe she was his brass ring."

"I don't think so. I just thought it was going to happen. I mean, I think he felt the same way I did. I'm sure about it."

"But he made the same choice you did, and probably for the same reason."

"Isn't that stupid? It's like an old French movie," she said, "and they're probably broken up now, don't you think?"

"Nothing kills a relationship faster than when it's not 'true love,' I would guess."

"I think—no, I just know, that he felt the same way about me as I did about him. I don't think I could have felt that strong a connection to him if he wasn't feeling it too. That's sort of how I think true love works. It doesn't qualify unless it is reciprocated."

"If he'd left her for you," Ben said, "or you'd left your boyfriend for him, would that change how you felt about each other—like, would you think, 'Maybe he's not that good of a guy?' or 'Maybe he doesn't think I'm that good of a girl?'"

"Exactly," she said. She thought about it "And no. It's because you're afraid of what you might think of yourself for doing it. Which, honestly, years down the line, I'll think I'm a schmuck for not realizing that I would probably have a lot of respect for myself for grabbing the ring and running with it."

"There's another way to look at it," Ben said. "You chose less-than-perfect what-his-name, who's gone, and he chose less-than-perfect what's-her-name, who is likely gone, too. Should two people who make such poor choices really be together?"

He gestured toward her again with the pack.

"Take one."

She smiled. She was a cutie.

"Oh, you evangelicals! Always on the clock. Thanks, no. I can't. That used to be, like, my religion. But now I'm an atheist.

I don't go to that church anymore, just sometimes stand outside and enjoy the smell of others worshipping and remember what it was like to worship regularly."

"I've tried to follow that path, but one drink and I start feeling the spirit calling."

"Yes, that can be a temptation."

He couldn't keep up with the church/smoking theme. He'd never gone to church, didn't know more than the stories that had been mixed in with his other fairy tales.

"Are you throwing this event?"

"No, I'm just a cog in the event-producing process. I'm in charge of set-up."

"So you're not staying?"

"Not if I don't have to. Someone's supposed to come break me before things really get started here. Then again," she said with a sigh, "You never know who is going to come through for you. I'm hoping to be out of here soon, but we'll have to see how it goes."

"My name is Ben."

"I'm Christy. Nice to meet you. Are you here for this?" She gestured at the platform.

"No, just in the area doing some business. Just good timing, I guess. What is all this?"

"It's some kind of party to celebrate and watch the lunar eclipse. My company contracts with a client who throws a lot of, I don't know how to say it, events related to space, astronomy, that sort of thing."

Someone called out her name.

She yelled, "On my way!" She turned to Ben, offered her hand, and they shook.

"Nice to meet you, Ben."

"You, too. Good luck with everything. Good luck getting out of here. And if you don't, then find me and I'll give you a hand with clean-up." The moment he'd made the offer, he didn't know why he'd said it.

"My hero."

"See you."

From the stage, the view of the undeveloped amusement park was unobstructed. Standing on it, Ben saw there were newcomers out in the middle of the Stonehenge area, people he hadn't noticed before. He couldn't see very well what they were doing, and decided to walk over toward the planet models, thinking he might have a better view from there.

But not much better. Standing under Mercury, he could see that they were women, apparently women of the country club variety, with matching light-colored floral dresses and sun hats and gloves on their hands. The lady who had confronted the reporter was one of them. There were five others, and they were busy doing something that very much resembled gardening. They were spread out over a small area, and all of them were crouching and working with their hands on the ground. Once done in one spot, each one stood and moved to the next. They weren't talking. There seemed to be an intentional pattern they were following, and they appeared to be working methodically, although he had no idea what that pattern was.

They had hung sheer fabric between the larger concrete blocks, creating something of a barrier to viewing what they were up to. But since the larger blocks didn't go all the way around, the view from Ben's position was better than he would get elsewhere. There was a single orange-and-white striped construction barricade between Ben and Stonehenge. Finally, he decided he would like to know what they were up to and, curiosity trumping the desire to give them their space, he started walking in their direction. When he reached the barricade, he saw there was a sign on it that read PRIVATE FUNCTION. INVITEES ONLY.

He didn't want to attend—he just wanted to see what they were doing. He saw that at least one of the women looked over at him as she crouched and worked with her hands in the dirt. She didn't want him to come any closer, he thought.

So he wouldn't.

He wondered if he might get a better idea of what they were doing if he went to the roof of the hotel to take a look. But oddly, once he was back at the hotel, he started feeling like he could use a nap. A beer, a cigarette, and a walk in the hot sun were the perfect preamble for a nap.

In a way, Ben thought as he walked down the hallway to his room, he recognized something of his situation in the words of the blond model in the restaurant. A kid is given this image of what he or she is supposed to be when they grow up. It all seems possible when they start, but then they realize that something about their personal situation maybe doesn't quite fit the mold. Their thought never is: What's wrong with the mold? It's always: What's wrong with me? Why am I this way? Why do other people all seem to fit and I don't?

The truth is, Ben thought, no one fits the mold. The mold is some half-cooked invention of what someone thought would be best for us all. The mold broke apart as soon as they started pushing it on everyone.

He wondered, however confused the blond model was feeling about himself, how much better it would make that buttfucker feel about his own proclivities if Ben told him that he was married to his twin sister. It would definitely give him a new ending for the phrase that began "Well, at least I'm not . . . "

No one ever knows for sure what they'll do when the world serves them a big plate of nothing they could have expected. Versatile didn't begin to cover what a person was capable of when called upon.

Chapter 16

Ben Chamber was fifteen when he looked at what the world was going to have on hand to offer him when he graduated, and realized that if he stayed in his hometown, he was likely to get stuck there. Lily was a cop, which was perfect for her because she was always the cop of the family, and Josh was doing his bodybuilding—Josh always came up with something different, some different way of using what he was born with and what he knew and what he could imagine. Carolyn was the prettiest, most popular girl in her class and was going to find herself someone to marry and she would have babies and be just fine. Cole was a great student, and Zoe, who was better at school than Ben, was going to have more options than he would.

Ben was not a great student, not like the other kids. He could only seem to perform at a certain average level, no matter how hard he tried. He wasn't athletic, not at all like Josh that way. Ben had some mechanical skills. He could do hard labor. He was good at fixing things, learning a lot of things sitting next to Josh with the two of them just taking a thing apart, figuring out what was wrong with it, and putting it back together.

He started thinking about what he could do to evade what seemed like a sad fate—to be stuck there forever, with no chance of escape, that was what it seemed like to him. He didn't hate the place, and he loved his family, but he sure felt like he'd had enough of his life in Clay. Ben knew his hometown wasn't where he wanted to be for the rest of his life. He didn't think any of his siblings felt the same, so he made a point of never going beyond a snide comment or a snort when anyone said much of anything about the hometown that was positive.

He didn't mind the lack of money growing up, because

there wouldn't have been much to do with it—and anyway someone in town would be watching every penny you spent and what you spent it on and then sharing that information with someone who would find a way of bringing it back around to home.

He spent time looking into different things, among them every branch of the armed forces, farm labor programs, and camp counseling programs. He read up on the details of taking his G.E.D., but couldn't do that until he was seventeen. He stopped short of telling anybody about any of it because there would have been too many repercussions at home. His eyes were open at that point, though, and he was watching for anything that came along that might open a path he could follow.

He thought more and more about joining the army. He thought about building a boat and riding the river down south as far as it would take him. He thought about hitchhiking his way to New York. Several times he tried walking as far as he could go, getting farther each time, but always he gave up and then had to walk home.

Not long after their sixteenth birthday, Ben and Zoe were in the field behind the house practicing their dance for a ballroom scene in the Snow Queen musical production at their high school. They were one of three dancing pairs that circled around the leads at a royal dance.

The dance had been simplified many times due to the awkwardness of the high school dancers. One, two, three steps, face each other, then one, two, three steps, open and parade. Zoe believed they had it down, but Ben was nervous, and wanted to keep running through it. Zoe started counting along with him, but then instead of saying either "Face each other" or "open and parade," she would say "Burp out loud" or "Fart and move on" or, when he kicked her by accident, "Break her leg," or "Drop and roll." Whatever came into her head. It made him laugh, too.

Then, when they were facing each other, she said "One, two, three, Kiss," and she stepped in close and they kissed. When she pulled back, his heart nearly exploded in his chest, it started beating so hard. It wasn't a peck, and it wasn't open-mouthed, but it was a long, straight-on kiss.

When she pulled back, she said, "One, two, three, open and parade." Ben knew her head was spinning, too, because she hadn't been able to think of something silly to say.

It didn't happen again that day, and they kept practicing another 15 minutes before they stopped and went back into the house. No one was around, no one had seen, so nothing had changed, right?

It happened two more times, both times really very chaste, and not pawing affairs—their hands were never part of it, other than that they held each other afterward the third time. They weren't groping sessions. It was then Ben knew he had to put one of his plans into action. It was time for him to get out before things could progress. It wasn't like they were seeking each other out, or making love eyes at each other, or sneaking around everybody at every chance they had. That was where he was feeling like it was about to go, though, and that just wouldn't do. Because they were twins, it was normal for people, even their family, to leave them together, and, if anything changed at all, it was that they chose to spend less time together. Even when they were together, and nothing was happening, they both knew that it was only a matter of time before they were revealed.

All of Ben's plans and research were suddenly put to use. Before he started to prepare to leave, he told Zoe what he was planning, and she told him she was coming along. He wasn't sure if he was okay with that or not. He didn't know if that was what was best for her, or for them—he only knew this was the best option for him.

They didn't spend their time on romance at all. They

did what they always did—talked about the others, worked on homework, did their chores. But Ben planned that whole time—mapping out their route, researching train and bus schedules, reading through hostel listings online at the library and about youth shelters and churches with homeless services, looking for job opportunities and schools in Midwestern states. At that point, both of them thought they knew that they wanted to end up on a farm somewhere someday. But it seemed that in order to get there, they would have to be ready to make do with anything they could get.

They were both almost seventeen. Between them, they had a few hundred dollars and the two gold coins. He knew that if one of them tried to sell one of the coins on the road, they were going to get dicked on the value, because they would so obviously be kids desperate for whatever they could get. Ben promised himself that the gold coins would be for emergencies only.

One morning when they left for school, their school backpacks were packed for traveling. They skipped the school bus, and headed instead to the north, toward their first stop in the path he'd mapped out, Knoxville, Tennessee.

Starting out, the three days it took them to reach Knoxville were challenging. They slept outdoors all of those nights. The world seemed less safe and more menacing, that was for sure. He felt inadequate for the job of looking after Zoe, who seemed so not ready to be dropped out into the world.

Zoe, of course, had surprised him—she was the one who had protected him, made smart choices, followed her instincts, and asked questions when his decisions were not so good. When presented with two choices, Zoe had a gift for choosing the smarter option, for seeing the landscape of the big picture, where with Ben, it could go either way. Wasn't that the way it had turned out? She was a great judge of character—she knew right away if someone could be trusted. While for Ben, in his time with her, he'd learned not to believe everything he was told, and to ask questions even if he knew he was being annoying. Information wasn't a substitute for instinct, but he'd found it improved his odds of maybe sometimes making the right choices on his own.

Once they reached Knoxville, there was indeed a hostel as advertised, and they were able to stay a night for $18. The woman running it called them a cute couple and they took this as a hopeful sign. Things did go better than they'd hoped from there in, but they were always aware of the fact that things could turn—they weren't kidding themselves. It was an adventure that could have gone seriously wrong, and because they tried to stay away from the more populous places, they saw a lot of people for whom it hadn't gone so well and knew they were walking a fine line. They worked as day laborers on a farm. They found a youth shelter located on a church property, and stayed there two weeks, working for various members, making a little bit of money, being invited into their homes for dinner, receiving guidance as to what social services were available, and when they moved on, getting all sort of leads to places down the road.

Ben was very reserved about talking too much about either of them. Zoe managed to avoid giving up anything without seeming like she was doing it. At first, he wouldn't tell anyone in a current location where he might be thinking of going next, because in his head that bit of information was going to be what led their family to wherever he and Zoe went. Zoe convinced him there was a strategic advantage to sharing a little with some of the people who were willing to help them.

They ended up staying different amounts of time in different places. Sometimes, a day was just a day, and sometimes it turned into weeks or months. Never more than a few months. A babysitting job for her would lead to a busboy job for him. The busboy job would lead to a temp job for her as a cashier in the pet store next door to the restaurant. There was never, never enough money, and somehow, every month, they got by. And they had fun. They sought out every free entertainment they could, any kind of thing open to the public for free, and if they couldn't find anything they'd lie around wherever they were staying and talk about stupid things and laugh.

They traveled through Tennessee, Kentucky, Missouri, Illinois, and Iowa over about two years' time. They had an apartment in Iowa, and Zoe was working at a chain restaurant, and Ben was apprenticing with an electrician. Zoe completed a community college course of classes on art instruction, thinking she could teach. It still didn't feel like the right place for them, but the economy in the country was pretty bad and they felt lucky to have any kind of paying jobs at all.

Then an old man drove his car into the restaurant where Zoe worked as a waitress. A man who was too old to be driving, who momentarily was overcome with confusion while barreling down the highway, who lost control and plowed through the cars parked on the street and right through the glass front window. A waitress and a busboy were killed, and another nine people, mostly customers but also a few employees, including Zoe, were injured. The car never touched her, but she was cut up pretty bad by glass.

Ben got there within fifteen minutes and found that they were seeking blood donations. He didn't tell them he was Zoe's brother. Here, in their new life, he was her husband; although they hadn't married yet, they pretended they had. Cutting off their last names, which they used only for official documents, they were Ben Nelson and Zoe Nelson. So he gave the donation and while doing so explained that neither he nor his wife knew their blood types—could they find out from this?

He found later that Zoe had needed blood, and that they had found a few matches. Ben also found out he was not among the matches. This confused both he and Zoe to no end, until someone on an online helpline told them that although identical twins have the same blood type, for fraternal twins that was not always the case.

True that might have been, but something about it didn't quite settle comfortably with him. He was so uncomfortable with it that he made her uncomfortable with it. Zoe suggested that they have their blood tested to see if they were okay to have children. They did this by mail. They waited four weeks to find out that there was an extremely low probability that they were related. Yes, theoretically they would be fine to breed, but in fact both samples showed hormone imbalances that in the female suggested ovulation issues and in the male suggested sperm production problems. A second set of tests, these conducted in a doctor's office, and made possible by the blessing of employer-provided health coverage, confirmed this. They were not related, and they were both infertile.

This news was really too much for them to absorb all at once. First and foremost, it removed a barrier from their relationship. It wasn't 24 hours before there was a shoebox on the kitchen table in which they gathered condoms, sponges, a 3-month supply of birth control pills, Spermicide, a diaphragm, and a pamphlet about a 5-year anti-pregnancy implant. Their sex life improved dramatically. Turned out that the very idea that he was fucking his sister, or for her that she might get pregnant by her brother, had added a level of inhibition that was suddenly removed.

On the other hand . . . it was a lot. They weren't related? Who were their mothers? Who were their fathers? Were they really both born on the same day at nearly the same time? They'd all known the story that Rose shared with the town when they first arrived, about his and Zoe's supposed polygamist father, was not true, and that Rose had purposely told that lie because she was fresh in the fear she felt for their true father. But was the story that Lily had long hinted at, that their father was a violent man who'd chased them out of Oregon or Northern California, also made up?

The possible scenarios seemed limitless. Had Rose stolen them from a hospital? Had she bought them from a patient, or been paid by a patient to take them? Was there some perfectly good, justifiable reason she might have adopted them and never told them the truth? Maybe each of their parents' stories was so terrible that Rose meant for them never to have to hear them. Maybe she thought she had been protecting them, even saving them? Or maybe she had stolen them, and that was why one or both of their fathers had chased them out of the West.

Their fathers and mothers might still be looking for them. The thought of it turned his stomach a little sour. What about the siblings? What did they know? What could they know? They were children back then. Except for Lily, she was a little bit older. Ben and Zoe both agreed that Lily likely knew more than she let on.

Early on after the blood tests, he got so tied up wondering about it, thinking about it all the time, that he started talking about confronting Rose, which he'd started calling her half the time, and Lily, and telling the rest of the kids what they had found out. That was where Zoe drew the line on the topic.

"I don't want to go back from here, Ben. I want to go forward. Away from them. Maybe before we learned this there was a small part of me that still wanted to feel connected to them. Knowing this now? Well, let's just be done with it."

So they had. Ben pushed it away, set it aside, and together they moved to South Dakota, to the northern part of the state. Where the recession had slowed down the economy just about everywhere they had been, in South Dakota there was an oil boom going on, and with the oil flowing, everything else was too.

Every town they passed on the bus ride over had new construction going on, houses and businesses going up everywhere, billboards touting new planned communities, help wanted signs all over every place they went.

Ben found a job as an electrician, working for a company that sent teams from new development to new development, wiring up house after house. They had clients booked for nine months ahead, even though everyone talked about there being an economic bubble, about someone here or there passing a ban on fracking, which was behind much of this boom, or just about the fact that the boom would one day end.

Ben kept that in mind, and they continued to live conservatively and to save money. Zoe got a job at an arts center, where she taught beginning art classes for teens and adults. They married, in a very private ceremony, before a justice of the peace, with his secretary as their witness. Ben sold his gold coin for several thousand dollars, and used that money to buy rings, to pay for a honeymoon in Yellowstone, to purchase the dress Zoe wanted, to let them have a ceremony they would remember.

They were renting a small house now, and were talking about buying but were also afraid to get stuck overpaying for a place right if the oil rush ended.

They still got along well. They still spent their free time together. They'd made some friends, and had fun spending time with them. They lived in a neighborhood, with houses up and down the block, and for two people who had grown up in near isolation, far from everyone, it was almost unbelievable that they had landed in some version of the suburbs. It was so normal for everyone else there, it seemed, but for Ben and Zoe it was like an alternate dimension. And strangely, it worked for them. It was an adventure in normalcy. The only things that caused any tension between them beyond what he considered the normal ups and downs of any relationship were his occasional flare-ups of jealousy, and when he started off again on his rants about Rose.

Something would come up, and he wouldn't be able to let it go. He'd start in on the "I'd like to ask Rose this," and "I want to tell Rose that," and Zoe would start tuning him out. So he'd come up with what he thought would help him finally be settled with Rose. He would drop by unannounced and have it out right there and get the answers he wanted. Without telling Zoe, he talked to a private investigator about gathering DNA from his siblings to test it to find out who was related to whom, so that if Rose tried to lie to him he would be able to call her on it. That was what he was hoping to do—confront her—when, of all things, Rose Chamber died.

He and Zoe had been in a window booth seat at The Square Coffee Shop, both of them staring at the menu shellacked to the tabletop, when Zoe had grabbed his hand. He'd looked up at her, and saw that she was staring out the window with a shocked look on her face. He'd looked that way, and there she was, Rose Chamber, standing two feet back on the other side of the window, watching them with a slight smile on her face.

"Oh my," he'd started to say, shocked. And like that, Rose was gone. Ben said, "What the hell?"

"That was goodbye," Zoe said after a few seconds. "She's dead." They were both stunned.

It was a week before an obituary and a notice of the service appeared on the website of the local paper in North Carolina. Ben confessed to what he had been intending. Zoe blew up at him, angry at the elaborateness of his plan and the amount of thought and money he was planning to put into it. They went back and forth on the topic for weeks. Finally, she stopped talking to him two days before he left.

Having been shut out of speaking with her for half a week, after nine years of sharing everything, every day, it had thrown him for a loop, into a less secure frame of mind. On this trip, how much time had he spent wondering what she was doing, if she had secrets she kept from him, if there might be someone else she was interested in, if maybe his absence was secretly a joy for her because she wanted time with some hidden lover? Ben could make himself crazy when he really got started, thinking about the men she had regular contact with at her job, how she talked about them, where she might have met someone without him knowing about it, how she might be communicating with him without Ben knowing, even wondering if some guy had been sitting in a parked car on the street outside their house early Thursday morning, just waiting for Ben to leave so he could get started with her.

It was a dark and insecure place to live, outside the aura of Zoe's blessings. Ben hoped this was worth it. He hoped it would give him something to settle that unsettled place inside of him. Ben hoped Zoe would be there when he returned. He hoped he was able to emerge from this more of the man she wanted him to be.

Chapter 17

When Ben woke, the controlled environment of his hotel room immediately disoriented him. With the curtains closed, it could be night or day. With the pervasive quiet, punctuated by a central air-conditioning system that kicked on and off on its own schedule, it could be the middle of the early morning tomorrow, or middle afternoon today. He found the clock, and it was 3 o'clock. Morning? Afternoon? He looked at his phone, hoping for a flashing light that would let him know there was a message waiting. It was still today.

But no. He worried: Had he missed his appointment? Was that possible? Didn't the investigator work for him?

He felt his way to the window, pushed open the curtains. It was broad daylight outside. The street was busy with people.

In the lobby, he checked with the front desk. No package. No message.

He peeked into the restaurant. There were still eight people sitting around the outside patio. The blond model was still there, but with a group of four others around him, none of them the other models. He looked like he was explaining something. Ben wondered how many were listening to him and how many were just enjoying looking at him.

"So, there's a more detailed version," the model said, "that described the original humans as having four arms, four legs, and a single head with two faces. There were three genders . . . "

Someone said with mock wistfulness, "Remember when there were only three?"

" . . . man, woman, and androgynous. Each of the men and women had two sets of genitalia, and the androgynous ones had both male and female genitalia. The women were children of the Earth, and the men were children of the Sun, and the androgynous ones were the children of the Moon.

"But the humans were very powerful in those forms, and they were a threat to the Gods. The Gods' only choice seemed to be to kill them with lightning—which was how they tended to get rid of people—but then they wouldn't have anyone to worship them or make offerings to them.

"What Zeus decided to do was to split the humans apart as a punishment for the rebellion. Not only did that diminish their power, but it also doubled the number of the Gods' worshippers. Win, win. The humans, split apart, were so miserable that they weren't eating, and they were dying of starvation. So Apollo, the God of the Sun, saw how miserable they were and sewed them up, making them new bodies. The belly button was the only leftover piece of their old bodies. That's supposed to be how we all ended up in bodies with only one set of genitals, and why we are always searching for our other half, who we will supposedly recognize when we encounter them again, and then we will find contentment from being unified again."

"I don't know if I buy it," one of the listeners said. "It sounds like a line for picking someone up, and it sort of can be used on anyone, regardless of gender."

"Of course, I'm more of an Adam/Eve, woman-from-the-rib of man, sex-for-procreation type of person anyway," another person said slowly. Ben realized the speaker's twang was close, but not quite right. Someone was mocking the locals, he thought with mixed feelings. He wasn't a Christian, but that didn't mean he thought it was okay for everyone to mock them.

. The whole group laughed before the blond continued.

"It's too long for a pickup line. It's a metaphor for . . . "

Ben stepped out of the restaurant, headed for the hotel's front door.

The smell of the barbecue was the first thing he noticed outside. The swirling clouds of smoke from the grill drew him forward. This was one of the best things about living out here, the food at a gathering, he thought. At any kind of freakin' gathering in the South, the food.

To his right, across the street from the parking lot, about a quarter of the seats in front of the stage platform were filled, mostly with people staring at their cell phones.

There were only a couple people in line for food, and three waiting for their orders. It smelled like heaven to Ben. It took him a minute to notice the walkie-talkie snapped to the belt of the girl standing to the side, another to realize who it was.

"Christy? Hey. You're still here."

She looked at him, rolled her eyes.

"There's an accident on one of the roads to get here, and my replacement is supposedly on his way, just running late. As you can see," she said, gesturing toward the barbecue, "I'm hedging my bets."

"Good plan."

"So, I didn't get your last name before. It's Ben, right? What's your last name? In case I need to have you paged over the P.A. because, you know, I want to pray?"

Want to pray? He didn't understand it. She gestured with two of her fingers as if she were either making a crude gesture or, then he got it: smoking a cigarette. He thought, Gosh, I hope that was what that was. She was saying she would have him paged if she needed a cigarette? Or was she flirting with him? Right out in the open in front of everybody, him with a ring on his finger?

"Chamber," he said. He slipped like he hadn't slipped in years. Once it was out, he couldn't take it back.

"Ben Chamber," she said. He felt a mild horror grip him as she seemed to run that name through her head, and then recognize it.

"Chamber," she repeated.

She smiled cryptically, and looked right through him for a moment. Then she'd worked through whatever it was in her mind, and she returned her attention to him with renewed curiosity. Whatever it was she had planned to ask him next, she changed course.

"So I remember you said you were here on business. Does that mean you have no interest in watching a lunar eclipse?"

"Oh, I'll come out and check it out. I don't know about watching the whole thing," he said.

"I know, right?"

He asked, "Who is paying for all of this?"

"Well, I know who is paying for some of it. The company I work for has a contract with a non-profit called the Framework Foundation. We've done a bunch of events for them. They're pushing this idea of space travel for the human race, like they think that we need to be moving in that direction, so they've been sponsoring all of these, I want to say, space-themed events?"

"I've heard of their museum in Washington. I want to go there to see it some time."

"Yeah, well, I guess they've taken it on the road. I feel almost like I'm a member, except I really know only the rough outline, and that's because I end up doing everything in promotions at some point—usually it's advance stuff, like hiring staff for an event, but sometimes I'm there handing out flyers and doing set-up like this," she said, gesturing toward the stage.

"This is unusual, because this is planned by a bunch of students, and not by the foundation. The students are sort of anti-Framework, because I guess college kids need to be anti something, but they took the money anyway. There are events like this going on tonight all over the world, from what I understand. The students applied for a "Star Grant" and this fit entirely within the foundation parameters, so they put up X amount of dollars, and to make sure it's spent well, they put us in charge of spending part of the money to make sure the event works the way the planners wanted it."

"For free."

"I don't work for free. But the donation to the students that also pays me is free to the students. That's one of the donation guidelines. It has to be open to everyone, and really, they frown on people trying to hoard their donations for purposes other than the events."

The counter girl called, "Christy." Her food was ready.

"See you around, Ben."

Ben ate his plate of ribs and potato salad seated in front of the stage, with the plate balanced on his knees. He saw the scene around him as a Tennessee version of A Sunday Afternoon on the Island of Grand Jatte. It was a nice day, sunny but with a breeze, and there were people out picnicking and playing and strolling all about. It was the ones who were strolling with umbrellas that made Ben think of that painting.

The sound of a police radio made him jump a little, and a guy in a fishing hat who must have been a plainclothes officer, a guy who'd just walked past Ben, reached to his side and pulled out a walkie-talkie.

Into the walkie-talkie, the cop said, "Yeah, I'm here now. Lost time chasing reports of a man on a tractor driving through the hills. It's been a nuisance since yesterday."

The walkie-talkie made a scratchy noise that Ben thought was unintelligible, but which the cop responded to with, "Nah. Couldn't find him. It's either the next shift's or the next county's problem now."

Ben looked up the block and saw a police car double-parked in front of the professional building. It was the first car he'd seen on the Galaxy Park business district street since he'd been there. He hadn't even noticed an accessway for vehicles. Ben didn't have anything against cops—although during the early months on the road with Zoe, and pretty much until he turned 18, he'd been nervous to ever have them around. That fear never quite went away—that he was moments from being busted. When he saw the police, he went back to being a kid, stammering and compliant with whatever they told him to do.

There were three teens in neon orange vests now managing the parking situation in the parking lot. It was a good turnout. It wasn't Mardi Gras, for sure—there was room to move around, space for people to set up their own deck chairs and towels and blankets for the viewing later—but for a place that had been so vacant the last few days, it was nice to have some kind of a crowd. He realized after a minute that the social club ladies were dispersed among the people along the block, their creamy, shimmery dresses and shawls giving them a distinctive, easy-to-spot look.

Ben saw the reporter interviewing Dot and Walt while the younger guy captured it all on a handheld camera. Ben's timing was terrible, because the bright light on the camera flashed off as he approached, and Dot and husband turned to each other, and the cameraman and the reporter swung around, and there Ben was in their path.

"Hey, hi!" The reporter said, not missing a beat. "We're doing some background interviews before the event starts. Want to be on film?"

Ben stopped and said, "No, thank you."

"Then maybe just let me ask you a few questions? No camera? Like, are you from around here?"

"No, I'm in town on business."

"What a great surprise for you, right? You have this giant lunar celebration happening right on your doorstep."

"I guess."

"You're not going to give me much to work with, are you . . . what's your name?"

"Ben. Ben Nelson."

There was no reason for the guy not to think it was true. It was true. But Ben thought that the guy reacted as if Ben had lied to him. "Okay, Ben. Ben Nelson," he said. "Are you going to watch the eclipse out here tonight with everyone else?"

"I might," Ben said. "The ribs are mighty good."

"That's more like it. Now, let me ask you, do you know anything about the event's co-sponsor, the Framework Foundation?"

Ben studied the reporter. He asked, "What's your name?"

"Art. Arthur Sinclair." The two shook hands.

"Are you really a reporter for a radio station, Art, Art Sinclair? I'm not sure that you are."

This made the reporter and the camera guy stop. The reporter stepped back and looked Ben over.

"Okay," Art said, "I won't bother you. I'm sorry. I'm just trying to earn a living."

They parted ways.

Ben returned to the hotel. The blond model was outside. Ben said hello, and for some reason, couldn't keep himself from asking, "Did you find a ride out of here?"

The guy looked at him, and smiled.

"Maybe. One of the other models lives somewhere in Georgia, and he invited some of us to go there tonight to party. It doesn't get me exactly to where I want to go, but it does get me closer to the car rental agency."

Ben was curious. "Everyone else is staying for the thing tonight?"

"The photographer and his crew went home, but their van was too packed to fit one more. I'm trying to get out of here, but it's just not working out so far. Maybe I'm meant to be here for one more night. What can you do? You can't fight what the universe wants."

Ben asked, "Can I ask you something?

"Something else? Sure."

"What does your girlfriend think of your search for your, um, friend?"

The guy studied Ben for a moment.

"Right. So I took this job because I knew I wanted to do this, and at first I told her I was going to spend some days driving around, but didn't say anything specific about my friend. Later, she said something like, 'So I don't have to be worried that you're heading out there just so you can start up again with Cole, am I right?'"

Ben would have said "Ouch" at that point, but he was stuck on the name the guy had just said. Cole.

It couldn't be, Ben thought. In his head, he heard the same guy saying earlier Mason County.

"I think she understands that I have to at least make an effort to apologize, to let him know we're still friends if he wants to be. I think she gets that the other part was just . . . what? Taking advantage of a window of opportunity? But I think she thinks I'll be a better person if I can file it away. I'll be honest with you, I miss her, like, five times a minute right now, and the frequency is increasing. Part of me just wants to call it a draw and fly home to her."

He studied Ben a minute. He saw the ring.

"What about you? Where's your wife?"

"She doesn't want me to be here. She wants me home. She's not, actually, talking to me while I'm here. I have to do this, I guess, too. But she's not understanding about it. She doesn't believe it will help me put things together. She's afraid it will take residence and never leave. She thinks it's the first step in everything unraveling."

"Heavy."

"It doesn't have to be. I just need to know."

"I hear you."

"I wish she did. Your girl sounds like she trusts what you say, I guess."

"Right, plus she knows, like, I'm not moving to the old South for anything! No offense."

"I've got to go check something inside," Ben said.

"Truth will play out, no matter how you do it," the blond said. "Whether your girl sees it or not. No point in wasting time hiding from it. Better to face it and be done with it. Good luck."

"Right. Good luck to you, too."

Inside the lobby, as he approached the front desk for what seemed like the thousandth time, he spotted the oversized envelope sitting on the shelf behind the clerk. He slowed his pace as he stared at it. That was for him, he knew with certainty.

He walked to the desk, the clerk smiled, and with a nod, turned to the shelf to grab the envelope. Ben nodded as the clerk handed the envelope to him, and wordlessly, they both turned away from each other to move on to the next thing.

For Ben, the next thing was a booth in the restaurant, with a beer on the side, the envelope opened and set aside, the documents in his hands.

Over the next hour, he learned that Lily had a two-story house, two children, and she was no longer working for the police department. It had information about the kids, the kids' school, income tax information, but really nothing very surprising. The investigator found several samples in Lily's trash, including a used menstrual pad, a chewed pencil, and a hairbrush.

Josh now owned a bug farm. Ben would never have guessed a bug farm specifically, but he would have thought Josh would be doing something unexpected. According to the report, Josh was also a handyman, and maybe he'd messed around with some of his customers in town, but did not seem to have an established relationship. The investigator had taken one of Josh's drinking glasses from the wake. Carolyn was apparently an alcoholic and a widow and had some money to her name. She owned a thrift shop, partially owned a restaurant, and had money in the bank. She did a lot of online selling. The investigator had stolen several of her cigarette butts. Cole had received a full scholarship and was now a graduate of the University of California, Los Angeles. He'd had a job in Los Angeles, and several different addresses, but seemed to have moved from the area. The investigator had not been able to find very much about him because he'd hardly started establishing a trail, but in the closet of his old room at the house the investigator found a pair of tennis shoes, a mouth guard in its case, and a sweat-stained high school baseball hat from Cole's graduating high school class.

Rose Chamber died of natural causes. Her funeral was attended by Josh and Lily among the family members, close to a hundred people from the local area and, apparently, the investigator. There was a list of attendees, and photos, and Ben recognized most of them as town faces, and the few he didn't recognize had the look of also being locals. As he thought that, he read the line in the report that said everyone in attendance lived locally or had family that lived in the area. Rose was buried at the northeast corner of the property. No will was yet on record.

Finally, after pages of lab reports, the summary said that it was highly unlikely that the seven individuals tested shared any familial connection. That number included his and Zoe's DNA, and whatever sample the investigator had managed to gather from Rose.

Common markers indicated different genealogies for all seven samples.

There it was, he thought. I knew it! None of us are related. None of us.

Having thought this to be true, and having considered what the next step would be when it was confirmed as true, Ben had always imagined he would confront his mother. He'd always known, even before his mother died, that if his mother wouldn't admit to anything, there was one of them who knew more than the rest, and he was going to confront her next.

Well, Lils, you're at the top of the list now, Ben thought. You're next.

He felt so satisfied for a moment that he almost wanted to share it with someone else. He looked around the restaurant patio area for someone, even a waitress. No one was around. His eyes settled on a cell phone on a chair near him.

He walked over to pick it up, pressed a button on it, and a picture of the blond model and a beautiful woman who must have been his girlfriend flashed onto the screen. Damn, they were good-looking people. She was even prettier than him.

He swiped the screen to see if the phone was locked. It wasn't. He went to the contacts section, and scrolled down, looking for the name Cole Chamber.

There it was. He selected Cole. Below his phone number he saw there were 27 g-mail messages and 134 text messages to and from Cole. Since it was listed first, Ben selected the g-mail. There was a list of messages with no responses. Ben scrolled to the start of the list.

Two months ago:
Hey, Cole. Howzit? Send me a message so I know you're okay.

A week later:
I thought we taught you better. Three days without returning a message is a snub. You gonna check in or what?

A week later:
I guess Tony and Trina are dating now. They bonded over their shared mutual loathing of you. That guy is a wanker—can't believe he was your friend. I think he's so smug because he knows about you, me, and Alexa, and he thinks that makes him better. Trina and Alexa are trying to get back to a normal place after the Great Betrayal, so we're all having to spend excessive amounts of time together. Alexa hates him, too.

Two days later:
Ah, a clue. Alexa said that Trina had been trying to track you on your phone, and that your phone had been coming up disabled. So maybe you're just hiding out? I'll see what I can do about it. Maybe I'll just push her (and her phone) into the pool. Let me work on it.

Five days later:
So I got paid this week for that job I was doing this spring, a nice fat check. Alexa and I are going to go to Hawaii for a couple weeks. I took the money you left behind for me and Alexa, divided it up, added a little of my own and then had it delivered to your Asian roommates. They're paid off now. Just in case you decide you want to come back here, thought I would eliminate one of the obstacles. I didn't give anything to Tony, that sucker. One of the few entertainments I've enjoyed the last few days has been watching him as he tries not to completely lose his cool over them being paid back and not him. I guess I'm missing having you around. Hope you're doing all right.

Two weeks later:
Two things. I didn't have to drive my car over Trina's phone. Tony the turd got her a new G7 with a different carrier, so she's no longer linked to your phone. Number two is that in Hawaii, Alexa

"rented" us an attractive woman so we could check another item off the sexual bucket list. I think after a similar experience you'd agree, and won't be offended to hear, that it's far more physically enjoyable to be the owner of the only penis in the room in such a situation, because that was generally where the focus fell most of the night.

A week later:
Dude, where are you? I've been feeling sort of confused about some things lately. Signed up for a Philosophy class at the community college. Thought it might help me with . . . I don't know with what. I've been thinking about you a lot. I don't mean that in a sexual way, but I miss having you around enough that it is throwing me off my game. I feel like the only thing that will make me feel better is hearing you're okay. You just went off into the void. If you don't call soon, I'm probably going to take this job in Tennessee so I can come looking for you. I don't know if that's more likely to make you call or make you not call. Call me, buddy, text me, something.

Last week:
I just want to be more honest with you. The therapist I'm seeing said it was the first step toward restoring order in my head. Maybe you won't ever read this, but at least I will have put it into words, and that will be therapeutic for me too.

I had a steady flow of work going on when you and Trina started dating, which was when you two started hanging out with Alexa. We were having some tension, Alexa and I, because I was getting lots of work but she was not, and Trina was busy spending a lot of time with you, and it was going to Alexa's self-confidence that no one was around for her and no one was hiring her. She wanted me to be making more of an effort to find time.

I'd met you when we'd all gone out together a couple

times, and I think we hit it off. I liked you better than any of Trina's previous boyfriends, for sure, but my radar sort of kicked on with you. Not that you were making moves on Alexa, or that she was thinking that way about you, but I felt like there was a potential situation developing.

Then Trina started her school thing. She told us she was going to be busy, and that you really enjoyed hanging out with us, so could we make an extra effort to keep you company while she started her pre-law school socializing? Alarms went off. I knew Alexa wouldn't say no to Trina, and I knew that if I weren't around, she would hang out with you by default. I could envision you and Alexa both getting mad at being neglected by Trina, and Alexa getting mad at being quote unquote neglected by me. I thought it was a formula to push you two together.

I know this was all in my head, but I canceled two jobs so that we would all three be able to hang out and do stuff together. And that was fun long before the events that led to our downfall. It was a great summer. But the unstoppable progression of the situation continued, with you basically getting kicked out of your place and ending up on our couch. Then I felt like I had to be around the house all the time, so as not leave you two alone at all. It was kind of schizo on my part—I wanted to help you out, and I liked having you there, but then I also wanted you to get the hell out.

The thing was, if I'd acted jealous or threatened in any obvious way, I was sure that would have the opposite of the hoped-for effect. I didn't have any other argument for turning you away that wouldn't lead back to me seeming to be threatened by you. So finally, I decided the only solution was to take the opposite tactic—I was just going to embrace it. Alexa and I have our bucket list, so I suggested to her that we check off number 17 with you.

I was right that she was mad enough with Trina to consider it. I think you knew that Trina was ready to break up with you, even if she never voiced it, and Alexa was bothered by the way Trina was sort of keeping you in reserve before she delivered her final decision. I also believed it was evidence I was right, too, about there being some attraction between you two also, because, again, Alexa went along with the idea.

So that's how all that was initiated on our part. I was really in some crazy headspace. I was like, "Whatever he does to her, I'm going to do to both of them," and "Whatever she does to him, they're both going to do to me." I know it wasn't like that when it happened, but ahead of time there were a lot of games going on in my brain.

I told Alexa most of this after we spent the night with the woman in Hawaii. She admitted to being confused by my choice of you for number 17, but decided to go with it anyway, and basically for the same reasons I was doing it. She thought the fact that I'd expressed an interest suggested maybe she had to worry about you and I getting together when she wasn't around. This way she'd be present to assess the threat and also remind me that she's got the stuff I really want. She also said that the reason she'd wanted to check off number 16 in Hawaii with me was because Trina had spent so much time ragging on her about my sexuality, even though our threesome had fairly convinced Alexa that I was basically straight. She wanted to make sure I loved boobs and pussy as much as I professed and that I'd just been displaying my openness when we screwed around with you.

So, after telling you all that, I am also going to tell you how sorry I am for my part in your exile from California. When that big check came in, I realized that if you'd stayed just another month, we could have figured out the money thing. If I'd not been insecure about my relationship with Alexa, I wouldn't have pushed the things that happened, and even if you had broken up with Trina, you wouldn't have felt like there was a cloud over your head that you needed to escape.

So that's my confession, and my apology. I'm sorry. I still miss you enough that I haven't written off the idea of heading out to find you. I love you, Bro. I miss your face. I'm always hoping for the best for you.

Ben closed everything up and set the phone on the table and looked around self-consciously. He was going to leave it where he found it. Thinking this news had given him a lot mull over during the party, he went back to his room to drop off the package. He wanted to call Zoe now, but he wouldn't—he was going to make himself wait.

It was starting to change to dusk outside.

On his way to the elevator, the door of a room swung open as he passed, and he caught a quick glimpse inside as the young cameraman walked out. The room was filled with video monitors, and the girl with the news team was seated in front of the monitors with a headset on.

This was their control room, Ben thought. The door closed.

The cameraman gave Ben an irritated look, then shrugged and turned in the direction of the elevators. Ben did a quick two-step to catch up to him.

"So," Ben said, "What kind of program are you making?"

"When it's done, it'll be a 7- or 8-minute segment."

The elevator door opened. The guy didn't want to talk, and thought about not getting on. When Ben didn't move, the guy stepped in. Ben did too.

"You need all that for 7 or 8 minutes?"

"We'll probably leave here with 300 hours of tape, and then edit that down."

"A video for a radio station?"

"The company that owns the station has other outlets. We'll prepare different product for a bunch of platforms."

"Sorry I ask so many questions. My name is Ben."

"I know. I'm Fong."

Ben thought he heard him wrong.

"Fong?"

"Yes"

"But you're . . . you're not Asian."

Fong looked at him blankly.

"I'm sorry," Ben said. He wanted to continue, but caught himself and repeated the apology.

The elevator opened in the lobby, and the cameraman didn't wait to see who would get off first.

"I can't talk anymore," he said as he hurried away, "I've got to get to work."

Outside, the big difference, other than the fading light, was the sound of live music, a bluegrass band playing their version of "Moon Over Bourbon Street." The chairs around the stage were filled, and there had to be a good two hundred people out besides the ones who were seated, and they were roaming all over the block. The band played a very country rendition of "By the Light of Silvery Moon" and followed that with what the male lead singer said was a request for a very special friend far away, "The Whole of the Moon."

The original crowd from the restaurant this morning was dispersed along the block. Dot and Walt were seated in the first row of chairs in front of the stage. Ed and Martin were in the barbecue line, looking like they'd gone out fishing in between. The models were mixed in here and there and across the amusement park property. There were a lot of college students, but then there were more people who looked like they were locals. There were license plates from North Carolina, Alabama, Tennessee, and Georgia in the parking lot.

When the band finished the Waterboys' song, a voice

boomed out over the mic.

"Hello, Moon Watchers! Thank you all for joining together with us tonight for this very special event brought to you free of charge by our amazing universe! Know that you are not alone . . . "

A round of applause went up from a section of the seats.

"We are joined in celebrating tonight's lunar eclipse by more than 50 other events just like this all over the planet under the Syzygy banner. North America, South America, Western Asia, Africa, and across Europe. What is Syzygy? Well, loosely defined, syzygy refers to an astronomical alignment of three celestial objects. Some of the more romantic among us see it as more than an event, or a moment in time. They see it as signaling the initiation of some kind of change. There are two bodies in fixed orbit, and then a third body comes in between them, resulting in changes to one, two, or all three of the bodies involved. In tonight's syzygy, the Earth is the interloper. The Moon's influence on our planet is powerful enough to affect our tides, and our planet's influence is powerful enough to cause quakes on the moon.

"The current pop theology that attempts to explain why we are here in the universe—and let's not kid ourselves, it is being rolled out as science, but it is a theology—would have it that unseen and distant aliens instigated the processes of life on this planet by means only speculated at and for purposes not yet determined. It is modern sounding, and it is scientifically presented, and for the followers of the Framework Foundation it is perhaps a consensus view, but at its heart, this is still high priests sealed away from the rest of us telling us to worship star gods for bringing life to Earth.

"What we choose to celebrate tonight at this Syzygy is the power of interconnection. It is what we see as the power of our small pocket of the universe to incubate life on its own, with no external tampering required. We know that the planets in our solar system are abundant with all the elements needed to create and nourish life. What we know less about are their relationships to each other. We think of Earth as the only living planet because of its magnetic core, but it is the whole planetary system functioning together that makes life possible here. When life is extinguished here, it's very possible this system will raise and feed another race on another one of those surfaces, if it hasn't already. It is the purpose of the creation machine that is the universe to manifest and encourage life.

"Our universe is not a field of planets, some randomly dead, others alive. It is a life-sustaining, life-creating system of four terrestrial worlds—the first four—and five gas planets, interconnected at the solar system's foundation, each one necessary for the others to do what they're meant to do.

"Similarly, we see the interconnectedness of life on this planet, the push and pull that leads to great advancements and great shortcomings. We are all a part of one another's existence. Syzygy is about the power we wield over those around us simply by the fact of our existence, by the fact of our presence.

"The Syzygystic celebrate that moment when the bodies of the solar system move each other during alignment. We don't understand all that occurs when we slip into alignment, or when we slip out of it. In each celestial syzygy, energies are created, energies are transferred, to what end we do not know. We are simply here to celebrate the powers and the power that exists here naturally before us.

"We will go back to the music in a few minutes. We have a lot of different entertainments for you to enjoy for the next few hours, and then at 10:45 we're going to go dark so that we can enjoy the event without distraction when it starts at 11:12 pm."

Another round of applause from the crowd.

The band returned. The female lead singer said, "This is 'We're All Made of Stars,'" and then they started playing. Ben thought they sounded pretty good, and that they were doing a great job of putting their own spin on the songs—he kept thinking pop bluegrass was going to be corny, but they were doing it great.

Ben looked around the street for Christy. Her truck was still parked in the lot, although the clipboard and the walkie-talkie seemed to have been transferred to someone else, a skinny, balding guy in a tank shirt hustling here and back between the stage and the BBQ. Ben didn't see Cole's blond model friend, either.

Ben sneered at the thought of what two men might do to each other. It was disgusting, in his opinion. He would never have thought Cole would be like that.

Then, randomly, he wondered if maybe Christy and the model might be off somewhere together? He didn't know why he thought that, maybe just because they were both blond and better looking than everyone else? Why wouldn't they end up together? Didn't blondes gravitate toward each other instinctively?

Why did the thought of them together make him feel envious?

As the band started "Bad Moon Rising," Ben decided he wanted to celebrate a little bit. Maybe the investigator's report wasn't really an achievement, but he felt vindicated, and it felt like a victory. He thought there would be a next step, and wasn't sure what it was, but he was at least in a place, mentally and physically, where he could set it aside for a minute to enjoy what was going on around him.

Two beers later, and he was back in his hotel room, calling Zoe. As he expected, the call went to voicemail. He left a message: "Hi. It's me. I miss you. I'll be thinking of you during the eclipse tonight. I think I found out what I needed to know. I'll be heading home tomorrow. I love you. Bye."

He shared the elevator down with one of the ladies' guild women, much younger than the others, maybe only in her twenties.

She wore a sticker that said Hi, I'm Kendra. She seemed flustered. Ben didn't even have to ask. Christy had told him earlier about the accident on the road in.

"Traffic," she said. "I'm late."

"What is it exactly that you ladies are doing out there?"

"Oh, that," she said, with a disarming smile. "It's similar to a solstice ceremony, but built around a celebration of the eclipse." Something about her voice made her sound older than she looked. More mature, or something Ben couldn't put his finger on.

"Sounds interesting. Are they . . . "

"Oh, it's members only." Again that smile. "Have to pay your dues, you know."

The elevator doors opened, and she was off. He stepped out of the elevator, and noticed there was a googly eye on the wall next to the elevator.

Ben leaned toward it and said, "Hello."

Chapter 18

Ben returned to the restaurant. The cell phone was still on the table. He sat down next to it, and as he pushed it away from him, he heard Ed and Martin entering the lobby and greeting the front desk receptionist. A moment later, they were sliding into the favored personal spots that they'd had to sacrifice earlier because of the crowd. Now that all the tables and chairs had been returned to their original positions, it was as if order had been restored. The band was playing "Moonlight Sonata."

Ben stood and gestured to the open seat across the table from them. Ed nodded his head, so Ben took the seat, and ordered another beer.

"How you guys doing?"

Ed said, "Good." Martin nodded.

Ben asked, "You got some fishing in today?"

"Yup," Ed said.

"Well, how'd you do?"

"Not a lot today. Martin did a little better. No records broke."

"Did you try the ribs? The ribs are good."

"Yup."

"Just trying to enjoy watching the crowd with no one talking?" Ben studied Ed's eyes. "Is that what we're looking for?"

Ed smiled, which was not a big change from his neutral expression.

Ben turned his chair slightly, so he faced more toward the window. He sipped at his beer without another word.

A little later than promised, after a very spare rendition of "Walking On The Moon," the lights around the platform flashed and began to go dark. The last few stayed on while the band cleaned up, and there seemed to be some dispute about whether or not the sound guys should pack everything up or if the program called for any further communication with the crowd.

Eventually, the band cleared out and the sound set-up remained, and everyone around the stage started to disperse to find their viewing areas.

That was when the K-NOX news guy walked into the restaurant for a break. He sat on one of the stools, staring at his phone while he typed at the keypad.

It didn't take him long to notice Ben was watching him. Ben figured the guy had every reason to ignore him.

Instead he waved at Ben.

Ben waved back.

"No," the guy said, "come over here."

Ben stood, maybe a little unsteadily after his latest beer, and walked over to Art. He stood next to him until Art turned the barstool next to him toward Ben, then gestured for Ben to sit down.

"They don't want our camera lights moving around out there right now. So we've got some downtime."

"Did you get a lot of interviews?"

"Yes."

"Did you talk to the social club ladies? Do you know what they're doing out there?"

"You're a curious guy, aren't you, Ben?" Art studied him a minute. Ben thought he was going to say that Ben should be a reporter. "No, the ladies wanted to talk on camera about as much as you do."

"When will this be broadcast?"

"It'll be a little bit. Listen," Art said, "I heard you got a peek at our room earlier. You want to come upstairs and have a full look?"

Shortly thereafter, Ben was walking into room 304. It looked like a control room. There were laptop-sized flat screens arranged across the wall behind the bed and propped up on the bed. The girl Ben had seen Art with earlier was seated on a chair behind a keyboard and studying her own laptop screen.

"This is Ellen. Ellen, this is Ben."

They both said hello. Although Ellen masked it better than Fong, she wasn't thrilled at Ben's presence.

There were views up and down the street, and across the Galaxy Park property. The barbecue, the stage from different angles, the landscaped gardens behind the hotel, and the planet sculptures were among the images flashing across the screen. One camera was focused on the astronaut, which seemed to be glowing.

"You've got everything covered."

"We hope so."

"What is it that you think is going to happen? The moon is going to be covered up, and then it will come back? What's the story?"

"We just do the assignments that we get," Art said. Another lie. Art was not a good liar.

Ben moved closer to the screens. There were people all over the Galaxy Park property. Stonehenge looked unoccupied for the moment—where had the ladies social club members gone? On one screen was the moon, with a small portion at the side of it darkened. On the screen showing the barbecue area, Ben saw the plainclothes cop. For a long minute, his face was right in the middle of the screen, and in that time, Ben recognized him as a friend of Lily's from the policy academy. His name, if Ben remembered right, was Elias.

This was someone who had been in the family home, who had met all of Lily's family. This could be a problem, Ben thought. He was going to have to avoid running into Elias. If Elias hadn't already noticed Ben.

When Elias moved from the barbecue area down the street, he disappeared from one screen and then appeared at a different distance and from a different angle on another screen.

"This is pretty cool," Ben said, "Would it be okay if I hang out here for the duration?"

"We also have the adjoining room," Ellen said. "It's got a better view of the street. That way you won't get in my way."

Ben saw one of the cameras was on the roof of the hotel. Nothing fancy there—a railing, a bench, and a planter.

"Oh, yeah," Ben said, "I was going to go up there to have a look, see if there was a better view of Stonehenge."

"It's not, really—there's a lot of structures on the roof that obstruct the view, and the access is limited to a very small area. The hotel went to some efforts to make sure no one could get too close to the edge."

As they watched, the cameraman stepped into view, his camera pointed at the sky.

"That's Matt," Art said.

"Told me his name was Fong."

Art snickered.

"Fucking with you. There's nothing to see up on the roof. Let's get out there on the ground and check it out."

Ben saw the screen that must have been linked to Matt's camera. In that view, as Matt panned the camera across the sky, Ben could see the moon was more than a quarter covered.

Ben was relieved when he, Art, and Ellen were back outside, The night was clear and beautiful, and the huge moon hung, remarkably imposing, in the sky. There was something magical about the whole thing—the tame and happy crowd enjoying the natural spectacle. People strolling the small street like it was daylight.

Ben asked, "Why is the moon so big?"

"Super moon," Ellen said. "Happens when the moon's orbit brings it to its closest distance from Earth. It's rare to have that in conjunction with a lunar eclipse. The sun will block out most of the light, but some of the light will still get past because it gets bent toward the Moon by the Earth's gravity. That will make the moon red, which is why it is called a blood moon. It will be a super blood moon."

Art said, "If we were standing on the moon, looking toward the sun, it would appear as if the Earth were surrounded by a ring of fire."

The moon was big, and it was darkening. It was more than halfway gone. They crossed the street, then walked out onto Galaxy Park. There were a few campfires going among eight or ten campsites on the amusement park side of the property.

As they walked, he tried to picture where they would be on the legend of the park. This side of the park was supposed to be the NASA-ish section, intended to house a section of spinning cylinders, which was called Pressure Test, another spinning exercise called Orbit—a giant metal post with multiple arms sticking out of it, and each arm with a seat connected to it by a long rope—and LaunchPad, a roller coaster ride. When a parkgoer got off LaunchPad, he or she would be at the entrance to the Lunar Village area.

Beyond the Lunar Village, they reached the astronaut. He had indeed been painted with glow-in-the-dark paint. He looked like a cartoon villain. To add to the effect, whoever had done it had made a set of glow-in-the-dark footprints that started off in the distance, continued down the concrete path approaching the astronaut, and then ended at the astronaut's pedestal. It was supposed to look as if the astronaut had crossed the park and then climbed up on the pedestal.

From this side of the park, their view of the encampment in Stonehenge was no better, although glimpses of movement between the blocks suggested the ladies' social club members had returned to the site.

They followed the footprints backward to the place where they started. There they came across a large family camped out on blankets. The kids were running around with glow-in-the-dark necklaces. There looked to be two families, two wives, two husbands, and two other men, one younger looking, and one much older looking. Ben was sure there was a can of glow-in-the-dark paint hidden somewhere among their belongings.

"Hello," one of the women said in a friendly voice.

"Hello there," Art said.

They walked a distance from the family, to the Space Mine section, where there were more of the concrete blocks set about. They decided to stop there to watch the last sliver of the moon disappearing.

They waited until the moon was completely hidden. A loud cheer went up from the crowd. In the sky, the moon was indeed dark and reddish in hue. Ben thought it resembled the Death Star from *Star Wars*, hovering menacingly in the sky.

Ellen got the shot and lowered the camera.

All three of their phones started making their various notification sounds.

"No wireless signal," Art said.

Ben and Ellen read similar messages on their phone screens.

When the cheering died, another sound replaced it. It was music, but from a source other than the sound system on the stage. Art had his head cocked, listening for what it was. Then Ben could hear it, too. Something about Art's expression gave Ben the feeling that Art recognized the sound, and that he was trying to swallow his discomfort. Art looked hurriedly at Ellen, who didn't seem to care about it at all, then at Ben.

Art said, "You hear that, right?"

He stared at Ben, and Ben stared at him as the music grew louder. Ben nodded his head slowly. It was a song. Women singing a song. They both turned to the area where the ladies' social club was meeting as the ambient glow from that area brightened.

Matt's voice broke the silence.

"You guys there?"

It was Ellen's walkie-talkie.

"Yeah, got you," Ellen said.

"So short range is working, at least. The hotel wireless is down and I can't find any signals or Internet to grab onto."

"Yeah, we're disconnected, too," Ellen said. "Can you see what's going on with the social club? The blocks are obstructing our view. We'll try to move around to a better position."

"Stay where you are. I have them from the inside. Got some eyes in Stonehenge before they claimed it. Right now seven or eight women are walking around in a circle inside the blocks. It's the circle they were marking out earlier. They're still in their hats and chiffon dresses, and they are holding lights—maybe it's fire, like each one has a candle—in their hands."

The sound of their voices singing grew stronger, louder. The light emanating from the Stonehenge area brightened.

Matt said, "They've got the attention of everyone in the immediate area." To himself, Matt said, "What are you doing out there?" Then he said, "Okay."

"Okay, the lights they're holding are getting brighter. And, Ho! There it is. They just lit something on the ground and there are lines of fire springing up inside the circle. They should be careful. Those dresses would probably torch faster than an old Christmas tree. Oh, the lines are all lit. It's a pentagram. A witch circle."

A rumbling sound filled the air.

"Oh, I felt that." Matt said, "That's got the onlookers who were getting too close backing off a little."

Ben felt what he thought was a slight tremor under his feet. His heart jumped. He hated it when the ground moved that way.

"Look there," Matt said. "Something is coming up in the middle of the circle."

To Ben, it looked like a big top tent pole as it quickly rose up above the glow of the ladies' gathering. It was tube-like, and translucent. It seemed to have a purplish line of neon running down through the middle of it like a vein. In a slow few minutes, it rose up until it was twenty feet or more tall. Then the pointed top of it twisted slowly as its glistening and glowing petals peeled away from the stalk and spread wide, opening toward the red moon in the sky. While the petals of its blossom settled, Ben saw that there were four other stalks, also purple, slowly rising behind the first one, and opening up and blooming. As the petals unfurled, the glow of the neon from the plants grew brighter, coloring the landscape a violet hue.

The crowd oohed and aahed and applauded. Ben looked at Art, confused. Was this part of the night's entertainment? It was very much like watching a fireworks display, or a show with lasers played on mist. Art and Ellen looked concerned.

Ben couldn't imagine how it was being done. It looked too lifelike to be a light show. It was astonishing to watch, and the smooth, unhurried way each new plant unfurled itself was hypnotic even though, or maybe because, there was also something creepy about each one, and about the wormlike appearance of their appendages—the plants' skin looked translucent, slick and glistening, jelly-like. Other sprouts with internal systems glowing in different colors sprang up in a way similar to the first plants, as stems that extended into the air—in green, pink, soft blue, and yellow. Some were narrower in width, and some were wider, but each one, when it bloomed, was almost primordial in appearance.

Ben was astonished, and again wondered how it was being

done. Was that what they were putting in the ground earlier?

He asked Art, "This is why you're really here, isn't it?"

Art looked at him.

Ben said, "Who are they?"

Without looking at Ben, Art responded, "A rumor. An urban myth. They're a cult that believes they are ushering in a new age by waking the sleeping consciousness of the planet."

Ben snorted. "You don't believe that, do you?"

"I don't know what I believe any more, Ben. We don't know what it is they're doing," he said.

Ben thought you had to draw a line somewhere. "It's a show."

"We don't know what it is, do we?"

It was amazing, Ben thought, watching the towering plants.

"We only know them from fairy tales, don't we?"

Ben looked at him, thinking, Oh, great, another nut job.

Art said, "We don't even know if they know what they're doing."

Ben almost asked, Who are you, really?

"Yes," Art said, finally answering his question. "We've been wondering what they were up to for a while now. This time, we hoped to make a record of what happened."

This time, Ben heard.

What was happening was really quite spectacular, and if the people on the Galaxy Park parcel thought it was some bizarre kind of performance for their benefit, maybe they couldn't be blamed. Ben found it mesmerizing. The plantlike things were giant. It was like a glowing section of primordial forest was springing up in front of their eyes. When the first, largest plant had opened, the air had freshened noticeably. As the other stalks opened and took on their own shapes—a pink plant that, when it bloomed, looked like it was covered with giant grapes; a light green plant that resembled a mushroom until it opened up into tendrils that wiggled weirdly, like neon-colored grass—they filled the air with beautiful floral fragrances.

Ben realized that the women had stopped singing.

Art did, too. He asked Matt what the ladies were doing.

"Now they're all lying prostrate around the edge of the circle. I think they're praying. I can tell by the way some of them are looking around at each other that they are very pleased with themselves. There have been a couple of thumbs-ups."

There was a reddish tint to a cauliflower-like plant that opened up, revealing little shoots in the center that looked like the skeletons of Christmas trees. What appeared to be the web of its nervous system was lit a neon blue. Another plant opened to reveal an interior that looked almost gelatinous, with spires forming in coiled blue shapes that resembled snakes.

The crowd loved it.

All of this unfurling and opening had taken about half an hour, Ben had realized, until the Stonehenge area was filled to bursting with this glowing, unearthly-looking bouquet. The moon was still dark red, with no sign of light on it.

Then Ben heard a noise that didn't match all the others.

It sounded as if a tractor were approaching.

Art asked, "What's that?"

Another sign they were city folk, Ben thought. Clearly, it was a tractor.

Matt said. "There's a guy, a farmer on a tractor. He must be the one the police have been chasing all day east of here. He's crossing the park. He's got something in his hands . . . "

They heard the tractor in the darkness to the east. Soon it was within the aura of light cast by the neon-lit fauna. It wasn't coming fast, but it was steady.

Matt said, "What's he carrying? They look like duckpin balls. I can't run a check on anything, right now. But I've captured the image so I can do that later. My best guess? Meteor orbs."

Art rolled his eyes.

Ellen explained, "Matt initially assumes everything unexplained is of extraterrestrial origin."

The tractor drove right across the parkland, toward Stonehenge. As quickly as it had been in Ben's field of vision, the Fordson was hidden behind the Stonehenge blocks.

"Right into their set-up," Matt said. "Right into their circle."

There was a terrific flash, and a huge, muffled, wet explosion. The air was filled with a burst of sparkling light as the plants came apart in pieces that were flung in a wide, glittering circle that seemed to reach across the whole of Galaxy Park, followed by another bright flash and a fine spray of moisture that spattered Ben and the others. The stalks and stems collapsed like tissue, their neon electrical systems gone black, seemingly short-circuited.

"None of the ladies are getting up," Matt said a minute later. "Can't tell if they're still being religious or if they're dead, but I'm thinking they're dead. They don't look right. One of them had to move to get out of the tractor's way, and she's down on her back after that second flash.

"Damn," Ellen said, "Crap on the camera."

Ben said, "What just happened?"

"I don't know," Matt said. "Gunk on my eye cameras, too. I'm looking at the tapes right now."

The plant-like things inside the Stonehenge ring were all but gone. The remaining stalks wavered and collapsed, disintegrating as they fell. The Fordson tractor could be heard running inside the circle of blocks, but it wasn't long before the engine choked and stopped.

With the neon lighting gone along with the plants, Ben had a better view of the whole of the Galaxy Park again. It was so strange a sight, and it seemed contained. There didn't seem to be any danger of whatever happened there spreading beyond the zone it was in. When Ben looked around, other people were still standing there, watching the spectacle with their phones out, recording it all. They couldn't dial out, but they could still capture the moment. A few people were running over to check on what had happened to the social club ladies.

"Let's see if we can get some footage," Art said. "Or if we can help."

"Clean off some of my lenses, too, if you have a chance," Matt said.

Ben rubbed his arm, and found the moisture on his skin was gone, evaporated already.

As he followed after them, Ben said, "I don't understand. Was that part of the show? Was that a show?"

They headed for Stonehenge, and had just heard a guy in that direction yelling out that he was stuck and couldn't get his foot out of the something there when Ben felt his stomach turn violently. Another two steps and his brow was wet with perspiration. He wiped his forehead with his wrist, and took a third step. His body went weak, and he collapsed to the ground.

"Oh . . . ," he said.

He heard Matt on the radio saying, "It looks like one of the social club ladies is still alive, and that someone chased her into whatever it is that is left where those plants collapsed. Inside the inner ring of stone blocks, it looks like a pool of goo."

Ben pushed himself up to sitting, embarrassed, about to ask the others to hold on a minute, when he realized Art and Ellen were down on the concrete ahead of him. His arms were weak, almost quivering.

"It looks like she's stuck there," Matt said. "Can't move her legs. I wouldn't go over there, if I were you. Two guys who went in to grab her arms and pull her out are both stuck there, too. It's like a great big glue trap."

Ellen vomited violently, and Art did too. They both looked in disgust at what they had just thrown up, and threw up again.

Ben threw up, too. It was the worst thing he had ever felt in his life. His heart pounded, and all the sound went out of his world. He looked down to see a dark, stringy pile in front of him. It smelled like nothing he had ever smelled before. It resembled black, wiry pieces of metal. He threw up again and it was like he was blind—the world around him vanished. It was such a pure, inescapable pain that at that moment he couldn't have said whether or not he was in Galaxy Park, South Dakota, or any other place in the world. Maybe he'd never left North Carolina. He closed his eyes.

In his imagination, he saw the night sky, a heavy, liquid darkness populated with flashing lights, brilliant and fiery white. He couldn't look away from the stars, couldn't look down or around to see where he was standing. He felt there were others around him, watching the same scene, but he couldn't turn to see who they were.

Looking up at the stars, he thought he could detect subtle differences in shades between them, some darker, some redder, some brighter, and some further away. His eyes settled on one that stood out against the field of black and shades of white. It was blue. It was not a star. It was Earth, seen from the edge of the solar system, so appealingly blue compared to the lights around it—how could it not attract someone's attention?

Ben blinked.

He was in a cabin in a forest in the mountains. It was daytime. Outside the window he could see rows of dead, grey trees. It did not smell like the forest or the mountains. It smelled unpleasant, almost like dead things, but there were strange chemicals in the mix, too. When he looked back from the window, where the stars were visible, he wasn't in the room alone.

The most terrifying man he had ever seen was standing in front of him. Old and chalky and dirty and dressed like he just got back from dying in the 1900s.

"They're farmers, like us," he said, his thick accent making the words difficult to understand. "They found their plot. They put a fence around it. They formed it according to their needs. They cleared it of predators. They hoed their rows and planted their seeds and waited for them to grow, helping in what ways they could. A part of them resides in all of us.

"But the seeds are corrupted, and the crop needs to be culled. They're not going back to the way things were before they were here. Their hooks are too deep. This world is theirs."

Then the man, the room, the cabin, all of it was gone.

Ben was back in his home in South Dakota. It was nighttime. Zoe was asleep, and he was doing his last sweep through the house, turning off lights, dead-bolting the front door, and latching the windows. He turned off the light in the kitchen, and there was only one lamp left, the one in the living room, which he would pass on his way to the bedroom. With the windows closed, the house smelled musty.

When he walked into the living room, his mother was there, sitting in a rocking chair that he didn't remember owning. She smiled at him, a warm smile, as if she saw him every day. She even chuckled at his look of surprise. She nodded her head toward the clock on the wall. It was a digital clock, showing the time 5:06 a.m. While he was watching, the 6 turned into a 7. 5:07.

She said, "Ben, if you're not out of the house by the time the clock turns to 8, it'll all be over."

Ben woke up, as if from a bad dream. He was still in the South Dakota house, in his bed, in his bedroom. It was dark outside. The lights were off. He looked over at Zoe, next to him in the bed, and smiled at how peaceful she looked. His eyes drifted up to the alarm clock beside the bed, reminding him of the digital clock he'd just seen in his dream. It showed the time 5:05 am.

He panicked instantly. His mother's words fresh in his mind, he momentarily considered waking Zoe up, but the 5 changed to a 6 and instead he announced, "I'm sorry if this is a false alarm, but we have to get out," and he picked her up and headed out of the bedroom, charging through the living room as she woke up in his arms. It seemed not only like he was moving slowly, but also that time was rushing past him.

Zoe's eyes were wide with worry as he crossed the kitchen. The door was locked. She reached out to turn the deadbolt, and he was sure they were going to make it . . . until Zoe hesitated, her hand inches from the knob. The earthquake started with a roar. The clock had turned . . .

When Ben came to he was curled on the concrete in a fetal position. He had no idea how long he had been in this delirious, shaking, sweating, vomitous state. He thought of Zoe, and hoped she would be all right without him, but thought the dream was telling him that it was already too late. He hoped that she might be able to reach out to their siblings and that they would support each other when he was gone. Otherwise, she would be alone.

Ellen, coughing, said, "What the fuck was that?"

Matt's voice coming in over the walkie-talkie was somehow comforting. "You guys okay?"

Art said, "You saw that?"

"Yeah, it's been like fifteen minutes since you guys went down. I guess I . . . I might have phased out for a little while."

Art said, "What does that mean? Did you get sick?"

"No," Matt said. "Just saw some things in my head. We'll save it for my next session with the shrink."

Ben stood up. He felt shaky, but surprisingly better than he thought he should feel. It felt like he'd maybe cleared it out, although he would have to wait and see.

Ellen stood up. "Oh, so much better," she said.

Art asked Matt, "And?"

"And, well, sorry to tell you this, but I think there was something in whatever it was that sprayed you. I think it was either in the spray or something transmitted by those flashing lights."

"No shit," Art said, spitting. "What was it?"

"If I was that guy in the movies who could rewind the film, study it, and arrive at a scientific explanation to tell you, I would. Unfortunately, I'm a guy with an A/V degree. I would guess the guy on the tractor had something that made their magic plants go boom. The only information I have other than that is a lot of dead bugs stuck to the cameras."

"They're all dead?"

"They're all dead. And they appear to be decomposing at an accelerated rate."

Ellen said. "What the hell?"

"So," Art said, "How many people got sprayed?"

"About 500 yards in every direction, with Stonehenge in the center. It hit every one of our spy eyes."

"So everybody here was exposed."

"Yeah," Matt said. "I think that literally everyone but me was outside watching."

Ben pictured someone in the sky spraying a blast of bug spray at a colony of people that looked like ants.

Art said, "What are you not saying?"

Matt answered, "Some people are down already. Some went down right after the plants came down, some while you were getting sick. It's all happening on my screens, so I don't know for sure if they are sick or dead other than the way people around them are reacting."

Ben, Art, and Ellen all looked at each other.

"It's not looking too good at the front end of the park."

They decided to return on the route they'd taken from the hotel.

It was only a few minutes before they came upon the family they had passed on the way in. The older man was laid out flat on the ground. One of the wives, and the younger man, maybe her younger brother, sat by the body. Off a bit, and watching them anxiously, were the other wife and all five of the children. One kid was holding his stomach like it hurt. Ben thought the older man was the father of the woman seated next to him, the younger man, and at least one of the other adults in their group—either the woman standing with the kids or one of the two men who'd been there earlier.

"Hello? Can everyone hear my voice?," someone said over the microphone off in the distance. "We're going to ask everyone in the area—everyone—to meet over on the street in front of the stage in the next 5–10 minutes. I repeat, we are asking everyone in the Galaxy Park area to return to the parking lot and the street in front of the hotel. Let's get moving, people."

Ben wondered if that was Elias.

As they approached the family, the woman by the body said, "My father just collapsed after that explosion. My husband and my sister's husband went to get help." She was crying, and so was the man next to her.

Ben looked at the sister. She looked like she was afraid to come near the other three, and she didn't want the kids near them, either.

"What happened?" The younger brother was angry. "Everything was perfect. Why did they have to do that?" He gestured toward Stonehenge. "What was that?"

Ben said, "I know as much as you do. We're going to go see what we can find out. I'm sorry about your father."

The woman near the body started crying anew as they walked away.

The speaker repeated the message again, adding this time,

"Please do not bring any bodies to the street. We will organize teams to collect them. If you are still able to walk, please come join us immediately."

"Matt," Art said, "How many people are dead so far?"

"So, yeah, maybe 50. A lot of the older folks went right away. Just collapsed."

Ben guessed that Ed and Martin and Dot and Walt were all dead on the hotel restaurant's patio.

"There were also a number of what I think were coronary-related incidents after the first group dropped."

Ben noticed a sleeping bag on the ground about 20 feet to the right, lying on concrete. Clearly someone was having sex in there. There was no hiding the humping movements. One last screw before the end of the world? Or just oblivious to everything that was going on around them? He decided it must be the second, because in the first case, knowing death was impending would definitely be an obstacle to completion.

He was slightly curious who might be in there. He thought briefly of the blond model and Christy—it could just as easily be them as anyone else. Why did that idea bother him?

There was a large group of college kids and models playing what looked like a game of football over to the right. They seemed unconcerned with whatever might be happening outside of the end zones.

Although they were no longer very close to Stonehenge, the structures there still blocked some of Ben's view of parts of the park. They had to walk a short distance farther before the view of the landscape toward the hotel opened up, making the dark corner of the park where they'd just spent the last hour seem tranquil in comparison. They could see the street and the back of the professional services building. There was the parking lot. There were people down all over the landscape, and clusters of people all around, and a lot of other people racing from one place to another, from one cluster to another, the lights from their cell phones and flashlights bouncing erratically with them as they went.

Ben understood that was what they all were to whoever had done this: ants.

Wasn't this what happened when he sprayed an anthill? First, a lot of them died right away. Then there was a portion of the colony that the poison took a little longer to kill. Their movements slowed, but they didn't die. Some of that group would try to head back toward the anthill, but wouldn't make it. And last there were the scurriers, the ones on the edge of ground zero, the ones that seemed like they might have been immune or might not have been in range of the spray. These were the ones that returned to the anthill dragging other ant bodies, still strong enough to make it back inside, and healthy enough to deliver their poison-laced bounty to the queen before they, too, succumbed.

While Ben was standing there, absorbing the scene, they were passed by the woman and the five children they had seen near the body of the old man. They were with a man. Ben thought perhaps it was the woman's husband. Her face was pained, intensely concerned as she clutched the youngest in her arms. The father, too, was grim-faced, and he too was tightly holding one of the kids. Some of the children had tears in their eyes, but the rest were wide-eyed as they surveyed the scene.

One of them said, "Mommy, my stomach hurts," and although the mother told him she was sorry, that it would be all right, her eyes bulged with fear.

"Oh, no," Ben said to himself. His first inkling of how bad this was really going to be.

Ben understood the look on the Mom's face. What could they do? Where could they go? Both parents would do anything at this point, anything that would give any one of their family members a chance.

Ben looked back the way they had come. It looked as if the other woman was lying on the old man's body, and her husband was there, discovering that she was gone, too. The younger man had his face in his hands.

Ben turned away. He wanted to run away also.

More than anything right now, he wanted the eclipse to end. He wanted one thing to return to normalcy. How long did a lunar eclipse last? To him it had seemed to have lasted forever already. It had started to seem like the moon wasn't ever going to come back. What if this were what it would be from here on in? Endless night.

There were two loud noises behind them. Instinctively, Ben ducked down. Gunshots. Ellen gasped. Now four bodies were in a pile, the husband on his wife, the younger brother on top.

The sound of gunfire would continue sporadically, from random locations around Galaxy Park, for the next thirty minutes.

Ben longed to see the face of the moon lit up again.

Why was he here, really? Rose Chamber was gone. Nothing he had learned here would physically change anything in his life. Why couldn't he just have been content to build a home and a life of his own? What really was he going to get out of knowing even a little tiny bit more than he did the day before?

He would ask Zoe, "Doesn't it matter to you who you are?"

"Yes, it does," she would say. Something along the lines of, "It matters so much to me that I don't want anything to mess with it anymore. I know who I am. I know what my whole life has been up to now. Knowing where I was born isn't going to change who I am."

"It doesn't matter that it has all been a lie?"

"What is a lie?" Zoe said, "The life I've lived hasn't been a lie. The lies started before we were even born."

"Everything she told us is potentially a lie."

"Everything we experienced with her was true. It was real. This is the person I became because of it. Anyway, isn't that what adopted kids all want to think? That there is some better, truer life they could be living? That their real parents are some sort of awesome, rich, well-connected near-celebrities who have been waiting all this time to be reunited? I'm not kidding myself with all that. We had a good mother looking after us growing up—she took care of us and raised us well."

He asked her, "If it was so great, why did you leave?"

"You weren't the only one who was tired of living in the middle of nowhere," she said. "I just wanted more . . . choices . . . than I could see myself having there. I didn't want to leave because it was so terrible that I had to get out. I was just, I don't know, ready to go—it could have been then, it could have been five years later. It was going to happen. But when you said you were going, I knew I was going, too. It felt right that way."

Maybe, Ben thought, he did feel guilty about leaving. Guilty about his relationship with Zoe. Guilty about any hurt he had caused his family. They really had never done anything but be his family, with all the good and bad, fun and frustration that all that entailed. Maybe this search for the truth was a way of justifying his choices after the fact. To maybe confirm he had been right to abandon his mother and his family, to take up with Zoe, to ignore whatever impact that would have on them. The one thing that seemed true in Ben's life had been Zoe, and he wasn't going to let her go.

Chapter 19

When Ben, Art and Ellen were only a short distance from the street, they came across a middle-aged woman who asked them for help carrying the large body of her fallen husband over to the street where everyone was meeting.

Ben said, "Ma'am, I don't think we should be handling the bodies without the right protection."

She glared at him. "I'm not going to leave him here."

He thought about it. If it were him, the last thing he would want would be Zoe dragging his dead body with her.

"I'm sorry," Ben said. "They'll figure out a way to help you out."

"They won't," she said, "No one will. We're on our own."

"Ladies and gentlemen, everybody present here, my name is Elias and I am a police officer. Thank you all for gathering here. I know that what is happening here is incredibly stressful, and we are going to need to work together if we are gong to get through this. Together.

"We don't know what we were all exposed to, but I believe and my partners agree that we have to assume that whatever it was, we do not want to go out into the world and expose our loved ones to it without having a better idea of what it is.

"One of the officers who was working here tonight has already left with the intention of contacting folks who can get us the medical attention that we might need."

There were about a hundred people up and down the street. Most that Ben saw looked haggard even in the dark. A few were leaning on others for support, or sitting because they couldn't stand up. Everyone looked worn and unwell. Ben assumed it was the combination of stress and very bad lighting, until he saw one of the models doing a subtle double take when he walked by Art. Ben looked at Art and realized that Art didn't have that same look about him that the others had, and neither did Ellen. They looked fine.

"What we want to do now is get organized so that when help does arrive," Elias continued, "we can direct them to the people who need them the most. So to that end we are going to be making a list of every person present, and ranking all of you in terms of your condition.

"We will not be opening the parking lot until we have been reviewed by health personnel. As I said before, if we have been exposed to something, then we do not want to go and expose others to it until we understand that it is safe to do so. If you are thinking you can make it out of here on foot, there really aren't enough officers present to stop you, but the end result is you will be that much farther from help when you most need it and when it arrives here."

In a low voice, Ben said to Art, "Do you think all these people threw up like we did?"

Art said quietly, "I don't know. If your question is do you look as unhealthy as everyone else here does? No."

After Elias repeated his request that people stay in the area, reminding them that someone would be coming by to get their names and information, he thanked them, and walked purposefully up the street. Some people watched him as he went, but most seemed to be more focused on how crappy they felt, or how poorly someone with them was doing.

This, Ben thought, was where the movies got it wrong. There was not going to be a riot or an insurrection. The people here weren't going to break into factions, start tearing each other apart in panic, or stampede for the exit. Everyone felt like crap. No better way to incapacitate a person than through their stomach. Why would aliens try to take the planet with military force when an alien stomach flu might work better? If there were samples of Ebola and the plague in labs on this world, a person probably couldn't imagine what an ancient race of extraterrestrials had sitting in their test tubes. In the movies, it was usually the aliens that got sick from human germs. In reality, Ben thought as he looked at the crowd, it would be like the Native Americans' immune systems facing off against European germs—a battle for which no one on Earth was prepared.

Ben had his eye on Elias as he headed in Ben's direction, and grew increasingly uncomfortable as the distance between Elias and himself grew shorter and shorter. When Ben realized Elias was going to pass right in front of him, he tried to turn away, but didn't get more than a couple steps before Elias was standing right in front of him.

"Ben," Elias said, his voice surprisingly calm. "Hey. It is you." The two shook hands.

Ben didn't know what to say. He managed a sickly, drawn out, "Yeah . . ."

Elias looked over Ben's face, although Ben wasn't sure for what. Elias had the same look about him as everyone else. He was sick, too.

"Come with me," Elias told him.

Ben didn't know what to say. "Okay?"

Moments later they were headed down the street at a fast pace, cutting across a corner of the Galaxy Park land to the post with the park legend, and then walking toward the planets.

"I'm sorry about your Mom, Ben," Elias said as they passed Mercury. "She was a great little lady. After my Mom died, she started having me over for lunch every once in a while." He smiled. "She was smoking weed sometimes, for her glaucoma, and she used to really try to clean up all evidence of it before I'd come by, and then we'd walk in the garden and pass by a giant weed plant she was cultivating." He laughed, shaking his head. "I just . . . well, there's worse things people do and for worse reasons. I never told anyone."

Somewhere near Jupiter, they passed two women, maybe in their 30s, who were sitting off the road, on either side of a body, talking. They looked over at Elias and Ben, but kept talking instead of responding to their presence.

Ben didn't know what to say. They all sort of acknowledged each other with their eyes. The farther they walked, the more Elias seemed like he had a slight limp.

When they passed Pluto, they came to the open gate. Elias went and grabbed one of the gate arms, and pulled it around until it was closed. He did the same with the other arm. He was breathing heavily with the exertion. There was an old chain, no padlock, hanging from one of the arms, and he wrapped that around a rod on the other arm, so that it looked closed.

"You think people are going to try to rabbit."

"Hope not. This won't stop them if they're determined. Might make the first few turn back."

They turned around and started back. As they neared Jupiter, they saw that the two women had decided to try to move the body of the third.

One of them said, "Just over to the road." There was something odd about the brush they were moving through. They would step on a plant, or brush against a bush, and it would fall apart. It had all been green this morning, when Ben had walked by it. Now it all looked dead.

They picked up the body of a woman who looked much older than either of them. One woman held the ankles, and the other had her hands under the shoulders. They took a step and one woman said, "She feels soft and wobbly," and they took another step before both of the woman's legs separated from the rest of the body.

One of the women said, "Oh, shit!" Both of them fell backward, screaming. Ben didn't see any of the blood he expected would result. The one holding the legs dropped them, still screaming, and the one holding the body dropped it to the ground, where it separated into a few pieces, as if whatever had been binding it together was gone.

Elias kept walking while their screaming turned into sobs. From a distance came the sound of a gun report.

One of the women wailed, "Jesus! Is that what's going to happen to us?"

Ben stared at the women, feeling he should do something. There just seemed to be literally nothing he could do for them. He hurried to catch up to Elias.

With Ben walking beside him, Elias said, "I loved your sister. I still love your sister." He thought about it a moment and said, "Damn. Feels nice to say it out loud. Never thought it would. I think she always knew, but I never told her. Not straight out, at least—more like in a code she couldn't break. So I might as well have never loved her, I guess," he shrugged. "She knew it, and even though I was crazy about her, looked forward to seeing her, wrote poetry about her, sometimes even imagined my ex was her during . . . you know . . . I couldn't admit it to myself that it wasn't just about the chase, like it had been with most every girl before. I told myself it was because of Richard that I held back, that I loved her so much that I wasn't going to wreck everything else in her life just to have her. The truth is, somewhere in there I might have had a chance—she might have loved me, too, but I was so into my own head that I didn't even see it until it was too late."

"I didn't know," Ben said. There two more gunshots from somewhere in the park. Elias winced slightly at the sounds.

"Richard's a good guy. A steadier guy for her than I would have been. Although, maybe being with her made him better than he was before. Maybe I would have wanted to be better if I'd been with her, I don't know. Or maybe I would have raised her up, too, if I was with her. I think I wouldn't be a police officer without her pushing me just to keep up with her. She helped me figure out my life by making the job seem worthwhile."

They were almost back to the street.

"Listen," Elias said. "Your sister and your mom were both hurt when you and your sister ran away. Lily and I would have come after you if your mom hadn't insisted that we didn't. Your mom thought if we found you and dragged you back, it would tear your relationship apart and you would just leave again, this time with anger in your hearts. She knew that you wouldn't be as easy to catch the next time. She was a smart lady."

"We didn't leave to hurt anybody," Ben said. "It was time for new lives for us."

He stared at Ben. Ben didn't know if Elias had heard what he had said.

Elias said, "I wish I'd seen her one more time is all. I could have done that, but I was afraid to, for a lot of reasons that I had to work really hard to come up with. Now I wonder why I was making so many damn excuses."

In the fifteen minutes they were gone, the crowd had nearly dissipated. Not only had people dispersed, heading off to places where they would rather die than on the street, but also there were more bodies all over. There were a couple groupings of people crying, groaning in discomfort, moaning in pain, and there were even more of what Ben could call stunned survivors, solitary folks sitting here and there who looked like they'd lost anyone and everyone they cared about, sick themselves and overwhelmed by it all.

Ben thought, This is what the ant colony looked like slightly more than forty-five minutes following the application of the spray. No one was scurrying about any more.

Ben saw a woman with dark hair who was obviously in great pain being helped to a sitting position on the ground by another woman and a man, neither of whom looked much better. After staring at the dark-haired woman, the man pushed himself to his feet and started walking toward the parking lot. He didn't hurry, and it seemed to take some effort, but he got there just the same. He climbed between the metal bars of the gate, went to his Buick, and started it up, which caught Elias' attention.

He was blocked in, so he tried to get out by smashing his way out, first accelerating into the car parked ahead of him, then slamming in reverse into the car parked behind him. He did this about six times and managed to clear enough space to get over to the gas station at the back of the parking lot. From the gas station, he drove over the curb, onto the main street. At some point he was driving over bodies. It was senseless, because the street he was driving down was a dead end and the direction he was headed was the opposite of the way he would have to drive his car to get out of Galaxy Park. More, Ben had expected the guy to stop to pick up his female companions, but he cruised right on by them.

The few people remaining in the street tried to clear off of it as he drove down the block. The cop at the end of the street yelled for the driver to stop. When the driver did not slow down, the officer tried to pull his gun, but instead collapsed as the car accelerated toward him.

Then there were two shots fired, and the car immediately lurched as it stopped accelerating. It continued down the street at a slow speed, curving slightly to the right until it came to a stop against the brick front of the professional services building with a crunch of metal.

It was Elias who had fired the shots. He limped over to the other cop, who was down on the street.

Two men ambled into the street to look at one of the bodies that had been run over. Ben saw that there was no blood.

One of them kicked at one of the bodies, and whatever he kicked broke off, rolled about a foot, and then broke down completely into crumbled pieces. Ben looked at the two women the man in the Buick had left behind. The eyes of the one they'd helped get seated were closed, and it seemed like she was gone. The other was crying soundlessly into her hands, her whole body shaking.

Art and Ellen were watching it all from the sidelines, standing quietly among the dead plants in the hotel's front garden. More than before, up close they looked young and fresh compared to everyone else. Seemingly well aware of this, they were keeping to themselves, back a bit from the street, shaded by an awning from the hotel's lighted windows. Art had the rim of his cap pulled down over his eyes and Ellen had her hoodie over her head. Ben told them about the women he'd seen when he walked with Elias, the ones who tried to move the body, and the way the body had fallen apart.

"Matt's been calling it mulching," Ellen said quietly. "That's what he said happened to the bugs on his lenses. Decomposed into dirt."

Ben spoke in a low voice for what he said next.

"What is doing this? Who did this?"

Ellen said, "An old man with a couple bombs? A group of cultists? The United States government? Aliens? An unnamed corporation? It's the standard conspiracist's list."

"More questions than when we started," Art said. "We were following the women. I don't think this is what they intended. I don't think they planned to die. Maybe someone else didn't like what they were up to?"

Ellen snorted, "Like Monsanto?"

"Why are we the only ones who aren't displaying symptoms? Why are we the only ones who threw it up? Do you know?"

Art said, "We don't know."

"But you know something about this."

"Believe it or not, this is a new frontier for me, Ben. I came here expecting to investigate something I didn't understand. I didn't know it would be this."

Ben couldn't imagine people voluntarily exposing themselves to something like this. Or risking that it might kill them instead of making them puke.

Ben asked, "What did you see when you were throwing up?"

Ellen and Art both stared at him, then looked at each other.

Art said, "You saw something?"

Ellen said, "Yeah. You did?"

Ben said, "I saw an old man who I think said aliens did this."

Ellen said, "I didn't see anything like that, but, weirdly, that was the message I got from my dream, too."

"Maybe mine started out kind of like that," Art said, "but then it dissolved into another murder attempt by my mother against me." Ben noted this was the second time Art had mentioned his mother trying to kill him.

Art somehow recognized what Ben was thinking.

"That's another thing to worry about on another day when there aren't things going on," Art said. "Besides, I was at least five years older in my dream. I've got some time to prepare."

When Elias had turned off the Buick, he walked to where Ben, Art, and Ellen were standing. He was limping more dramatically when he reached them. He looked like he was in pain.

"I wish you could tell Lily that I want her to have a good life. That she made my life a better life to live, just by being herself. I had a bad time a couple months back, after your mom died. I was ready to go and propose to Lily, even though she's married, just out of the blue go try to talk her into starting a new life with me. Realized I still have a lot of unsettled stuff inside. Tell her it didn't mean anything." He studied Ben's face. "You don't look as bad off as I feel. Maybe you will be able to tell her that."

"I'll tell her if I can."

"Thanks, Ben." For a moment, he shed tears with his eyes squeezed shut. "I'm sorry," he said, and looked regretful. "I shouldn't put this on you. You don't have to say anything. I don't feel well is all, with all this going on. I'm okay with how things turned out with Lily. I know it's for the best. I know we weren't ever in love. I know we weren't meant to be."

He was lying and it clearly pained him.

You love her, Ben thought. I wonder if Lily loves you?

Elias turned and walked off. They watched him limp up the street. He went over to the stage area, and sat down on a folding chair, his arms resting on his knees as he leaned forward.

He closed his eyes for a moment.

Then he leaned back, pulled out his gun, and shot himself in the head. His body collapsed forward, slid off the chair, and fell to the ground.

This did not cause the commotion or despair Ben would have expected among those remaining. Most everyone still alive had withdrawn, either alone or with their dead loved ones. For the most part, they all stayed where they were, waiting for their turns to die. Ben, Art, and Ellen did the same, standing a silent vigil in front of the hotel. It wouldn't be long before it seemed that it was just the three of them left.

A sliver of the moon was visible, glowing in the sky.

Ben thanked whatever powers there were that had kept him alive this long. He wanted to go home now.

Matt said he was coming down. The hotel had locked its doors, and he was the only one left to let them in. After he opened the doors, he walked out to the street, but looked decidedly uncomfortable about it.

"Let's see if I get sick, too," he said.

Ben thought about this as they entered the hotel. Something about Art, Ellen, and himself had protected them from whatever this was. What made Matt so sure he was immune, too? What did he share in common with the other two that made him so confident? What did all four of them share in common?

As they walked through the lobby, Ben looked out into the patio area and saw Ed and Martin's bodies were in their spots, slumped over the table. There was no one at the reception desk, and Ben wasn't even tempted to look behind it. Matt showed no similar reservations, going behind the desk and, after a minute, stepping away from it with a videocassette in his hand.

Ben said, "So you're afraid to walk outside, but not afraid to walk around the bodies?"

Matt said, "Yeah, I guess that's true. I'd have it by now if it were still out there. Or if it were contagious."

They were a somber group, silent on the elevator going to their floor. On autopilot, Ben followed them to their room, most of which had already been dismantled and placed in bags around the room. He'd been running on adrenaline since he'd gotten sick, and now he felt it starting to catch up with him. Had that only been an hour ago?

Ben was still stunned as they grabbed the equipment. He felt like he was still playing catch-up.

"What . . . Why are we still alive?"

"Listen," Art said, "we're getting ready to leave. If you have anything in your room . . . " Ellen and Matt were zipping up duffel bags and setting items that were ready by the door.

"Oh, right," Ben said. He jogged up the hall to his room. Everything was packed because he'd never really unpacked. He threw the investigator's report into his bag, zipped up the bag, and then headed out the door with it. The others were also coming out of their room, each carrying multiple bags. Ben joined them as they headed to the elevator.

When they were down on the street, Ben tried to ignore and avoid looking at any bodies as they walked to the parking lot. Art went to the gate and unwrapped the chain that held the gate arms together. He and Matt pulled them open. The four of them went to the K-NOX van, which was parked near the front of the lot, and Ellen and Matt loaded all of their equipment inside.

"Oh, I almost forgot," Ellen said. She reached into one of her bags, pulling out a small remote. She pressed the red button on it.

"Googly eyes deactivated," she said.

Ellen and Matt climbed into the front two seats, and Ben was going to follow Art in through the side door when Art turned to face him.

"Let me ask you a question, Ben," Art said. "Is your mother still alive?"

"I'm not sure. The woman who raised me just died. She was the only one who knew who my mother was."

"Interesting."

"Why?"

"Well, we think the truth is that who your mom is makes you special. Especially, it seems, on a night like tonight. I thought you were one of us the first time I saw you." He tapped his temple with his pointer finger. "Now we know.

"If I had any idea who you are or where you came from or how you happened to be here tonight, then I would be able to bring you along with us. But we can't take chances with unknowns."

"What?" Ben took a step backward. "No, you're kidding."

"I wish I was. We don't know who you are."

"What is going on? What is all this? What happened here? Are you kidding? Are you really Art Sinclair?"

"Are you really Ben Nelson?"

Ben didn't answer.

"We're trying to figure all this out, too. This is not what we expected." Art shook his head. "How could we expect this?"

"You said this happened before," Ben said.

"Something different. Same end result," Art said. "A lot of empty homes left behind. But that was one town. Tonight, there were 50 events like this going on. That was just a small handful of those women, when there were hundreds of others headed to those other sites. What if this is just one out of fifty crazy happenings tonight? What if the scale of this is growing?"

Art paused, took a breath.

"Sorry. Getting myself worked up. I didn't think I was coming here to watch people die."

Ben thought about it.

"You're talking about that town in California. But I don't remember reading about people turning into mulch."

"Anyway," Art deflected, "I'm confident our paths will cross again. But we have to go without you."

Ben thought about it.

Maybe he didn't want to be a part of whatever they were a part of. That was all he needed—more people keeping secrets from him, more secrets to keep from everyone else. All he wanted was to get back to Zoe. Going with them was obviously not the path that would take him there.

"Fine."

"Good. One other piece of advice. I'd clear out of here soon. You'll have to take my word for it—survivors tend to come under scrutiny. I don't know that they will ever let you go if they find you here and everyone else dead." He pulled out a K-NOX cap from one of his bags, handed it to him. "If you put this on, they won't be able to see your heat signature as easily from the sky."

Then Art was in the van, and the side door was sliding

closed and locking, and the van was pulling out.

Ben watched the lights of their vehicle pulling away. When they reached the end of the planets, the van paused for Art and Matt to open that gate as well. Then they were around a bend and gone from sight.

Ben looked around Galaxy Park, and knew he was not going back there. Art's last words of warning about the authorities echoed in his head.

They would want to know, wouldn't they? An eyewitness to what had occurred here? The government would be able to find him anyway, wouldn't they? Hit rewind on a satellite surveillance tape, and watch the death of everyone in a small valley, maybe in infrared. They would see there were four heat signatures left, and that three of them took off in a van, leaving only him for miles around.

Where would they track that last person going? He slid the strap for his bag over his shoulder and started walking toward the mountains to the East. It was the stillest, quietest night he had ever heard. Everything around him was dead.

He was going to be retracing his escape from childhood, was what it was going to be.

Not far from the park legend, inside that tangle of rebar that was supposed to be a crashed rocket ship, Ben found a teenage girl seated on the ground with her arms crossed, her elbows on her knees, her head in her hands. In front of her was a pile of the black stuff she'd thrown up.

She was maybe 16 or 17. When she looked up to see who was approaching, he saw that she did not look sick. He also found that he couldn't simply walk away.

"Are you okay?"

"I feel better now," she said. "Except my foster family is gone. Everyone is gone. Again."

"I know. Everyone but us. And I want to be gone too. Can

you stand up? Can you walk?"

She stood up in the tangle of rusted metal.

"Do you want to leave here?"

"I don't have anywhere to go," she said.

"We'll find someplace that isn't here."

He looked at the girl.

"What's your name?"

"Emily," she said.

"Emily," he repeated.

"Emily," she said again.

"Well, Hi, Emily. I'm Ben. I hope you're good at walking. We've got a ways to go."

She looked at him doubtfully.

"You can't stay here, Emily."

"I'm afraid you'll hurt me. I don't know who you are. I don't want to stay and I don't want to go. I'm scared."

"I'm going to start walking," Ben said. "I hope you will come with me. I don't want to hurt you. I won't hurt you. All I care about is getting away from here. I won't feel right about it if I leave you. If you want to walk ten feet behind me the whole way, that's fine. I just don't think it's safe for anyone to stay here." He then decided he was going to play unfairly. "I don't know if whatever did this will be back . . . "

Her eyes widened.

" . . . but I'm not waiting to see. So, come with me. If you don't, I wish you well, but I'd go hide someplace good until the police come. If they come."

He started walking. He looked at the parking lot sign instead of the bodies of the two women he and Elias had passed less than half an hour ago. The sign read TOMORROW BECKONS. After he'd gone a little way farther, Emily started following behind. He nodded grimly to himself. The last two ants fleeing the anthill. Ben Nelson Chamber was headed home.

PART 4

Chapter 20

As agreed, ten days after the night of their first family dinner in years, the Chambers were getting ready for their first vacation together since most of the kids were in their teens. Joshua showed up at the house at noon and alongside Cole started loading the truck. Carolyn's suitcase and handbag had been set outside the front door.

"Geez, man," Cole said, "I thought I'd seen the biggest drinkers ever when I was in college, but this is another level of play entirely."

Joshua averted his eyes when Cole waited for a response. Joshua never liked to speak badly about family. It used to take some pushing for that to happen.

Cole continued, "It doesn't even tire her out! For a few minutes she'll seem like she's going down. She's leaning against something, or tilting over on the couch, but then she gets a lift from something out of somewhere and off she goes again."

"Well," Joshua said, "She always did like to party."

"That's not what this is. She's a drunk."

"Yeah, she sure is. In the past, Lily has tried talking to her some. It got worse after she married Don, and we didn't really see with our own eyes how much worse until after he died. He was hitting her, you know."

"How would I know?"

"Well, someone in town knew. Someone I know said he saw it once and I told Momma when I heard it, and that led to an all-out crazy scene here with Carolyn drunk and carrying on and on and on about me talking to Momma about her personal life. I was just about ready to hogtie her and she knew it and that's the only reason we got her off the property that night. She's civil with me most of the time, but when she gets real drunk it tends to surface again.

"Look here," Joshua said, leading Cole over to the hedge wall. "It's growing crazy slow, but it's growing. It's getting taller. Momma said it was a plant and that it would grow like a wall, but I didn't believe it—still only kind of believe it, but look at it."

The wood part of the hedge was about six inches thick, and there was no green to it anywhere except the top. Instead of feeling like wood or stem, it felt rough, like stucco. It looked manmade, Cole thought.

"What I've noticed," Joshua said, "is that it's porous—the way the branches grow over each other leaves a lot of little holes, almost too small to see unless you're actually looking for them."

There were, indeed, little pinholes, and in some places, notches in the wood.

"There's all kinds of things living in there. It's got its own ecosystem going in there."

While standing at the wall, they heard the sound of a tractor, an old tractor, running to the east.

"Oh, crap," Joshua said, "That one of those old guys driving his tractor up the road."

Cole asked, "Where's he coming from? Do people live over there now?"

"Not that I know of. Who knows? Maybe he's out for his Sunday drive. Some of the older guys around here just do it if they want to. If we get stuck behind him getting out of here, it's gonna hold us back an hour. Tell Carolyn to get a move on."

Had they remained only a short while longer before leaving, they would have seen a most unusual sight on the road near their home. No less than Wiltern Baylorson, or what was left of him. Awakened by a string of early morning tremors, he was now astride his classic Fordson tractor, headed west.

Cole had been to his brother's ranch, which was kept in a way that was nothing like the way Joshua kept things at home. Everything outdoors was manicured and perfectly in order. Inside, it was immaculate—even the garage. Cole had never known his brother to cook, to clean up after himself, to do his own laundry. He'd always acted like that was the others' responsibility, since he took care of so much of the outdoor physical work. At the ranch, he met two of his brother's workers, one of whom, Marco, not an English speaker, was clearly just crazy about Joshua, and happy to meet his younger brother.

Joshua had made nearly all of the furniture in the house, and everything had little flourishes, from the icebox built into the track-lit coffee table in the TV room to the unfolding spice rack in the kitchen to the bed frame with the attached nightstand, with drink holder, remote holster, and built-in clock.

Cole enjoyed spending time with Joshua. After five years of guys he hardly knew calling him Bro, and telling him he was like a brother to them—that was Tony all the time, until it wasn't—it was awesome to actually have a brother who lived up to the title. Cole felt like he could relax with Joshua, and they could laugh about people, and he knew awkward topics weren't going to come up, because God knew the last thing Josh wanted to do was start up something awkward.

Josh told him he knew Cole would need a bit to figure out a plan, but that he could make a job for him at his ranch. All Cole had to do was ask.

During the week, Cole had also gone with a morning-after sober Carolyn to eat at the Southern Baked restaurant and afterward to shop at the thrift store. The restaurant smelled like a fryer and of course the reason was that practically everything but the butter and the salad was dipped in batter and/or fried. Even the collard greens were served looking like potato chips.

At both jobs, Carolyn was very comfortable when she was on the floor. It wasn't that she did a big makeover or anything, but it was as if she underwent a personality adjustment. She hummed away happily when she was cooking, and she was a conscientious waitress without hovering. She made saucy jokes along the way, and didn't seem so much like a lush, just a happy worker having some fun.

Oh, my, Cole thought. Who is this person?

There were a few customers in the morning who seemed like regulars. He noticed that some of them, when they walked in the door, turned to a chalkboard on the wall, and pulled off a nametag. The nametags were napkins from the bar. He noticed that when his sister greeted them, she did check their nametags before giving each one a warm hello. She knew their personal stories, if not their faces, once she knew who they were, and they all seemed fine with that way of working it out.

At the thrift shop, Carolyn had urged him repeatedly to find clothes for himself. He found a bunch of stuff. She told him he should wear it out and burn his old stuff.

The thrift shop was busy.

She said, "Recession is a great sales tool."

The free shopping whetted his appetite. "I want to see the mobile home that's stuffed with the rest of the goodies."

"That's something I've been thinking about, Cole. Maybe I should be doing more with it. Are you good with computers? Maybe you could put it all online and sell it. What do you think?"

"Let me think about it," he'd said at the time.

Seated between Carolyn and Joshua in the front seat of Joshua's truck, Cole was hoping Carolyn wouldn't repeat the offer. He didn't have any excuse other than working for her doing inventory and selling thrift shop goods left by her ex-husband did not sound like something he wanted to do.

But shouldn't he do it, because he had nothing, and then

81

be in a better position for job-hunting later? It was hard to get work right now. But wouldn't it be weird working for her? And wouldn't he hate the work? Wouldn't Carolyn be great to work for until that day she got drunk? Wouldn't it change the dynamic in the relationship, where he would be more at her beck and call? Wouldn't he just hate her as his boss? Would it really feel like a legit job, or just doing someone else's busywork?

Carolyn wasn't drunk, but she still wasn't talkative at the start of the drive to the cabin, which was owned by Richard's family. Lily and the kids were driving there separately with Richard. Carolyn kept her head sort of turned toward the window, and when Joshua spoke to her—Cole was avoiding talking to her because he didn't want to poke at her when she was down—she answered in a purposefully measured tone.

Joshua said, "How you doing over there, little sis?"

Carolyn answered, "Well, I'm doing very well, big brother. How about you?" She leaned on the words big brother when she said them, but her tone was otherwise very measured. "How are you doing over there?" She was mirroring him.

Joshua and Cole both rolled their eyes.

Cole asked her, "Did you feel those tremors last night?"

"What time?"

"Maybe two this morning."

"No. Must have slept right through them. Big ones?"

"No. Little rumbles. Always a little worried they'll turn into something more, but it was mostly like a train rumbling by. Enough to wake me up, rattle things a little, that was it."

"I was having a bad day yesterday," she said, without turning to look at them. "I decided it was enough with Harris."

Joshua looked at her blankly.

"My latest boyfriend. Something was going on with him, I figured. I don't need to see it or provide him with evidence or prove it to him, that stupid son of a bitch. When he said 'Where's your proof?' I gave him fifteen minutes to get his things together and get the hell out. When 15 minutes wasn't enough time for him I started throwing what was left outside for him to pick up out there. I was pissed, and he was scared, so I was thinking somewhere in the back of my head maybe I'm not right, if he is this scared and he's sticking by his story. But I went ahead and did it, slammed the door on him.

"I went through the house, top to bottom, every room in the house, and found little remnants he'd left behind and I put them all together in a paper bag to set out with the rest of his stuff, and you know what? Half the stuff that we'd already dragged out? It was gone.

"I look around, look two houses up the block, and he's walking up the neighbor's walkway, and in through the door, and he's carrying an armful of his stuff. And the neighbor, I don't know who she is, she's got an armful of his stuff too, and the two of them walked right into her house."

"Oh."

"Yeah, I knew it was something like that. At least I can appreciate that he didn't sleep with me when he was screwing that dirty bird. So the whole situation there has me in not the best of moods. And I won't be drinking because nothing is worse for me than drinking when I'm on the down, no matter what anyone might say."

"I'd say sorry, Carolyn, but it sounds like you did the right thing," Joshua said.

"But, you know," Cole said after a few beats, "You sure do drink a lot."

"Thank you," she said, fluttering her eyelids. "You shouldn't pretend you're perfect."

"I'm not perfect."

She snorted. Cole didn't know where she was going with that.

"It's not normal to get drunk and sing on the roof in the middle of the night."

"Tell the roosters."

Joshua and Cole both smiled. Cole shook his head, but didn't say anything more.

"What about the Whelan girl," Carolyn said. "Did you go by to see her?"

"No, but I did go by to see her brother . . . "

"Wasn't there," Carolyn said under her breath.

". . . but he wasn't there. He's serving overseas right now, I guess."

Carolyn prodded, "Who told you this?"

"It was his sister," Cole admitted, bowing his head in mock shame.

"Erin," Carolyn said. "And what did you think?"

"I . . . "

"I?" Carolyn looked at him.

"I . . . "

Joshua looked away from the road, at his brother, chuckling.

"Got a problem there, brother?"

"Yeah, she's pretty hot. We dated once."

"I heard," Carolyn said sarcastically. "You were in diapers at the time."

Cole had gone over to find out about Sean's whereabouts, but it had been Erin who opened the door. They had gone to school together, him two years ahead of her, for about 10 years. They had dated for four days in high school, and if he remembered right, she broke up with him because a boy she'd had a bigger crush on for years had just broken up with his girlfriend and Erin wanted to go after him.

That was how he remembered it. Not that he had dwelled

on it—the fact that she was Sean's sister had added levels of complication that he was fine avoiding in high school.

Erin was in town for four days with four of her friends from school. They were just hanging around the house, doing homework, doing girl things, Erin said, getting away from campus life, which, as juniors, they were just about done with. There was something so very comfortable and real and normal about the group of them that he immediately wanted to stay, and he jumped at it when Erin asked if he wanted to hang out with them.

It was like going back to college for a couple hours. They sat in a group and all of them talked about anything that came up—school, politics, some movie half the girls had seen—and Cole felt like he had a better understanding of everyone in the room than he would have if he'd been meeting them one by one in small conversations at a party. They weren't drinking or smoking, because Erin's parents wouldn't have approved, but they giggled and laughed the whole time like they were all on something.

At some point Erin explained to him that his memory of their relationship was fuzzy. It was Shelley Mack who broke up with Cole because someone she wanted more became available. Erin had broken up with Cole because she could see that he just wanted to fool around with her, and she was too young for that, and Sean would kill him for it, friend or not. Erin said she knew that if she did fool around with Cole in any way, there was a good chance that, having conquered her, he would quickly move on to someone else. Likewise, she knew that if she said no, Cole would also move on to someone else. And he did! That bitch Jindi, as Erin told it—giggling the whole time—who Cole dumped before another week was over.

"Probably because Jindi wouldn't put out either," one of the girls said.

"Yeah, right," Erin said. "That is an unanswered question from childhood—did guys like you ever score?"

Cole couldn't even remember what Jindi looked like.

"Let's just say there were small accomplishments along the way that kept me at it, but never the prize I was searching for," he said.

"No one slept with you in middle school? Not even Dirty Mandy?"

"Ew," he said. "And no. Standards. No one from school, that was for sure. Remember that girl in my class who got pregnant at the beginning of senior year? They said it was a Homecoming conception." Cole smiled. "I think her name was Shari. She was like a daily service announcement for the girls in my grade about the dangers of premarital sex. I probably had one of the most chaste back country classes of the decade."

Something about a couple of the girls' comfort and closeness with each other had him speculating about their sexuality. He asked Erin about it when he followed her to the kitchen for a drink.

Erin clarified.

"No, they're not. Not that anyone has ruled anything out. I mean, who knows? I think they're keeping a respectful distance from you because they don't know what my relationship with you is. Who were you picturing was with who?"

"I don't know," Cole said ignoring the notion of defining his relationship with Erin. That had come up fast.

For some reason he let them weasel out of him some details about his living situation before he left California, his relationship with Trina, and then with Alexa and Zane. When he said they were models, the girls looked them up on their phones and debated over whether or not they were really that good looking. (They were.) He talked about how it started, and, weirdly, the mechanics of it. When he was only willing to go so far as to describe some aspects as being surprising and uncomfortable, he noted a couple of them were nodding along sympathetically. He told them about Zane's messages after the fact—how if he thought about the whole situation, it left him with a lot of confused emotions about his last months in California— and that he preferred not to respond to Zane or deal with it yet because it no longer seemed relevant to his life.

When he'd told them about his embarrassment about being naked with pretty people in any kind of light, a long funny discussion followed about nakedness, and being naked in front of other people for the first time, being naked in front of people that were notably more attractive, being naked in front of people who were notably less attractive, and reasons why at one point or another each of them had refused to take off their clothes in front of someone. They talked about how much more attractive a naked woman's body was than a man's, and then there was an extended session between the girls about the way clothed men most often were far more attractive than the same men naked and then they ran through examples and laughed and laughed for a long time.

Saying goodbye while they all stayed to talk, he assumed, at least for a little while, about him, he regretted having said anything personal about himself, while also feeling relieved to have said what he had said aloud. Even though he hadn't called Zane back, or texted him, Cole wasn't mad at him at all. He just didn't want the awkwardness that he assumed would be part of any conversation with Zane going forward. Not yet, at least. He wanted to get himself more settled, more secure, more . . . more . . . something. He had to figure out who he was going to be, and he needed to figure it out without that knot of relationship confusion as a distraction.

Erin walked him out the door and out to the driveway, stopping just short of the trees that held the hammock. He asked her not to share any of his personal stuff with her mom.

"Because you don't want her praying for your immortal soul? I'm sure she already is, Cole."

"No, it's just . . . I don't need it around here. In L.A., it's just one funky story in a neighborhood where there are several thousand weirdo stories within a short radius. It leaves no lasting impression there. Here, there's not enough of those stories getting out, so everyone just feeds on anything that comes along. It'll form the only impression they have of me."

"You don't want me to write a letter to Sean telling him you are ambivalently, ambiguously ambidextrous? Thanks, no. I'll let you do that." They both smiled.

"So, thanks for walking me out. Thanks for letting me be part of the normal world for a few hours."

"You know what? I might be back next week for a day or two. Sean's wife is going to fly out to see him and my Mom is watching his baby."

"Sean has a baby?"

"Yes, he does. I might need to be here to help out a day or two. If you see my car outside, stop by."

"Okay. Okay. I will."

"So," Cole asked Joshua, "You seeing anyone?"

"Nah."

"He's mooning over that girl," Carolyn said.

Joshua blinked slowly, shook his head slightly.

Cole asked him, "Is that true?"

"Yeah, maybe a little. I just . . . I just feel like I blew it."

"Blew what?"

"I think she was the One."

"The One that got away," Carolyn said. Was she needling him, or sympathizing? Cole wasn't sure.

"First rule: If she got away," Cole said, "then she wasn't the One."

"You know what? I used to believe that, too. But I don't think that's true now. She was the One. And I'm going to spend the rest of my life missing her, missing what could have been."

"You don't know," Carolyn said. "Everyday life with her might be different than chance flirtations. Most definitely would be. It's better this way. This way she can be more perfect in your mind than she could ever be in reality."

"I do know that I can't stop missing her," Joshua said. "Thinking about her. It's never gone away. I just feel like there is a place reserved for her, and it's empty, and it's always going to be empty. Shouldn't that feeling have gone away?"

"I don't know, Josh," Cole said. "I thought I'd been, you know, 'in love' before. But maybe I've just had crushes that had the potential to grow into more, if I'd let them. I've never been head over heels."

"The way I've been feeling," Joshua responded, "when 'in love' happens, it's not something you wonder if that's what it really is. It's ass-kicking."

Cole said, "How do you know that it's not just some crazy OCD form of a crush?"

Carolyn asked, "Is that how college kids describe lusting after someone?"

"Yeah, I guess so."

"College kids." She snorted.

"I think I know what I'm feeling," Joshua said.

"Yeah, okay," Cole said. "I feel like you should be more hopeful. You're a great guy, and there's a lot of fish in the sea. But I'm sorry you're feeling that way."

"Me, too," Joshua said. "I'd rather have never met her if I was going to end up feeling like this."

"Except . . . well, you would never have met her."

"Exactly. The quality of my life would be diminished, but I wouldn't know it."

"Are you, you know, seeing anyone while you're holding out hope for her? Because that's the best cure."

"I've fucked a few of the ladies in town. Nothing regular, no one regular, just happens once in a while."

"Lovely," Carolyn said to the window.

"A guy's gotta do," Joshua said.

"At least until something better comes along," Cole said. "I get it." Carolyn snorted again, and looked at them both, shaking her head, then returned to staring out the window.

Chapter 21

Lily had worried about the family trip from the moment it was decided upon. She worried Carolyn would get drunk and lose control of her mouth in front of the kids. She worried Joshua and Carolyn would argue. She worried about bringing enough food and about coordinating the timing of the ride over so she could pick up the kids and Richard and still be at the cabin before her siblings, and she worried that someone was going to notice she and Richard were away for the weekend and rob their house. Sometimes she thought that she encouraged herself to fret, because the anxiety was the best way to motivate her to action.

She developed back-up plans. When her siblings arrived at the cabin, and she was showing Joshua to his room, she told him that she and Richard wanted him to build a swing set and jungle gym for the backyard of their house. Which was true, they did want one—it just wasn't a priority item on the to-do list. She told Joshua she didn't care how he did it, but that she knew the kids had certain features they hoped to have, and she named them all.

"What kind of space do you have?" He seemed skeptical of her sincerity.

She pulled a folded piece of paper out of her pocket with measurements and a hand-drawn sketch of the backyard layout.

He said, "Thanks."

She felt like she should be thanking him. But that was how Joshua was. He wanted a mission. He was already studying at the paper.

She said, "No problem?"

Not only did it give Joshua something to occupy his mind, which was always restive, but also it gave him a conversational starting point with the kids. He would be able to recall every feature she had rambled off to him. He was fine once he got started.

Carolyn was more challenging, and the best thing Lily did for her sister was to give her repeated opportunities to spend time with the kids, both of whom had nametags on their shirts the whole weekend. Did she want to do a puzzle with them? Did they want to make cookies with her? Could they all watch the new animated musical cartoon movie together? Carolyn really enjoyed it, and so did the kids. Both sides could be so shy.

Lily realized Joshua was of a similar mind when he announced to everybody that he'd brought a telescope so they could watch the coming lunar eclipse even more closely. Both Joshua and Richard loved new toys. With Richard, there was an extra bit of fun, because he so rarely let himself go off to play. When Joshua introduced him to fly-fishing, Richard became far more interested than Joshua ever was, taking lessons after their first trip, booking himself a weekend with a tour group. He was the same way when one of the kids gave him a Rubik's cube, carrying it around with him for weeks until he solved it.

Richard was similarly enthralled with the telescope, and when Joshua basically handed it to him and put him in charge of it, Richard had his own project for the weekend.

Joshua enjoyed Richard's enthusiasm, but had mentioned to Lily that sometimes he felt like the Dad with three kids when he spent time with Richard and the children.

This would be born out later, when the kids were bickering with Richard about him hogging the telescope, and Joshua took a five-minute hourglass timer from a board game, made a list of their three names—with Richard at the bottom—and told them to take turns, starting from the top, in order, every time the hourglass turned. Then he went down to the porch below, where Cole and Carolyn were sitting in deck chairs, to watch the eclipse, leaving Richard and Lily to have some quality family time with the kids.

Richard had found an old almanac in the cabin, and he read, "The harvest moon is the full moon closest to the autumnal equinox. The hunter's moon is the first full moon after the harvest moon." He paused in reading. "We went to a festival in Lafayette once, the Feast of the Hunter's Moon."

Lily said that her mother told her that some Native American tribes had names for each month's full moon. Richard said his Boy Scout handbook said the same thing but that he thought it might have been made up by some old white guys.

"For example, this month's moon is called Chester." The kids groaned.

When the moon was just a giant, red-black circle in the sky and the stars were out, the kids, then Richard, then Lily took five-minute turns looking through the telescope, and then she called out to her siblings, "If any of you want a peek, come on up and we'll cut you into the rotation." But no one answered.

She sat with Richard beside her on the deck chair while the kids continued looking at the moon, then at the stars, then at anything they could that looked interesting. There was really nothing but darkened treetops to see.

It was a gorgeous night, and the plus of having the moon so dark was that it brought out the Milky Way that much brighter. She might have drifted off for a few minutes, although Richard stayed wide-awake.

She got up, went downstairs to check on the others, and was surprised to find the porch so quiet, and her siblings unmoving. Just standing in the doorway, she could hear their deep breathing. She went back inside the cabin, pulled out three throw blankets, and returned to the porch. She turned off the light.

She brought a blanket to Carolyn first, tossed it over her lightly, leaned in to adjust it, and then realized Carolyn's eyes were wide open.

Lily swallowed her gasp of surprise.

Good heavens, she thought. Did Carolyn sleep with her eyes open?

She turned to Joshua, and was startled by open blue eyes that seemed to be staring back at her. This time, after she jumped, she couldn't help snickering.

She turned on the porch light. Cole's eyes were open, too. If they weren't all three breathing so regularly, she would be worried they were dying. She covered Cole exactly as she'd covered the other two, then snapped a picture. She stared at the three of them for a few minutes after that. It looked weird, all right. Another genetic bullet she had avoided?

She moved in closer to Cole because she thought his skin looked blotchy. It looked rashy. It wasn't terrible, and it seemed to be fading. She thought about waking him gently, but decided against it. She rested a hand on his forehead, and felt an incredible heat coming off him. It almost burned her fingers.

Lily stepped back and looked at him. She pulled the blanket off of him, set it next to his arm. Maybe he ran warm when he slept? She decided she would come back in a bit to check on all three.

Fifteen minutes later, when she returned, Richard came with her. They both chuckled about the open eyes, and they took pictures, first with Lily beside them, then Richard. Cole had cooled off, and the blotchiness had gone away. She covered his lap with the blanket.

After the eclipse had started to clear and she was ready to go to sleep, Lily stopped by one more time. All eyes were closed, thankfully. They looked so settled that she just decided to leave them there, with the door unlocked, on the chance they woke up and wanted to come inside.

While she was asleep, Carolyn saw the future. She knew it for what it was, the second she woke up in it. For a moment, it was dark outside. She sat up in the bed in her mother's room, and stared out the window at the night sky. She felt like there were other people in the room behind her who were seeing the same thing.

She grew bored with the stars quickly. When she rolled out of bed, and as she walked to the window, she watched the night give way to full daylight as she crossed the room.

The house smelled of coffee. Things were modernized within the family house—there were new pieces of furniture, there was new flooring in some of the rooms. It was nice inside, in a way their house had never been when they were growing up. Pieces of furniture matched one another, and the colors of the rooms blended in pleasing ways, and none of the furnishings looked like they had been taken in just because someone else was done with it and left it on the curb.

Carolyn was in her mother's home, but it was clearly Carolyn's home now because it was filled and decorated with her possessions. Her mother's old room was now Carolyn's bedroom.

In the kitchen, she opened the liquor cabinet. It was packed with preserve jars containing herbs. For some reason, this pleased Carolyn. Much as she would have liked to have a drink—even in her dream she felt the urge!—she thought maybe this was a sign that somewhere down the line she would kick it.

Carolyn stopped at her reflection in the floor-to-ceiling mirror that had been installed beside the front door. Her face was lined with age, her hair cut butch short and the color of steel. Her body had grown a little larger. She opened the front door, stepped outside.

The hedge wall that encircled the house was now fifteen feet tall, and the top of it curved in slightly but noticeably. It now seemed clear that one day it would form a dome and the entire house and vegetable garden would be covered by it. It was impossible to see over the top of the wall, where she knew endless fields of golden plants were ready for harvesting.

As she stood there, one of the giant rings that now encircled the Earth slowly rotated across the sky. There were two of them, and she knew from news reports that the two particle-thick bands, each hundreds of yards across, crossed the sky at higher than 50,000 feet in the sky at different times of the day, a giant gyroscope that acted as a defensive shield against unidentified objects from space. She hardly even noticed it anymore. It didn't blot out the sun as it turned or create the band of shade one would expect. The sunlight passed through the bands.

Half of the field behind the house was a forest once again.

Carolyn of the future knew that people in town thought she was a witch. People were using herbs in their medical treatments more often these days, and they came to her, because her garden held so many varieties. Some of those varieties wouldn't grow in a field—they needed the canopy of the forest to thrive—so the trees had been allowed to spread once again.

On Halloween, her house was the most popular one in town to visit.

It was a different world outside the family home, although Carolyn was only dimly aware of the details. Despite the rings, and the protections they offered from the heavens, even though guns didn't work anymore on the surface of the planet, even though rape wasn't a threat anymore, still far-off wars raged on.

There was someone coming in from the fields who she did not recognize. A young woman, in a lovely dress, with lavender fabric that Carolyn remembered from her mobile home. Who was this, now?

"Hi, Carolyn. It's Emily. Good morning!"

Joshua opened his mouth and butterflies erupted from it.

He dreamed he was in a college movie theater again, but in a front seat this time, watching a film about the Earth being terraformed to make it fit for life. The theater seats around him were filled, but he was too engrossed in the movie to look to see who was there. He was sure, for some reason, that some of his siblings were there, too.

The film began with larger-than-nuclear explosives being delivered at the poles of the planet, helping to kick-start reactions that heated the surface and boosting the atmosphere to a place where the planet would support life. The special effects, showing the post-explosion reactions in fast-forward, were especially convincing. After the atmosphere was established, meteor strikes carved the surface while at the same time delivering a collection of amino acids necessary for life, along with massive amounts of ice to augment what was already there.

He looked down and noticed he held his sketchpad in his lap.

He was working on an idea. He drew a picture of a plant, with a long, transparent stem, and long, drooping leaves. It's nervous system would be visible through its skin. It would be a carbon eater. The trick was in the root system, tendrils of which would extend much farther into the ground than was generally true for plants. It would not only absorb large amounts of carbon and convert some of it to oxygen, but also it would pump excess carbon through its own root system deep into the Earth where it would serve other purposes.

At his ranch he would one day grow carbon eaters. The one design would not have to be the only one. As he finished his drawing, he flipped through the pages of his sketchpad, and saw there were designs for carbon eaters in many different shapes and colors. He drew several more, imagining his field planted with rows of them. In the daylight, they would all look like a field of jellyfish, but at night the rows would glow in a neon rainbow selection of colors. His small ranch would help improve air quality for miles around. Of course larger plants would be more effective, but Joshua didn't think that was a possibility yet—that would have to be a goal over time. He would keep working on it.

Cole dreamed he was standing in the front yard of the family home, listening to explosions in the distance. The hedge wall was as tall as him, and thick and sturdy, yet somehow the sunlight filtered clearly into the yard through it. His mother had been wise enough to make room for two openings in the hedge wall. Years after their planting, with the walls so tall, those openings were like doorways. Cole ran to the open section in front to see what was happening in the outside world.

Many miles distant in the sky, hovering high above the Earth, was a spaceship. It wasn't a saucer or a disc, Cole thought. It was more like a cruise liner or an aircraft carrier. It looked huge, despite being so far away. There were other, smaller ships in the vicinity of the behemoth. They seemed to be firing at the ground, and were perhaps responsible for the far off explosions he heard.

Straight out from where he stood, past the wall, past the house parking spots, and a little bit down the driveway, there was that tree. As he had always expected would happen, that section in the middle of the trunk, about thirty feet up from the ground, that large bump in the middle with so many branches coming out it, the one that had always looked like a giant spider to him, it started to move. The branches that were not its legs snapped violently as it separated itself from the wood of the trunk and started moving toward the ground. The brownish, furred body alone was six feet wide, the legs another seven feet long and each of them half a foot wide if not wider.

The sight of it terrified Cole, and he was frozen in place, his rational thoughts replaced with a fear that he would have described as instinctive. If it charged the house, he didn't even think he would be able to force his legs to run. But the brown spider, he could see, was not interested in the Chamber house. It was there for another reason, and to that end, it started moving in the direction of the spaceships.

Behind that fat brown tree was another, with a white, long, narrow trunk that rose maybe 80 feet tall. At 40 feet were its lowest branches, on either side of the trunk. These branches were moving as Cole watched, as if they were arms. The right arm reached up to the top of the tree above it, and pulled off the section there—maybe the top 10 feet of the leafy branches at its crest—removed it like it was a hat, and dropped it to the ground below with a crash. There was just a bald nub at the top of it—it looked like a giant stick bug. It rubbed its tree branch arms together, knocking leaves and large pieces of wood to the ground. When it was done, there was no green left on it, and it started pulling its roots from the ground, which it managed with not a lot of effort. The trunk split apart into legs. Free, and mobile, it immediately followed in the direction of the spider, which already was nearly out of sight.

The rest of the extended weekend was notable for its lack of drama. After sleeping late into the morning following the eclipse, everybody relaxed. Carolyn and Lily took turns making meals, and Cole and Richard did kitchen clean-up afterward. Lily was thrilled to eat meals that she hadn't personally prepared.

Joshua was generally left to entertain the kids before dinner. He was their action uncle, and they loved to see what he would come up with next—which, on Sunday, was an oversized slingshot he'd fashioned from a bike tire inner tube and a carefully selected tree branch. He attached it to the railing with a fishing rod holder that would normally be used on a boat. He had also set up a few circular trash bins out in the yard behind the house. They used the slingshot to try to land large pine cones in the trashcans.

The kids warmed to Cole, although it was obvious that

Cole was a little scared to be the center of the children's attention. He felt he'd sort of made a start when the younger one stopped trying to hide her face every time he looked at her, but he was still not confident at all with them.

At some point over the weekend, Richard spoke with his parents, and they talked about taking an old table out of the cabin and bringing it to their house, and exchanging it out for something that didn't give everyone splinters. Joshua offered Richard his truck, and Lily decided that he should take the kids with him to his parents, and she would take her siblings back home in the SUV, and then they could meet up at home later.

Once they'd all said their goodbyes and were settled in their respective vehicles, Lily waited for Richard, who was parked behind her, to figure out that he needed to release the emergency brake or the truck would never move.

"You really did get lucky with him," Carolyn said while she stared ahead out the car window.

"That's nice, Carolyn."

"Usually, you can look at a couple and see that there's one who loves the other more than the other. One who goes farther, one who puts up with more, one who does more of the work. I look at you two, and I can't figure out which is which."

Still not looking at Lily, she said, "He got lucky with you, too. We all did."

Lily thought it was the nicest thing her sister had ever said to her. She didn't say a thing, but she did reach out and give Carolyn's hand a squeeze, and Carolyn squeezed her hand back. For Carolyn, that was a lot.

Chapter 22

Carolyn said, "King of Hearts."

Cole sat in the back seat, beside Joshua. Cole dropped the King of Hearts, where it fell to the floor mat, joining a handful of other cards.

He flipped the top card.

"Jack of Hearts."

He dropped the Jack of Hearts. Flipped over the top card, clowning around about shielding it from Carolyn.

"Nine of Clubs."

Carolyn sat in the front seat, facing forward, eyes closed beneath her sunglasses. She had her right hand pressed against the door, as if she were bracing herself. Always with dramatics, Lily thought.

"Jack of Spades," Carolyn said.

Cole flipped a card.

"Seven of Hearts. Thought I already said that one."

"You did!" Cole said. "Josh tried to slip one in off the floor. Here's another one."

"Six of Diamonds."

Card flip.

"Two of Clubs."

Card flip.

Lily looked back quickly. Joshua was staring at the card Cole was shielding with his palm.

"Seven of Clubs," Carolyn said.

"Okay," Lily said, "You guys are not going to go through the whole deck right now."

Cole said, "Aww, why not?"

"Because I'll lose my mind."

Carolyn made her tsk tsk noise.

"Okay, Lils," Cole said brightly. "I just wanted to see it in action again."

"You all used to just make me crazy with those weirdo things," Lily said. "No playing hide-and-seek, because you always knew where to look. No hiding presents in the house because of the same thing. Cole had this weird thing he would do when he was little where he would tell Mom or me that someone was going to have a cold or be sick, and usually within two days, that person was sick."

"More like a jinx than a prediction," Joshua said.

"Exactly," Lily continued, "Joshua used to always guess who was calling on the phone—when we finally got a phone—before he would pick it up, and he was almost always right. Sometimes he would say something like, 'Uh-oh, that's Mr. Hamilton calling,' and none of us would answer while it rang and rang. Then there were times when it just felt like some of you could read my mind. Once I was in the kitchen, thinking about something I'd read in a book—I think it was one of the Narnia books, and I wondered where my copy of that book was so I could look that part up. Five minutes later, before I was even done with the dishes, Zoe came in and said, "Here, Lily, your book was in my room—and it was the exact Narnia book I was thinking about."

"Sometimes I get feelings, too," Carolyn offered.

"Like what?"

"Well, lots of things. The one I can remember most clearly right now was on the night that mother passed. I was at the restaurant, about to leave to drive home, and I had this sensation of my car being hit, something just slamming into the door . . . "

Joshua's eyes widened.

Lily said, "On the night Mom died? Are you teasing me?"

"Yes, that's how I tease—so that no one, not even me, knows what I'm making fun of."

Lily's eyelids fluttered rapidly as she thought. She held up her hand to silence her sister.

"Stop that. I got hit that night while I was driving home. Blue pickup slammed right into my door."

"Oooh. I just got the chills," Cole said.

"Blue pickup?" Joshua said, "Gotta be Bill Swasser. Drives like the ass in his name."

"Spun me around to the other side of the road, and then he took off."

Joshua said, "Really?" Everyone in the car heard his tone turn to anger.

Cole looked at his brother.

"What the hell is that? You're going to go beat him up now?"

"You didn't recognize 'em?" Josh looked irritated. He ignored Cole.

"Al still doesn't have my car fixed," Lily said. "But a couple weeks ago he asked me to drop by because he thought he knew who it was." She shrugged. "It was just random chance that I was driving my old car and not this one. Anyway, Al showed me the pickup that hit me."

"You're kidding," Joshua said. "It's gotta be Bill. Right? Where else would Bill go to get his car fixed? Did you find out who it was?"

"You know, Al was going to get the information I need to give to the insurance company. But you know that old car. If I get $400 for it I'd be lucky."

"Still," Josh said, "the guy that did it should still pay for everything. Can't just let him get away with it. "

"The thing is," Lily said, "The truck Al showed me, the one that hit me, was trashed. It looked like someone had taken a bat or a crowbar to it, just beat the heck out of it. Broke the windows, cut up the tires, bashed the shit out of it."

With that, Joshua relaxed, and looked satisfied. His eyes lit up, and he nodded his head in agreement.

He asked, "Was it someone else he bumped?"

"No, actually, I don't think so. Al got the impression it was a cop."

Cole said, "Yikes."

Joshua nodded his head more, clearly thinking *Justice.* "So it was Elias," he said.

"I think so, too," Lily said.

"I always knew that guy was all right," Joshua said approvingly.

Carolyn said, "You weren't hurt? In the crash?"

"No. Just pissed off at the other driver. After talking to Al I sort of weirded myself out thinking about Elias. I mean, haven't really heard from him for a while, not much more than what's cordial when I try to contact him, and then something like this as a way of checking in?"

"You know," Carolyn said in a tone that was close to gossipy, "He came by to visit with mother regularly. Maybe that night he was feeling some grief, too, over losing her."

"What do you mean regularly?"

"Twice a month. Every other Tuesday or so he came by to visit and have tea with her. He started doing that a couple months after his own mother died."

This bothered Lily to hear. Not the thought of him spending time visiting with her mother—Elias had always gotten along with her—but that Carolyn had seen Elias multiple times and knew personal things about his life and state of mind that Lily did not. What had Elias said about her to them?

"The poor man! Still carrying a torch for you. Oh," Carolyn teased, "He never said that. Maybe didn't even know it or admit it to himself. He always asked about you. He always looked like he was trying not to look sad talking about you."

Lily wanted to know, "Why tell Mom?"

"Oh my, Lily. Well, he didn't tell her anything directly! Whatever was in his heart, he knew he hadn't been brave enough to act upon it. Because of that, you were married, and he'd lost the chance. Those were the rules. I did respect that he honored those boundaries. You know, for all his fickleness with his relationships, his being unable to commit, at the least he was too moral of a man to interfere with your marriage. I think even if he thought you were hot-to-trot for him now he wouldn't touch you without a divorce or an annulment in the works."

Lily said, "Are you sure you weren't the one who had a crush on him?"

"No," Carolyn cackled, "Mother was the one who had a crush on him! She was very touched that he visited her because he missed his own mother so much."

"What did they talk about?"

"Well, not you all the time, if that's what you were worried about. They talked about everything. He talked about his job and about the people at the department. She usually prodded a little if she thought there was good gossip there somewhere."

Lily knew her mother was not a gossip in that she never liked to tell stories about people. She didn't do that at all. What she did enjoy was hearing stories about people and all their shenanigans and keeping them to herself.

"But, I'll tell you, Lily, charming as the package is, I think you dodged a bullet with that one," Carolyn said. "It's all sweet to be talking about you like a lost secret love, but not so sweet to his wife—his second wife, mind you—or her two children. Now if you were a lovesick puppy, you might believe his two marriages weren't so great because he was really in love with you. Or, if you're a wide-eyed skeptic, you might realize that if he'd ended up with you, there is a good chance you would be where wife number one is now and where wife number two will undoubtedly one day be headed. You can be sure, too, that if you switched places with wife number one, in your marriage to him she would be the one whose absence he would be lamenting. That's the type."

"Where do you think that comes from?" Lily asked. "Why is he like that?"

Joshua said, "Because she's the relationship expert?"

Carolyn ignored him. "It's a way to distance himself, maybe? I would guess the most likely culprit is Elias' mother. I think she just adored her firstborn little boy so much and never wanted him to love anyone more than he loved her. You know what some mothers do with their firstborn boys! When she delivered the 'Don't let a woman trap you' speech, he took it to heart."

"Love is a trap," Lily said.

"Right. Better to keep it at a certain distance. Wife one and wife two are people he could do that with, or so he thought, until wife one wanted either all of him or none of him. No one in a good relationship is happy at a distance. Not a good thing," Carolyn said, shaking her head. "Maybe he knew that if he got involved with you, he wouldn't be able to keep you at a distance. Whether that scared him or tempted him or both, that's a big jump to make, especially if his history with relationships hasn't been that great, and especially with another suitor like Richard in the background. Lack of confidence in himself."

"There's no reason for it, either," Lily said.

"I think you dodged a bullet."

"I'm not disagreeing."

Lily turned on the radio, flipped around until she found a news station.

A male announcer said, " . . . reports of unusual activity during the weekend's eclipse continue . . . "

"The lunacy continues," the female announcer said, emphasizing the loon. Rim shot sound effect.

"You are not kidding, Sparkle," the male announcer said.

"Let's just go over some of the stories that have come in over the last 48 hours, since Saturday night's total lunar eclipse."

"The Syzygy. Mark," Sparkle said.

"Gesundheit, Sparkle," Mark said. "So far we have heard about sightings of Greys in Vermont. . ."

"Those anime-eyed aliens," Sparkle said. "Those guys creep me out because they never talk. They're just thinking at you with their big heads and their little person bodies."

" . . . Reptilians in Kentucky . . . "

"Which," Sparkle said, "Is another space shape-changing species, supposedly one of the earliest races to inhabit our planet, living underneath the Earth's surface and infiltrating our governments . . ."

Mark said, " . . . and there are reports of sightings of strange, and I will quote, 'unidentified and exotic subterranean and prehistoric flora and fauna . . . "

"How does that happen?" Sparkle returned. "Is it the gravitational force of the moon just pulling all these things out of the ground?"

"Speaking of out of the ground, at Graceland, several folks reported seeing . . . "

"Zero points for guessing it right, folks," Sparkle said.

" . . . Yeah, I guess that's fair. They said the King was spotted in a crowd that was holding a vigil at Graceland as part of a lunar eclipse celebration, and that at some point, he separated from the group and was observed slipping into the house through a secret entrance."

"It used to be a secret entrance! For a fried peanut butter sandwich! Meanwhile, in Mexico," Sparkle said, "several hundred members of a death cult sacrificed 24,000 chickens in the shadow of a pyramid as part of an ancient ritual that appeals to the Gods to return the moon to the people."

"And we all know it worked!"

"Thank goodness for those death cult worshippers."

"You know, that's a lot of offal."

"It is a lot of awful, Mark."

"No," Mark said, "Offal. O-F-F-A-L. When they make sacrifices to the Gods, right after they kill the animals they separate the offal—you know, they look at the liver, the heart, the kidney, the neck, to see what the future holds . . . "

Lily clicked off the radio

It was quiet a few more minutes.

Cole said, "What the hell was that? The more they talked, the more I felt like we were in a *Twilight Zone* episode."

"Speaking of," Joshua said offhandedly, "I saw Momma in a tree at my house a few minutes before Lily called me to tell me she was gone."

Cole took that in, then looked at Joshua, slightly disbelieving.

"You did?"

Carolyn said, "What did she look like?"

"Like Momma."

"Men! What was she wearing?"

"Uh . . . "

"Was she happy? Was she sad? Was she angry or sorry?"

"I'm . . . "

"Useless," Carolyn snorted.

Lily looked over at her sister.

"I just thought she was letting me know," Joshua said. "Saying goodbye."

"You know," Cole said, "That is the weirdest thing I've ever heard you say."

"Yeah," Joshua said, looking at the back of his hand. "But I guess I'm not one of those people who needs to believe something to the exclusion of all the rest. I mean, there's the quote unquote facts or theories, and then there's your own eyes."

"Just because you can't explain it doesn't mean it didn't happen," Lily said.

Cole asked Joshua, "Does that happen to you a lot? Like, visions?"

"No, not at all. I generally don't see dead people. I just thought, in that case, maybe she sent something out when she went."

"I thought I saw someone like her on the bus," Cole said. "Right before I got Lily's text. I didn't pay close enough attention because I was all in my own head. There was a lady on the bus when I got on, which was when the bus started moving. Then I got that text, and when I looked again, the lady was gone."

"Okay, okay," Lily said. "Let's talk about something real that I can prove happened. On the night of the eclipse, when I came down to check on you, you were all asleep. You all had your eyes wide open. Cole, my phone is in the center console. Open up the pictures. I took a couple of you all.

"So, guys and gal, what was that? Where did you all go?"

The car was quiet. They all regarded her with some anxiety on their faces. Then Carolyn picked up the phone, and, after a few seconds, started snickering. She passed it to Cole, who showed it to Joshua. They all chuckled. Cole and Joshua tried to pose themselves so they looked like they did in the photo.

Lily rolled her eyes.

"At first I thought you were sleeping, and didn't give it much thought. But a little bit later, when I saw you from the front and realized all of you were sleeping with your eyes open, I was a little worried. So what was that all about? Do all of you actually sleep with your eyes open regularly?"

They all three looked at each other, surprise and then curiosity on their faces.

"I was dreaming," Carolyn said. "I don't remember what

it was about."

"Me, too," Cole said. Joshua echoed his agreement.

"Really. None of you finds that weird?"

None of them knew what to say.

"Fine. Well, maybe after a few hours in the car together, someone will come up with something."

Carolyn giggled a little.

"If you tell me you're disappointed in us," Carolyn said. "I'm going to laugh at you for acting like everyone's mother. I won't mean it in a bad way. "

At some point in the drive in the mountains, they passed a convoy of six large semi trucks, all painted black, all Alabama plates, working their ways up the grade. Something about them seemed unusual to Lily, but she assumed they were out doing their jobs, and left it at that.

They got off the highway past the state line, and soon after saw two people—two tired, bedraggled people—walking beside the road. One was a man, the other, a young woman— maybe a teen. Lily felt bad for them. They didn't look like typical hikers or hitchhikers. More like people whose car had just stopped working.

She had room for three more in the SUV. She figured they had to be from somewhere around here. She slowed.

As she pulled up beside them, she opened the passenger window.

She asked if they needed some help.

It took her a moment to realize the man wearing the K-NOX hat was familiar, and another two before she knew she was looking at her long-missing brother, Ben. He looked at her like he could not believe his eyes. He also looked a bit delirious.

It was even longer before she realized the person with Ben was Emily.

She stared at Ben. Cole, who was sitting on that side of the car, stared at Ben through the car window. Carolyn had no idea what anyone was seeing in the strangers, and Joshua, who had seen Emily out the window, was so fixated on the probability of running into her again under these circumstances that he hadn't yet moved on to recognizing Ben.

"So," Lily said automatically, "Get in. We're headed home."

Without a word, Ben slid into the back seat, catching the eyes of his confused sister in the front seat and both his brothers in the middle row of seats. No one said anything as Emily climbed into the back of the car.

Then they were on their way home again. No one said anything.

Ben and Emily were both asleep in minutes. They looked like they had been outdoors for a while, and like they hadn't been on the roads all that time—they were covered in scratches and cobwebs and pieces of leaves.

Lily looked at the others in the rear view mirror.

Cole mouthed, "Is he asleep?"

Carolyn said loudly, "Who the hell is it?"

Cole leaned forward, and whispered in his sister's ear, "It's Ben."

Carolyn looked confused. She thought about it. She looked relieved, and then she glowered. It was a cycle she would repeat most of the way home.

Lily closed her eyes and thanked whatever higher power existed in the world. They would sort this all out, like family should. Still, no one said anything more the rest of the way home.

Chapter 23

When they reached the family home, Joshua carried first Ben, then Emily inside the house, putting Ben in his bed in his old room and Emily into Lily's old room. Carolyn dropped her luggage just inside the door, and made a beeline for the kitchen. Joshua could hear the bottles rattling, and he imagined her hands were shaking as she tried to figure out what kind of drunk would be most appropriate for the circumstances.

He stared at his brother lying in his bed—for the second time in less than a month, he was seeing one of his brothers for the first time in years. Ben looked much older than Joshua remembered him. His hair was long, grown out, and he had a good couple days of stubble. He had some wear and tear on his face, although he looked healthy. His hands looked like he worked with them—cuts and bruises and blisters—and he had some lean muscle on him, too.

Where Cole had looked like he'd grown up a bit, Ben looked like an adult version of the kid Joshua remembered. He looked like he took care of himself—no missing teeth, no tracks on his arms. Maybe he smelled like he smoked some.

He had a wedding ring on his finger.

Now that Ben was here, Josh wanted the last missing part of the equation: Where was Zoe? That would complete the answer to one of the great unsolved questions of Joshua's life—well, the questions that he cared about the answers to. Some unanswered questions could stay that way, and he'd be fine with it.

"Hey, Josh," Cole called in a hushed voice from the kitchen. "Come in here."

Joshua followed the sound of Cole's voice. When he

walked into the kitchen, he saw the table was moved to the wall, revealing the concrete floor underneath it, and the ring cut into the concrete, and the hole in the center.

"Do you know what that is?"

"Yeah, in the old days, before electricity, they used to set something in the hole, like a lantern post, and then there was a base that went over the top and slid into the ring to keep the post from falling."

Cole asked, "You're sure of that?"

"Momma told me a post went in there. I might have sort of made up the rest the way I thought it would work."

Cole was holding his belt buckle in his hand. He'd disconnected it from the leather. He opened the stem so it stood straight out from the ring, and then he walked over to the hole. He lined up the stem with the hole, and slid it in. The buckle ring fit neatly into the larger ring cut into the floor.

Joshua asked, "When did you figure this out?"

"Just a few minutes ago, I was getting my gold coin from the place I hid it, and I pushed the table over to the wall. There's a slot up there you can't see unless you're up there. So I got the coin, but there was a big fly that was buzzing me, and I was trying to kill it with my belt. And when I held up the belt buckle, I saw one," he gestured to the floor, "and then the other, and it just clicked. I wanted you here, you know, in case it's a trap."

"A trap," Joshua repeated.

The floor clicked. The circle of concrete inside the larger ring pushed up a short inch.

Cole tried to pull it straight up, but it didn't give. Joshua tried, too. Then Joshua tried to turn it, and, surprisingly, it turned. It was screwed in. He turned it and turned it and the cylinder rose further out of the floor. While he was doing that, it was so quiet that they could hear Lily on the phone in the next room explaining to Richard in a hushed voice what had happened on the way back and why she wouldn't be home tonight.

Finally, it wouldn't unscrew any further. Joshua pulled at it and it lifted out. He set it down and inspected the resulting hole, fingering the grooves on the sides, noting the handmade set of springs at the bottom, and finally, a metal hook in the middle. He tugged on that to no effect. At this moment, he felt a closer connection than he'd ever felt to his long-dead great grandfather. His great grandfather had had an idea, and then he'd built the thing that made it work. He'd done it without a hardware store, modern tools, or electricity.

Joshua looked up, and saw that the ceiling fixture neatly aligned with the circle. He stood and lifted off the fixture, exposing the ceiling hook with which it had been attached. He went out to his shed for rope, and when he returned, he tied the rope around the buried hook, and then ran the other end through the ceiling hook.

He stood back, rope in hand, and started pulling

The response was almost immediate. The section of the floor surrounding the hook moved, and then lifted. Joshua pulled until it was a couple feet off the floor. Underneath was a dark cubbyhole space.

When Joshua looked left and right, there was his mother's mirror on the wall.

Joshua said, "Cole, take that mirror down."

It was a simple mirror with a simple metal frame, big enough for Rose to see only her face. Cole lifted it up, revealing another hook.

"There it is," Joshua said. "There the whole time," he said. He looped the rope through the wall hook, and then told Cole to push the compartment cover over to the side. "Then we'll set it down over there."

That done, he tied the rope, just to make sure the cover wouldn't slide.

"Lily, you want to come over here?"

Soon enough, Lily and Carolyn were in the room, which was just barely able to accommodate four adults without that section of the floor. Carolyn had a mixed drink in her hand, glass filled two-thirds of the way to the top. She was going for a hard landing. Almost couldn't blame her, Joshua thought. Almost.

Cole pointed at the floor. "Did any of you know that was there?"

Lily, Joshua, and Carolyn shook their heads.

Carolyn crouched in front of it. She reached in and pulled out the item on top, a cloth book with a fastener on the front. When she opened it, it was filled with small, folded pieces of paper with writing on them. She pulled one out to see what it was. It said Lemon. Inside the folds were three seeds.

"They're seeds. It's an old-fashioned seed notebook?" She handed it to Joshua. "Maybe we can use these here," she said.

She started naming some of the other things she saw inside.

"There's a pile of old books, with lots of old papers sticking out of them. A little purse here with, with, what? Some kind of spice jars. Ooh, there's one more gold coin. There are maps. The most modern thing looks like this . . . "

She handed it to Lily. It was an envelope. Inside were some documents. A property deed, an old contract, her grandmother Rose—Not Roslyn—Chamber's birth certificate, a will, and another will.

"I think this is grandpa's will, and I think this might be Mom's will. It looks like she might have just copied what he wrote, and stuck in our names instead of her mom's."

After a while longer, they decided to remove everything from the secret space, and to bring it into the living room for closer study. Carolyn made more than one comment about no one taking anything without everyone agreeing, but then it seemed to everyone that if she had a chance, that was exactly what she wanted to do with the seed notebook.

"Can we not start with dividing things up?" Lily was less patient with Carolyn once the drinking started. "Look, it says here, 'Divided equally among my children, Lily Nelson Chamber, Joshua Nelson Chamber, Carolyn Nelson Chamber, Ben Nelson Chamber, Zoe Nelson Chamber, and Cole Nelson Chamber.'

"Right now, let's just start with the rule that everything stays here in this house," Carolyn said. "Let's just see what it is before we start disagreeing over it."

While they unloaded everything, Joshua continued to admire the quality of craftsmanship that went into the storage area, into the mechanism to hide it. He figured it had sat here for a hundred years, maybe 50 of them exposed to the elements and to every kind of wanderer and gravedigger and still everything was intact and no one had discovered it. He wanted to immediately start building one at his own house.

He waited until the space had been emptied, then closed it up again so he could watch the mechanism in action once more. He pulled the table back into place and stared at the setup, scratching his head. Hidden right in plain sight all the time he'd been here.

For several hours afterward they combed through everything. Carolyn admired the old jewelry, pricing everything out loud as she went along, admiring gem quality more than the settings ("A diamond is a diamond"), pooh-poohing some of it.

"Look," Cole said, "Collected Stories of Faulkner."

Lily stared at the cover. She'd always thought that book came from the bookmobile in Texas. She held out her hand to Cole to have him pass it to her. She flipped through it quickly, looked for something, a stamp, a marker, that might indicate where it was from. Nothing. Was that a relief for her?

"She read us those when we were little," she said, realizing the others were watching her.

"These are great-grandpa Nelson's journals," Joshua said after a bit. "I think this is the order they go in." He picked up the first, and started thumbing through it. "I want to read them, but I also just want to look."

"I'm going to refresh," Carolyn said. "Anyone else?"

Cole wanted to, but somehow thought that would upset Lily.

Joshua thought that even if anyone did—and he'd like a beer all right—the idea of encouraging Carolyn in any way didn't seem the right way to go.

He looked at Cole. His brother looked back at him, shrugged.

"Two beers, then," Joshua, said, then immediately regretted when he saw the spring it added to Carolyn's step as she returned to the kitchen.

"One beer," Cole said, reading Joshua's expression. "One beer only. We'll share it."

Joshua volunteered to make dinner, to the girls' shock and surprise. He was mildly insulted, because here he was, 31 years old, and it hadn't been someone else making sure he ate every day of his life that he wasn't eating with family. He didn't do anything fancy, taking from the food supplies Carolyn brought home for them from the restaurant: a salad, mashed potatoes, steaks with a mushroom sauce.

"Not bad, brother," Cole said.

"How's your cooking?"

"I know how to boil an egg."

Lily said, "See, how did that happen? Mother taught all of us to cook."

"There were so many cooks when I came along that I stayed out of the kitchen."

Carolyn finished off her drink. She was not slurring her words yet, but when she wasn't engaged in conversation, her eyes tended to drift around the room, away from her siblings. When she got up for a refill, Cole said, "Carolyn, maybe you should take it easy."

It took her a minute to be sure who had spoken. She then turned her head and left the room, her arms sort of awkwardly at her side. Everybody remaining in the room exchanged looks. When Carolyn returned, she was almost strutting when she walked into the room.

"It's not your business if I drink. I like to drink. I'm not hurting anyone."

"Well," Cole said, holding her stare uneasily, "You're not really a pleasure to be around when you drink so much."

"Oh, Mr. Perfect. Mr. Perfect College Student Brother."

"Oh, come on," Cole said.

Joshua clenched the hand he had resting on the table, and then relaxed it.

"You're not so perfect, Cole. Mom's precious miracle child."

Cole was seeing what Carolyn could be like. It almost made Joshua's stomach turn to witness it.

"You know what, Carolyn? You've been making cracks for days now." Cole's voice was steady. He didn't want to get sucked into acting like her. "What's up your butt?"

"Haw Ha," she said, covering her mouth in mock shock with one hand while pointing at Cole with the other.

"I know about your little boyfriend and girlfriend," Carolyn said. "Did you guys know? Cole's a bisexual now. He has gay sex."

Joshua sat frozen. He thought that if he looked at Cole's face, and saw any kind of upset there, he was gong to end up punching his sister.

"Isn't that right? Just taking it up the butt?

Lily said, "Oh, good heavens, Carolyn."

"What's that like?" She was so ugly, leering in Cole's face.

Cole said, "You know what? It hurts, then it goes numb, and then it gets pretty intense, if I remember right."

This made for a stop in the flow of the conversation.

Lily said, "Really, Cole."

"Oh, come on, Carolyn," Joshua said slowly, "Can't tell anyone in this room you didn't already know the answer to that question, can you? I'm sure there isn't a dirty thing he's done more'n you have."

The room went silent again.

Carolyn glared at Joshua. They all saw that she was ready to throw her drink at him, and they all saw the moment when she suddenly found it too precious for that. She also saw clearly the odds in the room were against her. She picked her plate up off the table, and retreated to the kitchen.

"You're all teaming up on me! It's not fair! And it's not fair to bring up Don! I loved him once."

Lily said, "No one mentioned Don."

"Jesus," Cole said. He almost laughed.

Joshua wanted to say that what he found out when he was being "interviewed" in the next county over about anything he might have seen on the night Don died was that Don had been fooling around with a number of women over that way, including the Sheriff's niece, and he was about as gentle with those women as he was with Carolyn. That was likely part of the reason no one was ever arrested after he died—because it turned out no one minded that he was gone.

But Joshua didn't say that. A person always imagined they were going to have the last word with an alcoholic, and it just wasn't ever the case. Instead, he turned to Lily, and said, in a low voice, "How did Emily get into this house again? Is that not the strangest aspect here?"

Lily said, "I really hope that is going to be the strangest thing in this picture."

Carolyn was not gone for long. She returned to the room, again seemingly refreshed. She was holding a cell phone in her hand, the charging cord dangling from the end of it.

"Watch this," she said. This was her attempt to reset the mood.

She pressed a button on the phone, and listened.

She said, "Oh." She held up a finger to signal to them to wait. It was a voicemail message she was listening to. When she spoke again, her voice was composed and full of sugar.

"Zoe, honey? This is your sister, Carolyn. We have Ben here at the house right now, and we were just wanting to talk to you." Here, she lost her train of thought. When she started speaking again, it started out almost sputtering, and then ended with her repeating herself, "Yes, Ben is here right now, and we're . . . we would love to talk to you. Bye." She dragged out the last word a little musically. When she set down the phone, there was no apparent residue from the fact that she'd just drunk-dialed her long-lost sister.

Cole said, "That's Ben's phone? You're just a little cell phone hijacker aren't you?"

Carolyn, dismayed that this was what Cole was drawing from the situation, read aloud from the phone screen, "Zoe Nelson."

"Seriously, sis, you're spy material," Cole said, shaking his head.

"Oh, don't be like that. Your phone just started laughing like a maniac when you were asleep one night and I had to turn it off. And you know how it is when there's a message on the screen . . . "

"It's not okay, Carolyn," Lily said.

" . . . and I can't tell," she said thoughtfully, not seeming to be teasing now, " . . . if he is gay for you or if you are gay for him or if either of you really have any idea what you want to screw around with . . . "

"I'm not gay, Carolyn. Which if I was, thanks for your sensitivity at my outing. It was just . . . "

"Something you fell into?" Joshua couldn't resist.

Lily smacked Joshua in the stomach.

Cole and Joshua both laughed.

"I wasn't planning for it," Cole said. "It wasn't one of my goals, and then it happened and . . . whatever. They were nice people. It's done. I'd like to date a girl next, just one, and that's all I'm looking for." Why was he still talking? "Just a nice girl. Keep it simple here on out."

It was around eight in the evening that Carolyn came in from the gardens with some sage. Lily was in her car, having a private phone conversation with the kids and Richard. Carolyn set about trimming the cuttings, then binding the bunch together with string, eventually making it into a smudge stick. She went into the kitchen, filled a metal mixing bowl three-quarters full of water, and when she returned she set the bowl on the floor by the front door.

Cole, seated on the couch looking at numbers in one of Nelson Chamber's journals that meant nothing to him, watched her out of the corners of his eyes.

She returned to the kitchen and came back with the smudge stick and a box of matches.

Cole asked, "What are you doing?"

"What I should have done when we first got back here after she died. I'm cleansing the house. There are too many spirits here."

"Now? Ben and that girl are still sleeping."

"It will only wake them up if they're possessed," she ventured.

She lit the end of the smudge stick, let it burn a little, then blew it out and continued to breath softly on it, until it glowed and smoked. And stunk.

Starting with Lily's room, where Emily slept, and moving from room to room through the whole house, Carolyn walked slowly through the house, the smoke spreading everywhere, expanding heavily through the air.

Joshua, who was also sitting in the living room with a journal in his lap, heard a noise around the water bowl, and when he got up from the couch to investigate, he saw a ripple spreading across the surface of the bowl. And then another.

As Carolyn moved room to room, the water's surface became more active, until it was slowly bubbling. Joshua wanted to feel it, to see if it was hot, but something told him not to, and then Carolyn called out, "Don't touch that."

Finally, there was a light, pungent haze throughout the house, and Carolyn handed the smudge stick to Cole.

Her eyes widened in surprise when she returned to the bowl of water, and found it bubbling. She thought about it, then decided to go on with what she was doing. She opened the front door, and reached carefully for the water bowl.

Joshua saw out the door that Lily was coming across the porch, about to step inside, her car keys in her hands. She looked around the house, at the smoke, curiously. She looked at Carolyn, and then at the bowl she was picking up.

Something came over Lily. Joshua saw it—head to toe, she changed. Her eyes filled with anger, and with tears, and her teeth clenched together. Screaming, "No!," she leapt at Carolyn like she was going to knock her to the ground. Joshua threw up his arms in time to grab Lily, holding her back while Carolyn recoiled backward without spilling the water.

Carolyn walked around Lily and Joshua, her brow furrowed in suspicion and confusion, her eyes fixed on Lily. Drunk as she was, she recognized all of this, particularly Lily's reaction, as unbelievably strange. She walked around the arc of Lily's grasp. Lily, it seemed, was ready to hurt Joshua to stop this from happening, so he pulled her away from the door.

Carolyn was on the porch before he could too far with Lily, who yelled in protest as Carolyn poured the water on the ground past the front doorstep.

Carolyn explained to Cole, "Spirits can't abide by the stink of sage, and they can't hide in the people present either, because they're breathing the smoke, too. The water is the only place to hide, and water is a bad medium for them. When you pour the water out past the doorstep, you are sweeping them from the household so you can begin anew." She stared at the empty bowl. "It's supposed to be symbolic."

Lily yelled, "That's our mother!"

"Well," Carolyn said loudly, "She'll be happier in the garden than in the house, don't you think?"

Cole stared at her, at the empty bowl, and then at Lily, dumbfounded. Then he jumped at the sound of a voice coming from the hall outside the bedrooms.

"Has anyone seen my phone?"

It was Ben.

Chapter 24

Ben said it again, "Does anyone know where my phone is?"

"Oh, I have it," Carolyn said, and she moved for the kitchen. "I just found the phone and plugged it in so it would be charged for you when you woke up." She emerged a moment later, holding the phone in one hand, the cord in the other.

Ben looked around suspiciously.

"Why does it smell like that in here?"

"Driving out evil spirits," Cole said. When Ben stared at him, he shrugged.

Everybody stood frozen for a long moment, just staring at each other, before they settled into character.

Lily said, "Ben, are you hungry?"

He was starving. It was still hard to think about his stomach without thinking about what had come out of it. He nodded his head.

"I really am."

Cole walked over quickly, and gave his brother an awkward, but also heartfelt, hug. Lily followed behind and did the same while Carolyn and Joshua watched skeptically.

"Okay, then let's do that before anything else," Lily said. "I know we all have questions, but I can't look at him without wanting to feed him. We have leftovers in the kitchen. I'll make you up a plate,"

"I'll make him up a plate," Carolyn said, and she turned kind of awkwardly, keeping her eyes on everyone in the room as long as she could before exiting the room. No one really seemed confident about what they were supposed to do in this situation. Ben inspected the room, poked his head in the kitchen to look around, but didn't say anything as he did so.

He walked to the table. He slid right into his old seat, sat there awkwardly, with his arms at his sides.

Carolyn brought him a plate with leftovers from the dinner Joshua made, slid it in front of him, then handed him a fork and knife that were wrapped up in a napkin. He thanked her.

After giving him a few minutes alone with his plate of food, Lily slid into the chair that had traditionally been her seat. When he took a sip of his water, Lily gasped.

"Is that a ring?"

"Um," he said.

"Are you married?"

"Yeah."

"Do you have children?"

This was probably not where he wanted to start this conversation, Ben thought.

"No children."

Lily asked, "What's her name?"

When Ben paused for a longer moment, Carolyn jumped into that yawning expanse, the ice cubes clinking against the sides of the glass in her hand.

"Oh. My. Lord."

Everyone but Ben looked at her.

Cole said to Ben, "Don't mind her. She's a mean drunk. And she's on her way to drunk right now."

Ben missed Cole. That was a surprise. Cole was all grown up now. He looked around the room, at his white eldest sister, his half-Hispanic eldest brother, his supposedly half-Hispanic sister (he thought Carolyn was more likely all white), and his half-Asian little brother. He wondered, how could they not have known they didn't really belong together? Or was the picture just so weird to start with that a person would never suspect it was weirder underneath?

"Oh, you can mind me," Carolyn said. "Where is our

sister? Is she okay? Are you . . . married to her?"

Lily, Joshua, and Cole all made weird faces.

Lily said, "Carolyn! What's the matter with you?"

"She's been saying shit to everyone all night," Cole said.

Ben looked at Carolyn, and then nodded his head. The others recoiled with various expressions of distaste. The look on Cole's face was as if he'd eaten a sour lemon.

"Wow," Lily said. "Is that why you . . . is that why you two left?"

"No," he sort of lied. "We left because we felt like this place was a dead end for us, and we wanted to, you know, try to find something that was better for us."

"And then you got married," Carolyn said.

"Yeah. After a long while. Something like that."

"It's an abomination! You're going to have little troglodyte children."

"We can't have kids. Neither of us can have kids. She doesn't have the eggs and I don't have the swimmers."

Lily asked, "Why isn't she with you now?"

"Zoe didn't want me to come here. I wasn't planning to come to Clay. She's fine with our new life. She was afraid my coming here would ruin everything we've put together."

Joshua finally chimed in, "So why are you here? Why now?" Before he could answer, Carolyn went off on another tack.

"Can we call Zoe? I'm probably not the only one who wants to talk to her."

"No, we can't do that. I told you, she's not into this. If you located her through me, without me asking her first if she wanted to be located by anybody, she might just run away all over again. But this time to get away from me."

No one said anything as Carolyn zipped out of the room again.

Cole said slowly, "Carolyn called Zoe on your phone a

little while ago, left a message that you were here."

Whatever color had returned to Ben's face, it all drained out.

"You're kidding," Ben said.

"No," Cole said.

"Shit!" His phone was out in his hand in a flash, his back turned to them just as quickly, and then he was in his bedroom, and the door was slamming closed.

They could only hear the muffled sound of his voice talking, but they could tell he was leaving a message. After another space of time, they heard him yell, "God damn it! Fuck! Fuck! Fuck!"

It was another while before Ben returned. Cole could see that he had cried some—his eyes were red. He wasn't seething when he came out, as they all had expected—he was defeated.

No one needed to ask if he had spoken with her, but still Ben said, "She didn't pick up. Maybe it's a good sign that she hasn't blocked my number. But maybe she hasn't heard any of the messages yet. Or maybe she's already gone and she just left her phone on the key stand in the front hall for me to find when I get back."

Lily wanted to tell him it would be all right, but thought that would only provide him an opportunity to snap at her.

"Ben," she said slowly. "Where did you find Emily? Why is she with you?"

"You know her?"

"Mom brought her home before. Seemed to have sort of picked her up off the street and decided she was going to take her in—without bothering to find out who she really belonged to. Probably," she said, "would have been better looked after by a nearly senile woman than by her own parents or any sort of public safety net. But we got Emily back to her home, back to her mom.

It was about two years ago. It's kind of odd for her to be showing up this way again, with you."

"That's the first I heard of any of that," Ben said. "She hasn't talked a lot. I think she's kind of in shock. I'm amazed that she kept going, and made it as far as we did. I couldn't just leave her there."

"Leave her where? Made it as far from where? Where did you meet her?"

Ben wasn't sure how to approach this. He assumed the whole country was probably freaking out about what happened in Tennessee, and that he just had to say the name.

"At Galaxy Park."

They didn't react as if that name held special significance. He was puzzled. It had been at least 48 hours. Whatever their motives, whatever their real mission, wouldn't the radio station crew have released at least some of their footage to the media by now?

"Well, what were you doing over there? Is there anything over there anyway? Where did you stay while you were there?"

"There's a new hotel there." He struggled with this. He still hadn't said anything specific. Still didn't have to say anything.

"So you . . . picked up Emily somehow and for some reason from the hotel?"

Joshua said, "Was this at one of those Syzygy things? Is that where you found her?"

Ben said, "You know what that is?"

"Yeah," Joshua said slowly. "I was thinking about going . . . just thinking about it, but we planned something else instead."

"Good choice," Ben said.

The others looked at Joshua curiously.

"What's a Syzygy?" Cole said. "I've seen that word somewhere."

"The lunar eclipse. That's a Greek word for a celestial alignment of three objects. For the eclipse, it was the sun, the Earth and the Moon in a line," Joshua said. Joshua thought about it a minute, and then his face clouded over.

Then Joshua slowly said, "So what happened to you? What happened there?"

Ben had thought about this while they were walking from Galaxy Park. What would he say about what had just happened? Who would believe him? When the police came and found a couple hundred mounds of dirt, and each with identifying items in them— phones, watches, glasses, wallets, keys, and whatnot—everything but the people they belonged to, what were they going to do?

Add to the equation five people, five survivors, with an unbelievable tale that seemed to match up with all of the footage they would gather from all the cell phones left behind. What was going to happen to those people? How much were their lives going to be changed? How much of his life would be ruined?

What Ben would say he wanted more than anything would be to be back with Zoe, and to never mention any of this again. To go back to a point in time where, on this subject, he had listened to her and moved on.

It wasn't that he disliked his "siblings," in fact, he loved them. He loved seeing them grown up and filled out as people. He loved that in each of them he could still see the person he'd always known them to be. That when they spoke to each other, it felt as if no time had passed and that whatever had been set down nine years before could be picked up with ease.

But there was too much pain here, too much buried too deep down for anyone to have noticed the wound. He looked at himself and Zoe as the first casualties, and Carolyn was clearly in line to be the third. He didn't want to be a part of that pain. He didn't want to be tied to it, when there was no truth he could reveal that wouldn't make it worse.

Yet, he was not fleeing for the door, not trying to arrange the quickest way home to see if Zoe was still there. He was here instead of trying to get back there, and there had to be a reason.

Before they'd gotten too far from Galaxy Park, he and Emily had passed a Prius stopped in the road. In the driver's seat was a cowboy hat, which Ben recognized as belonging to one of the undercover cops who'd been working with Elias. The older one, the one with the mustache. Ben opened the door, reached in, and lifted off the hat, revealing a clothed, crumbling body with odd objects poking out of it, a walkie-talkie and a cell phone most prominent among them.

He'd wondered then if they were wrong to be leaving the park. If they shouldn't just wait for someone to come find them. What if they were still carrying whatever it was?

By the time the SUV had stopped for them, nearly two days later, they were both exhausted but afraid to stop moving for long, and worries of a contagion were secondary. It was his family, and if Ben and Emily were going to live, it was too late to do anything but get in and hope for the best.

He'd thought that the only people he would tell this story to were Zoe and his so-called family, the latter in case something sinister happened to him and he never made it back to Zoe. He wasn't sure any of them would believe him, even if the story was already in the newspapers. Zoe would believe him.

Or would she?

So, he'd thought, maybe he wouldn't tell anyone. Maybe that was the best way for everybody. Just not say anything about being anywhere in the vicinity and be grateful to have a life and a place away from here to go live it. Hadn't the person who killed his great-grandpa managed to keep it secret a hundred years? Such a thing was possible, and had probably happened, and probably more often than anyone was aware.

It was possible, Ben thought, it would just go down as an unsolved mystery, just like that town in California. Maybe those people didn't disappear, he'd thought, maybe they were just turned into mud. Even if he emerged with the story of what had happened at Galaxy Park, it would just be one more unverifiable account. He'd done a lot to cover his presence there.

Or maybe it wouldn't. Maybe everything was recorded somewhere by someone other than the people who were pretending to record it for public showing. The K-NOX crew might have been documenting it, but they were apparently doing it for another reason than they said. Regardless, parts of the whole night were recorded on a hundred different phones. Everyone would know by those alone, right?

Now he had some doubts. No one in the room knew. What if no one ever saw that footage? What if no one ever knew to ask if there was footage? What if the only things keeping the whole thing from being an unknowable secret were the five people who left the site after it was over?

In the end, he decided to tell his story, whether they believed it or not. Then, if he and Emily ever disappeared without a trace—that was what his mind kept bringing him back to, that black ops out of the movies were going to kidnap him and drop him from a helicopter over a cornfield—there would at least be some chance someone would know why.

He had also vowed that before he went to sleep again he would write it all out, everything he'd seen, and then hide it someplace no one would ever think of looking for it—as a backup. In case anything happened to him.

"Okay," he said, "All right. I'm going to tell you guys what happened. I'm going to try to get through it all, so please let me tell the whole thing before you start acting like I must be either crazy or making up stories."

It took him a while to get through the whole story. He didn't tell them everything—he started with the photo shoot. He told them about the news radio people. He told them about the women at Stonehenge and the set-up for the Syzygy event.

There were moments in the telling, even before he got to the serious parts, where he got strangely choked up. As he talked about some of the people there, he felt especially aware of the fact that he was among a small group of people who saw the last moments of hundreds of others. Those hundreds of others had family, friends, and other people who cared about them who would wonder what their loved ones' last moments were like. Without his testimony, without the others' testimony, those people might never know.

He omitted a lot of details about the people he met. He told them about Ed and Martin and Dot and Walt. He didn't mention the blond model, the one he'd thought was trying to locate Cole. That was a can of worms he wasn't going to touch.

Joshua asked, "You didn't happen to meet a girl named Christy, maybe working for the event, perky little blonde?"

"Yeah," Ben said, staring back at his brother. "I did meet a person who met that . . . exact . . . description." He continued to stare into his brother's eyes. Joshua's countenance darkened. "I think her truck was still there when I left there, but I don't remember seeing her . . . seeing her after a certain point in the day."

Carolyn and Cole watched this exchange very closely.

Ben wasn't sure what was going on.

"You knew her?"

Joshua told him to go on with his story.

As Ben started describing the happenings after the moon was in eclipse, he didn't know as he was speaking if they believed anything he was saying. He told them about the weird and spectacular neon plant display, and the tractor, and the explosion. He told them about his dream after the explosion. He described the hour of dying that followed. He saw them repeatedly looking at each other and raising their eyebrows. Joshua was worried. Ben thought that maybe they were thinking that yes, everyone in Galaxy Park might be dead, but maybe Ben had killed them and this was his crazy cover story? Maybe they thought he was out of his mind? Ben couldn't tell what they were thinking.

He stopped his story to ask, "You guys haven't heard anything, no news, not anything, about Galaxy Park?"

They all looked back at him blankly.

Lily said, "When I talked to Richard just now, he said he saw they'd closed Highway 40 going west."

Cole said, "Sounds like there was weird stuff going on everywhere during the eclipse."

Lily listened intently when Ben described running into Elias as Elias was directing the crowd. Her eyebrows raised and didn't seem like they were going to come down.

Very carefully, he said, "He told me to tell you that he'd always had a thing for you. He wanted the best for you."

She asked, "What happened?" She leaned forward. "Tell me what happened." Ben thought sadly, She does still love him.

When Ben described Elias' death, Lily rose up from the couch, and walked into the kitchen. Moments later, her voice rang out clearly. It was quivering when she spoke. "Hi Claire, it's Lily. Yeah, no, right, having a rough night. You cannot imagine. Listen, I'm trying to contact Elias . . . "

"All right, so that's official sounding. That's how you're responding to inquiries?" Her voice was calm. "And you can't give me any more than that?"

"Was he over in Galaxy Park a couple days back? I heard he was on loan for something over there.

"No, I haven't heard anything. That's why I'm asking.

"I . . . I just want to talk to Elias, Claire. Do you know where he is?

"No, no . . . don't start reading that again. I wish I could say that I understand . . .

"Okay. Bye, Claire. I'm sorry. I'm sorry, too. We'll talk again soon. Take care."

When Lily returned to the room, she lingered in the doorway. Her eyes were slightly swollen, and the focus of her gaze was far off and uncertain.

"I don't believe it," she said to Ben. "It's too crazy. Did you come here just to screw with us?"

Carolyn asked, "So how do you know you're not carrying something around?"

"I don't," Ben said. "Not for sure. I'm not . . . you know, dead. Food's going through us normal. Things aren't dying around me. Don't feel sick. Says something."

They looked skeptical of this.

"I think I'm okay. It was a poison, not a virus. The people who had it, they knew something was wrong. It's not like that for me. After I puked it up, I felt better. Emily, too."

Joshua asked, "Why only you two?"

Ben shrugged.

"I don't know. And there were five of us."

"Right," Joshua said. "The other three mysterious unidentified people who were using fake names pretending to be people they weren't. People we don't know or have any method of contacting."

Cole said, "So five people out of three hundred? Same question. Why you?"

"I don't know," Ben repeated.

"It would be good to know, don't you think?"

"Maybe if our mother was here still, we could find out," Ben said.

Chapter 25

Lily said, "Someone's going to want to talk to you. If what you're saying is true, they're investigating now! How are they going to figure out what happened? Someone's going to want to know what happened. Something will lead them to you. Your name is on the hotel registry, at the very least."

"It's not. I paid cash. I used a fake name."

"Which leads to my next question," Lily asked, "Why were you there, Ben? Why come back so close to us if you don't want to see us? If you might run into someone who knows us all? Were you trying to come back here? Did you know Mother died?"

He told himself he wanted to say yes, that was why he was here. Instead, he said matter-of-factly, "I hired a private investigator. To collect DNA samples from all of you."

"What? Why?"

Ben said, "To figure out who I am."

Joshua said, "What the fuck is wrong with you, Ben?" He asked Cole, "Can you believe this?"

"My brain's still twisting in the wind from the sister-wife thing."

Ben ignored them. He stared at Lily.

"What do you think I found out, Lily, when someone looked at all of our DNA? Anything you want to share with everybody?"

Lines of worry deepened on her face. "What now? Why, Ben? Is that why you're home? To wreck everything you left behind? It wasn't enough to just up and leave? Is there any reason we should believe anything you say is true? Why are you doing this?" Lily was yelling by the time she was done.

He continued to stare.

"Fine," she said. She turned to Joshua, Carolyn, and Cole. She drew in a breath. "I'm adopted. Mother adopted me."

Her body swayed with emotion, though she managed not to cry. She breathed out a short breath, lips pursed, like she was blowing out the vapors after a shot of whiskey.

Cole said, "I'm so glad you didn't just say you were really our mother."

"I was at a foster home with some really, really terrible foster parents who basically locked me up and hurt me," Lily said, "and Mother was the bookmobile lady who actually cared enough to notice how miserable I was."

"She didn't adopt you," Ben said. "She kidnapped you."

"She rescued me. My foster parents never even reported me missing, even though I was five at the time."

"Foster parents," Ben repeated.

Lily looked at Joshua and Carolyn. Looking at their faces, she started crying again. "She said it didn't matter. That she would be my mother, and I felt so lucky for it. It was like being saved.

"I've always, always, always wanted to tell you. To have it out there in the open. But growing up I thought if anyone found out they would take me away from Mother, and maybe even send me back to Texas, where I never wanted to go again.

"I'm sorry for hiding that from you," she started choking up again, and Joshua crossed the room to give her a hug. Carolyn stayed in place, her eyes moving from person to person in the room.

Cole said, "Family is family, Lils. I can't afford to be losing any more."

Lily looked at Ben. She was angry.

"What do you think is going to happen when they come here looking for you? It's going to put a spotlight on the whole family. Don't you know you've gotten us involved now?"

"Who says they're going to come looking for me? Who

says they'll come here?"

"You better think of something, Ben," Lily said "I'm not pulling your ass out of anything. I'm not sure I know who you are these days, or what you're up to . . . "

Carolyn said, "I think she's right. You've done enough damage here. Go on home to your incestuous marriage and have little mutant babies . . . "

Cole said, "Carolyn! Shut up with that shit!"

Carolyn said, "What? He's all about the truth. Well, the truth is that he's married to his twin!"

Ben had been thrown slightly by Lily's confession, and had tried to understand if that changed his view of the situation. When Carolyn lashed out, he decided it didn't change anything.

He said, "Zoe and I aren't twins. We had blood tests, DNA tests, too. We're not related to each other."

Lily said, "What?"

"None of us—none of you—are related to each other or to me. Not by blood. And none of us is related to Mom, either. Lily's not the only one she took."

Lily said, "What?" She looked perplexed.

Ben said, "I don't know, Lily. How is that possible? You tell us."

"What?" Disbelief overwhelmed Lily, but she understood the accusation. "I don't know," she said, momentarily offended, "I just remember, each one of you—well, after Joshua—with each one of you she came home after being away from the house for an extended time. I never met any of the dads, but that was because she said she didn't think it was right for the kids to be a part of her romantic life, and she didn't want to bring strange men into our lives if she wasn't sure they were going to stay."

"You never thought that was weird?"

"I was eight with you and Zoe. Six with Carolyn. Eleven with Cole. No, I didn't think that was weird. I believed everything she ever told me."

"What happened to your parents, Lily?" Again, Ben's tone sounded accusatory.

"They died in a car crash. I don't remember them at all."

"But you have one over the rest of us," Ben said.

"Right," Cole said. "Who am I?"

"Oh, my goodness," Carolyn said. "Maybe my mother was an old whore who wanted to kill me."

"Would explain a lot," Joshua said. Carolyn glared at him.

The room was very, very quiet. Carolyn turned and walked out.

"I always . . . ," Joshua finally said, "I always liked that she said I was like my great grandpa."

"It seems kind of like you are," Cole said, gesturing toward the journals. "Regardless."

"Yeah, but it feels like what that meant just changed."

"We're family," Cole said.

Ben said, "Are we?"

Lily said, "Where did you spend the first sixteen years of your life?" Where did you learn the life skills that are still carrying you along? Who did you learn those things alongside? Yes, we are family. Blood isn't the only way to define a family."

"We were taken," Ben said.

"Maybe someone gave you to her. Maybe she saved you, the same way she saved me. Look at Emily there, that poor girl has nothing! No one, nothing. When I tried to find her family the first time around, her mom was a heroin addict who "loaned" her to someone in exchange for a fix. Her new "parents" dumped her off when they were done with her. Emily was living under a bridge when Mom found her," Lily said. "It seems like even when she was starting to lose it, that instinct kicked in. I think that's what it was."

Lily asked Ben, "Did you try to find your father?"

He bit his lip.

"No. Even though I wasn't sure if it was true that he was some horrible monster, I didn't . . . I was afraid, kind of . . . I couldn't get past being afraid it was true."

"Truly," Lily said, "the night mom brought you and Zoe home, that was the most terrifying night of my life. What she was afraid of wasn't something like getting busted by the cops. We were running for our lives."

"Maybe she stole me from someone who wanted me back."

"Obviously. Desperately. But what did they want you for? You know, not only have I spent the last 15 years keeping an eye out for my fosters, I've also been obsessively monitoring missing children reports from around the times you were all born, because the longer the Internet is around, the farther back they've been able to go back for cases to put online. I've been watching for the dads. And there has never, never been a missing child report that even faintly resembles any of us."

"Whoever she got us from didn't report any of us missing?"

"Not yet, they haven't," Lily said. "What does that tell us? At the very least, that they aren't the type of people who would report a missing baby. That says a lot right there."

Lily looked around the room. Were they listening to her? Was she listening to herself? Everyone looked lost in their thoughts.

She heard the clink of ice cubes in the kitchen.

"You know," Lily said, "I think I'm going to go outside for a little bit, walk around the yard. This is a lot. A lot for all of us. And then I'm going to go sit with mother for a while, if anyone wants to join me. I hope you all understand. She gave me everything, she gave me a family, a life where I could do more than stare out a window, hoping for better. She gave me love. She gave all of us her love. Nothing we've said here can change that."

She stepped out the front door, and closed it behind her.

Lily sat beside her mother's grave under the moonless night sky. A butterfly appeared out of a bush behind her, and fluttered over the grave in the dark.

"So, you had your secrets," she said. "My, oh my. I don't blame you. I always saw you doing everything you could to make it work. I am going to assume this isn't anything different. We all have secrets, I guess. Even when we tell ourselves we don't."

She wasn't able to accept what Ben had said about Elias. That wasn't real, she thought. She thought her bond with Elias, however strained and distant, was such that if something happened to him, she would know. She believed she would know if he were dead, but there was no deep-seated feeling to tell her whether or not this was true. Why would Ben return with such a story? Why would he make up such a story? How could it possibly be true? Was it possible she would never see Elias again? That just seemed . . . impossible to her.

She would hold out hope, she told herself, until she could find out more. Even though it was a relationship that was strained, she wasn't ready to say goodbye to him, to the comfort she had always taken from knowing he was still out there somewhere, doing no less than she was, making the best of life.

Joshua went into the kitchen, where Carolyn was taste-testing her latest drink.

"Pour it out, Carolyn. It's enough, isn't it? We don't need another dead body around here. At least not tonight."

She looked at her drink. She tried to glare at him, but couldn't quite manage it to full effect.

"Fine," she said. She reached out her arm, poured the filled glass down the sink, then quickly put all of her bottles away. "Fine. For now."

Joshua said, "Thanks."

"You know," she said, "You don't get to tell me what to do anymore. Turns out, you're not my brother."

"Thank goodness for that," he said. "Don't have to bait your hook when we're fishing, don't have to pull your high school boyfriend's car out of the gulley before his dad finds out he's driving without his license, don't have to bail you out of jail for underage drinking, don't have to pick you up at cheerleading and get you over to softball and then pick you up and get you to bowling, don't have to listen to you bawling because your haircut is too short . . . "

She said, "Don't have to pretend I don't mind that because you're a man you don't have do your share of the cooking and cleaning or that I like watching you dancing around on a stage in a bikini . . . "

" . . . Don't have to intimidate stupid high school boys telling tales out of school about you," he continued, "don't have to . . . "

She lifted her hand to signal that was enough, and he fell in step with her as she started for the front door. Joshua put an arm around Carolyn, gave her a quick little squeeze before he let her step through the doorway ahead of him.

Carolyn rolled her eyes.

Never before had Cole so felt that he was the youngest one in the family. He'd basically just sat back and let them all hash it out, calling offsides when it seemed like it went too far, but otherwise not contributing anything.

He'd already been working on an identity crisis. After more than two months away from California, he'd come to feel that the person he'd been there was not the person he truly was. There he had been so alone, so cut off from the people and the world that he knew, that he'd latched onto anyone who was nice to him. That's how he'd ended up hanging out with Tony, someone he'd done a lot of fun things with but about whom he'd always had reservations. That was how he'd ended up with a string of girlfriends, all of whom he'd had fun with until he didn't, ending with Trina, who he'd really liked but never been in love with. Trina was the only one for whom the feeling of not being in love was clearly mutual. They'd both known it was not a chemistry built to last, but it had been fun. Even the thing with Alexa and Zane, that would never have happened if he hadn't been so, so, so on the edge of giving up.

Well, maybe that wasn't entirely true.

It was a time when his head was confused and stimulated and always telling him it was okay to try a new thing once to see what it was all about. Then the window closed on that world, and the cacophony ended, and he could hear himself thinking again.

This was where he would be happy to live his life, he thought, at least for a while. He liked hanging out with Josh and Lily and Lily's family. He liked having family—and he wasn't going to let them pretend that wasn't what they were. Even Ben wasn't bad to be around.

Carolyn . . . well, Carolyn was a problem that one day was going to need solving.

Cole walked to his mother's bedroom, pulled open the bottom drawer, and took out her can of smoked joints. He looked in the can, and saw the corner of a small plastic zip bag, which he tugged out, revealing a packet of rolling papers.

With both the can and the rolling papers in his hands, he headed out the front door.

Cole thought that he was like any other kid in the world who didn't know his father—he'd always hoped and wanted to believe that his father was anything amazing he could imagine— from super rich to super famous to Asian royalty. His family story was different from the others in that their fathers might have wanted them back. Cole's father couldn't get away quick enough.

Now he not only didn't know his father, but he also had a mother out there? Was she still alive? Had he spent time with her when he was little, or did Rose get him at the very start? What was their story? Had Rose simply pretended his biological mother's story was her own? Was it some kind of Stockholm syndrome he was experiencing when he couldn't feel anything but love for Rose and all she did for them?

He came across Ben in the vegetable garden. He looked confused about where to find the others.

"They're back in the field," Cole said. "Her grave is at the back corner of the property."

When they reached the gravesite, Lily, Joshua, and Carolyn were all seated there, not talking. Cole sat down. Ben remained standing a short way back. Cole looked around at everybody, then cracked the lid of the box, pulled out the rolling papers, then pulled out one sheet, and set it flat.

Lily said, "Oh, no . . . "

"Relax, Lily. We need to smoke a peace pipe, and we can do it in honor of our mother, in the method she would have most preferred herself."

He ripped open one nub of a burnt joint, and a small pile of green fell onto the sheet. He repeated this several more times until there was a small pile of crumbled marijuana in the middle of the sheet. Then, in a matter of seconds, he rolled it, licked it lightly, and twisted the ends slightly.

"Pretty smooth," Joshua said.

"In California, people do every kind of thing to get high. This was what I generally chose over the other options that were available." He shrugged.

"To mother," he said. He lit a match, and took a drag,

puffing on the joint until it caught. He passed it to Joshua, who took a deep drag, held it in, then coughed violently. Joshua held it out to Lily and Carolyn, both of whom declined. He held it out to Ben, who took a drag and passed it back to Cole.

Ben said, "I'm going to go home tomorrow. I need to see Zoe."

Lily said, "If what you said is true, I think people are going to come looking for you. You're on a surveillance camera someplace. You're in someone's cell phone photo. They're going to start matching up names and faces and personal items and then cross-checking their lists and there you are going to be."

"I've thought about it, and if I'm home, and I'm with Zoe, in my house, in my neighborhood, maybe then I can figure out a way to deal with it from a better place than I'd be if something starts now. I just need to know she's okay."

"What if she's not there?"

"Then I will find her. And if they get me before I find her, then you will know that I am horribly, horribly alone as they bring me in to dissect me."

"Are you going to give us contact information, like your phone number and your address?" Lily was certain Carolyn had copied all of that down somewhere, but asked anyway.

Ben said, "I'm going to leave that up to Zoe. I've got nothing against it. I'm really glad I've gotten to see you all again. But I haven't really been fair to her, or done much to respect how she wanted to handle all of this, so I'm going to just lay it all out for her and let her tell me how she wants to proceed."

It was his turn, and he took another drag, which resulted in him coughing, too.

"Shit," Ben said, "Rose smoked some good stuff."

Cole said, "Right?"

Ben offered it to Lily, and she nodded her head, yes. He passed it to her, and she pulled lightly on it. When she breathed out, a narrow stream of smoke came out.

Lily asked, "What are we going to do?"

Joshua said, "What do you mean?"

"I mean, are we going to tell people?" She looked at Ben, at Carolyn. "Are we going to tell people?"

Cole said, "Does Richard know about you?"

"He will tomorrow. I don't think it will matter to him beyond how much it matters to me."

Carolyn said, "No, we are not going to tell anybody. Why would you want to go and do that? Do you want us to be on the cover of People magazine for that kind of story? With us on the cover with the word KIDNAPPED? Across the front? Nosireee, no we are not. 'A North Carolina Family's Tales of Child Abduction, Murder, Incest—no offense, Ben—and More.' Does anybody want that? Because that's what it's going to be. I'm sure that will drag all of our fathers, and probably a lot of people who aren't our fathers or mothers, out of the woodwork."

They all shook their heads at the thought of it.

Ben said, "So, we're going to keep this a family secret?"

Cole asked, "Which part of it?"

"Anything we've said tonight," Ben replied.

"I'm being honest, Ben," Lily said. "I don't think I can lie to the police if they come looking for information."

"That's . . . that's, I guess, for each of you to decide. Except maybe instead of going out and offering anything to anyone, we can wait to see if someone asks. Again, though, it's all up to you. I don't own you guys."

Ben saw something that made him jump a little.

Carolyn asked, "What was that?"

"Nothing. A shadow. I keep thinking those trees in the dresses are going to be standing behind me. What the heck is that about?"

"That was just something I did with Mother," Carolyn

345

said wistfully. "She liked them, for some reason."

They all sat quietly.

Cole said, "Hey, you guys. When Ben was talking about the dream he had, the start of it, with the stars? Did that sound familiar to anyone? I think my dream that night was like that, too. Aliens."

Joshua said slowly, "I think we were all there. Except Lily. The rest of us were together there." He scratched his head. "Someplace." Carolyn, Ben, and Cole all nodded.

Lily rolled her eyes. "Oh, great," she said with sarcasm, "Already you're excluding me. What do we do about Emily?"

Carolyn jumped in. "I'm going to look after Emily. I think I'm supposed to. We're going to let her stay here."

"Really?" Lily looked at Joshua skeptically. He shrugged.

"Yes, really," Carolyn said. "Something tells me it's going to work out best for both of us. And I've been thinking that the last gold coin, the one in the space, should go to her. The poor girl has nothing."

No one said a word in disagreement.

They chatted for a while longer before they all returned to the house, and it wasn't long before, one by one, they all went to bed, the first time in ten years that all of the Chamber children's beds were filled.

Chapter 26

Thinking he was the first one awake, Cole slipped out of the house quietly the next morning, and walked over to the Whalen house, where he knocked on the door. Erin answered, a baby in her arms.

Seeing the baby, he took a full step back from the front door. He wondered if he should be around a baby, if maybe he could unknowingly pass on something he might have been exposed to from being around Ben.

"Whoa," Erin said. "He's not radioactive." She tried to push open the screen door. He held it closed.

"Oh, I know!" Cole laughed. "I just saw him and realized I haven't cleaned myself up enough to be around a baby. I don't want to get . . . germs or anything on him." She looked at him weirdly. "It's too early to be coming in, anyway," Cole said. "But I thought maybe you'd want to go to breakfast? We can walk to Morrow's?" One of the only places to eat in town. "Bring the baby? I can come back in 20, 25 minutes to get you."

"Okay," she said. It was that easy. He felt a small thrill. "Sounds nice."

"I'll be back for you soon."

After Cole returned home, he washed up and changed his clothes. He wrote a note to Carolyn and pulled a twenty from her wallet. He would surely hear about that during the next bender.

Carolyn woke on the sound of Cole closing the front door behind him for the second time. She looked around her bedroom, disoriented for a moment. Her head hurt a little, and for one lovely moment, she didn't remember at all the things that had gone on the evening before.

The moment did not last.

She wanted a drink—knew the hair of the dog was the best way to clear her head—but she wanted food in her belly even more, and generally breakfast wasn't a meal that was improved on with alcohol.

Joshua walked into the kitchen as she was deciding what she could make. She saw the note from Cole, and it took her all of a couple seconds to decide he was taking that Whalen girl to breakfast.

She seemed like a nice girl, Carolyn thought.

She stood close to Joshua. In a low voice, she said, "I've been thinking about it, and I think we should turn Ben in. Who knows what kind of trouble this is going to bring down the road? If we call the police now, and he's taken away quick, no one will know why, and we won't have to tell them, and when they do find out, they won't think we did anything wrong."

"We're not turning in family, Carolyn. Certainly not if there's no one looking for him yet," he said. "No one around here will respect it, if that's what you think. We look out for our own."

"What if it was a terrorist attack? Aren't we looking out for our own, but instead of our own family, we're looking out for our own people? What if it's something worse?"

"Then we'll talk about it again. If it's as bad as he said, they'll find their way to him, and we'll work it out from there."

She looked at him, up and down.

He said, "Same would go for you, or for me, or for Lily, or for Cole. Even Zoe. Can't say we're bound by blood, but I can say we're bound by life."

"Excuse me?" There was an unrecognizable voice in the doorway to the kitchen.

Joshua mouthed one word to Carolyn, "Emily."

They both turned around.

Carolyn turned it on, much to Joshua's amazement. She became the restaurant hostess, greeting Emily warmly, ushering her over to the table, pulling out her chair. She became the waitress, asking Emily how she had slept, how she felt, what kind of food she wanted for breakfast—Biscuits and gravy? Bacon? Flapjacks? Potatoes?—and when Emily couldn't voice a preference, Carolyn became the chef, and set about making all of it, doing her best to coax some conversation out of the girl while she cooked.

Joshua went to the back of the house, to Ben's room. He only stood outside the door a moment, half-suspecting that Ben might already have left. He was tempted to look in, but decided that he would let it go a little longer.

Then, a moment later, he peeked in anyway. Yes, Ben was gone. He stepped out of the room, closing the door. Joshua would notice later that a sealed envelope had been left in the slot above the table in the kitchen, he would assume by Ben. The handwriting on the outside read: Galaxy Park. The next time the vault was open, Joshua would store that envelope inside for safekeeping.

Lily came out of their mother's room. Although she was wearing the same clothes as the evening before, she'd done something that made her look fresh and ready for the day.

"You're going?"

"Yes."

"No breakfast?"

"I can't. I've got to get back to Richard and the kids. This here is going to go on and on forever, and while I want us to continue the conversation, I've got to go back to my life with them." This was Lily as he knew her, putting everything back into place when she needed to.

"You're not . . . going to bail on us?"

"What? No, Josh, no. Not ever. But yes, I've got some things to do, and my head's not going to be together to even think about all of this until I do them. I've got some calls to make. I need to process some things, and there are things that need to be done because no one else is going to do them, but I've got to figure out a way to do that while remaining functional."

"It's what moms do."

"Yeah," Lily said. Her eyes teared up. "The good ones." For a moment, with pure exasperation, she added, "It never ends." She rolled her eyes. "That's what I think, anyway." They hugged, and then she went into the kitchen, gave Emily a short hug and Carolyn a much longer one, promising to call in the next few days, and then she was on her way.

Zane was parked at a gas station a few miles west of the Chamber home while an attendant filled the gas tank. He hadn't had much luck tracking down Cole. If Alexa were here, she would insist that Zane ask the attendant if he recognized Cole's name—but Zane couldn't bring himself to do it. A wild night of partying with two of the models at Atlanta clubs had subtracted about 18 hours from his expedition time. He was ready to go home.

Before this trip, if someone had asked, he would have said North Carolina was in the middle of the country, not out on the coast. He would have guessed it was an arid dust bowl, not lush and green. It was no wonder people liked living here, he thought.

A door opened at the restaurant across the street. And who but Cole stepped out behind an attractive, long-haired girl who was holding a baby. For a moment, Zane felt surprised and happy—but he didn't get out of the car. Instead, he watched for a short while. He thought his friend looked okay. It couldn't be Cole's baby, Zane knew. Maybe it was part of the package, came with the girl?

Zane wasn't sure why, but when he saw Cole, he felt like somewhere inside he was able to exhale the breath he'd been holding since Cole left California. Part of him wanted to run over and wrap his arms around Cole and hold him tight. He'd missed

Cole so much.

Geez, he thought. Maybe I *am* gay for Cole.

But it was too easy to look at Cole and this girl and think that whether or not the baby was Cole's, he and the girl could be happy, at least for a while. The last thing they would need would be for someone from the world that chased him away to come drag the unresolved past into the picture.

Was that why Zane held back? Had something changed about his feelings? Or was this just about as long as he could stand to be away from Alexa without needing the comfort of a welcoming body? She'd texted earlier in the morning that her job had ended, and that she was back in L.A. and missing him. Would he be home soon?

When he read that message, he'd thought L.A. was the only place he wanted to be.

Alexa: Also, your agency has left around 12 messages for you, asking for you to call in. Sounds like they're freaking out over something. Did your shoot go okay?

He texted: Thought it went great. I'll check in with them soon. Can't wait to see you.

Now that he knew where to find Cole, Zane knew he could come back if he changed his mind about dropping by for a visit.

Cole never looked away from the girl's face long enough to notice Zane was there. They didn't stop talking the whole time. That was probably for the better. When the attendant finished and Zane had paid, he drove off, headed out of town.

On the drive home to his farm, Joshua was nearly overwhelmed by a feeling of loss. He was sure Christy had been at Galaxy Park, just sure of it. Where else would she be on the night of the full moon but wherever the space people were hanging out? He should have been there, too . . .

He could rewrite a better weekend. Instead of going to

the mountains with the family, he went to Tennessee to watch the full moon. Instead of playing with the kids, he ran into the girl of his dreams. Instead of staying to die, she left with him to go someplace more private so they could start the conversation that would begin the rest of their lives together . . .

He pulled into the driveway. He was sure Marco would have everything under control, but would want an explanation for his boss' extra day off. Marco was a worrier.

Joshua was less affected by the news of his origins, he thought, than he would have expected. He figured it didn't change who he was. Whatever it was that happened before he was on the scene, he was Joshua Nelson Chamber now. Had a birth certificate and a Social Security card to prove it, and however his mother might have come by them, they were accepted by the U.S. government as legit.

His mother had given him a good life. She'd worked hard every day of her life that he knew her to make their lives better. A bad person? There wasn't any way that wouldn't have shown through over the years, and he'd never seen sight of it. He wasn't going to believe she had nefarious intentions. He was going to believe that she'd saved him when she took him.

In front of the house as he drove up the driveway was a car. It was a rental, he thought. Was this the cops already? He knew Lily was right, after all. It was just a matter of time before it showed up on his doorstep.

As he drove closer, the car's door opened, and out stepped a woman. A blonde.

It was Christy.

She waved at him. He looked at her, stunned. Then he thought to wave back before he parked.

Well, yes, he thought with certainty. *Thank you.*

Mother was right.

The universe has its own plans.

Also by James T. Riley

HILL PEOPLE

MY NAME IS JARED

www.ingramcontent.com/pod-product-compliance
Lightning Source LLC
Chambersburg PA
CBHW022147010726
47493CB00002B/371

* 9 7 8 0 5 7 8 1 8 7 6 8 6 *